CR

IN THE

CITY

with contributions from

ANDREA BADENOCH
ANN CLEEVES
MAT COWARD
DAVID STUART DAVIES
CAROL ANNE DAVIS
LINDSEY DAVIS
EILEEN DEWHURST
MARTIN EDWARDS
JÜRGEN EHLERS
MARJORIE ECCLES
KATE ELLIS
JOHN HARVEY
REGINALD HILL
BILL JAMES
PETER LEWIS
PHIL LOVESEY
VAL McDERMID
RUTH RENDELL
KATHRYN SKOYLES
CATH STAINCLIFFE
JERRY SYKES
ANDREW TAYLOR

Crime in the City

edited by

Martin Edwards

First Published in Great Britain in 2002 by
The Do-Not Press Limited
16 The Woodlands
London SE13 6TY
www.thedonotpress.com
email: citc@thedonotpress.com

B-format paperback: ISBN 1 90316 04 2
Casebound edition: ISBN 1 90316 05 0

British Library Cataloguing in Publication Data. A catalogue
record for this book is available from the British Library.

1   3   5   7   9   10   8   6   4   2

Crime in the City

LIST OF CONTENTS

Foreword

Lindsey Davis

'Crime in the City'? Well, I'm not going to argue with that. I live near Deptford, a famous venue for murder, at least since Christopher Marlowe had his argument about a tavern bill and was fatally stabbed in the eye (whether or not at the behest of a government spymaster). Around here men are still regularly found drowned in gore outside pubs that claim to be respectable, women are punched unconscious by car thieves at roundabouts, and the dear Millennium Dome hosted a fabulous jewel heist – all within an ace of the United Nations Heritage site at historic, respectable Greenwich. So I am used to the world where the disadvantaged jostle the overly fortunate on a daily basis, where there is a strong criminal tradition, where the police struggle, and where their actions are sometimes open to question in intriguing ways.

I have to say that for me it beats crime in the country, with all those unlucky gamekeepers being knocked over the head by antique dealers who need to protect dark secrets. In the city, criminal antique dealers are more likely to be a sophisticated front for international drug-running than weedy perpetrators of tea-time adultery with doctors' wives thirty years ago. Our doctors are too busy to care, as they face charges of negligence for dodgy plastic surgery, wilful euthanasia, and sheer incompetence. Even our dentists are probably running vicious branches of the sex trade. As for a secret love-child harbouring murderous grudges about its origins – oh, this is useless as a plot! Why would any love-child worry, when half the kids in their class are love-children too? And so is their teacher, in all probability (that's as well as being an illegal immigrant who is blackmailing the head of the crime squad, of course).

You have to admit, when people are shot in the city, nobody asks if the gun went off by accident. Here, persons in possession of weaponry will definitely not hold a gun licence, their ammo is never kept locked in the gun cupboard (it's behind the lavatory cistern or in their girlfriend's baby's crib) – and when they shoot, they mean it. This is all so much more exciting, if I may peek out briefly from behind my gently swathed Greenwich net curtains and express a prejudice. So it is with particular pleasure that I am introducing this latest anthology from the Crime Writers' Association, in my role as their current Chair.

These are short stories, however. My starting point in what I have said already tends to be the form I know best, both as a writer and reader. The *novel* about city crime will normally be labelled 'gritty' and 'dark' (oh, as if some crimes were as sunny and light as margarine!); it is frequently crime on a big scale, to match the teeming metropolis. I find it interesting that the writers in this collection have altered their stance to fit the delicacy of the form. Even those who usually write novels have lightened their touch. You will find no serial killers and very little organised crime here; we are among individual jealousies and sometimes a striking crunch, where a murder depends on events that just happen to fall into place because someone turns up somewhere at a particular moment. Death (it is usually death we are talking about, of course) comes, if not quite as an accident, at least as an apt coincidence. Even the premeditated crimes have subtle resolutions.

I don't mean that the stories are soft. Psychological twists can be just as stirring as detailed, hardboiled gut-wrenching, perhaps more so, many of us would feel. In these stories, the plot resolutions creep up on you with dangerous skill. Ordinary people, or people in apparently ordinary situations, find that crime jumps at them out of nowhere – though the point is that the resolution seems inevitable once it occurs. Traditionally, this was lauded as the 'twist in the tail' and the more twists there were, the more skilful a practitioner was reckoned to be. That's fine, and you will find good examples of that art in this collection. I do think there can also be much mileage in watching a dread climax unwind itself inexorably, so look out also for well-sustained narratives that make you forget that your bedtime hot chocolate is cooling rapidly… it is the writing that counts (as always). Here too, our members are as skilled at handling tension as anyone writing today. Heck, I'll be prejudiced again and say they can do it better than most. They do a nice line in demure irony too, which is particularly to my taste.

Read on; you are in for a feast of delights.

But be warned. There are chills ahead. Foreign travel may soon scare you. Life's uncertainties will become just that jot more certain to threaten you. You won't want to phone your accountant late at night any more – and believe me, Welwyn Garden City will acquire a whole new resonance!

Lindsey Davis
Chair, the Crime Writers' Association

Introduction

Martin Edwards

rime in the City opens a new series of anthologies compiled by members of the Crime Writers' Association. Of the 21 stories gathered here, all but two have been written especially for this volume and they provide a vivid demonstration of the range of talent currently working in the genre. The contributors have garnered countless awards: Diamond Daggers; Gold Daggers; Daggers for the best first crime novel, the best short story and the best historical mystery; Sherlocks; Edgars; Anthonies; you name it. Here you will find all those distinguished authors at the top of their form.

In choosing these stories from the mountain of manuscripts submitted by CWA members, I was keen to avoid restricting myself to endless tales of urban *noir*. Variety is crucial in a book such as this. I was seeking to focus on imaginative takes on the 'crime in the city' theme, and I was not disappointed. The ingenuity of several contributors is quite dazzling. This year the stories are set in the past, the present and the future, and range across the globe: the USA, Russia, Rio de Janeiro, Egypt, Tanzania and Welwyn Garden City are just some of the backdrops. Wit, social awareness, crafty plotting: all are displayed in abundance. An important feature is that the contributors include both household names – Ruth Rendell, Reg Hill, Val McDermid and so on – and newcomers such as Kathryn Skoyles. The health of any organisation depends on the talents of its younger proponents: suffice it to say that a successful future for the CWA seems guaranteed. We hope, of course, that readers who enjoy this book will be tempted further to sample the work of the authors represented, perhaps above all those who are at the start of their writing careers.

This is the first CWA anthology to appear under the imprint of The Do-Not Press, a company which already has an impressive track record in contemporary crime fiction publishing. Previous titles include the acclaimed *Fresh Blood* collections, as well as *Mean Time*, edited by Jerry Sykes, who has a story in this volume as well. I would like to thank Jim

Driver of The Do-Not Press for his admirable commitment to the project from the time we first discussed the 'Crime in the City' theme – naturally in a bar – at a Crime Scene convention in London. Russell James, the then chairman of the CWA, and Fiona Davies, the treasurer, offered invaluable help; so has Lindsey Davis, Russell's successor, in kindly contributing the foreword. Eileen Dewhurst kindly checked the proofs and I am most grateful for her help. In addition to the authors and their agents, I must also thank my family. They have shown their customary patience whilst I have been working to bring this anthology to publication.

Martin Edwards

BELTER'S MUGGING

ANDREA BADENOCH

This accomplished story provides further proof that Andrea Badenoch is
one of the major British crime writing talents to have emerged in the past
few years. Andrea hails from the North East, but – unlike Belter Skelton
– is far from being a 'professional northerner'. *Mortal*, Andrea's first
novel and the book that immediately established her as a writer to watch,
benefited from its London setting, and this writer's versatility has been
further evidenced by her later work. This includes *Blink*, a novel which
evokes with wonderful clarity a close-knit community of the 1960s.
Belter's Mugging features a protagonist who, although fictional, seems
strangely familiar. A pugilistic, conceited and two-faced government
minister – who on earth could Andrea have been thinking of when she
created such an unlikely individual?

Bob Skelton, or Belter Skelton as he was known in the papers, stretched and yawned, relaxing in the first-class compartment of the Great North Eastern express. He riffled through a pile of papers on the table in front of him. These should never have left his office and he felt a small concern, which he hastily suppressed. They were marked 'Confidential' on each numbered page. The top copy was stamped in red ink 'Secret' and 'Not to be Distributed Further'. They were Cabinet discussion documents dealing with a sensitive policy issue. He smiled ruefully. Who knows what the newspaper hacks would do to get a glimpse of *these*, he thought to himself. They'd *kill* to see *these*.

Bob stared through the glass, trying to discern landmarks in the fast fading light. There was little to see apart from horizontal, undistinguished fields cut by sparse lines of hawthorns, which had once been hedgerows. Now that agribusiness had made these old boundaries pointless, they leaned sadly eastwards in the wind. He rubbed his eyes. The dull glow of day was sinking towards the horizon, obscured by winter cloud. The Vale of York, he told himself, confident in his knowledge of the landscape. This meant there was an hour or so still to go before he reached his destination. He looked at his watch. The train was on time.

Bob was a northerner. His gruff, flat and unadorned way of speaking was at its best direct and at its worst aggressive and rude. He was a larger-than-life northerner, a professional northerner – a northern politician whose public persona was shaped by his direct statements and blunt speeches. Monosyllabic and fierce, his words, like his manner, were never embellished by any soft southern flourishes. 'I'm off home,' he'd told a couple of journalists as he left the House of Commons. Once on the train he tried to work out how he felt about the idea of 'home', and decided he felt nothing. It means nowt, he told himself. *Nowt.*

This train journey was his first trip to Newcastle in a very long time. Despite his northern brass tacks image, and his strong and deliberate identification with his roots, his constituency was away in the opposite direction, in the extreme south-west. As well as this, he never travelled anywhere in Britain for reasons of nostalgia or pleasure. He had no fond memories of his youth or his childhood and his journeys were always taken out of necessity – mere punctuation marks in his busy schedule. His early years in the north-east were a time of loss and hardship, and he remembered feeling especially miserable at school. Bob was a northerner because of political expediency rather than sentiment.

Now, smoothing the close-typed government papers under one fleshy palm, he allowed his thoughts to wander for a moment, and to his surprise he saw in his mind's eye two half-forgotten and ghostly faces, first of Sugsy and then Sugsy's little brother, Ernest. As he concentrated, they became clearer and clearer. For once, as he sped north, he held them in his consciousness and allowed them to pull him back into his past. He was twelve years old again in a flash. He was scruffy, swinging his duffel bag, his blazer ruined, his trousers torn at the knees. The three boys – himself, Sugsy and little Ernest – were walking home together, not because of friendship but to avoid name-calling from the bullies who always followed them with taunts and stones. The three of them were different from the rest and it was safer not to separate. They were different because they lived in a small flat above the chip shop where their foster Mam, a woman who wasn't their real Mam, looked after them.

Bob closed his eyes, felt the movement of the train and listened to an announcement. The guard talked of stations and times in a strong Geordie accent, similar to the politician's own. Without meaning to, Bob's mind jumped to that chip shop, decades before, and the stairs that led up from the street. These were dingy and their ancient carpet was greasy and torn. Bob could smell the batter and the hot oil as he remembered the piled-up sacks of potatoes and the layered, pungent trays of cod brought in a van, every afternoon, from North Shields.

He tried to picture Auntie Marge, his foster Mam, but failed to bring her face to mind. All he could remember was her faded pinnie and the fact that she'd lived in that flat rent free, in return for helping out Mister Singh downstairs. She'd helped Mister Singh with the frying every night time when the queue stretched down the street. Mister Singh was also a shadowy figure in a turban and a brown overall. Of course, Bob reminded himself, the council gave her something for having the three of them – himself, Sugsy and little Ernest – the ratepayers covered their keep whilst they camped out like lodgers in her front double bedroom.

Bob rewound his memories, going back again to the walk home from school. Little Ernest was undersized and suffered from asthma. He was gentle and timid and tried to hold Bob's hand. They walked a different route every night, trying to give their tormentors the slip. Sometimes they bought bubblegum from a machine because they wanted the football cards. Sugsy had been a pasty-faced, fat kid with a skin condition. He always seemed to have a lot of copper coins. Bob suspected he pinched them from coat pockets, in the cloakroom. In his imagination Bob could see the cobbled lanes, the sweet shop and the junction they called the Big Lamp. He could picture little Ernest's skinny knees and Sugsy's busted shoes as clear as yesterday. Not only that, he could also remember one big, important thing about these two foster brothers. Their real Dad had killed their real Mam with a punch to the head and afterwards he'd been sent to prison for life.

Bob forced his mind back to the present and stared down at his own beefy hands. A steward poured him a first-class cup of coffee from a silver jug. He fished in his pocket for a tip then regarded his hands once more. He tried to imagine the brothers' ordeal. A punch to the head. He himself had never hit a woman. He'd knocked out quite a few men in the boxing ring, and he'd once seriously hurt a Sunderland supporter after a match, decades ago, although he'd always managed to keep this out of the press every time he'd stood for election. He turned his hands over and then back again, examining them. They were square and enormous. He made one into a fist. Without wanting to, he thought about Sugsy's and Ernest's Mam's frail skull. A punch to the head. As far as he was aware, no one he knew had ever hit a woman. However, all this was beside the point. His personal experiences and recollections of violence meant nothing and could not alter the true, horrific fact of Sugsy's and Ernest's story. It had been all over the papers. A punch to the head. Death. Imprisonment. **Kitchen Fight Murder Shock** the headlines had screamed. Followed by **Wife-Slayer Gets Life**, then **Tragic Two in Council Care**.

Bob listened to the rhythm of the train. It was soothing and endless. He turned over the pages of his complimentary copy of the Newcastle Journal, expecting, in what he knew was a ridiculous way, to see photographs of people he'd once known. His thoughts were flowing now and there was no stopping them. Throughout his boyhood there had been another big, bad thing that he'd understood and reflected upon. This was the detail that marked *him* out as different, like Sugsy and Ernest, for he was on his own too. His own real Mam had gone off to Birmingham and left him behind. She'd left him in the bus station.

Bob stirred sugar into his coffee, bit his lip and blinked away the threat of two unmanly tears. His real mother was even more indistinct to him than Auntie Marge. There was no point in trying to remember her now because he'd not been able to remember her then. All he'd ever managed was a blurred image of a slim, retreating figure with a suitcase and an umbrella. She was not real, he knew, but just someone he'd once seen at the pictures, who was acting the sad part of a woman who was leaving, disappearing. She was in a film and somehow she'd become mixed with his real Mam in his child's mind. He'd never really believed in her. No, not then and not now. Thinking about it, she was probably Mary Poppins.

Bob signalled to the steward who topped up his coffee. He added three more sugars and stared at it thoughtfully. He'd lived in the flat with

Sugsy and little Ernest and they'd watched a black-and-white television set after school. There'd been a coal fire with a fire guard and a kettle that whistled on a gas ring. China birds had perched on the mantelpiece. Little Ernest used to give him things that he'd made at school. He could recall a toilet-roll pencil holder and a tiny chest of drawers made from match boxes. He searched around in his mind but, in the main, his memories were sparse and lacked detail. Foster care, he thought to himself, turning the words over in his mind. Foster care. All three of them were in foster care and faceless Auntie Marge had called them *our* Bob, *our* Sugsy and *our* Ernest. They'd got on fine and looked out for each other, loyal and somehow united, in a cheerless world, but there'd been a lot of arguments. Bob remembered that Sugsy used to take all the hot water. He frowned now at the recollection. The doctor had given Sugsy special white stuff to put in the bath to help relieve his red-raw skin, so Sugsy was in the damned bath all the damned time. Never mind the rest of them, Bob recalled. Sugsy took all the hot water and bathed his sore skin in the white stuff. He was a selfish bastard. They had to get in the bath after him and use his dirty, scummy, whitish water or else do without.

Bob sighed and tried to picture the moment of arrival in Newcastle, when the train would cross the river, as high as a bird. Below, the slick of the Tyne would curve away and the succession of elegant bridges would retreat into the distance. Ahead, on the Quayside, buildings would pile upon buildings – the graceful spires, the modern blocks, the windows, the chimneys, the steps and the monuments – his very own home town clinging as ever to the sides of its steep gorge as the train ran through... just thinking about it brought a lump to his throat. He swallowed hard. Auntie Marge, he thought. Faceless Marge... Poor, kind-hearted little Ernest... That bastard Sugsy... Marge still sent him a birthday card every year. She signed it 'your loving Mam'. He never replied.

Bob Skelton the politician was loud, occasionally hearty and deliberately bad mannered. 'Belter' Skelton to the adoring press, he played up to their pugilistic, masculine image. Although privately fond of fine wines and haute cuisine, he drank beer and ate bacon sandwiches whilst within camera range. Moreover, as an accessory to his Savile Row handcrafted suit, he sported a Newcastle United scarf and, due to a nail-biting run-up to the FA Cup last month, he'd even been photographed in an unbecoming black-and-white striped woolly hat. He had a large waist, big hands and a fat neck, but somehow these didn't signify poor health, even though his colour was high. Rather, his bulk suggested force, determination and strength. He was uncompromising and ruthless. His unattractive eyes studied and evaluated the world without the aid of glasses whilst his mind accommodated or rejected what he saw with the speed and severity of a sprung steel trap.

He yawned then picked up the top copy of the secret Cabinet papers and began reading. He uncapped an expensive gold fountain pen and began annotating in the margins. Within seconds his wandering memories of boyhood were harnessed and pushed down to a rarely accessed place, somewhere in his private soul. Now he concentrated on undisclosed government policy and his thoughts became entirely focused, structured and controlled. These small secrets of state he knew he could manage, manipulate, comment upon – unlike his own. He read and evaluated and his pen flew. He answered his phone twice and ate a prawn-and-iceberg sandwich without mayo. He thought about cigars but resisted the temptation to buy one. He was a big man in an Italian handmade shirt with damp armpits. One or two people recognised him on their way to the buffet car.

Bob Skelton came across to the chattering classes as uneducated, but at the very same moment they made this judgement, they acknowledged its irrelevance. He could, they knew, outmanoeuvre and outwit anyone in the Commons. He could think on his feet, he had the common touch in spades, and he made one good decision after another whilst taking huge risks. He never flirted but he had bottomless reserves of bluff, working-class charisma. He was fearless and headline grabbing. '**Belter Bob Pulps Bosses**', the papers might insist one day, followed by '**Belter Skelton wipes floor with battered Unions**' the next. That very morning a leading broadsheet had shouted gleefully, '**Belter's knock-out leaves crushed Opposition reeling on ropes**'.

After a while, Bob returned the 'Confidential' papers to his briefcase and locked it. The northern countryside had disappeared into darkness and he could see nothing but his own face shining back at him from the window of the train. It was the countenance of a man used to getting his own way, a man sure of his direction in life. As he stared, he thought he could again make out the dim wraiths of Sugsy and little Ernest hovering behind his shoulder. They were still hanging about. He examined them, and as he did so his steely composure seemed to slacken. An expression of doubt seemed to form and then grow, altering both his eyes and his mouth, even though the imaginary pair looked poorly nourished and hopeless. He watched them, his uncertainty and discomfort growing until the smaller brother held out his hand. Then Bob let out a sharp breath. From little Ernest, this was a gesture so theatrical, so Dickensian and so ridiculously stagy that he shrugged with impatience and pointed his finger, ordering the two of them away. Get lost, he mouthed. He might have even spoken the words aloud. Get lost! He rubbed his eyes as his foster brothers melted away. There was nothing in the reflection now except his own bullish head and shoulders. A crackly voice made an announcement. It was the Geordie guard, sounding more than pleased. He said the train was approaching Newcastle.

On the station concourse, Bob took a deep breath. He expected to taste something tainted and industrial but instead he inhaled the scents of fresh coffee and flowers. The glass-domed atmosphere resounded with the slamming of doors and there was a bustle of late commuters. He looked about before moving in the direction of the taxi rank, outside on Neville Street. He was excited by the familiarity of the place and disturbed by a unique feeling of being *at home,* whilst at the same time being *far away*.

A mile off, at the Big Lamp, on a cobbled corner next to a fish and chip shop, Little Ernest, or Ernie as he was now known, polished glasses behind the bar of a public house. The city had edged outwards over the years and at the bottom of the hill, close by, there was now an arts centre, a *fin de siècle*-style bar with tiffany lights and glib eateries serving sushi and tapas. Nevertheless, the area once haunted by the three lonely foster brothers, the same threatening streetscape explored by Bob's imagination, was dismal, unwelcoming and unchanged.

'You seen our Sugsy?' Ernie called to his wife who was busy emptying ashtrays.

'He'll be out thieving no doubt.'

'He said he'd give us a hand later.'

'Yeah? I'll believe it when I see it.'

Ernie laid down his tea towel and took a drag on his inhaler. He choked in an exasperated way.

His wife was dismissive. 'I'm not having any more words.' She polished the plastic table top in a brisk, no-nonsense manner. 'You know what I think. Even if he *is* your own flesh and blood.'

Ernie was silent. The very thought of his brother made him feel discouraged. That Sugsy's a wash-out, he thought to himself, and here I am, doing my very, very best.

As a tenant of the brewery, he was trying to make a go of a no-hope pub. The place was too rough to attract women, too far out of town to attract teenagers and too garishly tarted-up by Scottish & Newcastle to attract older men. However, despite everything and trying to meet the needs of his limited clientele, he'd tried pie and pea suppers, topless go-go girls and big-screen Sky Sports. The first two of these ventures had failed but the third was proving popular. Tonight, a European game was expected to pull in a few extra drinkers.

'Shall I give Auntie a ring?' He meant Marge.

'She'll be out line dancing.'

'We'll have to keep our fingers crossed then. For old Sugsy. The bugger might show up.'

Bob Skelton stepped through the massive wooden doors of the Central Station and caught a glimpse of an orange-stained and starry sky. He was emotional. He wanted to laugh and cry. A cab nuzzled the kerb and shoving his feelings firmly aside, he gave directions. His voice was firm, authoritative. I'm a government minister, he reminded himself. I'm here for *one* night. This bloody jaunt means nothing. Nothing at all.

Suddenly, something solid careened into him from behind. He lost his balance, fell surprised and winded against the vehicle and, in a dazed instant, heard the driver shout. He felt the handle of his briefcase tugged from his grasp. He straightened, turned and roared like an animal. '*Stop!*'

The thief was running away. He wasn't young, for his gait was unathletic, even hobbling, but passers-by were frozen with surprise. A woman yelped. A newspaper vendor altered his regular cry mid-breath from 'Chron-i-cle' to 'Hoy! Ye!' A couple of Japanese businessmen stared open-mouthed. Bob's eyes took in his assailant's unwashed fawn Nike jacket, his beat-up trainers, his balding head and his droopy backside. '*Stop!*'

The mugger dodged in and out of the line of taxi cabs, their glowing sidelights picking up and dropping his shadow. He half looked back, unseeing, fearful, dazzled by a headlamp's full beam. For an instant he was captured as in a newsman's flash, immobile, lit up in stark black and white.

'*Stop!*' Bob blinked, almost blind with anger. He raised his fat fist and shook it. The image on his retina connected first with the train memories and then with his emotions of moments before. There was no doubt. The person who had just stolen his case of Cabinet secrets was Sugsy, his foster brother. 'Stop, Sugsy. *Stop*! It's me. Come back now! *Sug-SY!*'

Bob Skelton climbed the steep hill from the station having fled the commotion, the transport police and the danger of recognition. His back was straight and his shoulders squared. He felt himself fill a significant volume of space. He was an important person but he needed time to think. He knew from Auntie Marge's loyal, yearly cards that Sugsy and

Little Ernest worked in a pub, almost next door to the flat above the chip shop at the Big Lamp. She worked in there herself sometimes, even though she was nearly seventy. None of them had moved on. They were stuck to the place as if their feet were smeared with glue. He would deal with this himself. He had to stay calm. He had to get the briefcase back at all costs. Newspaper front pages kept popping into his mind. **Belter Mugged – Secrets Stolen**, or **Brother Belts Big Skelton**, or **Careless Belter: PM's Fury**, or **Belter's Dodgy Briefcase Shock**. The chance for gleeful headline hacks to exercise their talents seemed enormous. They had to be stopped.

The pub, when he arrived, was brightly lit and noisy. A group of men stood outside holding pints and cigarettes and exchanging banknotes. A quick glance around the door assured Bob that the same man who had robbed him was serving, alongside an unknown woman, behind the bar. He was, without question, his foster brother. Tatty, dog-eared and as defeated-looking as ever, Sugsy was now wearing a pair of old-fashioned, oversized eye glasses. Apart from this, he hadn't really changed.

Bob was self-conscious in his cashmere overcoat and tailored suit. He felt out of place and a little ridiculous. For some reason his heart was pounding. Wanting to confront Sugsy one to one, in private, without a scene, he retreated to the shadow of a doorway, waiting and thinking. I'll give him some money, he decided. He took out his wallet and counted the cash. He had three hundred pounds. I'll wait for him to come out, have a quiet word, pay him off, get the case back and then I never, ever, need see him again.

It was chilly and boring in the doorway but Bob's mind was in turmoil. He was standing on the street where he'd lived as a boy. He'd lived here, in *this* place, longer than he'd lived anywhere else, either before or since. The three of them – himself, little Ernest and Sugsy – had played football on this very corner. Over there was the grocer's, now a 24-hour Spar run by Indians. Next to it were the launderette and the hairdressers, which were unchanged. Over the road was the fish and chip shop, now a shining takeaway pizza outlet. The flat upstairs looked empty and forlorn. Tears filled his eyes for the first time in decades. He wiped them away with his handkerchief, ashamed and confused. What's the matter with me? he asked himself. I've got to get that damned briefcase back, that's all. That bastard Sugsy's not going to stitch me up over this. He blew his nose. He decided to retrieve the case, cancel tomorrow's meeting and return to London on the next train. The thought of going back to London was strangely comforting. I know who I *am* in London, he thought.

When Sugsy finally appeared outside he was with a couple of men. Bob followed them at a distance, in the direction of Rye Hill. He watched his foster brother go into a modern maisonette and open the door with a key. His friends disappeared around a corner, out of sight.

Bob hesitated outside the front door, uncertain. I'm much bigger than him, he reasoned. Much stronger. Thinking of this, his heart was in his mouth. He imagined ringing the bell, forcing his way in and shouting. He tried to picture himself intimidating Sugsy but he felt rooted to the spot. It was quite impossible to imagine overpowering his foster brother, or threatening him, because it would be an entirely new way of doing things. This was never how things had been. His old pattern of behaviour from the past was one of deference to Sugsy because he was older. I'm afraid of him, Bob realised with horror. I was always afraid of him, the bastard. I'm *scared*.

He walked around the side of the dwelling. Here, a light shone from a frosted window and Bob realised that Sugsy was taking a bath. There was the sound of singing and splashing. He listened to the familiar sounds, remembering how Sugsy soaked his scabby skin and took all the hot water every night when they lived together in the flat. He was *always* in the damned bath, he recalled. No one else ever got a chance. And now he's got my briefcase. He was selfish then and he's selfish now. There was a lump in Bob's throat and his heart was beating harder than was normal. He felt helpless, bitter and alone.

At the rear of the property was a small yard with a washing line. A cat meowed on a wall. To his surprise the back door was ajar. It had been left open for the cat and there was a saucer of milk on the step. Gingerly, he stepped inside. He passed the bathroom where the singing was robust and cheerful. Sugsy's voice was as tuneless as ever.

In the living room, the TV was switched on without the sound. He glanced around. It was a small cheerless space, a little untidy. It was the room of a single man, lacking the homely touches of a woman or, in Bob's experience, an interior designer. On a low table in front of the settee was his stolen briefcase. The lock had been prised off and the papers tipped out. His toilet bag, his clean shirt, socks and pants had been pulled from their silk pocket and tossed aside. The only valuable items – the gold pen, the phone and a bottle of Armani cologne – had been collected together on the floor. Hurriedly, Bob returned all the items to the case and grasped it in his arms. He was sweating with relief. The out-of-tune Mozart aria from the bathroom was reaching a climax. In the doorway, he hesitated. A framed photograph on top of the television set had caught his eye. It was a colour snapshot of himself, Little Ernest,

Auntie Marge and Sugsy taken in the park many, many summers before. They were all eating ice lollies and smiling happily. Bob's heart lurched in his chest. That's me, he thought. That's us. I can't just *leave*, he decided. I can't just *go*.

He stepped into the hall then pushed open the bathroom door. He loomed in the thick steam, his briefcase clutched to his chest. 'Sugsy, it's me. It's Bob. I've come for my case. I just want to say…'

The man in the bath screamed. He jumped to his feet, his hand scrabbling on the window sill for his glasses. Panicked, he dropped them into the water. Wet and vulnerable as a beached fish, he then lunged forwards. Bob saw his red, shocked face, the strands of hair plastered over his bald scalp, the big naked stomach, the shreds of soapy foam falling from his flesh. His mouth was open and he yelled like a terrified soldier going into battle. 'Aaaagh!' Climbing from the bath, both his hands were raised in a cowardly attempt at combat.

Bob Skelton was afraid of Sugsy. This had always been so. In an automatic boxer's reflex he pulled back one arm as if it was on a spring. As the startled man approached, defensively, without thinking, without pause, he followed his fighter's training and let this tensed arm fly. It accelerated like a piston, like a bullet, like an arrow from a bow. His big, meaty fist connected with Sugsy's skull and he thought he felt the bone crumple. Straightaway the man fell at his feet, jerked like a shot rabbit and was then immediately still. Blood appeared in his ear and trickled gently from his nose. Bob placed his case on a chair and knelt down to feel his pulse. There was none. **Bathroom Fight Murder Shock**, he thought. **Brother-Slayer Gets Life**.

Little Ernest, or Ernie as he was now known, was on his way to Sugsy's maisonette, round the corner on Rye Hill. He'd listened to another angry outburst from his wife and now, even though it was late, he wanted to sort out the matter once and for all. Ernie disliked arguments, unpleasantness and any form of sulking. He had a peaceful nature and a kind heart. He also hated unreliability and ingratitude. Thus he was torn between his wife and his brother, both of whom he loved dearly but who couldn't be reconciled. He had no choice. The problem had been unresolved for too long and his wife was right – Sugsy was a hopeless barman and he was dishonest in his handling of money. Because of this he was going to do the unthinkable and dismiss his own flesh and blood. Give him the sack. There was no other way.

He trudged along, apprehensive and sad. His mouth was dry. He kept imagining his brother's outrage, his self-justification, his determination to blame his sister-in-law for everything that had gone wrong between them. Maybe we'll still be friends, he thought, regretfully. Maybe we'll still go fishing together on Sunday afternoons, in the park.

To his surprise a man emerged from around the side of Sugsy's place. He was tall and bulky and important looking, in an overcoat, a suit, a shirt and tie. He was a well-dressed stranger, cradling an overstuffed briefcase in his arms as if it were a baby. The little publican stopped in his tracks and the two of them regarded each other steadily. The street lamp shone down on to Sugsy's visitor, illuminating his big head as bright as day. 'Bob!' gasped Little Ernest with pleasure. 'Our Bob! It's you, isn't it? It's really you!' He paused. 'Wasn't our Sugsy in, then?'

Bob Skelton wheeled around on one heel like a skater. He turned in the opposite direction and broke into a frightened run. A bottle of cologne fell from his case and landed unbroken in the gutter.

'Bob!' shouted Little Ernest. 'Bob! Come back. It's me. It's your Ernest. Don't run off! *Bob! Bob! Please!*'

It was no good. His long-lost foster brother, the big noise in the government who'd made them all so proud, was running off down the hill. He'd gone. Ernie rubbed his eyes. He felt upset. Well, I'll be jiggered, he thought. I must go and tell our Sugsy about this. He'll never get over it.

A ROUGH GUIDE TO TANGA

ANN CLEEVES

This story provides further proof, as if it were needed, of the versatility of one of our most gifted crime writers. Ann Cleeves has written two distinct series of whodunits, featuring respectively an amateur sleuth and the policeman Stephen Ramsay, before moving on to stand-alone novels of psychological suspense including most recently the highly acclaimed *The Sleeping And The Dead*. Although she seldom writes short stories, 'A Winter's Tale' and 'The Plater' are splendid achievements, well worth seeking out. Here, she has tried something completely different – a study of the way in which some of our compatriots behave when visiting Africa. This is a story that is typical of Ann Cleeves' work; low-key, subtle and likely to stay in the memory for a long time.

I picked up the lads in the coffee shop in Moshi. It was December, approaching the hottest time of the summer. There'd been a brief shower and the air was suddenly heavy as the puddles on the red-mud road evaporated. The boys were sitting just inside the door, complaining about the prices. They spoke loudly, not realising perhaps that the waitress could understand them and that her English was as good as theirs. The coffee shop *was* the most expensive place in town but it was run by St Margaret's and I always tried to support it. The passion juice was delicious and they served coffee grown on Kilimanjaro. I could see the snowy summit from my room at school, if it wasn't covered in cloud. Most of the time it was.

I say that I picked up the lads but that can't have been true. They must have picked me up. I'm not a confident person. It would never occur to me to start a conversation with strangers. I can't remember how the first contact was made, but when I left the shop I was laughing. It was as if I'd been swept along by a river in flood. I felt I was different and would never be the same again.

There were two of them: brothers, both at university, separated by a year. Fair-haired, brown-skinned, they had flat stomachs and long hands and at that first meeting I could hardly distinguish them. They were Will and Oliver, the nearly-twins. I asked what they were doing in Tanzania.

'Just travelling,' Will-or-Olly said. A confident voice. A voice that would never be embarrassed or shy. 'We couldn't face another Christmas at home, and the parents couldn't face us, so they gave us the fares.'

'We'd planned to do Kili, but it turned out to be too much hassle. Expensive too, with the guide and the porter, so we thought we'd chill here for a bit before moving to the coast. We want to be in Zanzibar for Christmas.'

And they leaned back in their chairs and drank Coke from the bottle and told of their exploits at the Namanga border, when they'd managed to get in from Kenya without paying for a visa. They weren't boasting. It was a performance. They'd played out their relationship many times before to entertain. I knew that but still I fell for them. The beauty and the humour. I was their audience, already their biggest fan.

I didn't know much about boys. My parents and the teachers at my Catholic school said I was a *good* girl, but goodness didn't come into it. I had fantasies that would have made their hair curl. The lack of experience was caused by shyness, a crippling fear of doing the wrong thing. Embarrassment, the English disease. At least the disease of the lower classes. It was a miracle that I'd got to Tanzania at all. I mean literally a miracle, a mystery, a religious revelation. I was standing in assembly listening to Miss Sykes, letting the words wash around me as usual.

'We've supported Moshi Tech, a state boarding school in Northern Tanzania, for many years with our prayers and our fundraising; now they've asked if we might provide a volunteer teacher of English. Perhaps one of our sixth-formers would be interested in spending their gap year there?'

She wasn't expecting an immediate response but my hand went up. It rose in the air of its own free will. And I could hear people muttering in astonishment, 'Bernie, Bernie Devaney!' Because I wasn't that sort of girl. I never put myself forward.

Africa changed me. It seeped under my skin. I felt it happening in a physical way, imagined it sliding under my fingernails, into my nostrils, under my eyelids. It was to do with the heat, and the music that played in the packed daladalas and the rhythm of Swahili voices. I became more relaxed and more confident. I slept soundly at night, only woken by Mama Julius's cow, and the chanting of the students when they went for their compulsory morning run.

The old Bernie would never have struck up conversation with classy boys with confident voices. She would never have agreed to see them again.

We met the next night at a bar not far from the school. I'd never go there in term time when the students might see, but exams were finished and everyone who could afford it had left for the summer. I left my house in the short dusk when the mountain was still pink; by the time I'd walked to the bar it was dark and the coloured bulbs on the mango trees were lit. The lads were already there, sitting at a table outside, their white hair a dull gleam. We drank Safari lager and ate spicy chicken, goat and roast bananas. I exchanged a few words of Swahili with the waiter and they were impressed, as I'd meant them to be.

'You should come with us to the coast,' Will said. By now I could tell them apart. Will was the younger, the more talkative and impulsive. 'Shouldn't she, Ol?'

Oliver was my favourite. I imagined him moody and poetic. I looked at him across the table, over the empty bottles and the pile of bones.

'Yeah,' he said. He smiled very slowly. 'Why not?'

'I can't. My sister's coming for Christmas.'

Will wasn't giving up. 'Not to Dar and Zanzibar then. But we were thinking of a short trip before that. Tanga and Pangani. Everyone says Pangani's stunning. You can snorkel. Go up river and see crocodiles. It's all in the Rough Guide.'

His voice burbled, a background hum like the insect noise. I watched

Oliver, who was frowning and staring at me. I felt that he was holding his breath, waiting for my answer.

'Sure,' I said. 'I'd love to.'

The bus trip to Tanga took five hours. I had the place by the window and Oliver sat next to me. He was very tall and he spread out, one arm along the back of my seat and his legs in the aisle where people were standing two deep. We stopped to let on a group of Masai – the men skinny, wrapped in their pink and purple plaid blankets; the women dripping with beads. A Masai man rolled up his flimsy bus ticket and stuck it in the hole in his earlobe for safe-keeping.

The bus went fast. When it slowed suddenly or jolted I felt the bone in Oliver's thigh against my own. We stared at the passing landscape and talked about music and books and Africa. He was studying American literature at university and made me promise to read *The Great Gatsby*.

You approach Tanga across a flat plain, leaving the mountains behind. It isn't a rich city, despite the Golf Club and the Swimming Club and the yachts moored in the bay. The inland suburbs are unlovely; everything is grey concrete with an air of impermanence, half built or decaying, it's hard to tell which. There are occasional flashes of colour-brash neon signs, *Tusker Beer, Coca-Cola, Cyber Café*; a market selling live animals, vegetables and twisted bales of yellow coconut palm.

The streets aren't made up and the bus station is full of people hustling. They throng around the buses and lift trays of bracelets, water, fruit and samosas to the windows. They shout and rap on the windows with a desperation I'd not encountered in Moshi or Arusha. And once you leave the bus, they offer taxis, hotels, reassurance. In Tanga there's a need for reassurance. Country people come to the city and feel lost. European travellers arrive and are overwhelmed by the noise, the heat and the smell. At the bus stand you can buy a guide and a friend.

I chose Godfrey to be our guide. He was slender, like a girl, with long wrists. We spoke English together because he was a student and needed the practice. Will and Oliver fidgeted, impatient for a beer and a shower, made uncomfortable by the hustlers, flapping them away like mosquitoes, but I negotiated with Godfrey alone. We needed a hotel for the night before leaving for Pangani, I said. Somewhere nice but not too expensive. I looked across at the brothers who were already sweating. Somewhere with air conditioning perhaps, a fan at least.

Godfrey nodded sagely. 'The Inn by the Sea,' he said, 'is very good, very clean.'

And a taxi to get there? Of course a taxi. The Inn was on the shore, too far to walk. A taxi would be 1,500 shillings. He would arrange it and come with us. All the time Will and Oliver were watching us, and I sensed a hostility. I thought then it was jealousy and I played up to it, smiling at Godfrey, thanking him profusely though I knew he'd take a cut from the taxi driver and the hotelier.

At the coast it's a different town. There are wide avenues lined with palms. From the taxi we had a tantalising glimpse through open gates of a lush garden or a big white house.

The hotel manager was a courteous Asian, with a grey beard and a soft voice. The rooms had been built in a row like an American motel. Each door opened on to grass and then the Indian Ocean. There was a view across the bay to a headland. A dow with a brown sail was coming into land.

'Fine,' I said to Godfrey and to the manager, without even consulting the boys. 'This will be fine.'

We swam in the tepid sea, then watched tiny crabs draw patterns on the beach with recycled sand. The sun was setting and it was night again, and the smell of grilled fish and spice drew us to the terrace to eat. The heat and the travelling had made us languid. Our movements were slow, the conversation sporadic. The brothers talked about school friends, their parents' house in the country, and their life seemed as exotic to me as tales of Tanga would have done at home in Manchester.

I think some sign must have passed between them, because suddenly Will made excuses about being tired and hurried away. Olly ordered more beer, and the talk became intimate, every word invested with significance. He took my hand and we walked back along the beach. Outside my room he kissed me. Eventually, when I said I should go to bed he held me away from him, staring for a last time at my face, then he let me go. He made no attempt to follow me inside, and I thought how different he was from the boys at my school. A gentleman.

For the first time since arriving in Africa I found it hard to sleep. It was the excitement and the heat. My first experience of romance. I pictured Oliver lying, brown, on his bed, soft-focused behind the mosquito net. The air conditioning was noisy but ineffective and in the end I switched it off. I must have dozed because I came to with a start to discover that the faint light above the bed was still on and my book was up-turned beside me. There was a noise, a small scratching sound. I thought it was a moth fluttering against the mesh on the window, trying to reach the light inside. But when I turned, hoping to make out its silhouette against the faded muslin curtain, I saw movement inside the room. A thin black hand had squeezed through a gap in the latticed window panes and was groping towards the watch that I'd placed on the bedside table.

I couldn't move. My fear was irrational – the gap in the window was tiny, too small for anyone to climb in – but I can't exaggerate the terror. I remember thinking, this is how people who are scared of spiders feel, this is panic. And the hand crawling painstakingly towards the watch could have been a big, poisonous spider. Not human at least. I didn't picture a man on the end of the arm. I lay frozen inside the net that hung over my bed, which I'd tucked carefully inside the mattress to keep out insects. Now it wasn't a protection. It was a trap.

I only froze for a moment and then I screamed. The hand withdrew, sliding noiselessly away. I pulled at the mosquito net, ripping it in my desperation to be free. It tangled around my face. It was fine as a web with an animal smell. I felt it cover my mouth and my nose, that I was breathing it in and began to choke. There was the bang of a door and the hiss of voices. English, not Swahili. The brothers.

When I reached them they had the man cornered on the beach. He was backed against the cliff. They didn't see me. The scene was dimly lit like a black and white movie by the escaped glow from the hotel. The thief was older than I'd expected. Frail. Stooped. No match for the boys. But they circled him like vultures or the black kites I'd seen over the rubbish tip at Moshi, as if they were scared of him. There was the same mix of hostility and fear as there'd been in their reaction to Godfrey outside the bus. It came to me that they hated the old man. And that I did too.

If I'd shouted again I could have broken the spell; I didn't speak. I tell myself I had no idea what would happen but that's not true. I had a picture of myself wrapped in the mosquito net, helpless, ridiculous, and someone had to pay. The man suddenly made a move. Oliver leapt towards him and pulled him to the ground in a tackle. The brothers knelt on the sand beside him and they began to hit him. One after another. His face had the look of an over-ripe fruit, a papaya, squashed and bruised. There was no resistance in the skin to the fists. Then they stood and kicked his body until his shirt was soaked with blood. Still I couldn't make a sound. Eventually they let him crawl away.

I climbed back up the steps and sat there, waiting for them. Oliver sat beside me and put his arm around my shoulder. I was shaking. 'It's all right,' he said. 'We've frightened him away. No one will disturb you again.' He stroked my hair away from my face. 'Shall I sleep with you tonight? Would you like that?'

And I let him because I was afraid of going back into that square, humid room on my own.

The next morning we were back at the bus station. We planned to travel down the coast to Pangani. The brothers seemed over-excited, slightly manic. It was as if they were sharing an in-joke. Everything was a giggle. I had that frail, washed-out feeling that often comes with a bad hangover. I hadn't been able to face breakfast and my anti-malarial pills always make me queasy without food.

Across the crowd I saw Godfrey and I waved him over, thinking he'd probably get a good deal on the bus for us. He held out his hand and I shook it, then he turned to the nearly-twins, his hand still outstretched. They pretended not to see it and continued their wild conversation.

Then I saw them as they were. No different from the boys on my estate who attended my school. The boys who went to football matches to pick fights with foreigners.

'I'm going back to Moshi,' I said. 'I can't travel with you any more.'

'You're upset,' Oliver said. 'It was a terrible experience. We understand.'

'Can you get me a ticket to Moshi?' I asked Godfrey.

I was walking with him, sheltered by his body from the onslaught of hustlers when Oliver called after me, as if it were a consolation, 'We didn't pay the hotel bill. They might take security more seriously now.' When I didn't answer he shouted, much more loudly than was necessary, 'After all, they have to learn.'

BACK TO THE LAND

MAT COWARD

Although he has recently begun to write entertaining novels, Mat Coward remains first and foremost a short-story writer of versatility and distinction. His refusal to be pigeon-holed is undoubtedly a strength. But, despite their variety, you can be sure that a Mat Coward story will offer humour and a touch of social comment. When we were discussing his possible contribution, Mat – a home-loving man who seldom ventures too far from his base in Somerset – told me firmly that London was one of the very few cities with which he felt an affinity. I was anxious that *Crime in the City* should not be burdened with too many stories set in London, but Mat's idea of a futuristic tale set in the capital held great appeal. And the finished product represents one of our up-and-coming writers at his best.

'You're always going to get murders.' DI Wallace tucked his Fidel T-shirt into his trousers, to avoid it flapping hemp particles over the evidence. 'You're never going to get a society without murders.'

Detective Constable Townsend, sweating in a suit and polished shoes, was frankly looking for an argument. He'd spent the weekend at his parents' place, squashed in with his sister and his brother-in-law, and he hadn't been allowed to raise his voice to his brother-in-law once, on pain of female disapproval. He was overdue an argument. 'I thought you lot reckoned crime was environmental, right? Caused by social factors. So why would anybody commit a murder in Utopia?'

Bending at the knees to get a closer look at the corpse's feet, which were naked though the rest of her was dressed, Greg Wallace ignored the Utopia jibe. If that was the best Paul could do, he might yet survive until lunchtime. 'Murder's different. You abolish extreme inequality, you get a lot less burglary. And so on. Not that simple with crimes of violence, crimes of rage and passion. They're in the genes, they're not socio-economic.'

Not that this was entirely true, as both men knew perfectly well – though only one was likely to acknowledge. Wallace had joined the Met, almost fresh from school, in 1998. Twenty years on, the murder rate was a fraction of what he'd seen as a kid. Social changes, different attitudes, altered distribution of power; they did have an effect on murder, just as on all crimes. Fundamental point remained, though: murder's human, murder's ineradicable.

'Definitely murder, is it?' Townsend pointed at the dead woman's throat. 'What I mean is, a wound like that – could be suicide.'

'No, look at this.' Wallace used two gloved fingers to turn over the victim's right hand. 'Defence wounds.'

'Yeah, fair enough.' Townsend wasn't going to argue about stuff like that. He'd never done a murder before, not one in his two years of detective duty. The DI had done loads, he reckoned, back in the old days. He looked around the small, tidy, well-furnished bedroom. 'Come to think of it, there's no sign of a weapon, is there?'

'True. And it'd be easy to spot, given the size of the wound. Big carving knife, something like that.' Wallace got to his feet, and moved away from the corpse. He hadn't been at a murder scene in a while; he'd forgotten how the smell got into your lungs and lodged there. Especially in this heat. 'Was she wearing tags?'

'She was. Big ones, too – 64MB.' Townsend slapped at the small plastic box clipped to his belt. 'Couldn't run them, I'm afraid – bloody thing's not working.'

You mean you forgot to charge it. 'All right. We'll do it when we get back. I doubt she died of anything chronic, anyhow.' Wallace looked at the woman on the floor; not at any particular aspect now, not searching for specific evidence – seeing her as a whole, for the first time, wondering who she was and how she got there. Young, perhaps early thirties; well-dressed; white. She looked healthy enough, apart from having had her throat cut. 'I've never heard of anyone having 64MB tags. What would be the point? What kind of medical history could need that much space?'

'X-rays?' Townsend shrugged. 'Scans? Maybe she had a big series of operations at some time.'

'I suppose so. All right, Paul, you get back to the office, get us an identification off those tags. I'll see how the door-to-door's going.' He got down on his knees again, with his nose at carpet level, and after a moment he said 'Ah!'

'Ah?'

'Found her shoes and socks. Under the bed.'

'They're Texan,' said the lab guy, turning the dead woman's medical tags over in his hand. 'Republic of Texas.'

'Oh yeah?' said Townsend. 'Is that why they're so big?'

'Point is, we don't have a Texan reader.'

'Shit. Does that mean you can't read 'em?'

The lab guy bristled. 'We can read 'em. Of course we can read 'em. It's just going to take a while longer.'

'Can't you just bike 'em over to the Texan embassy? Consulate? Whatever it is.'

'Ha! You don't follow politics, Constable, I take it.'

Paul Townsend, who most certainly did follow politics – just because he didn't agree with the sheep, that didn't mean he didn't follow politics – said: 'It's Detective Constable, in fact. Currently assigned to a murder investigation.'

The lab guy sat himself on a tall stool and crossed his legs. 'Look. The Republic of Texas and the Republic of the British Isles are not close at the moment. Yeah? Because of California.'

'They'd still want to know about the death of one of their citizens, surely?'

'That rather depends on what she's doing over here. We'll ask them, but they're not going to be forthcoming, I can promise you that right now.'

'OK, but listen – at her age, she'll have been born in the USA, won't she? So can't we check with…'

'Nope. No good.' The lab guy was enjoying himself now. Openly.

'The Former USA won't answer questions from the RoBI concerning citizens of the Republic of Texas, because they know that we'll also ask the Texans. Which means we are de facto recognising the national integrity of the Republic of Texas, which means we're not de facto recognising the national integrity of the FUSA – or, as they would see it, the USA – over that part of North America that they call Texas and that the Texans call the Republic of Texas.' He bounced in his chair. 'And, to a large extent, vice versa.'

'Do we have to ask both? Couldn't we just ask the FUSA?'

'Not if we want to maintain neutrality, no. Any further questions?'

'Just one,' said Townsend. 'Which idiot invented politics?'

Her name was Mella Nelson, the neighbours said; that's who lived at the address, the death scene, the little flat in Moorgate. She worked for the Land Reform Agency, and she was very nice. Problem being, Mella was black, middle-aged and Welsh. Not young, Texan and white.

A young, white woman with an American accent? Friend of Mella's? Yes, said one or two neighbours, that did ring a bell. Met on the stairs once or twice. Just recently. Name of… hold on… Janet? No, not Janet. Janette – that's it. American accent. Very pretty.

'Big question, then,' said Wallace. 'Where is Mella? The Texans and the Americans both deny all knowledge of Janette. So, does that mean she's a spy? Given that she died in Mella's flat, does that mean Mella killed her – or is Mella herself dead, by a third hand?'

'Several questions,' said Townsend.

The streets of that part of London known as the City were, it seemed to Wallace, as full of traffic as ever; albeit, faster-moving traffic, and better smelling, than in his younger days. There were electric buses, sun-buggy taxis, horse cabs, rickshaws, take-and-leaves, and all manner of user-propelled vehicles: bicycles, tricycles, boards and scooters. Wallace and Townsend were on foot, the DI having closed his ears to his colleague's whining. Motor vehicles were available to the police, as they were to other emergency services, when their use could be specifically justified. Detective work was rarely classed as urgent. Detectives, Wallace had told Townsend, don't often do life or death stuff. Death stuff, yes – but that's not urgent.

It wasn't a long walk. The Land Reform Agency's offices occupied several floors of an office block off Old Broad Street. Mella Nelson's supervisor, a woman in her sixties with white hair and huge eyes, met them at reception and escorted them to an empty conference room.

She'd last seen Mella yesterday afternoon. No, she hadn't seen her this morning. Yes, she should have been in. No, she hadn't phoned. No, this wasn't like her. She was more likely to work late than she was to show up late. Not like her at all.

Townsend wrote it all down diligently, then asked: 'How long has Miss Nelson worked in land redistribution?'

'Land reform,' said the public servant.

Townsend shrugged. 'What's the difference?'

She smiled. 'A difference of tone, if you like.'

The DC's face said he didn't like.

'In 1999,' said Mella's supervisor, 'ninety percent of land in this country was owned by ten percent of the population.'

'Jolly unfair,' said Townsend.

She shook her head. 'Not a question of unfair – question of inefficient. Climate change, flooding, international problems leading to uncertain supply, thus the need to produce a far greater amount of our own food, energy and so on, plus taking in our share of refugees from the Americas and elsewhere… inefficiency in land use is no longer tolerable. You can't have a thousand acres producing nothing more productive than an annual crop of game birds. Not in this world.'

Not in this world. Townsend's contempt for the cliché-of-the-age was spray-painted on his face. 'Anyway,' he said.

'Or perhaps you don't think we should take in our share of refugees?' The woman's white hair made her flushed cheeks seem red as tomatoes.

'Not at all.'

There was a silence. Vermilion cheeks versus perma-sneer. Because they were both irritating him, Wallace surrendered to a naughty impulse. 'As it happens,' he told the woman, 'my colleague's parents were both refugees. From eastern Europe.'

'Oh,' she said. Then, recovering quickly: 'From an ex-communist country? I see.'

As if that explained everything. Which perhaps, Wallace thought, it did. Except that what had happened here, in these islands, wasn't a revolution that someone had planned; it was one that happened because it couldn't not happen. The way we live now, he thought, it's not an ideology. It's an antibody. The thing was, though, even if what you're doing is just a spontaneous survival mechanism, there's always a price for someone to pay. There were plenty, and not only in the Former US, who'd prefer the price was paid by us. Hence the Land Reform woman's red cheeks. Hence, perhaps, her white hair.

'We got a bit sidetracked,' he said. 'You were about to tell us how long Mella has worked here.'

'Oh, yes. Sorry. About five years.'

'An outside appointment?'

'No, no. A career civil servant. Before us, she was with Floods and Erosion.'

'What precisely,' said Townsend, 'is Miss Nelson's job here?'

'Registry. Tracing and maintaining ownership and occupation records, that sort of thing. She's something of an expert on title research, from her time at Floods.'

Thinking of the Texans, Wallace asked: 'Is that sensitive work? I mean, in a security sense?'

'No, hardly. It's all publicly-owned information.'

The supervisor was unable or unwilling to help the detectives with any questions concerning Mella's personal life. She took them back downstairs, and as they reached the foyer, Townsend said 'What did this building use to be?'

She laughed. 'You don't know?'

'He's young,' said Wallace.

'It was part of the Stock Exchange.'

Townsend looked annoyed. With himself; with both of them. 'So what happens,' he said, 'if things change and people want their land back?'

'It's not their land.'

'That's now. But a change in government and it could be theirs again, couldn't it?'

She said nothing.

'Well, couldn't it?' he insisted. 'If parliament said it was?'

'We keep very good records,' said the woman from the Land Reform Agency, as she showed them the door.

Whether living spaces these days seemed bigger or smaller, Wallace realised, as they stood in the centre of Mella's living-room, depended on who you used to be.

On average, people lived in bigger spaces now – but only because there were so many people living in very small spaces before. That's the thing with averages. If you grew up in a large, poor family in the middle of a city, that was one thing; compare your childhood with now, with your own large, working-class family living in the middle of a city, and you'd wonder what you were going to do with all the space. Wallace, though – well, since Greg Wallace became single again he couldn't help noticing that his bachelor flats of twenty years ago were considerably bigger than his divorcé flats now.

To him, Mella's flat seemed tiny.

What could it have been, before conversion, when the whole building was the HQ of an American financial services company? The living-room, maybe a photocopying room; the bedroom, where they kept the toner cartridges and the boxes of paper. The bathroom? A lavatory, maybe. Even City whiz kids had to whiz occasionally. Now it was a lavatory with a shower.

The flat was tidy, but overcrowded: 'As if she moved here from something bigger.'

'Divorced?'

'Could be,' said DC Townsend. 'Not so common these days though, divorce.'

'More stable society,' said Wallace. 'Less stressful?'

Townsend snorted. 'Nobody wants to live in a matchbox, you mean. No matter how ugly their husband is.'

Post-Crime Science had given them an idea of what happened. Two people of roughly the same weight and height – and therefore probably the assailant was a woman, though not definitely – struggled by the door. Then they stopped struggling.

'How can they tell?'

'By the heatprints on the carpet, mainly. There was a struggle, presumably, as soon as the door was opened. Then they stopped, moved over to here, sat on the bed…'

'They both sat on the bed?'

'According to PCS, yeah.'

'That's a bit weird, isn't it?'

Wallace pointed. 'There's only one chair.'

'All right then. One of them sits on the chair and one of them sits on the bed. But both on the bed? Someone you've just been fighting with?'

'Good, Paul. Good point. Right: they sit on the bed for a while – the exact wording is more than thirty seconds, less than forty five minutes – then they stand up.'

'Simultaneously?'

'Probably not. They can't say. I'm supposing that one of them stands up, walks to the desk…'

'Opens a drawer?'

'Maybe. Touches two drawer handles, certainly. Then the struggle resumes.'

'For possession of whatever's in the drawer?'

'Sounds reasonable. At some stage in this struggle – quite quickly, given the number and distribution of the heatprints at that spot –

Unknown Assailant sticks a blade into Janette's throat, cuts her open, and she bleeds to death.'

'How soon does Unknown quit the scene?'

Wallace checked his notes. 'As far as they can tell, she doesn't hang around.'

'So she's not looking for anything. Or she's already found it.'

'If Unknown is Mella then she wouldn't be looking for anything, she'd know where it was.'

'Then why isn't she here? If she killed someone who attacked her in her own home, why didn't she just call the police?'

Wallace shrugged. 'Old habits die hard?' He didn't need to look at the DC's face to know what Townsend thought of that. Paul wasn't in the job in the old days. Honest citizens fearing the police was something he genuinely couldn't understand. Which was a cheering thought, when you came to think of it. 'All right. So there's a possibility of a third person being involved here. Mella's somewhere else when Unknown kills the Texan.'

'The guy who found the body?'

'We'll talk to him again. But whether it's two people or three, the question's the same: what happened to Mella Nelson? Murderer or murder victim or both, we need to find her.'

An old woman living upstairs, retired, told them she didn't really know Mella very well. She was apologetic, which was something else that had changed, Wallace thought; life, perforce, was so much more communal these days. When he started, Londoners almost took a pride in not knowing each other. But that just wouldn't work these days; not in this world. Lives were intertwined, now. People lived in neighbourhoods, not postcodes. If you didn't know your neighbours, who did you know?

'She keeps herself to herself a bit,' said the old woman. 'Not that I'm suggesting anything—'

'Of course,' said Wallace. 'How about boyfriends? Did you ever notice anyone?'

'There was a young man, yes: white, quite short, early thirties.'

'Fat or thin?'

Eagerly, she added the extra detail: 'Quite slight.'

'Did you see him often?'

'Occasionally. Just lately. Like this morning. I saw him knock on Mella's door, and then a bit later I saw him standing outside.'

'Outside her door?'

'Outside the building. On the pavement.'

They'd send a technician round, he told her, to do a morph.

'Like an identikit?'

'That's right.'

Wallace and Townsend were both thinking – well, a short, slight boyfriend could be the Unknown.

'There are definitely only two people in the flat when the killing takes place?'

'They're certain of that. So if the boyfriend killed Janette...'

'We still don't know where Mella went. Or even if Mella was there.'

Wallace tapped his phone against his chin. 'I'm going to list Mella Nelson as officially missing.'

'Not as a fugitive?'

'Not yet. What family has she got listed?'

Townsend checked. 'Just a mother, no-one else. Lives in Cardiff.'

'All right. Get someone to call the Welsh police, inform the mother. Then we'll talk to the witness who found the body.'

He was young, short, slight, white. That was the first thing they noticed about him. Lewis Bright, the man who reported the corpse to the police, worked as a rooftop farmer for an advocates' partnership in Holborn. According to the partnership's plaque, it specialised in land negotiations.

'That's all anyone does in this city,' said Townsend. 'Swap bits of land around. I mean, nobody actually makes anything any more, do they?'

Very hot day, nowhere near over yet; Wallace couldn't be bothered to argue. 'Paul, this whole square mile used to be the world centre of stockbrokerage and money-laundering, so I wouldn't worry too much.'

'All changed a bit round here since you were a boy, sir?'

Wallace wasn't looking, so he couldn't see Townsend rolling his eyes. Thought maybe he could hear it, though. Yes, it had changed: he remembered roads invisible beneath black cabs and cars, cycle messengers and motorcycle couriers, lorries and vans, and big red buses travelling slower than a fit man could walk. Except that even a fit man couldn't walk much faster than the traffic, because the pavements were just as packed: tourists of course, in those days of cheap mass travel – of any mass travel – but mostly office workers, wearing suits and carrying briefcases and looking like death. What did they all do? It was hard to remember. No – not so much hard to remember; hard to imagine.

'A bit,' he said. 'It's changed a bit. Roads are a hell of a lot cleaner for a start.'

Bright wasn't happy to see them. 'The other officer said I could come in after work, make my statement.'

'That's fine, Lewis,' said Wallace. 'You see, the matter's become rather more urgent.'

The witness screwed up his nose. 'More urgent than murder?'

'That's right. A missing person.'

Lewis Bright sat on the edge of a raised bed of corn salad, trying to fill a pipe and spilling most of it. 'Well, people go missing all the time in this world.'

'Do they?'

'Must do. Don't they? Floods and all that.'

'The missing person we're looking for is someone we think you might know.'

'Oh yeah?' He gave up and put the pipe away in his dungarees.

'Mella Nelson. You do know her, don't you?'

'Who?'

'You were at her flat this morning, Mr Bright,' said Townsend. 'You remember? You found a dead body there?'

'Oh, right. Sure, right. Mella, yes.'

Was he stoned? Wallace didn't think so. This early in the day? 'What were you doing at Mella's place this morning, Lewis?'

'What was I doing there?'

'That's the question, Mr Bright. You've had several hours to think of an answer.'

'What is that supposed to mean?'

'Let's hope you've used the time well. What were you doing at Mella's this morning, besides finding a corpse there?'

He shrugged. 'I went to see her.'

'So early?'

'On my way to work.'

'Do you often visit her so early?'

'I don't know. Sometimes.' More shrugs.

'Did you enter the flat?'

'No! No, like I told the other officer. I saw the body from the doorway, and called the police. They told me to wait outside until they arrived.'

'And you did?'

'Of course.'

'Because if you did go in there,' said Wallace, 'I'm obliged to warn you, your heatprints will be detected. And we can apply to the Ministry of Justice for a reading of your heatprint, in order to match it against those found—'

'You don't need a warrant.' No more shrugging now; much more confident. 'I'll give you permission to check my heatprint. I've never been in that flat in my life, you can do all the checks you like.'

'You've never been in that flat in your life?'

'Right.'

'So, sometimes you visit Mella at her home on your way to work… but you've never been in her flat in your life?'

He saw it too late, kicked one ankle with the other foot, scratched at his scalp. 'Are you arresting me?'

'No, Lewis, but I'm going to ask you to carry a tracker for the rest of the day. You understand this? It allows us to locate you at any time, and to send you a message asking you to contact us urgently if we decide we need to speak to you again. Will you agree to that?'

'It's voluntary?'

'It is voluntary, Lewis.'

After a moment: 'All right then.'

On the stairs on the way down to ground level, Townsend stated the obvious. 'If he's never been in the flat – and he sounded bloody sure – that means he's not the killer. So we're back to Mella.'

'Means something else, too.'

'What?'

'If he's never been in the flat, then he wasn't there to visit Mella. In which case—'

'He was there to see Janette.'

Wallace nodded. 'That'd be my guess.'

The lab phoned: 'We've found out why her tags are so big – it's a camera.'

'So she is a spy?' Wallace could hardly believe it. In fact, he didn't believe it.

'Maybe. Funny sort of spy, if so. More like an estate agent.'

'How do you mean?'

'Lots of photos of properties. Interiors, exteriors.'

'Local properties? City of London locations?'

'Who knows?'

'I need to know.'

'Hold on.' Silence for a few minutes. 'Yeah, could be. Certainly could be. We'll check. Take a while.'

'Always does.'

'We've got a name, anyway.'

'Janette,' said Wallace, winking at the DC.

'Oh… yeah.'

He relented. 'Janette what?'

'Janette Foster-Lane. Last address is a hostel up West.'

'Good, thanks. Listen – anything from the Americans yet? Either lot?'

'Nothing,' said the lab. 'Not even a "no comment".'

Wallace put the phone away. 'Paul, do you suppose the technicians can tell the difference between a struggle and a grope?'

'In their own lives, you mean, or in evidence?'

A rare joke from Paul Townsend. Maybe he was getting somewhere with the lad. 'Find out, will you? If Mella and Janette were embracing when she came into the flat, not fighting—'

'That would explain why they then sat together on the bed. Right!'

Also explains the naked feet. 'Then something is said, or happens, that does set them fighting.'

'Simple lovers' tiff,' said Townsend. 'No spies need apply.'

This time, Townsend's phone went. 'That was tracker control, sir. Lewis Bright is on the move. Heading for home, they reckon, by bicycle.'

'Right. We'll get a cab.'

Townsend's lips twisted. 'Be faster to hop there.'

'All right.' Why not? A reward for making a joke. 'Call in, get us a lift in a patrol car.'

Urgency would be a little hard to make a case for, Wallace thought, as Bright met them on the stairs, clutching a burn-bag. Even in this world, the cycle was faster through City traffic than the cop car. Maybe not too fast, though: depends how many bags he's already got rid of. They stowed him in the car, let the driver keep an eye on him, while they went for sandwiches and a cone of tea. Not so much to let him stew, more to keep them – well, Wallace – from passing out.

'I remember this place.' They sat on the stoop of Bright's building, letting him watch them eat. 'Used to go out with a girl who worked in this very building.'

'Yeah?' Townsend picked out bits of watercress and dumped them in a tenants' greenwaste bin.

'Yeah, used to meet her in that pub over there.'

'What, she didn't want a scruffy cop coming into the office?'

'Too right. Very high-powered place this; First Bank of Texas. And now look at it – decent flats for working people.' He didn't add: Argue with that, you cynical puppy. Tell me that's not progress.

'Texas?'

Wallace stopped chewing. 'Yeah…'

'Didn't you say Mella Nelson's place used to be an American busi-ness?'

'Yes, I did. Call it in.'

He finished his tea and wished he felt relaxed enough in Paul's company to ask him for his watercress. Greg Wallace loved watercress; it reminded him of tea at his gran's.

'Company,' said Townsend, 'called Texas Fire and Life.'

'The victim comes from Texas. The two chief suspects live in properties that used to be owned by Texan companies – live presumably as stakeholders, rather than just tenants?'

'Bound to be,' said Townsend, too excited to bother with a sneer. 'I'll check to make sure.'

'Right. And one suspect works for Land Reform, while the other is employed by a bunch of land lawyers.'

'Land,' said Townsend, and nodded as if supplying the missing answer to a prize crossword.

'Do you know what a land staker is, Paul?'

He shook his head. 'No. No, I don't think so.'

'Well, let's nick this poor cuckold for murder, then I'll tell you all about it.'

'You thought you'd beat us back here by more than a few minutes, didn't you, Lewis?'

'You're not allowed to use cars, detectives aren't, except in emergencies.' He seemed to be sulking.

'Good job we did, though. There'll be plenty of evidence in that last burn-bag, and in your flat, to suggest that you and Janette were cohabiting. Incidentally, you're not allowed to use burn-bags except in emergencies. The clothes you were getting rid of should have been sent to a garment centre. We'll be prosecuting you for that, whatever happens.'

'Whatever happens?'

'That's up to you. I don't want to do you for murder if you're only due for manslaughter. Maybe you didn't mean to kill her, or maybe...'

'I didn't kill her. That woman killed her.'

'What woman?'

'I don't know. Mella, is it? Black woman, older than you.'

'Right.' Wallace looked at Townsend, raised his eyes slightly. 'Let's start your statement fresh from the top.'

Lewis Bright was living with Janette Foster-Lane. At least, he thought he was. Admittedly, he didn't see much of her. But she was beautiful and exotic and she was crazy about him. At least, he thought she was. Though lately he'd begun to wonder. To worry. And finally, as is so often the way, to follow.

'You thought she was having an affair?'

'Bloody right, wasn't I?'

'By this time, had she become a stakeholder in your flat?'

'Joint stakeholder, yeah. With me. Why? I don't think she seduced me for my money, if that's what you're worrying about!'

'Go on.'

He followed her several times to Mella's; what he now knew to be Mella's. He didn't confront her. He wanted to make sure.

'And this morning you were sure? And that's why you killed her?'

No, no, he didn't kill her. That woman killed her. Today, he went up to the woman's door, knocked. Quietly, so the neighbours wouldn't hear. No answer, so he tried the door handle and it was open. They'd been too bloody busy to lock it, Lewis reckoned – and Wallace reckoned he was right, given the evidence of the heatprints.

Bright could see straight across the tiny living room, into the tiny bedroom. On the bed, locked together, Mella and Janette. He shouted something – didn't remember what. Wasn't saying, anyway. Not so much shouted, more hissed. Then he went back down to the street. Dazed. Stood over the road, smoking a pipe. Really… dazed.

'From the look on her face, from what you said to Janette – did Mella know who you were? Know who you were to Janette, I mean?'

'Oh, yeah.' Nod, nod, nod nod, nod. 'She knew.'

A few minutes later, the woman –

'The woman in this photo?'

'That's her.' Eight, nine nods.

That woman came rushing out, didn't see Bright, rushed straight past him, running like anything. Wearing this great big overcoat, despite the weather.

He went back upstairs, saw Janette dead. Couldn't go in, just couldn't do it. Anyway, he could see she was dead. Called the police.

'Why?' said Townsend. 'You called the police, but then you didn't tell us the truth. So why call us in the first place?'

'There'd been a murder,' said Bright, baffled by the question.

'So why didn't you tell us all of it?' Wallace wondered: old habits die hard?

'Because it's my fault, isn't it? It's only thanks to me she got killed.'

Townsend looked affronted; the answer didn't make sense. It didn't have to, as far as Wallace knew, but then he'd done murders before. 'If it's any consolation,' he began, and then he stopped, because what he'd been about to say was, 'If it's any consolation, it was nothing personal, Lewis. You weren't the only one she was doing this to.' Which, of course, wouldn't have been any kind of consolation at all.

'Supposing, like you said to that Land Reform woman, there was a change of government. Next year's election year. Yeah?'

'Yeah?' said Townsend. 'What, they giving the sheep brain transplants?'

'And supposing all the land that's been compulsorily purchased over the last few years, suppose it was de-purchased. Offered back to the people, and companies, it was taken from in the first place.'

'Yeah, I can just see that!' Townsend laughed. 'Thousands and thousands of people being kicked out of their bedsits, so the banks can move back in.'

'Exactly.' Wallace smiled. 'It's not as simple as it sounds. Which is where…'

Welsh police on the phone. They'd visited Mella's family, told them that Mella was officially listed as missing but that everything was being done to find her, and that if they did hear from her they should immediately contact the police.

'Right, thanks a lot. I presume they hadn't – wait a minute,' said Wallace, speaking to the phone and to Townsend. 'Who is they?'

'The missing person's family. In Cardiff.'

'They?'

'Missing person's mother, sir, and missing person's sister.'

Townsend checked his notes, double-checked with Births and Deaths, while Wales held on. 'No, she definitely hasn't got a sister.'

'Get back round and arrest the sister,' Wallace told Wales. 'If she's still there.'

They could have drawn a car for the journey to Wales, but it would have taken longer to travel on the small roads adjacent to the reclaimed motorway than it would by fast train. Besides, Wallace had enjoyed enough motion sickness for one day. He wanted to sleep on the journey. First he had to finish his sentence.

'Which is where the land stakers come in,' he said, stretching his back and his legs and cooling his forehead against a truly excellent half pint of cider. 'You could – and it's been done before, in other countries; they did it a lot towards the end of the twentieth century – simply get the World Trade Organisation or whoever to declare the original seizures illegal, kick the peasants out on to the streets where they belong, and if you're feeling kind you could employ them to help convert their lavs back into your photocopying room.'

'No way. People'd get lawyers.'

'Right. Lawyers, human rights groups, barricades, armed resistance. God knows what. The whole thing could go on for years. Meanwhile, you're losing money. So, what do you do?'

With a huge and horrible smile, Townsend replied: 'Buy 'em off.'

'That's it. Tell them they can have nothing when you eventually get your way – which you will, you being a huge corporation, and them being little peasants – or they can have a few thou now if they sod off sharpish.'

'So what's the staker's slice?'

'Well, you have two kinds of staker. Freelances and corporates. My guess is that Janette was corporate. At its simplest, the staker gets himself or herself a piece of the action – say, by marrying someone who is a stake-holding tenant in a particularly valuable building.'

'Thus becoming a stakeholder herself.'

'That's it.' The train began the long process of slowing down; half an hour to destination. 'Because the staker knows the system, she's likely to get a better price. The more honest ones even admit that, up front, to the existing stakeholder. In the month before the last general election, for-mally registered Significant Intimate Relationships in London increased by eleven per cent.'

Townsend looked disgusted. Then he looked annoyed with himself for being disgusted. Then he looked confused.

'There are various staking scams,' Wallace continued, 'most of which aren't actually illegal, which is why we in the detective force have so little contact with the whole business. I only know so much about it because my ex-wife was in Special Branch. They keep an eye on them, at least the foreign ones. The corporate stakers, their job is basically to make the eventual takeover go smoother.'

'By keeping the price down?'

'Or by ensuring rapid compliance. Or, if possible, by discrediting the tenant, the existing stakeholder.'

'That's not legal, surely?'

'Why not? If you can prove the tenant is breaking the bylaws, get him kicked out of the flat – well, it's his own fault, isn't it? Or prove he's spending six nights a week at his girlfriend's place, so his claim on the property is questionable.'

Townsend sat quiet for a while. Eventually, he said: 'I'm surprised they don't get murdered more often.'

'Only when they get too greedy,' said Wallace.

A sun-buggy taxi took them from the railway station to the local police station. Through her lawyer, Mella Nelson admitted accidentally killing Janette Foster-Lane during an argument. She admitted panicking and running. Which she deeply regretted. She had been in a state of shock.

She had thought Janette loved her, and then that man appeared, and it was obvious he thought the same.

'Did Janette deny it? That she was living with Lewis Bright?'

'No. She didn't. What she did, Inspector, was she made me a business proposition. She wasn't just an ordinary staker, you see – you know what that is, a staker?'

'We know,' said Townsend.

'Well, Janette had big ambitions. She wanted to get someone on the inside at the Land Reform Agency. If she could get the records changed, for some or maybe all of her client's former properties – we're talking about a fortune, Inspector. A great, big, old-fashioned fortune.'

'You told her you weren't interested.'

'I told her to get out. She got angry, she attacked me, and we—'

'She attacked you with your own knife?'

'Well… yes.'

'Right. So, where was it?'

'I don't—'

'Where was the knife? You keep a tidy flat. Surely the knife was in the knife drawer?'

'Well, I—'

'Come to that, where's the knife now?'

The lawyer held up a hand. 'My client can't be expected to remember every little detail after such a horrifying trauma, Inspector.'

'I can't remember,' said Mella. 'But there was a struggle and—'

'And you accidentally cut her throat?'

'My client,' the lawyer began, but Wallace interrupted.

'Tell me: what did you fetch from the desk?'

'The desk?'

'Heatprints, Mella. You – or Janette – moved from the bed over to the desk drawers. What were you looking for?'

'That must be when Janette got the knife.' She smiled.

'That was the top drawer. What was in the second drawer?'

No-one said anything for a long time. Then Mella smiled again, and said: 'My mum's keys. My mum's spare keys. In case she was out when I got there.'

They charged her, and arranged for her to be taken back to London by police van. Wallace and Townsend sat in the Cardiff Central police canteen, drinking tea and eating currant buns.

'The scientific evidence will support manslaughter, won't it?'

'Maybe,' said Wallace. 'But we've not quite finished yet. I want her mum's house searched. Properly.'

'She'll have dropped the knife down a gutter. Thrown it in the river, wrapped in the bloody clothing.'

'Not the knife. I want whatever else she took from the desk drawer.'

'You don't reckon it was mum's keys, then?'

'I'm betting her mum's the sort who leaves a spare key under a plant pot. Her neighbours would have had keys. We'd also better phone the woman at the Land Agency – ask her to see if she can tell what's missing.'

'I see,' said Townsend. 'Well, well. So: not only will you always have murder in Utopia, you'll always have corruption, too?'

'Might not be corruption. Might be love.'

'Same thing,' said Townsend, but his tone now was more teasing than gloating.

Wallace put his cup down and brushed crumbs from his T-shirt. 'Besides, Paul, it's not bloody Utopia.'

'You can say that again.'

'Nobody ever said it was. It's just London,' said Wallace. 'Making do, it's just London.'

A GOOD DAY FOR A MURDER

DAVID STUART DAVIES

David Stuart Davies is probably best known as editor of that excellent magazine, *Sherlock*: he also edits the Crime Writers' Association's in-house journal *Red Herrings*. He is a highly regarded authority on Sherlock Holmes and his publications include non-fiction, as well as novels concerned with the great consulting detective from 221b Baker Street. Very properly, though, David is keen to explore the potential of contemporary crime fiction and I had the pleasure of including his story 'Instant Removals' in a collection of Northern crime writing, which appeared back in 1998. This story is very different. For reasons that will become apparent, I shall say little about it directly, except that the central idea is one that I believe occurred to a number of writers at roughly the same time. But David was, so far as I know, the first to transfer the concept into a completed and highly topical story.

Sharon Rice stepped out into the bright sunshine. It was another warm, early autumn day in New York. The trees in the park were just on the turn and they glittered with myriad colours beneath a pale blue sky. It was a good day. It was a good day for a murder. That thought brought a smile to her careworn face. Today she would exact her revenge. She had wanted to for a very long time but only recently had she mustered the courage and determination to go through with it. Years of humiliation and pain had festered within in her and had at long last metamorphosed into a fierce iron resolve to get her own back. Today, this very day, she would kill that bastard of a husband. She would kill him dead! That bastard of a husband who had cheated on her and degraded her for years. Not for Jack the subtle affair with a colleague at work or the surreptitious indiscretion with a friend's wife. Jack didn't believe in affairs. He believed in sex. As often as he could get it and with as many different women as possible. He didn't wait for any flirtatious advances or indulge in them himself. He took the short route. He employed hookers. It was more practical and efficient. There was no need for the candlelight dinner, the tantalising foreplay and the red roses on the pillow. And there were no tearful scenes when the relationship crumbled – as they always do. There was no emotion involved – just sensations. It was like the old cliché: wham, bang, thank you, mam.

To make matters worse, he made no attempt to hide the fact from Sharon. After a few drinks, he would even boast about the whore he had bedded that day. At his office. It was always at his office. He seemed to get off on the knowledge that while he was straddling some tart across his desk, all around him his employees were busy working, making him more money.

A month ago after one such drunken recital, Sharon decided. It had to stop. She suddenly realised that it gave him an extra frisson to tell her of his encounters. He was actually aroused by humiliating her. She just had to get rid of him. She didn't want a divorce. She wanted him dead. And the only way to bring about that state of affairs was to kill the bastard herself.

So she formulated a plan and, now that all the pieces were in place, she was ready to carry it out.

It was a good day for a murder.

She walked a little way, clutching her small travelling bag, before hailing a cab at Columbus Circle and asking the driver to take her to Penn Station. She gazed out of the window at the crowded streets; everyone seeming to be in a hurry to get somewhere, pushing, jostling, and jaywalking in order to reach their destination. She wondered idly if there was anyone else out there on their way to murder someone. She hoped not. She wanted this to be her day, not contaminated with other crimes of passion.

At Penn Station, she mingled anonymously with the throngs of morning commuters, before disappearing down into the ladies toilets. Once inside the cubicle, she disrobed, neatly folding her plain linen dress over the lavatory cistern. Unzipping the travelling bag, she took out a fresh set of clothes. She smiled as she began to put them on. There was a tight, short, black skirt and a low-cut pink jumper, along with some gold bangles. She had tried the outfit on earlier before she left their apartment and was both amused and appalled to see how authentic a hooker she looked.

Pulling a mirror from her handbag, she deftly scraped her hair back and donned the pièce de résistance: a long, peroxide-blonde wig. She giggled at her own reflection. She hoped she wasn't approached for business before she reached his office. She couldn't wait to see his face when she revealed herself. And when she produced the gun. There it was at the bottom of the travelling bag. An automatic with a silencer. Fully loaded. It was amazing what you could get hold of on the Internet.

She packed her own clothes in the bag, popped some chewing gum in her mouth and slipped on a large pair of sunglasses. Beulah is ready to go to work, she thought.

She had chosen the name Beulah because it was so preposterous. She used it when she sent the anonymous note to her husband's office: 'Try Beulah, her extraordinary services are out of this world.' She'd even bought a mobile in Beulah's name, ready for when her sex-mad bastard of a husband called. Using a Brooklynesque drawl straight out of Damon Runyon, which completely disguised her own gentle English accent, she had described in graphic detail what she could do for 'dirty boy Jack'. He fairly drooled down the phone. For what she promised to do, he was prepared to pay very well. He didn't realise, she mused, that he would be paying with his life.

Sharon hit the sunny sidewalk as Beulah and, using her newly acquired accent, attempted to hail another cab to take her downtown. But the cabs sailed past ignoring her as though she was invisible. She glanced at her watch. If she didn't catch a ride now she would be late for the appointment. That must not happen. It was too far to walk in the time and so she had to get a cab, yet they continued to sail past her.

In desperation, she stepped out in the road in the path of an empty cab. It screeched to a halt and the driver stuck his head out of the window. 'You got a death wish, lady?' he screamed.

'I just want a cab,' she said, forgetting to use Beulah's voice.

The cabbie looked her up and down, puzzled by the refined English voice emerging from such a blousy hooker.

'You working?' he said, suspiciously. ''Cause if you are...'

'No, no. I'm... I'm on my way home.'

The cabbie gave a sigh. 'OK lady, get in.'

With relief, she slumped back into the cool of the car and gave the driver directions. Then she cursed herself for being so careless. The cabbie would certainly remember her now, the whore with the English accent.

By the time the cab dropped her three blocks away from her husband's office, she had regained her composure. Nothing, nothing whatsoever, was going to prevent her from blowing Jack's brains out. What happened afterwards was in the lap of the gods.

She had wanted to walk the last few blocks in order to enjoy the fresh air, the sunshine and more particularly the anticipation.

It was a good day for a murder.

In her mind, she ran through the scene in his office. Would she just shoot the rat as he was taking off his trousers? Or would she reveal who Beulah really was first? In general, she favoured the latter scenario. It would be delicious to see the worm wriggle with shock and fear. She had no doubt he would beg her to spare him. Now that would be wonderful. She might allow him to think this was a possibility – before she pulled the trigger. However, she realised that when it came to the moment, she would have to play it by ear. Whatever happens, she thought, by noon Jack would be a dead man and she would be free.

She gazed up at the North Tower, its many windows glinting back at her like eyes in the sunshine. Somewhere up there, on the 46th floor, Jack was already pacing with suppressed excitement. She couldn't help herself. She laughed out loud, as she entered the building.

11th September, 2001. Yes, indeed, it was a very good day for a murder.

PARK LIFE

CAROL ANNE DAVIS

Although her work is, at times, seriously funny, Carol Anne Davis occasionally writes short stories that, like a number of her novels, are bleak in mood. 'Park Life' is an example, although it benefits from an ending that offers unexpected hope. Although now domiciled in Wiltshire, Davis comes from Scotland and here she glances at the dark side of Edinburgh – on the surface, such a genteel city – with a precision as uncompromising as her compatriot Ian Rankin. Davis has not as yet attained the international eminence of Rankin as a crime writer, but she is unquestionably one to watch for the future.

He was late tonight so his preferred pitch was already being used – he'd have to work deep inside Holyrood Park's iced darkness. Jason pulled up the zip of his calfskin jacket and buried his hands in the pockets of his well-shrunk cords. Then he walked studiedly along The Queen's Drive, trying to look hard enough to deter muggers, yet soft enough for the punters who wanted a boy rather than a man.

Salisbury Crags towered above him, igneous and sedimentary rock tilted towards the skyline. *Whin* and *intruded rock*: he knew the terms from when they'd studied the park at school in fourth-year geography. He'd watched slides from his Liverpool Comprehensive of how the 400 million year old volcano had formed and reformed at the hands of pre-historic settlers and eighteenth-century quarrymen. The crags had shrunk and crumbled under tearing powder charges but had ultimately survived.

He'd known then that he'd move to Edinburgh and see the vastness for himself when he turned sixteen. Had bused from England to Scotland without telling anyone where he was headed, lit up at the prospect of living in a whole new land. He'd thought that with so much space there would be lots of houses, but the landlords wanted tenants who were in full employment. So he'd lied about his age and gone into a homeless men's hostel where a wino had told him about the park…

A man or a fox screamed behind the winter-stark trees. Jason jumped, then stared down the shadowy path that led to The Innocent Railway. In some ways he still felt innocent, somehow removed from what he did here behind stretching whin bushes and family cars.

He'd been an innocent with women until last year when he met Debs, was still unworldly when it came to community charges and national insurance. Debs had teased him about it. He'd earn enough for a day then go spend it on books for her and a CD for himself. He could never quite envisage next month or next year, couldn't picture a life to save up for. And so he avoided any financial sacrifice.

But standing on this ancient mountainside, it was easy to believe in *blood* sacrifice. It was an urban reality, with the gay-bashing that went on here most weekends. Despite the casual cruelty he'd known during his first five years, he'd never become inured to the random damage of a kicking boot or a hate-filled fist. That early damage had already scared off his more genteel clients, had attracted the rougher, poorer punters and had lowered his street market price. Men liked a pretty boy, not a pretty-mangled boy. Jason walked away from the park's lights into the shadowy sector, which would hide his scar.

In truth it was more of a healed-over gouge, an area on the centre of his cheek where the tissue had been slashed out and never reconstructed. Not slashed by a knife, though – by his father's ring. A huge bloody setting it had had, gold, formed of a woman's bare breast with an equally buoyant nipple. The full curve had dad's initials diamond-cut over it. Sometimes, when Jason was very stressed, his scar would glow reddish-purple and he fancied he could see the three sloping letters still engraved deep into his skin.

Debs' skin was flawless compared to his. She had her own scars, of course, but they were tucked away in the form of nervous stomach cramps and behind-one-eyebrow headaches. She was really cute but wouldn't believe she was attractive to anyone but him. She'd been christened after Debbie Harry, a curvy blonde '70s pop singer. His Debs had brown hair and flat planes and no desire to sing.

Strange how some adults created a whole new person – then expected it to clone their existing persona. Jason kicked out at some rockfall and watched it skim along the road with the transfer of melancholic energy. Debs' mum was a little known pub-singer, determined that her daughter would find fame.

The rest of nature didn't behave like this. Each gorse bush here in the park seeded a slightly different shape of gorse bush. Each clump of woodsage was minutely and healthily unique. But Debs had been expected to take centre stage like her mum, when she preferred to be thought-filled and bookish. Had been dragged to childhood musical auditions then told she wasn't trying hard enough when she didn't get the part. She'd left her native Glasgow at sixteen to train as a nurse in the ask-no-questions city that is Edinburgh. That's where he'd met her, when his appendix grumbled – hell, caused an all-out protest – for a week.

No appendix pain now – only the scar, the forever scar that his father had bequeathed him. He'd just turned five when the man had back-handed him for the umpteenth time. A sharp, radiating pain in his face, then his legs had itched fiercely, and… He'd opened his eyes to find himself lying on his bed with Mum a bit flushed, looking down. 'You know what he's like when he's had a drink. You should have kept out of his way.'

She'd put this big pad of bandage on his face and it had dripped bright red and she'd changed it for another and another. The good bit was that she'd kept him off school for day after day. The morning he'd gone back had been the morning that the nice teacher who'd already been asking him loads of questions had called the social. The same month he'd been taken into care.

He could take care of himself now, provided the business kept coming in. Jason turned slowly around to give watching eyes the chance of a good appraisal. He was slim and small and though seventeen could still pass for fourteen in a subdued light. The clothes helped and the way he carried himself – just that bit uncertain. The uncertainty, though, was not an act.

He'd never been any good at standing up for himself. Not to Mum or Dad or to the so-called care-workers that followed. *I'll just tuck you in, son.* Seeking crumbs of comfort in a children's home without visitors or phone calls or birthday cards. *Bend and stretch, reach for the stars...* He'd looked into the sunlight day after day, certain that Mum would come and get him. But he'd never seen either parent again.

The following year he'd dared to get on a bus and go all the way across Liverpool to his house, his gable-end semi. He'd thought that they must have lost the orphanage's address, that they couldn't find him, that they'd be sad. But new people with a baby of their own and a barking spaniel had answered the door. He'd started to cry: 'Where have you taken my mum?' He was always crying. Then they'd given him nut biscuits and mango juice and phoned the council home.

He had his own home now. At least he tried very hard to make Debs' flat his own. She'd rented it a month after they got together, had gladly left the cramped all-girls-together confines of the nursing block. How he loved both small square rooms. He'd bought yucca plants and Swiss cheese plants for each previously spartan corner. Had planted up terra-cotta tubs with spring bulbs and summer seeds. Later still he'd planted cuttings of autumn foliage, their reddish tendrils brightening up the winter-dulled space.

At least he had space to breathe nowadays, loved his daily freedom. Liked walking through Princes Street by day and buying CDs like any other teenage boy. On Saturdays he and Debs often took the bus to places like Portobello, spending the day at the beach and the funfair and in the wee cosy cafes.

It was only at night, when he came here to earn his keep, that he felt different. Felt small and alone and a little unclean and scared. The things they asked him to... even after all those years with the care assistants he found it difficult. But it was known territory and he didn't yet have the confidence to move on. Debs wanted him to – she didn't criticise his choice for she'd walked that soul-crushing road throughout her childhood. But she feared for his safety and kept pointing out more sheltered jobs. Just last night she'd told him about a new company that was taking on landscape-gardening apprentices. 'You'd be good at it, Jase. You've got this place like a gardening centre, so you have.'

'A cold one, huh?' His heart speeded harder as he heard a voice to his right. Jason turned swiftly. The man must have walked from the upper road, come down silent as a snake through the frost-sparkled grass. He was about twenty, body dwarfed by an oversized parka. He had a patchy triangular beard and the shadow of a moustache. They stared at each other, the punter's eyes weighing and measuring. Jason smiled. Then his smile faded as the man broke off eye contact and walked away into the perils and pleasures of the night.

Was he the wrong age, weight, height for business or was it the scar? You never got to know why you'd been found wanting. Jason stamped his feet and flexed his toes inside the two pairs of socks he had on. Wellingtons and a duffle coat were the best defence against such wind-chill temperatures but they would hide his vital selling power – his shape.

He sucked his stomach in some more. Maybe he should check out the gardening job? At first he'd liked one aspect of doing what he did – the daylong freedom. But now he loved Debs and she worked during the day so he only saw her in the early part of the night. If he took the land-scaping post they could both work days like any other couple and spend the evenings in their little Newington flat.

Someone groaned from beneath another clump of gorse and he walked quickly for a hundred feet or so, hand going automatically into his inside jacket pocket. His fingers traced the reassuring weight of the wooden handle: his protection was still there. Maybe it was the way the wind was tugging the trees into reaching arms, but his skin felt clammy with foreboding. Any of the gangs or smackhead individuals here could lead him to his death.

But new life was approaching. This punter was older – forty or so. Kitted up in a suit, which was bloody unusual for a walker. Usually the suits wanted a good time from the comfort of their *Caution: Baby In Back*-stickered cars. Probably some businessman from out of town who fancied slumming it, had a fantasy involving a bit of rough. Jason finger-combed his hair as the man got closer. 'Looking for business?' he asked quietly.

The man nodded then seemed to realise that the darkness might obscure such a tiny move. 'Depends,' he said gruffly. 'How much?'

Jason costed the man's outfit then reeled off his flexible price list. He set out the least invasive options. But the man snorted his derision, could presumably get these alone or with a girl.

'I want…' He clearly saw rent boys as human flotsam. Jason listened wearily to the man's Anglo-Saxon words.

'I don't like to…' The care workers had been there so often that he already wore a tampon to keep the anal seepage in.

'Yeah? Maybe this'll change your mind?' The man reached quickly into his inside pocket. The clouds skirted away from the moon and Jason saw the hellish metallic glint...

Much time passed before the Royal Parks Constabulary found the body the next day. Other men had seen it in the interim period – seen it and immediately developed temporary blindness. The sergeant knelt by the cadaver. 'Gay-bashing job, you reckon?' his new assistant said.

The older policeman shook his head. 'No – just one deep, clean knife wound. Gangs like to kick the patsy's head in or carve him up a bit.'

'A robbery gone wrong then?' the police constable asked, looking fruitlessly around for the murder weapon.

The sergeant carefully opened the corpse's suit jacket. 'Doubt it. He's still got his wallet and his credit cards.' He stood up to greet the approaching ambulance and Lothian & Borders police car. 'Looks like a stranger murder. Almost no chance of them solving it.'

Several hours later a CID officer bagged a glinting, breast-shaped, monogrammed ring from the hand of the dead man. And, clutching an employment form, a young boy walked shakily towards his new life.

OLD BONES

EILEEN DEWHURST

For the past quarter-century, Eileen Dewhurst has been an astute chronicler of contemporary crime. She has, at different times, written about a Scotland Yard man, a police officer and an actress who sleuths in character as a PI. She has, however, written equally memorable 'stand-alone' mysteries, both at novel length and in the short form. 'Masks And Faces', one of her best stories, appeared in the CWA anthology *Past Crimes* in 1998. It benefited greatly from Dewhurst's authentic evocation of life in the Second World War and, since then, I have sought on a number of occasions to persuade her to turn back the years again. I am delighted that she has responded to this prompting with this portrayal of life in a small Welsh city during wartime.

I'd been thinking for some time anyway about going back to Bangor, cathedral city of North Wales with its maelstrom of wartime memories, and when I read about the female skeleton that had tumbled into view at the feet of some city council ditch diggers, I set off as soon as I could find a few days' space.

I'd spent my school holidays in Bangor during the war while there was the likelihood of air raids on Liverpool, in the flat above my uncle's jeweller's shop in the High Street, only a flight of stone steps and a road-crossing from Bangor Mountain where the skeleton had been found.

The High Street! In 1942 it was my Champs Elysées. All human life was there, its apotheosis the BBC's Light Entertainment Department, which when the Blitz began had moved lock, stock and barrel from London. The glamour of it washed over us round the clock. Summer evening after summer evening, my cousin Bea and I would stand with our autograph books outside the old County Cinema round the corner, waiting for the likes of Tommy Handley, Arthur Askey, the cast of Happidrome and many other celebrities of the day to emerge and give us their signatures and a bit of chat. Neither of these blessings, if I remember rightly, was ever denied the two little girls, and I can still recall the number of Arthur Askey's modest car. And day after day we would stand at our first-floor sitting-room window, watching for stars on the High Street pavements below and seldom having long to wait. What our grandmother was waiting for was one of us to spell out aloud the shaky white letters chalked on the grey stone wall of the bank building opposite. Eventually it was my ten-year-old cousin Bea (I was a majestic – but no less innocent – twelve) who obliged. 'S-H-I-T... That's a funny word. Grandma, what does it mean?'

'Just something not very nice, chick. It's a silly word, no one with any sense would use it.'

Something else not very nice, according to Grandma, had invaded Bangor Mountain that summer of my keenest memory.

No one had ever monitored our frequent disappearances up the flight of steps at the end of the narrow alley separating our shop from the next one up the High Street, content to think of us on our way to our lofty playground. Until the day Grandma told us, with uncharacteristic hesitancy, that she didn't want us to go up Bangor Mountain any more because... well, because some dangerous snakes and lizards had been found there, beasts with poisonous bites. This behest followed the arrival in the city of a small contingent of American soldiers – GIs – but girls of my cousin's and my age at that time were far too innocent to interpret our grandmother's metaphor and understand that the beast she was afraid would soon be infesting Bangor Mountain was the beast with two backs.

Now, on my latter-day return, I discovered that my great highway is so narrow it's unable to accommodate two-way modern traffic: and that I couldn't stay at the Castle Hotel, that fondly recalled pinnacle of '40s sophistication near the cathedral precinct, because it had closed down. This wasn't the shock the other changes were because I'd heard the news, of course, when I'd been unable to reach the hotel by phone and booked into a place in the nearby countryside.

The biggest shock of my return was the overall erosion of the close-knit grey stone city, holes blasted first by the numerous extensions of the University, and then, offered the precedent, by the iconoclastic jerry-builders of the 1960s. Builders of roads as well as buildings: the High Street isn't just narrow, it's become irrelevant. Oh, sic transit!

I drove to Bangor the morning after I'd checked into my hotel, and when I'd managed to find a parking space I went on foot round my old haunts, and the places that had figured in the final drama. Not yet up the mountain – partly because my climbing days are just about over, but also because I was pretty anxious to get to the police station and try to learn more about the unearthed bones. But I did pause in front of my uncle's old shop and remember, as I looked sentimentally at its unchanged facade and the small recessed space where the two windows stand proud of the door, that the manager had once locked Bea and me into that space when the outside gate had gone up at closing time and we were being especially obstreperous, and left us there for a corrective ten minutes, to our chagrin and the amusement of passers-by.

A few doors up there was no trace of Dai Jones's the newspapers, and when I went the short walk to Dean Street I discovered that the County Cinema building had become an unsavoury-looking night spot called the Octagon.

So it was in a queasy mood of mingled nostalgia, sorrow and apprehension that I went into the police station, announced my maiden and married names, and asked if I could speak to a senior member of the CID.

'May I inquire what about, Mrs Anderson?'

'About the female skeleton that's just been discovered on Bangor Mountain. I was in Bangor during the war, my uncle was a jeweller in the High Street. The shop's still there. Nearly sixty years on.' So, surely, there was no one left I could hurt. 'If you haven't been able to identify the skeleton, I just might have some helpful information.'

A young-looking detective chief inspector was there within minutes, and took me into an interview room.

'A young woman?' I asked him, as we sat down. 'About five foot six? Blonde hair, though I don't suppose there is any of that still around.'

He didn't say yea or nay, but he looked cautiously interested and asked me to go on.

'It's a long story, and it may have nothing to do with the skeleton.'

'Of course. But I'd like to hear it.'

I recalled it as I told it: The story of Megan and Dai and Gladys Lewis and the American soldiers.

But I began with the BBC Light Entertainment Department, in order to lament aloud the less-than-complete attention my cousin and I had given the real-life drama.

'Perhaps you can imagine the excitement of one's radio heroes suddenly there in the flesh. I mean, my uncle actually got to know the cast of Happidrome, and invited them home. My cousin and I used to go to sleep with the live sounds of their signature tune floating up from the sitting-room. Even the American soldiers couldn't compete with that!'

'American soldiers?'

'That's right. I'm afraid I can't remember precise dates, how long they were there or how many of them, but they were there that summer – 1942, it must have been – when Megan Morgan disappeared.'

I can see Megan now, her health glowing through her pancake make-up, her enhanced blonde hair piled high in the front and flowing down the sides of her lovely, animated face à la Veronica Lake (I had to explain that reference to the DI), and the beloved locket she always wore bouncing between her big breasts as she leaned over to kiss us in succession in greeting or farewell. I once heard the word 'blousy' under my grandmother's breath (I remember it because neither Bea nor I knew what it meant and long pondered it together), but she was no more immune to Megan's charm than anybody else, and after all (my grandmother said) she had been chosen by that lovely boy from the newsagents to be his girl.

And whatever happened in the end, Megan and Dai did have a lovely relationship for a while, the sort that at one and the same time included other people in their laughing affection and proclaimed them exclusive to each other. The only jarring note was the frequent presence of Gladys Lewis, another local girl but as lumpen and unattractive as Megan was sexy and charismatic. (Neither of those words was current in 1942, but I used them because the DI seemed so young.) Gladys nursed an unrequited passion for Dai, which used to amuse Bea and me as much as it made us uncomfortable, the way her large mournful eyes scarcely ever left his face. But neither Dai nor Megan was put out by Gladys's devotion, they were so secure in each other.

Until the arrival of the American soldiers. And we had no idea they had affected that happy relationship until Bea and I, finding our indoor occupations suddenly grown stale, disobeyed our grandmother one warm early evening when she was out, and went defiantly up Bangor Mountain in the face of her injunction to keep away.

And came upon the beast with two backs.

And saw that half of it was Megan.

It was what modern politicians might call a double whammy – the beast itself, and half of it being so familiar to us. If it hadn't been Megan, I think the beast itself would have troubled us more than it did in the aftermath of our shock. We knew of course, in theory, what it would probably look like, but in those days there were no magazines or TV programmes or movies to fill out our timorous imaginings, and to find out the truth of it so totally unprepared had to be a trauma.

But one immediately on the back burner as the man tumbled sideways and we saw who the woman was.

She must have had plenty of sang-froid, our beloved Megan, because even in that horrendous situation – her legs apart and what was between them hidden by her crumpled skirt through luck rather than management – she put a finger to her lips as she stared gravely from one to the other of us. I remember we both nodded violently before we turned and fled.

Neither of us spoke until we had skittered almost to the foot of the mountain, and then Bea muttered, 'Grandma has to have done that!'

'Only twice,' I reassured her. 'Once for your father, and once for my mother.'

'So why should Megan...?'

'I don't know.'

Although we had managed to pick up the technicalities, we had no concept of desire, of sex for its own sake.

'Girls of ten and twelve, which my cousin and I were, were too young in those days to get excited about men in real life; it was our dream heroes that absorbed us. Which is why we didn't pay all that much attention to the GIs. Until we found one of them with Megan on Bangor Mountain. And then... well, it was too awful for us to be able to think or talk about it and we threw ourselves even more enthusiastically into the arms of our radio heroes. Metaphorically, of course.'

'Of course. I presume it was so awful because you caught them in flagrante delicto?'

'Yes. And it was awful too because of Megan going steady with Dai and Dai expecting to marry her.'

'Dai wasn't in the forces?'

'No. He was a bit of a wizard with gadgetry – I suppose today it would be electronics – and although he worked at a local RAF station he was a civilian in what was called a reserved occupation. If you were in one of those you weren't called up.'

The next day, in silent apprehensive accord, we'd taken ourselves off to the milk bar.

At first it was a relief to see that they were there, and on their own, but we were still in the doorway when we realized all was not well between them: there were no smiles, no movements towards one another of the hands. No conversation, just Megan with downcast eyes, and Dai's eyes pleading as he gazed at her.

So although she'd told him something, she hadn't told him that. And he hadn't found out.

Without a word between us we crept out of the milk bar and slunk home. But I remember that on the way we passed Ronnie Waldman, the head of BBC Light Entertainment, and his glamorous wife Lana Morris, and were distracted from our concern for Megan and Dai.

'This is interesting, Mrs Anderson, but how are we moving towards the old bones?'

'I'm sorry. It's just that there's so much coming back to me... That evening Megan came to the flat and asked our grandmother if she could take us for a walk.'

Sometimes the three of us had gone up Bangor Mountain together, but that night Megan led us another way, into a little local park. None of us said anything until we were lined up on a seat with Megan in the middle. I've just remembered that the sun was in my eyes and I was glad I couldn't see Megan properly when I turned towards her. As soon as we were settled she began to speak. She thanked us in a soft, sad voice we'd never heard from her before for not having said anything about what we'd seen, then told us she and Dai had broken up.

'I can't love him enough, can I, chicks, if I could do that?'

'You got to love the American soldier pretty quick,' Bea said.

'I don't love him.'

Then we sat in silence while Bea and I digested another shock: the knowledge that that could happen without love. I didn't look at Megan, but out of the corner of my eye I could see her hand playing feverishly with her locket. It was very unusual, that locket. Bea and I admired it so much we used to ask to hold it, the small round of gold framed in gold coils with a tiny emerald frog set in its centre. It had been left to Megan by her grandmother, and inside were tiny photos of both her grandparents, which she told us she had had to poke in with a pin, it was so fiddly.

'This is relevant to my story, Chief Inspector.'

Eventually I asked Megan if she would be seeing the American soldier again. Doing that again, I suppose is what I meant.

I remember she took quite a long time to answer, and then said 'Yes. If he wants to see me.'

She didn't make any excuses, try to soften it. Looking back now, I think there was a sort of nobility about that. And just before we got up and went home, she said 'Two people I do love are you both. That's easy.' Then she got up off the seat and stood looking down at us, making us meet her big troubled eyes. 'Do you both still love me?'

I think I spoke first, but the two of us assured her eagerly that of course we did, and I'm sure Bea meant it as much as I did.

'I wish I could ask her, Chief Inspector, I wish she could be here with me now, she'd probably be more help to you. But she died last year.' And that's something I shall never get over.

Megan said 'Thank you, chicks. And if I… if maybe you don't see me any more, you'll love me still? You won't stop?' There was a sob in her voice and I saw her breast heave (it's astounding, what the catalyst of the bones is telling me I remember) and we were both even more fervent in our assurances of undying love.

But then, alas, we were actually taken to see one of our favourite programmes being recorded and when we recovered from the excitement of anticipation, event and aftermath, we discovered that the Americans had moved on, Megan had disappeared, and Gladys Lewis was sitting with Dai Jones in the milk bar.

He didn't seem to be taking any notice of her – that was our one consolation. So perhaps she had just sat down at his table without being invited. Perhaps he hadn't seen her, his head was down in his hands. For the second time we stood still in the doorway, and for the second time we turned without a word and went out, when we saw Dai was allowing Gladys's extended hand to lie on his without shaking it off.

'As far as I could understand at the time, Chief Inspector, Dai Jones was given a bit of a hard time of it by the police. If Megan had managed to keep her secret from him he wouldn't have been able to cite the GIs in his defence, and he had to admit that he and she had broken up against his will, because just about everyone in town apart from BBC Light Entertainment knew what had happened, and were concerned for him and Megan both. The police even interviewed Bea and me because of being told how friendly we were with Megan, and when they asked us straight out if she'd perhaps been friendly with an American (like so many of the other pretty local girls) we did say yes, we thought she had, and that she'd sort of suggested to us that she might go away. I honestly can't tell you whether or not we'd worked it out – that if she'd gone off because of a GI it would take the heat off Dai – but I think that must have been what happened, because they left him alone after a while. And there wasn't a body, there wasn't a shred of evidence that Megan Morgan was dead. Until now, perhaps?'

Again the CI didn't look a yea or a nay, but he asked me if I knew what had happened to Dai.

'Yes,' I said reluctantly. 'He married Gladys Lewis. Not right off. When I came back to Bangor at Christmas I didn't hear anything about it. But by the next Easter holidays they were engaged, and they were married in the summer. My uncle told me... oh, it must have been ten years or more later, that Dai had had a heart attack and died. Chief Inspector, if there was a locket like the one I've described among the bones, would you tell me?'

'If there was a locket like the one you described among the bones, Mrs Anderson, there'd have been a close-up picture of it by now in the national press.'

'Ah... Thank you for telling me.' And for telling me the bones couldn't be Megan's.

'And thank you for telling me about the locket, Mrs Anderson. If your Megan always wore it, you could have given us some useful negative information. Our inquiries would, of course, have dug Miss Morgan up eventually...' The CI coughed, and asked me to excuse his unfortunate choice of metaphor. 'And without what you have told me today we might well have spent time considering her at the expense of other more likely candidates for ownership of the bones. Although we will still, of course, have to retain her on our list of suspects.' And here, for the first time, the young chief inspector smiled and then laughed. Which I thought was pretty stoical of him, seeing it looked like he had just lost the straw that had appeared to be within his clutch. 'May I get you a cup of tea?'

I declined, because suddenly, having imparted what information I had, I was eager to acquire more.

The Jones's had been chapel, and I went straight off to the most central one, directed by the PC on the desk.

It was easy. There in the register was the evidence of the marriage of Dai 'work of national importance' Jones and Gladys 'shop assistant' Lewis in 1943, and the minister told me for good measure that Evan Williams, son of the minister who had solemnised the marriage, was alive and well and living in Penrhyn, just outside the city.

So, by five o'clock I was in his immaculate semi, drinking tea, having told him on his doorstep that I was the niece of the jeweller who, for a spell during the war, had owned J Welch & Co in the High Street – the goodwill name over the shop that my uncle had retained and that was still there as I spoke, in its original handsome red-gold glass facade.

'What do you know, then?' he responded excitedly, when we were sitting down with the tea and his silent, eyes-down wife. 'J Welch... It gives on to the steps leading up to Bangor Mountain, don' it? Where they've just found some old bones. You heard about them, lady?'

'Yes, I've heard. I was interested because... I used to stay over the shop as a child during the war, and my cousin and I were always going up the mountain.'

'But you didn't find a body, bach, or we wouldn't have this mystery now, eh, girl?' This last to his wife, who looked up for a moment, half smiled and nodded, then returned her gaze to her teacup. Perhaps her ebullient husband embarrassed her, but he was just the type I had hoped for.

'You'd have been around during my visits, wouldn't you, as a very small boy?' He was clearly younger than me, but not all that much. I decided to take the plunge. 'When Megan Morgan disappeared, it was thought she might have gone with the American soldiers. D'you remember that, Mr Williams?'

The eager face brightened even further. 'Well, I don't rightly know if I remember it, or if I got told later on. Bit of a legend it became, you know.'

'So you're thinking, Mrs Anderson, that she might not have run away after all, Megan Morgan, that it might be her bones on the mountain?' Mrs Williams's straight question, asked as her head came up and her penetrating gaze was transferred to me, made me jump slightly.

'It's a possibility, isn't it?'

Mrs Williams shrugged, and her husband leaned forward and shouted 'Yes!'

'Nobody suspected at the time that she might have come to grief?' I asked, looking now from one of them to the other. 'Did the police suspect foul play?'

'I wouldn't know that,' Mr Williams responded reluctantly. 'But I do remember my da saying that young Dai Jones had to be feeling uncomfortable. Son of Jones the newspapers, he'd been going steady with Miss Morgan but she'd broke it off just before she disappeared.'

'I think I remember that, too.' He had brought me to where I wanted to be. 'And I remember he married...' I pretended to fumble for the name, and Mr Williams supplied it.

'Gladys Lewis,' he said. 'I remember my mother saying she'd got what she wanted, but that she wouldn't have had a look-in if Megan hadn't taken herself off. Dai worshipped the ground Megan walked on; my mother reckoned he only married Gladys because nothing really mattered to him after Megan disappeared.'

'Gladys Jones is still alive,' Mrs Williams supplied, as she poured me a second cup of tea. My hand was trembling as I took it from her. 'In the Craig Bueno nursing home in Upper Bangor. Not that I've seen her, but I've a friend who visits old people's homes with a dog for them to pat, and the Megan-Dai-and-Gladys drama's still just a local legend. No mind, I'm told, but a good appetite.'

'Gladys was terrible ugly,' Mr Williams said. 'And never a word to say for herself. Dai Jones must have been out of his mind to take so much as a second look at her. But I suppose that's what he was, seeing he'd been so crazy for Megan. I didn't go to his wedding, o' course, but I remember it because of all the drama that had gone on, see?'

Mrs Williams asked me then how I thought the Bangor of today compared with the Bangor of sixty years back, and I was happy to sit back and exchange nostalgias, having got far more than I'd hoped for.

Gladys Jones having no mind made it easy for me to present myself at the nursing home the next morning as being on a trip down memory lane and having known her as a child.

But I decided I might learn more if I didn't help the head of the establishment out when she tried to break Gladys's condition to me gently.

'So I'm afraid there's no possibility of her knowing you,' she concluded. 'She doesn't know anyone.'

'Not even her own children?'

'Mrs Jones has no children.'

I don't know why, but something inside me rejoiced for Megan, that no other woman had carried on Dai's line. And I was rejoicing for him, anyway, that he hadn't lived a long life with his second choice.

'Here we are! She doesn't walk now, but she can still give a good kick if she suddenly doesn't like someone, or thinks they're too close to her... So sit down here beside her, pull the chair round a bit... HERE'S SOMEONE TO SEE YOU, GLADYS! It's a long time since she's had a visitor. I'll be in my office if you like to look in before you go.'

I wouldn't have known Gladys. For a start she was so much smaller, her bristly dark hair was thin and white and the aggressive teeth had gone. Her eyes, though, were still large and mournful, larger even than I remembered them in what was now her thin little face. The hands, though, hadn't changed much, lying together in her lap. On a reflex I started to move one of mine towards them, then to my surprise drew it back.

'Hello, Gladys,' I said.

The head took a few moments to turn towards me, and there was no new expression in the eyes. 'Kill her, God!' Gladys said.

'It's Mary, Gladys. Mary Rowe. D'you remember? I used to see you in the milk bar in the High Street.'

I knew it was a total waste of time, but one can't help trying. And now Gladys's eyes softened, and she said, 'I love you.'

I was about to make myself say, 'And I love you too, Gladys,' when she shifted in her seat and something she had round her neck swung forward. A small gold circle framed in gold scrolls, with something green gleaming in the heart of it. For a moment I was light-headed, feeling my heart pumping in my throat. The next I had to hold my hands together, to prevent them ripping it from between her shrivelled breasts.

'She's fallen asleep,' I lied, in the director's office. 'At least I've seen her. That's a very interesting locket she's wearing, by the way. Did she come in with it?'

'She came in with a small locked strongbox,' the director said reluctantly, looking embarrassed. 'When she got bronchitis last year we thought we were going to lose her, and as she's no family we decided to open it. There was no key, so I'm afraid we had to force it. There were one or two other bits of jewellery, a few papers, and this locket. She seemed to have a bit of an excited reaction when she saw it, so we put it on her. Then when we tried to take it off she got so distressed we just left it. We like to keep them as individual as possible, even if they're unaware of it.'

'Very commendable,' I heard myself say. 'Any photographs in it?'

'No. It was empty.'

No doubt emptied with a pin, it was so fiddly. I felt my eyes fill with tears.

'It is upsetting,' the director said. 'It was very good of you to come.'

I thanked her and left, and left the car in the nursing home car park and went walking without deciding where I was going, the picture suddenly in my mind playing over and over: the picture of Megan pleading for her life before a pair of implacable hands. One moment they were fastening round her neck, the next they were lifting a stone for the lethal blow, the next they were pushing her down a slope. Each time they buried her.

At least I knew they couldn't be Dai's. Dai would never have taken her locket from her. But now there's no BBC Light Entertainment to distract me, and I'm terribly afraid that the picture will run and run. Even though I've done what I realized as I walked that I would have to do. Megan had pleaded in vain for her life, and sixty years on she was pleading with me for justice. Well, I could give her that.

So I went back to my car and drove down to the police station.

SUNSET CITY

MARTIN EDWARDS

This story deals with the aftermath of killings that occurred in Liverpool, a city in which I set novels featuring my regular character, Harry Devlin, but the actual setting is very different. The Isle of Man is a tranquil place, beautiful and historic, whose charms are often underestimated – as they are by the protagonist of this story, Alix. The genesis of the story came from my interest in those whose lives are turned upside down when a loved one is convicted of serial killings. How much, one wonders, did they guess – or know?

*S*he must have known.

    'I'm not accusing you of anything,' Alix said. She opened her eyes very wide. It was a favourite trick. Simple, sure, but she never ceased to be surprised how often it worked.

In the distance, seagulls were keening. The sun was still high but there was a sharp edge to the breeze and Alix was glad she'd kept on her suede jacket. It wasn't exactly beachwear, but she never trusted the British weather, least of all at the British seaside. If you could call this Britain. She didn't know the island's technical status; that sort of trivia held no appeal for her.

Jayne Ive folded her arms. She was standing on the step outside her bungalow, a compact middle-aged woman, neatly dressed in a lime green trouser suit. Alix, a relentless optimist, thought it a good sign that Jayne hadn't slammed the door in her face. Behind her, Alix could see a hallway with framed prints of moody sunsets on the wall. This could be Mrs Anyone of Anywhere. But it wasn't.

'You say that as though you're doing me a favour.' Jayne's voice was pleasingly husky, Alix decided. Firmness tinged with irony. This was no downtrodden woman, scarcely a natural victim. She would sound good on the box. 'Taking my part when everyone else is against me.'

Alix smiled and said, 'Well, it's not so far off the truth, is it?'

'I have all the help I need, thanks. And, you might like to bear in mind, I have a good lawyer, too.'

The bungalow stood on the cliffs, looking out over the bay and beyond to the Irish Sea. Alix glanced at the sandstone buildings spreading out below, towards the moated castle on St Patrick's Isle. The little island was linked to the larger by a short causeway. A pretty enough place, this, but hardly a centre of metropolitan sophistication.

'Really? The sole Manx specialist in the law on defamation of character?'

As soon as the words left her lips, she regretted them. She hadn't liked the hint of legal action. Court proceedings, injunctions, they could snarl up any programming schedule; sometimes they killed a project stone dead. But she knew better than to allow herself to be provoked and she'd intended no more than a flip aside. Yet it sounded as though she were mocking both Jayne Ive and her island home. A bad mistake. It would be crazy to antagonise the woman she'd travelled so far to see.

'He's a partner in a big firm in Merseyside, actually,' Jayne said dryly. 'Don't worry, I'm not entirely parochial. I did live in Liverpool for ten years, remember.'

Alix had been raised in Sydney, Australia, and resident for the past

eighteen months in Battersea. To her, Liverpool was parochial en[...]
but she didn't push it. Jayne Ive came from a different world, a wo[...]
Alix too would need to inhabit if this programme were ever to be made.

'After the trial, though, you came back to your roots. Back to the Isle of Man.'

'There's a saying round these parts: a Manx girl who marries a man from the mainland will bring him back to the island one day. William and I spent all our wedded life in Liverpool.' Jayne unfolded her arms and brushed a lock of fading fair hair out of her eyes. 'But I tell you this. One day, he'll come back to join us, Rosie and me.'

There was a catch in her voice, making Alix wonder if at last she might be ready to crack. Time to be gentle. Tea and sympathy?

'Do you think – we could sit down, have a quiet chat?'

Jayne frowned. She was about to say no, Alix was sure of it, when her expression changed. She was looking over Alix's shoulder and an anxious look came into her eyes.

Alix turned her head and saw a young woman approaching, her flat heels crunching the gravel of the unmade road. Tall, overweight, with a blotchy complexion. The loose grey top was fair enough, but the flowery leggings definitely a mistake. Her dark hair was inexpertly cropped, tufts of it sticking out at odd angles, as if she'd let an old mariner down by the harbour do his worst with a blunt knife.

'This is Rosie?'

She was guessing. The studio possessed no file pictures of William and Jayne Ive's only child. But the age was about right. Nineteen, twenty? She bore no obvious resemblance to her mother, but her father, now, that was a different matter. The lumbering gait and the widely spaced blue eyes were spookily familiar from photographs and TV clips of William Ive attending court.

'Yes, it is,' Jayne said.

As she drew near, Rosie Ive focused her gaze on Alix. She glanced quizzically at her mother, as if to say – *why are you, you of all people, talking to a stranger?*

'We can talk, if you like,' Jayne said hurriedly. 'Just for a little while.'

Alix nodded. She always liked getting her own way, but she didn't want to show how pleased she felt. 'Fine.'

Jayne made no attempt to usher her guest inside or effect introductions. Instead, she stood her ground and spoke to her daughter.

'I'm going out for a little while. We're going to have a cup of tea down at the front. I won't be more than an hour, promise.'

...d and said nothing. She walked straight past them into ...ulled the door closed behind her.

..., then,' Jayne said, waving in the direction of the sea front.

...ppreciate this, Mrs Ive.' Alix concentrated on investing her ... the maximum sincerity. 'Or Jayne – if I may.'

'...all me what you like,' Jayne said with a shrug. 'I mean what I say, mind. An hour, maximum.'

Alix inhaled the salty air. 'Wonderful. This really is good of you.'

She fell into step beside the older woman as they moved down the hill. Jayne Ive kept up a brisk pace, as if anxious to get away from her home. Stretched out below was the beach. Children were playing with bats and balls, their parents sunbathing or eating ice creams. Fishing boats plied to and fro. Only the jagged remnants of the castle, outlined against the sky, testified to Peel's violent past.

'This is a lovely place,' Alix said. It seemed the right thing to say and she had to admit to herself that the resort would photograph well. For her money, though, Mauritius was more like it as a holiday destination. Never mind the history, feel the heat.

'Beautiful,' Jayne said, almost whispering the word. 'I love it very much.'

'I gather the wind blows pretty fiercely.'

The bloke who had sat next to her on the plane to Ronaldsway had told her this. His name was Rupert and he wasn't a native, just a young City trader who was flying over to a branch office in Douglas to sort a few tax-efficient deals. By a happy coincidence, as he described it, they were staying at the same hotel, off the main road between Peel and Port Erim. He'd asked Alix to have dinner with him and she'd said yes. Why not?

'Man is a small island, it's a healthy place.'

'Bracing, huh?' Alix said, just about resisting the temptation to say *surely no man is an island?*

When they reached sea level, Jayne waved a hand at a cafeteria squashed between The Longboat Guest House and a tiny gift shop. Its signboard bore the name *Maisie's.* 'We can talk there. It's quiet enough.'

Maisie, whoever she might be, was obviously a gingham fetishist, Alix decided as they settled down at a corner table. The place smelled of fish and chips. Apart from a noisy family of six by the door, the two of them were the only customers under seventy. As for the menu, it was *very* British seaside.

'I'll have a pot of tea and a plate of bread and butter,' Alix said. Her tone was mildly satiric – she just couldn't help it – but Jayne didn't seem to notice.

'Me too.' Jayne waved at a fat waitress, inevitably clad in a gingham overall, and ordered for them.

'Thanks for sparing me your time,' Alix said.

'I don't feel you left me with much choice.'

'Don't worry. Look at me; I'm not taking notes, and I promise I'm not wired for sound. Like I said on the phone the other day, I just want to hear your side of the story.'

'I haven't got "a side of the story". I never talked to the Press, not once. You must have heard – I was offered money, big money as it happens, but turned them all down flat.'

Alix leaned across the table, her hands almost touching Jayne's. 'I respect your wish for privacy,' she said earnestly.

'Then why are you here? Why don't you take the next flight back to London?'

'Jayne, you must understand, I'm not a tabloid journalist. I'm a serious documentary maker. There's a world of difference.'

'Not to me. Wherever you come from, whatever your agenda is, you all have one thing in common. You want to re-open old wounds.'

'Please. It's not like that. I want to present the public with a balanced picture about the case. Something they haven't really had until now. It's been pretty much one-way traffic, don't you agree? The police have had a field day, that inspector with the squint and his blonde PR lady. After the trial, the media hung on their every word. You kept your own counsel, from the best of motives I'm sure. But time has passed and maybe you ought to start wondering whether silence was the best idea.'

'Why wouldn't it be?'

'Because tongues start wagging, that's why.' Alix shook her head sadly. 'I'm sorry, Jayne, but there's no point in beating about the bush. You need to get real. And the reality is that when people stop talking about your husband, they start talking about you.'

'About me?' Jayne Ive looked puzzled, as if the idea had never occurred to her. A bluff, surely? No one could be that unwise to the ways of the world.

'You're married to a convicted serial killer, Jayne,' Alix murmured. 'I'm sorry, I don't mean to sound harsh, but it's not a conventional situation. Besides, it goes further than that. You worked side by side with him, you lived together in the home where all the deaths occurred. Face it, you can't be surprised that questions have been asked. Why didn't you figure out what your husband was doing to the residents? Did you help in a cover-up? Maybe – I won't spare you this, Jayne, we're both adults –

you *knew* what was going on all the time. Trust me, that's what people are talking about.'

Jayne received the little speech in silence. She didn't even blanch at the dread suggestion – *she must have known*. But then, she was bound to have gone through it all in her own head a thousand times.

The tea and bread and butter arrived. 'Lovely,' Alix said and the fat waitress positively simpered.

'I'm not even supposed to talk about the case,' Jayne said presently. 'That's on legal advice. William's appealing against conviction, as you know.'

'Lawyers.' Alix raised her eyes to the heavens. 'Don't they see, an appeal against a miscarriage of justice needs the oxygen of publicity?'

'Besides, some of the relatives have threatened to sue me, to claim compensation. Even though there was never any suggestion of my being charged with anything. Even though I've suffered too. I've lost a loved one, but they never think of that.'

'You owned the Sunny Hours Home.'

'William put it in my name. It was a tax thing, I don't know the details. As for being sued, there's a lot of emotion about. A little bit of money. It affects the way some people think.'

'But not you?'

Jayne's lips formed into a thin line. 'Alix, my husband was given four life sentences for crimes he didn't commit. What do *you* think that I think?'

Alix tried her tea, but it scalded her tongue. The bread and butter didn't look promising, either. Things that you do in the line of duty.

'Well, that's what I'd like to discuss with you. You obviously remain convinced he was innocent.'

Jayne took a deep breath. 'The first time we spoke on the telephone, I told you I had no intention of pouring my heart out to you. But I still say what I've always said. William didn't kill those poor old people.'

'The evidence...'

'Don't talk to me about the evidence! It wasn't worth two ha'pennies. Those so-called expert pathologists, disagreeing among themselves. Even that jury, that stupid jury, had two members who realised it didn't add up. It took the best part of a week to screw a majority verdict out of them. The judge should have called a halt long before.'

Jayne's pale cheeks had reddened. It was the first time she had shown animation. Alix felt like hugging herself. The ice was well and truly broken. Jayne might say she didn't want to talk, but it was only natural that she would seize the chance of challenging the received wisdom.

Maybe, just maybe, she genuinely *believed* what she was saying. Or had made herself believe it.

Suddenly Alix understood something that had eluded her until now. 'You expected him to get off, didn't you? You really supposed the jury would acquit.'

'That was when I had faith in British justice.'

'But two of the deceased actually left legacies to you or your husband.'

'It happens, in residential care homes. We cared for people, night and day. They were full of gratitude. We didn't encourage them to make us gifts. But some residents can be very persistent. They wanted to show how much they appreciated the way we looked after them, that's all.'

'You have to admit the timing looked unfortunate. Both the wills were made in the fortnight before the deaths occurred. No wonder the families became suspicious.'

'Only one of them, the Devaneys. Pure greed. They were the people who alerted the police. If it hadn't been for them, William would never even have been questioned, let alone convicted. In each case the doctors certified death as due to natural causes. As for the legacies, William and I were only ever going to get peanuts.'

She was in full flow, the legal advice on *omertà* well and truly forgotten. To encourage her, Alix assumed her most fascinated expression and said, 'Really?'

'Yes! You must have researched this. Fifteen hundred or two thousand at most. Don't forget, our residents weren't rich people. Most of them had spent their lives doing manual work in inner-city Liverpool, or else on the dole. The council was paying their fees because its own homes were packed out. Why would my husband kill for so little reward?'

'Because he could?' Alix sampled the bread. It was dry, and a single mouthful was enough. 'So easy, you see. Old folks, come to while away their twilight hours at this home. Frail, defenceless eighty-somethings. Easily smothered. At that age, if someone dies, who makes a song and dance? Hey, death is what happens to old people. *He had* a *good innings,* that's what people say, isn't it? It's only to be expected. Maybe even to be welcomed. Passing away peacefully in bed, there are plenty of worse ways to go.'

Jayne drained her cup. 'You don't understand. It wasn't like that.'

'Then what *was* it like? Don't you see, Jayne? This is your chance. You can tell your story for the first time. Explain to the world how it feels to be treated in this way.'

Jayne got to her feet. 'Sorry, I just don't want to carry on with this. Please go away from here. I'm not prepared to talk to you any more.'

In the bar of the swanky four-star Seascape Manor, Alix finished her vodka and tonic and said, 'She's got something to hide, I'm sure of it. Maybe evidence that could wreck William's appeal if it came to light. She only talked to me to find out whether I'd discovered a clue to whatever it is she's trying to keep secret.'

Rupert thrust out his lower lip. It made him look about thirteen. 'Maybe she helped her old man to do in the geriatrics. So what?'

She punched him lightly on the stomach and he pretended to double up in pain.

'You don't understand. This is important to me. This could be such a great programme. What's it like, being married to a serial killer? Does it come as a terrible shock, to find out the man you've been sleeping with has committed a string of murders? Or is it really confirming what, deep down, you already suspected? All those little things you turned a blind eye to, the nagging doubts at last bitterly confirmed.'

Rupert laughed and Alix felt his leg brushing against hers under the table. 'This really turns you on, doesn't it?'

Alix unclipped her hair from the ponytail, letting it fall on to her shoulders. This evening was going to end the way most such evenings ended. More than likely she'd just lie back and think of the BAFTAs. Yeah. *Best documentary,* it definitely had a ring to it.

'This could make such great telly,' she said.

'Right,' Rupert said. She could tell from the way he was looking at her that he'd talked enough about murder. 'So, Ms Alix Lawry, what else turns you on?'

Next morning, Alix lingered in bed until it was after ten. She had a hang-over and didn't bother with breakfast. Peel was supposed to be famous for its kippers but the very thought of tucking into dead fish made her want to puke. Rupert left her early: he had meetings to attend and money to make. They'd have one more night together before he went home to his posh flat in Fulham and the accountant girlfriend who he said, not very convincingly, bored him rigid. Alix wouldn't be sorry to see him go: he wasn't the least selfish lover she'd ever encountered. Perhaps he might say the same about her. Whatever. They'd helped each other to while away the time.

She wasn't sure how long she would stay on the island. The booking was for a week, but more than likely she'd know sooner than that whether a programme about the Ive case was viable. The first time they'd spoken, she'd talked about a fee for co-operation, but Jayne had said at once she wasn't interested in money. A lie, of course, for everyone was interested in money. All the same, she could understand why Jayne was sensitive. Refusing the tabloid offers to tell her story might have cost her, but it was a good move in terms of maintaining credibility. Once you sold your soul to the red-tops, you were fair game. What chance then of insisting on personal privacy? Jayne was wise to keep her options open. What Alix needed to do was to keep on at her. Everyone was persuadable. It was a question of making her understand that a serious, balanced, and fair examination of serial killings from the perspective of the culprit's (sorry, alleged culprit's) wife would give her a right to answer everyone who said *she must have known*.

Alix scrambled out of bed and started getting dressed. She'd always realised it wouldn't be easy to tempt Jayne into talking. Perhaps she ought to play dirty. It was never the first option; she had professional standards, after all, and before long she would have a reputation as a serious broadcaster to protect. But it wasn't a last resort, either.

Before leaving London, she'd done her homework. Rosie, poor Rosie, her father's final victim, had found herself a part-time job in a book shop. Although Alix didn't have the name of the place, how many book shops could there be in somewhere the size of Peel?

Several, as it turned out, and it was a case of fourth time lucky when, around lunchtime, Alix arrived at an antiquarian dealer's dusty place of business in a side street near the harbour. The front window was given over to a display of Hall Caine first editions: whoever Hall Caine was. There were two big ground-floor rooms, crammed with books from floor to ceiling. The place reeked of mildew. In one of the rooms an old man with a flowing beard was talking to a doubtful customer about a volume of local history.

'It will tell you everything you'd like to know about that remarkable fellow Magnus Barefoot. How he built the first castle...'

Magnus Barefoot? For God's sake, this place was like something out of Tolkien. Alix moved away. A scruffy note on a piece of card: Upstairs to Children's, Reference and Sport. She climbed the steps carefully, holding on to the wobbly banister. The rickety staircase was a deathtrap.

A young woman stood facing a set of shelves devoted to the likes of Enid Blyton and Captain W E Johns. Her ample backside wasn't flattered by today's choice of leggings, in hideous mauve. A mobile phone was clamped to her ear.

'Honest, mum, I'm fine,' she murmured soothingly. 'Now, I think I heard a customer coming up. I have to go.'

As Rosie switched the phone off, Alix gave a little cough. Rosie turned to look at her.

'Can I – oh, it's you!'

The interrupted offer of help was expressed wearily enough; as soon as the girl recognised Alix, her hostility was undisguised. Her heavy frame seemed to stiffen, as if in self-defence. Alix felt a small stab of pity for the girl. She was unattractive and she was branded as her father's daughter. But pity never got a television show on the screen.

'Hi. I was wondering if we could have a quick word.'

'My mother told you yesterday. We just want to be left alone.'

'I tried to explain to her, Rosie. This programme's going to be made, whether you and your mum co-operate or not. What I'd like is to make sure you have your say, put forward your dad's point of view. Tell the viewers how things really were in the Sunny Hours Home. After all, it was a family concern, wasn't it? Your parents ran the place and you helped to look after the wrinklies. That was the title we were thinking of, by the way. *A Family Concern.*'

Rosie's jaw was square and solid. Uncompromising. Loudly, she said, 'No way. Why don't you just go back home and pester someone else? Leave us in peace.'

From downstairs, the Magnus Barefoot fan called, 'Is everything all right, Rosie?'

'In case you're wondering,' Rosie hissed, 'he's a cousin of my mother's. He was glad to give me a job. So don't even think of threatening to tell him that I'm the daughter of William Ive. He already knows.'

An afternoon spent asking around convinced Alix that Jayne Ive had made a shrewd move, returning to her native island. No wonder she hadn't needed to change her name, assume a false personality and keep on the move, the usual fate of serial killers' spouses. Plenty of people seemed to think that William Ive might be innocent. There were hints that the relatives of the dead were Scousers on the make, and that the defence pathologists might have been right after all and the aged victims had indeed died natural deaths. In the dim and distant past, Jayne Ive's long-dead parents had been well known on the island, and well regarded. Whatever the rights and wrongs of the trial, she and her daughter were widely regarded as luckless victims of one man's personal catastrophe.

'One thing puzzles me,' she said to Rupert over dinner that evening.

'Why bury herself away here when it's so far to visit her husband in prison?'

'Well, if she's among friends…'

'Sure, but she's also supposed to be the devoted little woman. Yet she hardly ever goes to see him. As for Rosie, someone told me she doesn't think the girl's visited him once since the sentence was passed. Not what you'd expect from a devoted family.'

'Why worry?' he said. 'You're a programme-maker, not a detective.'

'I'm not sure this programme's ever going to get made,' she said. 'Too many bloody contradictions.'

'At least you got a nice holiday out of it,' he said. 'A short break in Sunset City.'

'Sunset City?'

'Yeah, that's what they call Peel. Haven't you read the brochure in your room?'

'I seem to remember I was otherwise engaged last night. Too occupied to leaf through the literature, let alone the Bible so kindly left by the Gideons.'

'Well, to you and me this may be a seaside resort, but the Manx see it differently. Something to do with the reddish hue of the sandstone everything's built of, apparently. Hence sunset. And there's a ruined cathedral in the grounds of the castle. Hence a city.'

'Darling, you know everything,' Alix said teasingly.

'At least, after last night, I know what you like,' he said. And they spoke no more of the Ives that night.

When they drew the curtains the next morning, Alix was surprised that visibility was so poor. It wasn't September yet.

'I never knew a place like this for fog,' Rupert said. He was an authority on the island's imperfections. 'I tell you, this is nothing. Later in the year…'

She kissed him goodbye when his taxi arrived and let him promise to get in touch when she was back in London. She didn't think he'd bother. On too much of a good thing with the accountant girlfriend, probably. Oh well. Easy come, easy go.

After a leisurely continental breakfast – she still didn't fancy kippers – she caught the bus that took her back into Peel. The mist was clearing and, according to the forecast, the day was going to be bright, the temperature in the low 70s. Still not exactly Bondi, and the scarf she put on wasn't intended simply as a fashion accessory.

After making her way back up on to the cliffs, she pressed the bell beside Jayne Ive's front door.

'I thought I told you not to come back.' Jayne had opened the door, but kept it on the latch. Treating her like an unwelcome intruder, someone who might be wanting to ransack the house.

'Jayne, we need…'

'Listen, all I need, all Rosie and I need, is that you leave us alone. She told me that you'd been to see her while she was working. It's disgusting, the way you people harass children.'

'Jayne, she's not a child, she's a grown woman. You had her working for you.' A thought struck her. 'Did she guess what was going on?'

The face in the crack darkened with rage. 'Get away from here!'

At last, Alix thought, I've broken through her defences. No chance of co-operation now, though. So: may as well be hung for a sheep as a lamb. 'What are you hiding, Jayne?'

'I'm not hiding anything! Now, go and leave us alone, or I'll call the police.'

She slammed the door fast and hard, before Alix had time to think up an ironic rejoinder. In frustration, Alix banged hard on the door but all that happened was that she barked her knuckles and Jayne didn't answer.

For a minute or so, Alix stood outside the bungalow, swearing quietly to herself. She'd messed up, there was no denying it. She hadn't handled Jayne Ive well and, without her input, she didn't have nearly enough material to persuade the powers that be to make a fifty-minute programme about what it's like being married to a serial killer.

Could she put a different spin on her original idea? Her old boss back in Sydney had told her that that was the secret of all the successful programme makers. As she trudged back along the unmade road, she juggled the possibilities in her mind.

The mist had vanished, leaving the skies bright and clear. Slowly, too, the fog in Alix's head was beginning to disperse. What if Rupert had been half right? *Maybe she helped her old man to do in the geriatrics* – that was what he had said. What if William Ive had, indeed, been innocent? What if Jayne were responsible for all the crimes?

She quickened her pace. It made a kind of sense, if Jayne were the killer. The forensic evidence in the case hadn't been up to much. The Devaneys had focused their attention on William Ive, since he had been named in their late mother's will; maybe when the postmortems had revealed something untoward, the police had taken the easy option. For all anyone knew, William might even have connived in taking the heat off his wife. By all accounts they were a devoted couple.

Maybe this programme would turn into a detective story. A quest for truth that ended up with the unmasking of an unexpected culprit. Terrific. But how to pin the crimes on a woman who had, as she'd already pointed out, never been charged with anything?

She could see people scrambling over the grassy mound inside the castle walls. The sun was bright on the sandstone of the little houses crammed between St Patrick's Isle and the quayside. Sunset City, yes, the nickname made a kind of sense.

Rosie. She was the weak link, Alix was sure of it. Time for another chat.

In the bookshop, the bearded man was extolling a book about Viking burial customs to a wizened little chap in a tweed jacket. No sign of Rosie Ive downstairs.

Alix went up to the first floor. Rosie was bending down to look at the crowded shelves, trying to see where she could squeeze in the scruffy hardbacks she held in each hand. Alix read the titles off the spines. *Moominland Midwinter* and *Spitfire Parade*.

'Sorry, it's me again.'

Rosie straightened, put the books down on a stool. 'What is it this time?'

'We never finished our conversation properly and now your mother won't talk to me at all.'

'So why should I?'

'Because I want you to understand, the two of you can't hide the truth forever.'

'What are you talking about?' Rosie demanded thickly.

'I've figured it out. The two of you were right, up to a point. Your father never killed those old people.'

Rosie's cheeks had reddened. 'What do you want from us?'

'I'm right, aren't I?' Alix was exultant. It was an effort to restrain herself from punching the air.

Rosie took a step towards her. 'You can't prove anything.'

'Just tell me the truth.'

Rosie reached out a muscular arm and seized Alix's scarf, jerking it tighter around the neck. 'I'm saying nothing. Hear me? Nothing!'

And then Alix saw the look in her eyes and knew that she'd got it wrong after all. Not Jayne – *Rosie*.

'So it wasn't money,' she said. The scarf was uncomfortable. Rosie wasn't strangling her, but she felt vulnerable and afraid. 'A power thing? A cry for help? Munchausen's by proxy, something like that?'

Rosie's head was very close to hers. The breath of a murderer warmed her cheeks.

'Rosie, you need help.'

'My mum gives me all the help I need. Now leave us alone!'

Rosie let go of the scarf and raised a beefy arm, as if to hit her. Alix stumbled backwards, felt her feet giving way beneath her. She was off the ground now, arms flailing as she grabbed in vain for the railings that guarded the staircase. As she plunged head first, she screamed and Rosie cried out something about a terrible accident.

Falling, falling, falling. Any moment now her neck would snap. But what filled her mind at the last was the memory of Jayne Ive's angry, defiant face. Jayne, who had sacrificed the old folk, and sacrificed her husband too.

She must have known.

BANK HOLIDAY IN CAMBRIDGE

JÜRGEN EHLERS

Jürgen Ehlers is an overseas member of the Crime Writers' Association. In his native Germany he has, during the past few years, begun to carve out a reputation as a short-story writer of distinction, as well as an occasional anthologist. He speaks English fluently and, when he writes in the language, his terse style is well suited to a fast-moving tale such as this.

It had all been Peter's idea, that mad, short trip to England. Only three days, but long enough to turn my life upside down. This is the result: Peter and Bernd have been caught, Marianne is gone, and I am on a plane back to Hamburg, with a bag full of worthless scraps of paper.

By the time we arrived I was already fed up to the back teeth. All shops were closed, on the Monday. Bank Holiday they call it. So shopping was out. Peter was not amused either. He is our boss. He went to university. He really is a doctor or professor or something. Or at least he was. Until one day he suddenly dumped it all and founded our little company. Peter had never suggested we go on holiday before. But he said he thought we'd earned one after the Aldi job. And he'd spent some time in Cambridge studying. It was a nice place. Actually we did need a holiday. Although not such a busman's holiday. But now I tend to think it was all because of Marianne. Just to impress her.

Marianne, 24 years old, slender and blonde. She had been with us for little more than a month. Peter had spotted her from the car, when she was little more than a dot on the railings up at the top floor of some university high rise. 'Stop,' he'd said to Bernd, had jumped out of the car, run through the entrance hall to the lifts and pressed the 12. He'd been lucky; she was still standing there when he got to her. Much later, after their dinner at the *Vier Jahreszeiten* hotel, he had said to her: 'You were going to jump.' She had shaken her head and said that she had just wanted to enjoy the view. One of those lies you have to let pass, said Peter. He knew that it had been different. And she knew that he knew.

After having unpacked our things, we went on a little tour of the city. Peter pointed things out: 'That building over there, that is Trinity College. Lord Byron studied there. And Dr Crippen, of course. He's someone we all know, don't we? And also Hastings, the Essex Ripper...' Marianne looked at him doubtfully. She couldn't tell fact from fiction, but anyway Peter made a good guide.

Two hours later we are sitting in the drizzle on a bench, viewing the river and the colleges.

Marianne's green eyes are shining. 'Isn't it marvellous, all those medieval colleges and churches? Like in a fairy tale!'

'Yes.' Peter sounds just as enthusiastic. 'Have you seen the Church of St Mary the Great? And the Barclay's Bank right next to it, right in the centre of the pedestrian area? Four different escape routes, at least, and not a chance for a squad car to get through!'

Of course I've seen it. 'One-way streets galore,' I say. 'And parked cars all over the place.' Then even Marianne must have finally realised that Peter had his own ideas about what a Bank Holiday should be like.

Bernd, my brother-in-law, has taken off his shoes and is massaging his feet. He's our man for the rough stuff. And our gunman. In his best days he could hit a gin bottle at 50 yards with his Walther. But probably he's practised a bit too much. The gin bottles had to be empty, of course. And the Walther has ten shots. Also, last week Bernd got glasses, and he is not happy about them. They make him nervous, he says. Now he is complaining: 'A bank robbery like this isn't really going to pay, is it? What's in it, do you reckon? One thousand pounds? Perhaps two thousand?'

'It might well be five thousand or more. All those professors and high-tech managers, they must earn quite a packet!'

'All right, five thousand then. So what?'

'Don't forget that we're outside the Euro zone. The pound's exchange rate is high right now!'

I look at Marianne. She hasn't said a word. What is she thinking? She's like a cat. I wonder when Peter told her how we earn our money. After she went to bed with him? I don't know. I don't even know if they sleep together. Peter gives that impression, but then you can't believe everything he says.

Tuesday morning, we are talking over the details. Peter unfolds the city map and rubs his forehead. He used to be a mathematician in his earlier life. I can see how he's doing his calculations. He draws a big circle around Barclay's Bank, right in the middle of the map. He says: 'Three hundred yards between the bank and Lion Yard. Another hundred yards to the War Memorial. Right across St Andrews Street. Marks & Spencer, into one of those cubicles. Our car will be parked right here. Three, four hours later we'll be back in Harwich…'

If everything goes well. I look at him: 'When?'

'Tomorrow, at eleven o'clock, that's the best time. Then the police will be on their tea break. Well, some of them, anyway. And as for the others, we'll have to find them some useful occupation.'

'The police station is damned close though,' I say. Peter ignores me. Instead, he turns to Bernd to talk over some technical details. They will be the men in the bank. Marianne and me, we will take care of the field work.

Marianne seems absorbed in thought. Eventually she looks at me: 'What do you think about all this?' she asks in a low voice.

Nothing, to be honest. Peter is a show-off who would do all kinds of things to impress the girl. And Bernd, the gunman, without his glasses he is half blind and with his glasses he is nervous. And drunk in any case.

Not the best of preconditions for a successful heist. In fact, Bernd's drinking problem has turned serious lately, since Marianne joined us. I suspect Bernd is jealous of Peter. Just like me.

'Perhaps we should run for it together,' I venture.

Marianne laughs. So I laugh too. Just a joke, it means. Perhaps she doesn't really believe that I'm ready to defect. Of course, she knows that I owe my freedom to Peter. When, after that bungled robbery at Karstadt's, the two cops had chased me through the city, me and my carrier bags full of money, he had reacted at once. Pulled up alongside and kindly offered me a lift. Very decent, I must say. It was a narrow escape, although when you think of it, he could have guessed that the cops would not shoot. Jungfernstieg is a pretty crowded street, and they might have easily hit one or other of the passers-by.

People are predictable, that's what Peter always says, it's simple maths. Although with Gerda, his ex-wife, apparently he miscalculated. He still hasn't quite recovered from the shock when she went off, all of a sudden. When he realised that she'd gone, he sort of freaked out. Threw all his scientific stuff in the bin and started a new life. Much more exciting than anything he'd done before, he says. And rather crazy, somehow. Because he doesn't really need money. In contrast to Bernd and me and especially Marianne, he has a lot of money somewhere in the background.

Peter's short discussion with Bernd is finished. He sees Marianne's worried face. He says: 'Relax, girl. No need to worry. We're an experienced team, so nothing can go wrong. Anyway, we've a job for you to do. We need *Schwarzbrot*, if you can get some, and a tape recorder, a bag, a mobile phone – oh, and a car.'

Marianne seems baffled. 'A car? In this place? All you'll do is add to the traffic jam!'

'Exactly. That will be your job.'

Two hours later, Peter and I are on our own. Bernd has gone to arrange some details for the escape tomorrow, and Marianne is not yet back from her errands. A good moment to tell Peter a thing or two. 'You're crazy,' I say. No time for diplomacy.

He shrugs. 'It's all nicely calculated!' he claims.

'Not everything,' I say.

He raises his eyebrows.

'Forty-six minus twenty-four, for instance,' I say. 'That's quite a difference!'

He does not comment, though I'm sure he knows what I mean.

'You can't keep her! And it wouldn't be fair! She is not like us, Peter.

Not a bit criminal. She pretends to be cool, but haven't you noticed how nervous she is? She's nothing but a poor, troubled bird that'll fly away in panic. She might do for us all.'

'Are you scared?'

Yes, I am scared. I don't want to go to prison. I want to enjoy my life. That's why I save every Euro I can get hold of. But for two, three more years I have to carry on.

'It'll all work out nicely,' says Peter. 'And the girl – this is a kind of test for her. Here in this bag we have the Aldi money. More than a hundred thousand Euros. She knows all about it. Either she will take the bag and beat it, or she won't – I bet, she won't.'

I just stare at him. To be a little arrogant is fine, I think. No problems with that. But this, this goes far beyond reason. Absolutely mad, to bring along all that money. I honestly consider taking the bag and running myself. But probably only Marianne could do that. Of course, she's the one who shares a room with Peter. Not me. Consequently I don't have much chance of getting hold of the bag.

We spend the best part of the afternoon walking back and forth through Cambridge in the rain, checking escape routes and studying police behaviour. Of course, there are patrols on foot, but not many. Later, we get some free time. Marianne buys a whole bag full of stuff. Bernd, the only one of us who never completed school, comes back with a 'University of Cambridge' T-shirt and a Kings College tie. Peter sits in a café and tries to do the Daily Telegraph crossword. On our return, he has folded the paper and stares out of the window. I give him a questioning look. 'That was pretty difficult,' he admits.

At night, when I am almost asleep, there is a soft knock on my door. So faint that I almost miss it. I open the door, and there is Marianne. I notice that she is wearing a pair of Peter's pyjamas, with rolled-up sleeves and legs.

'Come in,' I say.

But she shakes her head. 'Here, the bag,' she says. 'Could you, please, take care of that?'

It's the new bag! No doubt about what's inside. 'And Peter?' I ask.

'Fast asleep! Here's your plane ticket. Departure from Heathrow at quarter past six.'

So she has changed her mind after all! We will run together! I should hug her, my god, why don't I?

She smiles and takes one step back. 'You are sweet,' she says. Then she tiptoes back to her room.

Next morning the rain has stopped. I'm one hour early. The bag has spent the night in the left luggage at the station. I will collect it as soon as this is all over. In the meantime I've come to know the displays in the windows of *River Island Clothing* and the *Designer Clothes Store*. Not that I care much for designer clothes. And I'm nervous. Of course I am well aware that this is by no means a good job, the risk being far too high. Probably we should have run last night, I think. Too late for that now. Marianne will be in position as well.

I glance at my watch. One minute to eleven. Now the mobile phone in our room at the B&B should start dialling 999, as we have programmed it. And the tape with the screams, I think we have really done a good job on that. Should keep the police occupied for a few moments. And if all goes well, Marianne will stall her car right now at the corner of Pembroke Street and Tennis Court Road, which should put an end to all traffic south of Barclay's Bank instantaneously. And I start singing *Swanee River* on Petty Cury, rather loud and out of tune, so that the people stop and block the passage.

But, of course, it all goes wrong. I have just come to the third verse. The *Tie Rack* staff are pressing their faces at the windowpane by now, and a nice crowd of people have gathered around me, but the passage is still far from being blocked. And just as I am singing, 'All the world is sad and dreary...' I see, all of a sudden, Peter and Bernd come running, and the police are right behind them. I wonder who might have called them so quickly. Of course, there is not much I can do. So I stop singing, say '*Feierabend, Jungs!*', which of course nobody understands, and push my way through the crowd in order to find out where the others have gone.

I emerge just in time to see them fly up the iron circular stairway outside some university building and disappear behind a steel door. The police right after them, rather brave, I must say, because in contrast to our boys they are unarmed. But when they eventually reach the steel door, they find that it is locked from the inside, and our people are gone.

Not for long, though. The police apparently have managed to seal off the building. Eventually, I see Peter and Bernd coming out – in handcuffs. The group moves directly past me. Bernd is limping and cursing, as he is led past. Apparently he has sprained his ankle on his flight through the colleges. 'Bloody bitch!' he moans, probably referring to Marianne. Marianne? Yes, indeed, that is somewhat strange. Traffic is running normally, for Cambridge, that is. No car with a stalled engine anywhere. And no Marianne.

No Marianne either, when I eventually arrive at Heathrow airport. She must come any minute, I think. After all, I have the money. But the time passes, and eventually I have to go to the departure area.

Only later, when my plane is flying somewhere over the North Sea, do I open the bag. There is the parcel with the money. I look aside. My neighbour is snoring. Carefully I tear open the wrapping. And then I see. No money, just plain paper. 'So it didn't work, getting rich this time,' I think. Oh well, I will survive. At least I'm free, in contrast to Bernd and Peter. Peter's arrogance. I wonder if all his money and connections will help him now. I beckon the stewardess to bring me another red wine.

And then, as we're descending towards Hamburg, it suddenly occurs to me that I don't have a chance. The passenger list! Of course the police by now will have seen the passenger list from the England ferry, and they will know pretty well who shared a cabin with whom. And since Bernd is my brother-in-law, they will get me at once. They will certainly get me with aiding and abetting. Most likely they are already waiting for me at the airport. I close my eyes and think of Marianne. Would she have thought of that, I wonder? Perhaps. That she is not here now may be a good sign. And that she has the money may not be so bad either. Being such a nice girl, probably she would give me my fair share of the booty, wouldn't she? Or at least visit me in prison, perhaps?

THE EGYPTIAN GARDEN

MARJORIE ECCLES

In recent years, Marjorie Eccles has quietly established herself as a leading exponent of the traditional English detective story. Like many novelists, she evidently enjoys the scope afforded by the short form to try something different: 'Remember Kazarian', which appeared in an earlier CWA anthology, *Whydunit?*, is an excellent example. Here, her chosen setting is Cairo. The picture of expatriate life shortly before the Second World War is drawn with Eccles' customary clarity and attention to detail.

'But what has happened to the garden?' asked Mrs Palmer. 'There doesn't appear to be one, I'm afraid, dear,' replied Moira Ledgerwood who felt obliged to take the old lady under her wing, as she'd frequently let it be known over the last two weeks. 'Just a big courtyard.'

'Well, I can see that!'

'No garden in Cairo *housses*,' the guide, Hassan, asserted sibilantly, with the fine disregard for truth that had characterised all his explanations so far.

'But there used to be one here. With a fountain in the middle.'

Hassan shrugged. The other twenty members of the cultural tour smiled tolerantly. They were accustomed to Mrs Palmer by now, after ten days together in Upper Egypt. You had to admire her spirit, and the way she kept up with the best of them, despite her age. A widow, refusing to let the fact that she was alone limit her choice of holiday to Eastbourne, or perhaps a Mediterranean cruise. Intrepid old girl, eighty if she was a day. They were always the toughest, that sort. But her younger travelling companions sensed that this trip had turned out to be something of a disappointment. Egypt was not apparently living up to expectations; it wasn't as it had been when she'd lived here, though that would have been asking a lot, since it had been in the Dark Ages, before the war.

'Taking a trip down Memory Lane then, are you, Ursula, is that why you've come?' Moira had asked kindly, when Mrs Palmer had let slip this fact on the first day, utterly dismayed at the tarmac road that now ran towards the once remote, silent and awesome Valley of the Kings; at the noisome phalanxes of waiting coaches with their engines kept running for the air-conditioning; at the throngs of people from the cruise ships, queuing up for tickets to visit the Tombs of the Pharaohs, which were lit by electric light. Before the war, when her husband had taken her to view the antiquities, they had sailed across the Nile in a felucca from Luxor, and traversed the rocky descent and on to the Valley of the Queens and the Temple of Hatshepsut by donkey, accompanied only by a dragoman. The silence had been complete. Now, they might just as well be visiting a theme park, she said tartly.

'They're a poor people. The tourist industry's important to them, Ursula,' Moira reminded her gently.

Mrs Palmer had so far managed to bear Moira's goodness with admirable fortitude, but she was beginning to be afraid it might not last.

Strangers ten days ago, the tour group were on Christian name terms within a few hours, something it had taken Mrs Palmer a little time to get used to. But nothing fazed her for long, not even the touts who pestered with their tatty souvenirs, and craftily pressed worthless little scarabs into your palm, or even slipped them into your pocket, and then held out their own palms for payment. Moira had asked her advice on what to say to get rid of them, but when she repeated what Mrs Palmer had told her: 'Imshi! Mefish filouse!', the touts had doubled up with laughter and Moira had been afraid that Ursula had been rather unkind and led her to say something indelicate. Ursula, however, said no, it was only the prospect of a middle-aged English lady using Arabic and telling them to go away because she had no money that amused them, when they knew that all such ladies were rich and only addressed the natives loudly, in English. But then, they were easily amused – childlike, kindly people who were nevertheless rogues to a man.

The group advanced through the courtyard and made an orderly queue at the door of the tall old Mameluke house near the bazaar – now a small, privately-owned museum with a café for light refreshments on the ground floor – buying their tickets from the doorkeeper, an enormously fat, grizzled old man who wore a sparkling white galabeya and smiled charmingly at them with perfect teeth. He kept his eye on Mrs Palmer, gradually losing his smile as she lagged behind. He noticed her casting quick glances over her shoulder at the benches set in the raised alcove of perforated stonework, at the many doors opening off the large, dusty inner courtyard, which itself held nothing but a couple of dilapidated pots haphazardly filled with a few dispirited, un-English-looking flowers. But after a while she turned and resolutely followed the rest of the party.

Inside the house, little had changed, except that it had been recently restored, and consequently looked a little too good to be true. Wide-panelled wooden doors, wrought iron and coloured-glass hanging lamps depending from ceilings elaborately carved with geometric designs; inlaid furniture and wide couches in balconies that jutted out over the once poverty-stricken squalor of the narrow street below. Mrs Palmer was so overcome she was obliged to rest on one of these couches to try and catch a breath of air through its carved trellis screening, leaving the rest of the group to be shown around the house. She had no need to go with them; she knew every corner and every item in it, intimately. She had lived here once, she had been the mistress of this house.

And there had been a garden here. She had made it.

Impossible to count the number of times she'd sat here behind the mushrabiyeh latticework, a device originally intended to screen women of the seraglio from passers-by. Listening to the traffic that never stopped, the blaring horns, police whistles, the muezzins' calls to prayer, the shouts and sounds from the bazaar, to Cairo's never-ceasing noise, noise, noise! Longing for the soft, earthy smell of an English spring, to hear a blackbird or the call of the cuckoo, and the whisper of rain on the roof.

'Rain? What rain?' her husband had repeated when he had brought her here from England as a bride, dewy-fresh, hopeful and twenty years old. 'It never rains.' She had assumed he was exaggerating, but she quickly realised it was almost the literal truth. He rarely spoke anything else.

In the short time since her wedding, she had already begun to wonder, too late, if her marriage had perhaps been over-hasty. Such a good catch, James Palmer had seemed, courteous, well connected – and well off, something that Ursula had been taught was of paramount importance in a husband. She knew now that he was essentially cold and reserved, and humourless, too. He was tall and thin, handsome enough, and his only disadvantage, it had seemed to Ursula, was an Adam's apple that seemed to have a life of its own. She had decided she could learn to ignore that disconcerting lump of cartilage, and also the fact that he was twenty years older than she. His lack of warmth and humour, his pomposity, however, was something she didn't think she would ever get used to.

As time went on, longing for the smiles and laughter that had once been a natural part of her life, she began to throw herself into the pursuit of amusement, easy enough to find in the cosmopolitan Cairo of those days. It was 1938. Somewhere beyond Egypt, the world was preparing for war, but here expatriate European society carried on as though it would go away if they ignored the possibility. Her time was filled with countless dinner parties, afternoon tea at Shepheard's, gossip, charity functions, and tennis parties if the weather was supportable. When James was away, there was always someone to escort her, to take her dancing and dining every night.

But fun of this sort turned out to be an ephemeral gratification. For a while, she had believed such frenetic activity could obliterate the loneliness and dissatisfaction with her married state, but it very soon palled. Increasingly, when James was away and she was left entirely to herself, a pensive melancholy fell on her. As an oriental export merchant, eldest son of his family business, he travelled all over the Middle East in search of carpets, carved wooden furniture, alabaster and metalwork to ship to England, and it had pleased him to furnish this old house he had bought with the best of what he had found, so that one had to accustom oneself to reclining on couches and eating off low tables, as if one were a woman in a harem. Indeed, her disappointment with the life she had let herself in for made Ursula reflect ironically that James might have been better pleased if she had been.

Spending most of her time listlessly in this very room, which was open entirely to the air on one side, drinking thick Egyptian coffee or mint tea, longing for Earl Grey – which could be bought if one knew where to look, but never, for some mysterious reason, in sufficient quantities – she had gazed over the balustrade to the barren expanse of sandy earth around the edges of the courtyard, the drifts of dust obscuring the lovely colours of the tiles, wondering if this was all life had to offer. Not even a sign of a child as yet, though her mother, in her weekly letters, constantly assured her there was plenty of time.

Time, it seemed, stood still, an hour as long as a day. A huge expanse of space, and inside its infinity she sat alone, while the friendly chatter and laughter – and noisy, if short-lived, quarrelling – sounded above the continuous wailing Arab radio music that issued from the kitchen quarters and made her feel more alone than ever. What was she to do? Nothing, it seemed, but assume a stiff upper lip and get on with accustoming herself to the inescapable facts of her new life. The food, for one thing: the tough, unidentified meat she was tempted to think might once have been a camel, the sugary cakes that set her teeth on edge, and the unleavened bread. She must get used to the heavily chlorinated water that James insisted upon, too. The flies. The beautifully ironed napkins, so fresh from the dhobi that they were still damp. And especially to the khamsin that blew from the south west, hot and dusty, giving her a nasty, tickling cough that wouldn't go away. Oh, that eternal dust and grit that insinuated itself everywhere!

When she first arrived, she'd been determined to emulate her mother and maintain an orderly English household, with the dust outside where it belonged, but she was defeated. In their attempts to clean, the servants insisted on using whisks, whose only effect was to redistribute the dirt from one place to another. The grit ground itself into the beautiful mosaic floor tiles and the silky carpets under your feet. The cushions gave off puffs of dust whenever you sat on them. Even simple tidiness was beyond her capacity to convey to them, and theirs to accept. Elbow grease was a substance as entirely unknown as the Mansion Polish and Brasso she ordered from Home. Gradually, despite all her natural inclinations and her mother's training, inertia overcame her and she began to think: what does it matter, why fight the inevitable? Perhaps the servants were right, perhaps it was as Allah willed, inshallah.

Even more did she feel that now, sixty years later, when ghosts, and her own perceptions of violent death, were everywhere.

Sometimes, for air, she used to sit in the cool of the evening on the flat roof of the house, overlooking the expanse of the lighted city, watching the achingly beautiful sunsets over the Nile, with the ineffably foreign domes and minarets of the mosques piercing the skyline, as the darkness mercifully masked the seething squalor of the ancient, dun-coloured city. There was an especially low point on one particular night, when she almost considered throwing herself off, or alternatively taking to the bottle, but she was made of sterner stuff and didn't really take either proposition seriously. Instead, when it eventually became too cold for comfort, she took herself down the stairs to her usual position overlooking the courtyard, where she faced the fact that, unless she did something about it, her life would dry up as surely as the brittle leaves on the single palm that gave shade to the dusty square below, that she might as well take to the chador and veil. Despite the lateness of the hour, she went outside and, picking her way over the rubbish that seemed to arrive by osmosis, stared at the gritty, trampled earth and thought of her father's hollyhocks and lupins and night-scented stock.

'Of course the courtyard's dark,' James said when she later began by mentioning, tentatively, how the walls seemed to close in on her. 'That's its purpose. Oriental houses are traditionally built around the concept of high walls providing shade. The natives like nothing more than to live outdoors whenever they can, and the shade makes it bearable.'

'No one lives outdoors in this establishment,' Ursula pointed out.

'We are not natives, Ursula. And while we're on the subject, it's not a good thing to get too friendly with the servants. They'll lose all respect for you.'

It wasn't the first time she'd been tempted to laugh at his pomposity, but she knew that would have been a mistake. She didn't laugh now, she was only half listening anyway, absorbed by her new idea. She didn't bother to point out that the only friend she had in the house was Nawal, the one female amongst all the other servants who, as one of Yusuf the cook's extended family, had been brought in to work for her. At first sulky and unco-operative, she had gradually accepted Ursula's friendly overtures. Now she was all wide Egyptian smiles and good humour; she delighted in looking after Ursula, making her bed, taking care of her silk underclothes, and being allowed to brush her mane of thick, red-gold hair. She brought magical, if foul-tasting, syrup for Ursula's cough when it became troublesome and had become fiercely protective of her, pitying her, so far from home and with no family around her; no one except that cold and distant husband.

The next day Ursula obtained – with difficulty – a spade, a garden fork and a hoe, took them into the courtyard and began to dig the hard, flattened earth around the edges of the tiles, where surely there had once been plants and trees growing – and would be again, after she'd arranged for a delivery of rich alluvial soil from the banks of the Nile, in which anything grew.

James predictably disapproved strongly when he'd got over his first disbelief at this crazy notion of actually tackling the making of a garden, alone. It was unnecessary. She could occupy herself more profitably elsewhere. Why not take up sketching, or Byzantine art, his own particular passion? But Ursula's inclinations didn't lie either way; she couldn't draw for toffee, and she found Byzantine art far too stylised to be either comprehensible or interesting. For once her stubbornness overcame his disapproval. Very well, he said reluctantly, but had she considered how such eccentricity would reflect on him in the eyes of their European acquaintances? They needn't know, said Ursula. And neither was it, he could not resist reminding her yet again, ignoring her interjection, something calculated to enhance her authority with the servants.

And of course, he was right about this last, as he always contrived to be. They came out in full force to see what she was doing and laughed behind their hands at the prospect of an English lady wielding a spade, even sometimes going down on her knees, getting her hands filthy, grubbing in the earth for all the world like one of the fellaheen. She didn't care, but was nevertheless a little discouraged. Digging in the heat was harder work than she'd anticipated, and meant she could only do it for short periods. It did not seem as though her garden would progress very fast.

On the third day, she saw the boy watching her. He watched her for a week. She didn't know who he was, why he was here, how he'd arrived. If she spoke to him, or even smiled, he melted away. He appeared to be about sixteen or seventeen, slim and tall, liquid-eyed, with curly black hair and skin as smooth as brown alabaster. A beautiful youth in a galabeya white as driven snow, with a profile straight off a temple wall.

'Who is he?' she asked Yusuf, at last.

'He Khaled,' Yusuf said dismissively, and Ursula, intimidated, asked no more questions. She wondered if Khaled were dumb, or perhaps not entirely in his right mind, but dismissed this last, recalling the bright intelligence in his face.

The first time he spoke to her was early one morning, when he said shyly, 'I deegéd the kennel for you.' His face was anxious.

Kennel?

Following his pointing finger, she saw that the first of the series of blocked irrigation channels, which led from the source of the fountain, had been cleared. He had anticipated her intention, to clear the conduits so that she could draw water for her thirsty new plants. She smiled. He smiled back, radiantly. He took up the spade and began on the next one.

Miraculously, he persuaded the fountain to work. Water began to jet into the basin again, and at once the courtyard was transformed with possibilities: colour and scent, visions of lilies and lavender, marguerites, blue delphiniums and phlox in white and pink swam about in her head. Roses, roses, roses. She saw her dream of a lush and opulent garden coming true at last, the tiles clean and swept and glowing with colour, with the reflection of light and shade dappling through the leaves on to the dark walls, under the burning blue sky, the cool, musical playing of the water into the basin.

He came most days after that to help her, unself-consciously tucking his galabeya up between his legs. She discovered he had a sly wit, and they laughed together, sharing their youth as well as the work – she was not, after all, so many years older than he. He sensed quickly what she wanted done, but shook his head when she showed him the plant catalogues her mother, over-enthusiastically, had sent from England. Roses, yes, Khaled made her understand – his English was picturesque but adequate as a means of communication, and he learned quickly – roses would flourish. Were not the first roses bred in Persia? But lupins, hollyhocks, phlox – no. She thought it might be worth a try, however, if she reversed the seasons, pretended the Egyptian winter was an English summer, then for the fierce summer heat planted canna lilies and bougainvillea, strelitzia, perfumed mimosa, jacaranda and jasmine, oleander... The names were like an aphrodisiac.

She arranged, mistakenly as it turned out, to pay Khaled for his work, and though it seemed to her pitifully little, after some hesitation he accepted gravely, while making her understand he would have done it for nothing. 'It help pay my bookses,' he said ingenuously.

Nawal, with a blush and a giggle and a lowering of her eyes whenever she spoke of Khaled, had told Ursula that he was hoping to attend the university of Al Azhar, to study architecture, in order some day to build good, clean houses for poor people, both of which ambitions his uncle, Jusuf, regarded as being impossible and above his station. Nor was Jusuf, it seemed, pleased with her arrangement to pay the boy. Shouting issued from the domestic quarters shortly after she had made him the offer. When she asked Nawal what was the matter, Ursula was told that Jusuf,

while able to shut his eyes to the help Khaled gave freely, could not entertain the idea of his accepting payment for it. The noise of the altercation
in the kitchen was so great it brought James from the house's upper fast-
ness, where he immured himself whenever he was at home. After a few
incisive words from him, an abnormal quietness was restored. He then
turned to deal with Ursula.

'When will you learn?' he shouted, marching out into the courtyard,
his face red with anger, his Adam's apple wobbling uncontrollably, his
patience at an end. 'Don't you see that paying him money, when he freely
offered his services, is tantamount to an insult? You will abandon this
ridiculous project at once, do you understand? No wonder the servants
look down on you, working out here like a peasant! If you want a garden
so much, I can have one made for you, dammit! There's no need to make
such an exhibition of yourself!'

'No! You've missed the point, that isn't what I want at all!' Now that
she had found her raison d'être, something that gave meaning to the
enforced idleness and aridity of her life in Egypt, Ursula was in a panic at
the thought of losing it.

Khaled had followed them outside. He had endured Jusuf's shouting
with equanimity but when James turned on Ursula, those liquid eyes of
his flashed, simply flashed.   He plucked out the garden fork that was
driven into the earth nearby and for a terrified moment she thought...
But he merely dashed it to the ground with a dramatic gesture worthy of
the wrath of God. Before anyone could say anything, after another murderous look, he was gone.

And that's the last I'll see of him, Ursula thought sadly.

She had no prescience then of the dark future, otherwise she would
have left, too, taken the next available ship. Left Egypt then and there and
gone back to England, as James had been urging her to do for some time,
in view of the ever-increasing talk of war in Europe. But that would have
been admitting failure, and a certain innate stubbornness was keeping her
here, a refusal to admit defeat. A tacit awareness by now had arisen
between herself and her husband that their marriage was not a success, but
divorce in those days was not to be contemplated lightly. Paramount was
the scandal, as far as James was concerned. As for Ursula, it would have
felt as though she were being sent home in disgrace, like a child, for not
being good, which she knew was unfair. She had been too young for what
she'd had to face, and her marriage had been a foolish leap in the dark, but
no one had attempted to warn her. And for another thing, although James
simply would not, or could not, understand, Ursula was not going to
abandon her project at this stage. He could not make her give it up.

The garden had become an obsession. Ignoring his disapproval, she worked every day, until the perspiration poured off her and her thick hair became lank as wet string, until the sun or the khamsin drove her indoors. Sometimes she was so hot she took off her hat in defiance of the sun and her fair skin got burnt. Her English-rose looks faded and she was in danger of becoming permanently desiccated and dried, as English women do, under the sun. It was obvious that James was beginning to find her less than attractive. But her garden was starting to take shape.

She had been wrong about Khaled. Eventually, without explanation, he returned. Nothing was said, he simply took up where he had left off. Ursula bought him books and gave them to him as presents, so that honour was satisfied. James, surprisingly, said nothing. Perhaps he hoped the garden would be completed all the more quickly and Ursula would regain her sanity. Then one day, he announced, 'I've found a live-in companion for you.'

'What?' She was so furious she could scarcely speak, in a panic, imagining a stringy old lady who would torment her with demands to play two-handed patience, and prevent her from gardening. How could he do this to her?

But the stringy old lady turned out to be a bouncy and athletic young woman, not much older than Ursula, called Bunty Cashmore. Three months out of England, with short, dark, curly hair, hockey player's legs and a healthily tanned complexion enhanced by the fierce Egyptian sun rather than ruined by it, as Ursula's was. And then she understood the reason for James's sudden concern for her friendless state.

Rather than regarding the brisk bossiness of her new companion as a threat to his own authority, he seemed amused by it, and showed not a trace of disapproval of her, or impatience with her meaningless chatter. In fact, he paid more attention to her than to Ursula, no matter that she showed enthusiasm for the garden project. But then, Bunty was enthusiastic about everything, most especially when it came to learning something of Byzantine art, about which she cheerfully admitted she was ignorant.

She knew nothing about gardening, either, but it didn't prevent her from interfering – or pitching in, as she cheerfully put it. She pulled up tiny, cherished seedlings, believing them to be weeds. Oops, sorry! Surveying the garden through its haze of dust, which was hosed off each night when the garden was watered, she informed Ursula that she needed bedding plants to provide more colour in the courtyard, that the yucca in the corner, chosen for its architectural form, was ugly, and should go. She suggested that 'the boy' was no longer needed, either, now that she was here to help Ursula, now that the garden was at last almost finished, apart from the very last strip of bare earth that Ursula was reluctant to deal with, since that would leave little else to do but tend the garden while waiting for it to mature.

Khaled bent over his work at hearing what was proposed for him, hiding his thoughts and the resentment in his eyes.

And Nawal, meanwhile, noted every look that passed between Bunty and James, enraged on behalf of her mistress, fiercely jealous of the time Ursula was now forced to spend with the usurper, Bunty.

As for Ursula herself, she gritted her teeth at Bunty's insensitivity and refused to let her get on her nerves, hoping that all she had to do was wait, and the untenable situation going on in her own house would resolve itself. For England had declared war on Germany in September 1939, and Bunty was forever talking of going back Home and becoming a WAAF. Ursula, entirely sick of her, couldn't wait. Yet talk, it seemed, was all it was. Something held Bunty here, presumably in the person of James Palmer: she was by no means as naïve as she seemed; she knew very well which side her bread was buttered.

Though he was too old to fight, James was presently offered a job with an army intelligence unit, and was threatening to close the house and pack his wife off Home whether she wanted it or not. An ugly atmosphere developed at her point-blank refusal to do his bidding. Egypt was neutral, maintained Ursula, she would be safer here than in England. Depend on it, James countered, sooner or later the war would be on their doorstep, and who knew what would happen then? But it wasn't her safety that was in question, they both knew that, it was a face-saving ploy for getting rid of her.

Yet how could she have willingly left the only thing she had ever created – her garden?

What had it all been for, the struggle and the unhappiness? More than sixty years later, despite all the love and dedication lavished upon its creation, that garden, that bone of contention, but still the one shining star in an otherwise dark night, had disappeared as though it had never existed. The old feeling of melancholy overwhelmed Ursula as she contemplated where it had once flourished. It wasn't only, however, that the garden had gone and the courtyard had reverted to its original air of sad, dark desolation, with the fountain in the middle as dried up as when she had first seen it; one could cope with that. It was something about the atmosphere itself that provoked such thoughts, a sort of pervasive accidie. A stain on the air, left by the events that had happened here. She felt oppressed by the thought, and the weight of her years. Or perhaps it was just that the last ten days had taken it out of her.

'Mrs Palmer?'

She turned with weary resignation, but it wasn't Moira Ledgerwood, being responsible. There was still half an hour of interesting things to see on the upper floors before the group descended for glasses of tea in the café. It was the doorkeeper who stood there. He said softly, 'I'm sorry the garden is no longer there. It grew wild. They cut it down, during the war, when the house was occupied by English officers.'

The filtered light from the windows fell on the ample figure of the doorkeeper in the white galabeya, and as he turned slightly, she saw his profile. He knew her name. And suddenly, she knew his. It was a shock. The dark curls were silvered now, but the smile was the same. She saw the young, slim, beautiful youth inside the grossly fat old man. And he, what did he see? A scrawny old woman in her eighties. 'Khaled? How did you know me?' she asked faintly.

'By your hair, first of all.'

Involuntarily, her hand went up to her white, serviceably short locks. 'How could you? I had it cut off, years ago, and it turned white before I was forty.'

'I recognised the way it grows.'

There was a silence between them. A feeling of what might have been, had they been born in other times, other places. Perhaps. Or perhaps not.

'Mrs Palmer.' He came forward with both hands outstretched and she saw he wore a heavy gold ring with an impressive diamond on his little finger. He clasped both her hands, something he would never have done in the old days, and she allowed him to. 'It is so good to see you.' Something had radically changed, apart from the fact that his command of English was now excellent. He didn't look like a moab, a doorkeeper, a man who sat at a table and took money. He looked like the sort of man who made it.

'But next year would have been a better time to come,' he went on. 'Then, there will be another garden. The men come next week to begin. I needed to have the house restored first.'

She stared at him. 'Khaled, are you telling me—?'

'Yes, the house belongs to me, now, Mrs Palmer. After the war, after the officers left, that is…' He paused. 'It stayed empty, as you must know, until seven years ago, when I bought it, through your lawyers. The condition, the neglect!' He threw up both hands. 'But I was too busy to do anything about it until now. A retirement project, you might say, hmm?' He smiled.

She digested the information that he was rich enough to do all this.

'You did go to university then? You became an architect?' The guilt that she had carried around for more than half a lifetime began to shift a little.

'Alas, no, that was not possible, in the circumstances.'

There was a long pause. 'And did you marry Nawal?'

His soft, dark eyes grew inscrutable. 'No, I never married anyone at all.' He shrugged. 'Malish.' That unquestioning submission to fate. Malish – never mind – it doesn't matter. Then he laughed. 'I became successful instead. I sell souvenirs to tourists. I have co-operatives to make them, and also shops now in New York, Paris, London. Many times I have thought of you when I am in England.'

The hopeful young man with his lofty ambitions, now an entrepreneur, a curio seller, in effect – albeit a rich one. To such do our hopes and aspirations come.

'Why did you run away, Khaled?'

He looked at his feet. 'It was necessary. Who would have believed me?'

'There were no questions asked; you should have stayed.'

'I heard that, but I was far away by then.' He smiled again.

Death due to extreme sickness and diarrhoea in this land wasn't so unusual as to cause many inquiries to be made, especially when it was known that the victim was not Egyptian and had been suffering from stomach upsets for ten days or more before dying. It had been put down to one of the many ills European flesh was heir to, and for that matter Egyptian flesh, too, in this land where clean water was unknown and a mosquito bite could kill.

She and Khaled had been pruning the shrubs. The jasmine had already grown into a tangle and the pink, white and red oleanders, though pretty, needed to be kept in check. Bunty, decidedly under the weather, was sitting in the shade of the stone alcove, too unwell to do anything but watch. Ursula threw her a long, speculative glance and pensively snipped off an oleander twig, careful not to let the milky sap get on to her hands. 'That's a nasty cough you have there, Bunty,' she said eventually. 'Why don't you ask Nawal for some of her cough syrup?'

'It's this wretched dusty wind,' said Bunty, coughing again, her eyes red and sore. 'This khamsin. I'm going indoors.'

'Go and lie down and I'll bring you the medicine. It's very good.'

'We-ell, all right. Do you think she might have something for my gippy tummy at the same time?'

'I go bring,' said Khaled, and departed with unusual alacrity.

The dry, rasping cough came again and another griping pain almost doubled Bunty up. It wasn't only cholera and malaria, or worse, that one had to fear, here in Egypt. Stomach upsets, and quite often being slightly off-colour for unspecified reasons, were unavoidable hazards, facts of life. Bunty looked wretched, but Ursula had little sympathy for her predicament. She had a passion for sticky native sweetmeats, and one didn't care to think about the flies. Ursula had actually seen her carelessly drinking water from the earthenware chatty by the kitchen door because it was always cool, and because the water that Ursula and James forced themselves to drink tasted so nastily of chemicals and didn't, as Bunty pointed out, necessarily make them immune; James himself hadn't quite recovered yet from the same sort of malaise that Bunty was suffering now, and was still extremely queasy, even with the care he took. As for Bunty, it was hardly surprising that her usual rude health sometimes deserted her.

Death, though! No one could have foreseen that. These things took unexpected turns, however, Madame, they said at the hospital, shrugging; affected different people in very different ways. A constitution already weakened by bouts of sickness and diarrhoea... Inshallah. There were few formalities.

Afterwards, the desire to shake the dust of Egypt from their feet had been mutual. Home was all there was now, wartime England. It had been Ursula, after all, who joined the WAAF, taking a rehabilitation course in horticulture when she was demobbed.

'I made another garden, Khaled, in England, in Surrey. It became a commercial success. Hollyhocks and lupins, as well as roses.' They smiled, remembering. 'But no oleander. The climate is too cold there for oleander.'

'Ah.' The smiles faded as their glances met.

That day, after she'd administered Nawal's medicine, which Khaled had brought, Ursula had come downstairs again and sat on the carved wood bench where Bunty had sat, to wait. The garden was tidy, and so still, apart from the splash of the fountain. The oleander twigs which had lain scattered on the brightly patterned tiles had already been swept away and cleared, she noticed.

Nerium oleander. All parts of which, including the nectar, are deadly, even the smoke from the burning plant, and especially its milky sap. Causing vomiting if ingested, sweating, bloody diarrhoea, unconsciousness, respiratory paralysis and finally, death.

The memory of that day was etched into her brain for ever: the sultry heat, the metallic smell of dust, the perfume of the roses. The silence in her head, as though the habitual din of life beyond the high walls had been stopped to let the world listen to what she was thinking. Even the Arab music from the kitchen was stilled. The waiting.

Within half an hour, the sickness had begun, and twenty-four hours later, it was all over.

Khaled was looking at her earnestly. 'And you, Mrs Palmer. Have you had a happy life, Mrs Palmer?' he questioned acutely.

A happy life! How could that have been possible? Living with the tedium of Bunty's bright inanities, year in, year out. But there were many ways of expiating guilt. In the end she'd become quite fond of her. A delicious irony indeed.

'I have – had no regrets.'

'Meesees Palmer!' Hassan's voice, rounding up his flock, echoed down the staircase.

'Ursula!' Moira Ledgerwood coming in, looking for her protégée, finding her. 'Oh, the things you've missed! What a pity you didn't come with us.' She looked curiously from the old lady to the old doorkeeper.

Ursula held out her hand. 'Goodbye, Khaled. Good luck with your project.'

She turned to go and then turned back, as he said softly, for her ears only, 'Your husband should not have died. Nawal's medicine was good.'

She smiled. 'It must have been intended, Khaled. Inshallah, hmm? He must have been too ill for it to make any difference. Who knows?'

Khaled watched her go. And perhaps Bunty Cashmore would have died, too, if she hadn't been so violently sick again, immediately after swallowing her own dose.

'Who knows, Mrs Palmer?' he said into the empty room.

LES INCONNUS

KATE ELLIS

In common with many other contributors to this volume, Kate Ellis has
seized the opportunity offered by an anthology to try her hand at a story
with a setting and characters very different from those familiar to her regular readers. The result is, to my mind, a notable success. Ellis conveys
the flavour of the French capital with conviction, whilst characters are
neatly integrated into a highly satisfying story-line.

'No window in Paris attracts more onlookers than this.' Jules Seurot ignored the remark. He stared at the scene behind the huge plate glass window feeling no revulsion, only a mild, detached curiosity.

The corpses lay on a row of slabs behind the glass, propped up slightly so that their features were clearly visible to the viewers. They were naked, their modesty covered by a small board upon which was written the details of where and when they had been found. Their clothes hung above them, dangling from a rail, providing a pathetic splash of colour in that white chamber of death.

The man who had spoken to Seurot was small, with a shock of dark hair and a pair of spectacles perched precariously on the end of his nose. He was dressed like a clerk, neat but shabby in dusty black.

Seurot turned to him. 'Where do they come from?'

'They are pulled from the Seine and brought here to the morgue in the hope that someone will claim them. Allow me to introduce myself, monsieur. My name is Charles Mery and it is my unhappy duty to investigate the deaths of these unfortunates. It is your first time in this place?'

'Indeed, monsieur.'

'You are not from Paris?'

Seurot wondered if his small-town ways had betrayed him in some way. He was painfully aware that the sophisticated Parisians saw him for what he was; a middle-aged provincial with an expanding belly and thinning hair.

'No, monsieur. Although it is my wife's wish to move to the city. I am in search of an apartment.'

'I wish you luck.' Charles Mery inclined his head politely and gave the henpecked husband a look of pity. 'I must take my leave, monsieur. I have matters to attend to.'

Seurot watched him disappear through a green painted door. Mery seemed amiable enough, although he was sure that he had detected a note of mockery in his voice.

The crowd before the window was growing fast. Mothers had brought their children to stare at the unfortunates behind the plate glass and the young seemed as entranced by the spectacle as their elders. People chattered and laughed as they gawped at the unseeing dead. Seurot had heard it was the best show in Paris, not to be missed, and it seemed that the rest of the city thought likewise. All classes of Paris society thronged into the morgue: from well-heeled gentlemen in silk hats arm in arm with their plump wives, to rough matelots and ladies of a certain calling with their cheap, bright plumage and hard, pinched faces. Death fascinates all manner of men and women.

Seurot mopped his brow: the place was oppressive with too many bodies, alive and dead. He turned to go: he would view the great cathedral of Notre Dame nearby before continuing his search for an apartment that would satisfy Madeleine's exacting requirements.

He glanced at the large notice on the wall as he was leaving. 'The public is requested to declare to the Morgue Clerk the name of any individual they recognise.' Seurot continued on his way. The notice did not concern him as all Parisians were strangers.

As he reached the morgue's main door, he collided with a roughly dressed man who mumbled an apology and hurried on his way. It wasn't until he entered the portals of Notre Dame that Jules Seurot felt in his pockets.

The Seurots lived just outside the centre of the small town of Moret, east of Fontainebleau. Jules returned from Paris to find the shutters open but no sign of life. Madeleine was out, which wasn't unusual. There were times Jules suspected that she had a lover, that she and Maitre Michet, the lawyer, were more than friends. However Moret – unlike Paris – was a small place where everyone knew each other's business and if his wife were unfaithful the town gossips would be bound to know of it.

And Madeleine's ardent desire to move to Paris reassured Seurot that there was no lover to keep her there. He understood her longing for city life: she had endured years trapped in Moret's dull provincial world by the need to be near her aging and miserly father. But now her father was dead and she had come into her considerable inheritance. Soon they would be in the city, in the centre of things, where Madeleine could show off the jewels and fine gowns she could now afford.

As Jules opened the front door a girl scurried from the back of the house. She bobbed a curtsey and smiled coquettishly. The sun had brought out the freckles on her turned-up nose: Jules liked that. And he liked the swell of her breasts beneath her starched white apron.

'Where is your mistress, Chantal?'

Chantal looked him in the eye, too boldly for maid and master. 'Visiting Madame Benot. Boasting of how she will soon be playing the grand lady in Paris.'

Jules flinched. 'You mustn't speak like that.'

'Why not?' Chantal reached out and drew him towards her. A few moments later he was kissing her, tasting her lips and running his fingers through her fine, fair hair, dislodging her white linen cap. He broke away, breathless. 'Not now, Chantal. It is not the time or the place.'

The girl pouted. 'But when we're in Paris…'

Jules's heart was pounding. He put his finger to her lips. 'We must be careful. My wife must have no inkling of…'

Chantal caught his finger and kissed it. 'Trust me,' she whispered.

The sound of footsteps on the stone steps leading up to the front door heralded Madeleine's arrival. Chantal ran down the hallway and opened the door, bobbing a curtsey meekly to her mistress who barely acknowledged her presence. Jules breathed deeply, his heart still thumping in his chest. Deception was an exhausting game.

'My dear, how well you look,' he said forcing a smile. He kissed his wife on the cheek but she hardly seemed to notice as she was busying herself with a hatbox.

'What news of Paris? Did you find…?'

'I found the most beautiful apartment near the Rue Saint Honoré. It has every luxury – such a bathroom. And it is spacious and light: you will love it.' He looked round and saw that Chantal had disappeared into the servants' quarters below stairs.

'And what did you get up to in Paris?' Madeleine asked, narrowing her eyes.

'I saw the sights, of course… Notre Dame, the Louvre and… I lost my wallet: I fear it was stolen.'

Madeleine looked at her husband disapprovingly. She put him in mind of an overripe fruit – plump and past her best. She frowned and he could see the fine lines radiating from her pursed lips.

'You should be on your guard in the city.'

'It was your idea to live in Paris, my dear.'

She ignored the remark. 'Did you report the loss?'

'I returned to the morgue and the gentleman I spoke to there was most agreeable, in spite of his grim calling. He said that there had been many such thefts there and that the gendarmes have been alerted. But he held out little hope of getting it back. Paris is full of pickpockets.'

Madeleine's face was a mask of horror. 'You went to the morgue?'

'In Paris it is quite an attraction. Whole families go to view the corpses pulled from the Seine. I will take you when we move to the city.'

He watched her face, enjoying her expression of disgust.

'I would never set foot in such a place.'

'How was Madame Benot? And her revolting little dog?'

'Both well. Although her nephew, that so-called artist, still causes her much worry. She fears that his immoral behaviour will scandalise all of Moret.'

Jules fought back a smile. 'What a trial it is to have scandalous neighbours. You do realise that in Paris it is possible that all our neighbours will be scandalous?'

Madeleine gave a snort of disapproval and swept off to try on her new hat. Jules watched her ample backside disappear through the doorway.

He was looking forward to Paris. In fact he could hardly wait.

A city, any city, bestows a certain anonymity upon its inhabitants. But Paris possessed a body of women who considered it their right and duty to know the business of others. The concierge was queen of her domain and observed all the comings and goings in her kingdom. Madame Dubois dwelt in her dark quarters on the ground floor beneath the Seurots' new apartment like a spider waiting in its web. Jules Seurot, who had never before lived in the capital, found her constant, vigilant presence disconcerting.

Seurot moved into the first-floor apartment in a small street off the Rue Saint Honoré on the last Wednesday in November. Madeleine was to follow at the weekend as she had business to attend to in Moret. Jules knew that this involved spending time alone with Maitre Michet and he still had an uneasy feeling that there was something between them. The lawyer was much younger that he was, a tall and attractive man, and last week at Mass he had been staring in the direction of their pew. Madeleine was still what some would call a handsome woman, rendered even more handsome by her substantial fortune. And Gaston Michet knew exactly how much she was worth, down to the last centime.

But soon Michet wouldn't bother them. Madeleine and their maid, Chantal, were due in Paris on Saturday at three o'clock and Seurot was to meet them at the station. On Saturday afternoons the concierge, Madame Dubois, visited her aged mother and as he waited on the platform at the Gare de Lyon he congratulated himself that he had timed his wife's arrival to perfection.

When the train arrived in a cloud of billowing steam, he watched as Madeleine strutted confidently along the crowded platform towards him; the new Parisienne preparing to explore her adopted city with the zeal of a convert. Behind her walked Chantal carrying a valise and a hatbox. Madeleine wore blue silk and Chantal plain brown; a sparrow in the wake of a peacock.

Madeleine stared, wide-eyed, out of the carriage window as they trotted along the Rue de Rivoli past the great bulk of the Louvre. When they arrived at the apartment, Seurot studied Madame Dubois' windows but saw no telltale twitch of curtains. The horse that had pulled their carriage to its destination looked at him with soulful eyes and Jules patted the animal's nose absent-mindedly. He liked horses; horses didn't ask questions.

He paid the driver and hesitated before entering the building. He knew what had to be done. And it had to be done quickly before Madame Dubois returned.

When Jules entered the apartment, he found Chantal busy in the bedroom unpacking her mistress's clothes. She hurried to and fro, avoiding his eyes; tense, frightened. He felt like taking her in his arms. But he had to be patient.

Madeleine was exploring each room, making noises of approval. 'What do you think of the apartment, my dear,' he asked, playing the dutiful husband.

'It will do very nicely... for now. But when we begin to entertain, we may need somewhere larger.'

Jules didn't reply. He studied his feet for a few moments.

'I thought we could take a stroll down to the river while Chantal unpacks,' he said casually. 'Then we shall dine out to celebrate your arrival: there are many fine restaurants in the vicinity.'

She looked like a cat who had just caught sight of a desirable bowl of cream. 'Why not? I am no longer a dull, provincial woman so why should I not eat at the best restaurants in Paris?' She laughed, the tinkling laugh that set his teeth on edge. 'But it is almost dark.'

'Paris is at its best in the dark.'

'Very well, Jules, let us take our stroll. Chantal can manage here.'

Madame Dubois had not returned so they left the apartment unobserved and walked arm in arm in the fading light through the bustling crowds, towards the Quai des Tuileries. And as they walked Madeleine Seurot took in every new sight, sound and smell and stared round in wonder like a child in a toy shop.

'Is it done?'

Seurot nodded. 'I saw the concierge return as I was coming in. She asked me if my wife had arrived safely.'

'And how did you answer?'

'I said she liked the new apartment.' Jules Seurot breathed deeply and realised that his hands were still shaking. 'Shall we dine out?' he asked, hoping his voice sounded normal, untroubled.

'I have nothing to wear.'

'You shall have the finest gowns now that you are...'

'Madame Madeleine Seurot?' Chantal tilted her head to one side. 'Are you sure we shall not be discovered?'

'Do you think I have not taken precautions? There is no reason why anybody here should suspect that you are not who you say you are.'

'What about Maitre Michet?'

'What about him?' Seurot snapped. Was there something he had overlooked?

'Nothing. He has been dealing with Madame's affairs, that is all.'

'He won't trouble us. He has said on many occasions that he never visits Paris. But it would be as well to find a new apartment soon, just in case Madeleine has given anyone this address.'

'You think of everything,' she said admiringly before kissing him on the lips. 'And... and Madame? Did she...?'

Seurot tried to smile. 'What a blessing it is to have a wife who can't swim.'

'And nobody saw you?'

'It was quite dark by the time we reached the river and I made sure there was nobody about.'

'And when she is found? They might identify her and...'

He stroked her hair, like a parent comforting a child. 'It is impossible, my darling. I visited the morgue. Many bodies pulled from the Seine are never claimed – I have seen it for myself. *Les inconnus* – the unknown ones – are common in a great city. Nothing can go wrong. As far as all Paris is concerned you are Madame Madeleine Seurot. I shall take you downstairs soon and introduce you to Madame Dubois as my wife.'

Chantal fluttered her eyelids as her hand travelled down his body. 'And tomorrow we will go shopping. I have nothing to wear and if we are to...'

'You shall have the finest clothes Paris can offer,' he muttered as he led her to the bedroom.

Chantal was everything Jules Seurot had ever dreamed of in a woman; passionate and uncomplaining, her slender body excited him in a way that Madeleine's never had. But after a week he began to find lust rather exhausting. And he wasn't sleeping well.

Each night Madeleine's face appeared in his dreams, drowned, bloated and accusing. Her murder had been so easy. She had been off her guard, excited at seeing the river she had heard so much about. One shove and it was over: a splash, a muffled cry, then her heavy clothes had dragged her down and the murky river claimed another victim.

Now he had control of Madeleine's money and Chantal's body. But he felt uneasy, as though Madeleine was about to rise, dripping, from her watery grave and bring him to justice. Perhaps if he saw the body, if he reassured himself that everything was going as planned, he would feel better.

One morning when he suggested to Chantal that they venture out to explore their new city, she pouted sulkily and stated that she would rather buy a new hat.

'My dear, you have enough hats. And as for gowns, why don't you have some of...' He hesitated. 'Why don't you have some of Madeleine's gowns altered. There are many good dressmakers in Paris.'

Chantal stared at him in horror. 'I would never wear a dead woman's clothes.' She turned away from him. That was her last word on the subject.

Jules said nothing. He was beginning to discover that Chantal, so compliant at first, possessed a stubborn streak – and that after surviving for so many years on a servant's slender wages she was becoming all too adept at spending money.

He would go out alone, which was probably best. There was one place he needed to visit again. He had to know if Madeleine had been found.

The first time he had visited the Paris morgue, he had been filled with curiosity. This time his only emotion was dread. But he couldn't rest until he knew that Madeleine was lying there, anonymous and unclaimed, awaiting her pauper's grave.

Even though he knew he would find her there, naked and bloated, behind the plate-glass window, the first sight of her body shocked him and his heart began to pound uncontrollably. As he stood in the milling crowd, breathing in the scent of the rich mingled with the stench of the poor, he couldn't take his eyes off her waxy, lifeless face.

He had never loved Madeleine: he had married her because he knew that one day she would be a very rich woman. And when she was visiting her dying father he would lie with Chantal in her narrow attic bed, formulating the great plan: the plan that could not fail. Once they were in Paris Madeleine would die but nobody would know because Chantal would take her identity, steal her life. It had seemed so simple. But now he was faced with the reality of what he had done, he felt sick and afraid.

'Ah, good morning, Monsieur Seurot. I had not thought to see you again so soon.'

The voice made Seurot jump. He swung round and saw Charles Mery smiling at him, a suspicious and mirthless smile.

'You remember me?' he muttered.

'I have a remarkable memory, monsieur. I never forget a face. I have some news for you. The gendarmes arrested a pickpocket here this morning. It may be the man who stole your wallet. He may say what he has done with it and…'

'Don't worry about it, monsieur. There was nothing of great value in it,' Seurot replied quickly, anxious to get away. He was aware of Madeleine, lying behind the glass a few yards away.

'You have moved to Paris now?'

'Yes.'

'Perhaps you would give me your address, monsieur – in case the wallet is found.'

It was a direct question that Seurot couldn't avoid answering. And in his panic, it never occurred to him to lie. He gabbled his address and was gratified to see that Mery did not write it down.

Mery smiled again. 'And how do you like our city?'

'Very much.' Seurot took his gold watch from his waistcoat and made a great show of studying it. 'I am late for an appointment, monsieur. If you will excuse me…'

'Of course. You do not recognise any of our cadavers today?'

Seurot shook his head and made a swift exit. Before going home to Chantal, he needed a drink.

Seurot tried to put Madeleine out of his mind but in his dreams she still rose from her slab behind the plate glass and pointed an accusing finger at her murderer. His stomach lurched every time he thought of that dark building in the shadow of Notre Dame. He would never go near the morgue again.

But Chantal, like a butterfly, had emerged from the chrysalis of the submissive maidservant and was spreading her beautiful wings. She walked past the concierge, Madame Dubois, with her nose in the air and she had discovered the delights of the Moulin Rouge and other fashionable haunts. The late nights were tiring Seurot out and he wondered how long he could keep up with a beautiful woman young enough to be his daughter. But they were tied together forever by what he had done. Neither of them could escape.

Then, a few days later on a damp, Tuesday evening, the visitor arrived.

Jules answered the door, thinking it would be Madame Dubois. But when the door opened he saw a familiar figure silhouetted against the gaslight on the stairs. Maitre Michet's hat and coat glistened with rain and he looked weary, as though he had spent the day trudging around the city.

His smiled as he took off his hat. 'Monsieur Seurot, it is so good to see you. May I come in?'

Jules opened and closed his mouth, uncertain what to do next. This was something he hadn't expected. He told himself to keep calm, to think clearly. Then he remembered that Chantal was in the drawing room wearing a fine gown of red silk, hardly the attire of a maidservant. Somehow he had to warn her that she had to resume her former role.

'I'm surprised to see you, Maitre. I understood that you never visited the city.' Seurot hoped that the terror he felt didn't show on his face.

'There are times when it is inevitable, monsieur. Your wife is at home?'

'I'm afraid she is not here. She's visiting an old friend in Rheims,' he said, hoping he sounded convincing.

Michet looked disappointed. 'I'm sorry to have missed her. I wished to speak with her.'

'I understood that her affairs could be dealt with in Paris.'

Michet smiled. 'Indeed, monsieur. But this concerns, er, a delicate, private matter. In Madame's absence, you might be able to help me. If I may come in...' He shivered and looked at Seurot expectantly.

Seurot had no option. He stood aside and the lawyer stepped into the hallway. Thinking quickly, he opened the door to the dining room, praying that Chantal wouldn't wander in: she had a habit of seeking him out when she was bored that was beginning to irritate him. 'Please step in here, Maitre Michet,' he said in a loud voice, hoping she would hear and be on her guard. 'If you would excuse me one moment.'

He closed the dining room door, leaving the unwanted guest alone, then he rushed to the drawing room. It was empty: perhaps Chantal had heard Michet's arrival after all and was in the bedroom putting on one of her old, plain gowns; something more suitable for a maidservant.

But as he left the drawing room, he saw to his horror that Chantal, in her finery, was at the dining room door. Before he could attract her attention she swept into the room as though she were mistress of the place. Seurot froze as he imagined the look on Michet's face.

He stood, paralysed with terror, as he watched her make a rapid retreat, closing the dining room door noisily behind her. She spotted him hovering in the doorway and their eyes met. They slipped quietly into the drawing room. Something had to be done.

'You didn't tell me he was there,' she accused.

'I didn't have a chance. Did he look surprised to see you?'

'Yes.' Her eyes widened in panic, verging on hysteria. 'My gown. I saw him look... I'm certain he suspects something. What shall we do?'

Seurot looked down at her upturned face and touched her cheek gently. He suddenly felt calm, in control. 'Do not worry. I will deal with

Maitre Michet. Go and get ready: we will visit the Moulin Rouge tonight if you wish.'

'But…'

'You are not to worry.' He patted the padded silk of her bustle. 'Run along.' He watched her leave the room, feeling the first tinglings of desire, and he realised that the danger had excited him.

He took a deep, calming breath before returning to the dining room where Michet was waiting.

The lawyer spoke first. 'Your wife has not taken her maid to Rheims?' The suspicion in his voice was almost palpable.

Michet looked his host straight in the eye and Seurot knew that he had seen through their charade. He had come this far; taken so many risks. He had killed once and he had heard it said that murder was easier the second time.

Now Jules Seurot recognised the sprawling, crowded city as his friend. If Michet joined *les inconnus* at the morgue, what did it matter? He had to kill again to keep his secret – to keep Madeleine's money and Chantal in his bed.

He smiled at Michet. 'I have a slight headache and I am in need of some fresh air. Perhaps you would walk with me. Paris is very beautiful at night – particularly the river.'

Chantal stood in the bedroom, her ear pressed to the door, listening to their departure.

An hour later Chantal rushed to answer the door. 'Is it done?' she whispered.

'It was easy. He suspected nothing.'

'I can't believe it has worked out so well.'

'We must move from here quickly.'

'To a bigger and better apartment?'

'We can afford it.'

They kissed, tentatively at first, then passionately.

'We are rich,' Chantal announced in triumph.

Gaston Michet smiled. 'And Jules never suspected?'

'He thought you and Madame Seurot…'

Michet snorted in derision. 'I have better taste.' He kissed her head. 'I was afraid Jules would lose his nerve.'

'Once I suggested the plan, it was easy. He was all too eager to get rid of her. She led him a dog's life: never let him forget who had the money.'

'So to everyone in Paris you are Madame Seurot?'

'Yes. The money is ours.' She put her arms around his neck. 'When are you returning to Moret?'

'Tomorrow – I must finalise my affairs. All Madeleine's money must be transferred to a Paris bank. You have been practising her signature?'

Chantal nodded. 'I think I could fool anyone.'

'In that case I have some papers for you to sign.' He smiled and kissed her nose 'And I have put it about in Moret that I am moving to Lyons to care for my aged mother. You must move to a new apartment at once before that old concierge downstairs begins to ask questions, and I will join you as soon as I can.'

'Did she see you return?'

'I don't think so.'

'And Jules? You are sure he is...'

He took her hand. 'Don't worry. Jules put up a fight but he went in the river. When his body is found they will think he is just another suicide – another victim of the city who ended up choosing the Seine to take their worthless life. But forget him. We are now Monsieur and Madame Jules Seurot.' Gaston Michet shivered. 'I am cold. The air by the river was damp.'

'Then take a bath. We have every luxury here.' She kissed him, her tongue exploring his mouth. 'And we have the whole night ahead of us.'

The water was running in the bathroom and the pipes in the apartment gurgled so noisily that Chantal didn't hear the first knock on the door. When the second knock came she froze, wondering who it could be at that late hour. Then came another knock, louder this time: the caller was persistent. Chantal hesitated. It was probably Madame Dubois who would know that there was somebody at home. She had no choice but to answer the door.

But it wasn't Madame Dubois who stood there in the corridor. It was a small man with a shock of dark hair. The spectacles perched on the end of his nose made him look older than his years. He grasped a hat with both hands and was turning it round nervously.

'Pardon me for intruding, Madame, but the concierge confirmed that I had the correct address. It is Madame Seurot, is it not? Wife of Monsieur Jules Seurot.'

Chantal's heart was beating fast. She nodded.

'I had the pleasure of meeting your husband recently, Madame. Is he at home?'

Gaston Michet chose that moment to call from the bathroom, asking her to join him. His voice echoed against the green tiles. Too loud. Too suggestive.

'My husband is in the bath, monsieur, and it is late.' She was surprised at how calmly she said the words.

The little man bowed his head. 'No matter, Madame. If you would
tell him that his wallet has been found. The gendarmes apprehended the
thief who has revealed where he disposed of his ill-gotten gains. The gen-
darme is a friend of mine and I offered to return your husband's property. The money has gone, alas, but the name inside confirmed that it was
his. If you would give it to him, Madame, with my compliments. My
name is Charles Mery.'

As Chantal took the damp, crumpled wallet from him she hoped he
wouldn't see that her hand was shaking. She watched as he hurried away
down the stairs; just another clerk. Now she had tasted riches, she was
starting to feel contempt for such people. But as she had assumed that
nobody in Paris knew Jules or where he lived, the encounter disturbed
her. The sooner they moved to another district, took advantage of the
anonymity the city offered, the better.

'Chantal.' The voice from the bathroom was urgent.

She walked slowly down the hallway. There was no need to tell
Gaston about Monsieur Mery. The man was a nobody, she told herself.
And she didn't want to spoil their first night in Paris together.

'Have we any new guests today, Pierre?' Charles Mery asked as he bus-
tled into the morgue the next morning.

A large man with a face like a death's head was sweeping the floor.
He looked up. 'Just three, monsieur. Two girls, one with her throat cut,
and a well-dressed gent.'

'I'd better make their acquaintance.'

Pierre nodded and led the way into a white-tiled chamber. Mery
passed the naked remains of a young female and bowed his head rever-
ently. A prostitute probably, he thought; another victim of the city. She
looked so young, so vulnerable.

He came to the second corpse and stopped.

'He was pulled out of the river by a couple of sailors yesterday
evening,' said Pierre. 'Hadn't been in long, by the look of him. They
thought he was a jumper but I reckon he'd been in a fight. Look at the
bruises.'

But Charles Mery was looking at the face. He never forgot a face. Or
anything else, come to that.

'I know him,' he said quietly. 'I called at his apartment last night at
ten o'clock and a woman who claimed to be his wife – although she was
young enough to be his daughter – said that he was home and in the bath.

I heard a man's voice call out to her.' He frowned. 'What time was he pulled from the river?'

Pierre ambled over to a high desk and consulted an open ledger. 'Half-past nine, monsieur.'

'You are certain?'

'Yes, monsieur. It is recorded in the book.'

Mery stared at the body of Jules Seurot for a few moments then moved on to the third corpse. Another young woman, and this time the yawning wound on her neck told Mery exactly how she had met her death. He stared at her in disbelief. 'Pierre, this is most curious. This woman is Madame Seurot. I saw her last night at Seurot's apartment. And now she is…' He paused, deep in thought. 'Pierre, my friend. I have a call to make.'

He walked out of the building and breathed in the smoky air. This time perhaps he could do something to bring the killer of Jules Seurot and his wife to justice.

It was what he wished he could do for all his *inconnus* – all the unknown ones of Paris.

Gaston Michet congratulated himself as the carriage crossed the Pont Neuf. Everything had gone as planned. Now he had control of Madeleine Seurot's fortune and he didn't even have to share it with the tiresome Chantal who had served her purpose well.

He sat back and listened to the clip clop of the horse's hoofs on the cobbled city streets. This was his reward for the dull, respectable years in Moret. Soon he would be at the apartment he had rented near the Palais du Luxembourg; a rich young man with Paris at his disposal.

The great, noisy, city sprawled around him, hiding all manner of evil deeds. For Gaston Michet, life was just beginning.

DUE NORTH

JOHN HARVEY

I have admired John Harvey's crime fiction ever since I read the first Charlie Resnick novel, *Lonely Hearts*, within a week or two of its publication more than a decade ago. Harvey is as talented an exponent of the short story as he is of the longer form, as his collection of Resnick tales, *Now's The Time*, demonstrates. This is, however, the first Harvey story that I have had the pleasure of including in a CWA anthology. Harvey has moved recently from Nottingham to London, and moved away also from Charlie Resnick – but here he offers another police story with an urban East Midlands setting. 'Due North' shows one of our leading crime writers at his very best.

Elder hated this: the after-midnight call, the neighbours penned back behind hastily unravelled tape, the video camera's almost silent whirr; the way, as if reproachful, the uniformed officers failed to meet his eye; and this especially, the bilious taste that fouled his mouth as he stared down at the bed, the way the hands of both children rested near the cover's edge, as if at peace, their fingers loosely curled.

He had been back close-on two years, long enough to view the move north with some regret. Not that north was really what it was. A hundred and twenty miles from London, one hour forty minutes, theoretically, by train. Another country nonetheless.

For weeks he and Joanne had argued it back and forth, reasons for, reasons against, two columns fixed to the refrigerator door. *Cut and Dried*, the salon where Joanne worked as a stylist, was opening branches in Derby and Nottingham and she could manage either one she chose. Derby was out of the question.

On a visit, Katherine trailing behind them, they had walked along the pedestrianised city centre street: high-end fashion, café latté, bacon cobs; Waterstone's, Ted Baker, Café Rouge.

'You see,' Joanne said, 'we could be in London. Chiswick High Road.'

Elder shook his head. It was the bacon cobs that gave it away.

The empty shop unit was just off to one side, secluded and select. 'Post no Bills' plastered across the glass frontage, 'Sold Subject to Contract' above the door. Joanne would be able to hire the staff, set the tone, choose the shade of paint upon the walls.

'You know I want this, don't you?' Her hands in his pockets as she pulled him back against the glass.

'I know.'

'So?'

He closed his eyes and, slow at first, she kissed him on the mouth.

'God!' Katherine exclaimed, whacking her father in the back.

'What?'

'Making a bloody exhibition of yourselves, that's what.'

'You watch your tongue, young lady,' Joanne said, stepping clear.

'Sooner that than watching yours.'

Katherine Elder: eleven going on twenty-four.

'What say we go and have a coffee?' Elder said. 'Then we can have a think.'

Even a casual glance in the estate agent's window made it clear that for the price of their two-bedroom first-floor-flat off Chiswick Lane, they could buy a house in a decent area, something substantial with a garden front and back. For Katherine, moving up to secondary, a new start in a new school, the perfect time. And Elder…?

He had joined the police a twenty-year-old in Huddersfield, walked the beat in Leeds; out of uniform, he'd been stationed in Lincolnshire: Lincoln itself, Boston, Skegness. Then, married, the big move to London, this too at Joanne's behest. Frank Elder, a detective sergeant in the Met. Detective Inspector when he was forty-five. Moving out he'd keep his rank at least, maybe push up. There were faces he still knew, a name or two. Calls he could make. A week after Joanne took charge of the keys to the new salon, Elder had eased himself behind his desk at the headquarters of the Nottinghamshire Major Crime Unit: a telephone, a Rolodex, a PC with a splintered screen; a part-eaten Pork Farms pie collecting dust in one of the desk drawers.

Now, two years on, the screen had been replaced, the keyboard jammed and lacked the letters R and S; photographs of Joanne and Katherine stood beside his in-tray in small frames. The team he'd been working with on a wages hijack north of Peterborough had just brought in a result and shots of scotch were being passed around in polystyrene cups.

Elder drank his down, a single swallow, and dialled home. 'Jo, I'm going to be a bit late.'

A pause in which he visualised her face, a tightening around the mouth, the corners of her eyes. 'Of course.'

'What do you mean?'

'It's the end of the week, the lads are raring to go; of course you'll be late.'

'Look, if you'd rather…'

'Frank, I'm winding you up. Go and have a drink. Relax. I'll see you in an hour or so, okay?'

'You're sure?'

'Frank.'

'All right. All right. I'm going.'

When he arrived home, two hours later, not so much more, Katherine was closeted in her room listening to Pharoahe Monch and Joanne was nowhere to be seen.

'*Decapitate his ass!*' confronted him when he stepped inside his daughter's room. '*Smack him, slap him in the back of the truck.*'

'Dad!'

'What?'

'You're supposed to knock.'

'I did.'

'I didn't hear you.'

Reaching past her, he angled the volume control of the portable stereo down a notch, a half-smile deflecting the complaint that failed to come.

'Where's mum?'

'Out.'

'Where?'

'Out.'

Cross-legged on the bed, fair hair splashed across her eyes, Katherine flipped closed the book in which she had been writing with a practised sigh.

'You want something to eat?' Elder asked.

A quick shake of the head. 'I already ate.'

He found a slice of pizza in the fridge and set it in the microwave to reheat, opened a can of Heineken, switched on the TV. When Joanne arrived back, close to midnight, he was asleep in the armchair, unfinished pizza on the floor close by. Stooping, she kissed him lightly and he woke.

'You see,' Joanne said, 'it works.'

'What does?'

'You turned into a frog.'

Elder smiled and she kissed him again; he didn't ask her where she'd been.

Neither was quite in bed when the mobile suddenly rang.

'Mine or yours?'

Joanne angled her head. 'Yours.'

Elder was still listening, asking questions, as he started reaching for his clothes.

Fourteen miles north of the city, Mansfield was a small industrial town with an unemployment rate above average, a reputation for casual violence and a soccer team just keeping its head above water in Division Three of the Nationwide. Elder lowered the car window a crack, broke into a fresh pack of extra-strong mints and tried not to think about what he would find.

He missed the turning first and had to double back, a cul-de-sac built into a new estate, just shy of the road to Edwinstowe and Ollerton. An ambulance snug between two police cars, lights in the windows of all the houses, the periodic yammering of radios. At number seventeen, all of the curtains were drawn closed. A child's scooter lay discarded on the lawn. Elder pulled on the protective coveralls he kept ready in the boot, nodded to the young officer in uniform on guard outside and showed his ID just in case. On the stairs, one of the Scene-of-Crime team, whey-faced, stepped aside to let him pass. The smell of blood and something else, like ripe pomegranate, on the air.

The children were in the smallest bedroom, two boys, six and four, pyjamaed arms outstretched; the pillow with which they had been smothered lay bunched on the floor. Elder noticed bruising near the base of the older boy's throat, twin purpling marks the size of thumbs; he wondered who had closed their eyes.

'We were right to call you in?'

For a big man, Saxon moved lightly; only a slight nasal heaviness to his breathing had alerted Elder to his presence in the room.

'I thought, you know, better now than later.'

Elder nodded. Gerry Saxon was a sergeant based in the town, Mansfield born and bred. The two of them had crossed paths before, swopped yarns and the occasional pint; stood once at the Town ground, side by side, as sleet swept near horizontally goalwards, grim in the face of a nil-nil draw with Chesterfield. Elder thought Saxon thorough, big-oted, not as slow-witted as he would have you believe.

'Where's the mother?' Elder asked.

Lorraine Atkin was jammed between the dressing table and the wall, as if trying to burrow away from the pain. One slash of a blade had sliced deep across her back, opening her from shoulder to hip. Her nightdress, once white, was matted here and there to her body with stiffening blood. Her throat had been cut.

'The police surgeon...?'

'Downstairs,' Saxon said. 'Few preliminaries, nothing more. Didn't like to move her till your say-so.'

Elder nodded again. So much anger: so much hate. He looked from the bed to the door, at the collision of bottles and jars across the dressing table top, the trajectory of blood along the walls. As if she had made a dash for it and been dragged back, attacked. Trying to protect her children or herself?

'The weapon?'

'Kitchen knife. Least that's what I reckon. Downstairs in the sink.'

'Washed clean?'

'Not so's you'd notice.'

There were footsteps on the landing outside and then Maureen Prior's face in the doorway, eyes widening as she took in the scene; one slow intake of breath and she stepped into the room.

'Gerry, you know DS Price. Maureen, Gerry Saxon.'

'Good to see you again, Gerry.' She scarcely took her eyes from the body. The corpse.

'Maureen, check with Scene of Crime. Make sure they've documented everything we might need. Let's tie that up before we let the surgeon get to work. You'll liaise with Gerry here about interviewing the neighbours, house to house.'

'Right.'

'You'll want to see the garage next,' Saxon said.

There were two entrances, one from the utility room alongside the kitchen, the other from the drive. Despite the latter being open, the residue of carbon monoxide had yet to fully clear. Paul Atkin slumped forward over the driver's wheel, one eye fast against the windscreen's curve, his skin sacking grey.

Elder walked twice slowly around the car and went out to where Saxon stood in the rear garden, smoking a cigarette.

'Any sign of a note?'

Saxon shook his head.

'A note would have been nice. Neat at least.'

'Only tell you what you know already.'

'What's that then, Gerry?'

'Bastard topped his family, then himself. Obvious.'

'But why?'

Saxon laughed. 'That's what you clever bastards are going to find out.' He lit a fresh cigarette from the butt of the last and as he did Elder noticed Saxon's hands had a decided shake. Probably the night air was colder than he'd thought.

There was no note that came to hand, but something else instead. Traced with Atkin's finger on the inside of the misting glass and captured there by Scene of Crime, the first wavering letters of a name – C O N N – and then what might have been an *I* trailing weakly down towards the window's edge.

Mid-afternoon the following day, Elder was driving with Maureen Prior out towards the small industrial estate where Atkin had worked, Head of Sales for Pleasure Blinds. Prefabricated units that had still to lose their shine, neat beds of flowering shrubs, no sign of smoke in sight: Sherwood Business Park.

If someone married's going over the side, chances are it's with someone from where they work. One of Frank Elder's rules of thumb, rarely disproved.

Some few years back, close to ten it would be now, his wife Joanne had an affair with her boss. Six months it had gone on, no more, before Elder had found out. The reasons not so very difficult to see. They had just arrived in London, uprooted themselves, and Joanne was high on the speed of it, the noise, the buzz. Since having Katherine three years before, she and Elder had made love less and less; she felt unattractive, oddly sexless, over the hill at thirty-three. And then there had been Martyn Miles, all flash and if not Armani, Hugo Boss; drinks in the penthouse bar of this hotel or that, meals at Bertorellis or Quo Vadis.

Elder had his fifteen minutes of crazy, smashed a few things around the house, confronted Miles outside the mews apartment where he lived, and restrained himself from punching him in his smug and sneering face more than just the once.

Together, he and Joanne had talked it through, worked it out; she had carried on at the salon. 'I need to see him every day and know I don't want him any more. Not turn my back and never know for sure.'

Elder had told Maureen all of this one day: one night, actually; a long drive down the motorway from Fife, the road surface slick with rain, headlights flicking by. She had listened, said very little, a couple of comments only. Maureen with a core of moral judgment clear and unyielding as the Taliban. Neither of them had ever referred to it again.

Elder slowed the car and turned through the gates of the estate; Pleasure Blinds was the fourth building on the right.

Constance Seymour, read the sign on the door. *Personnel*.

As soon as she saw them, her face crumpled inwards like a paper bag. Spectacles slipped, lopsided, down on to the desk. Maureen fished a Kleenex from her bag; Elder fetched water from the cooler in a cone-shaped cup. Connie blew her nose, dabbed at her eyes. She was somewhere in her thirties, Elder thought, what might once have been called homely, plain. Sloped shoulders, buttoned blouse, court shoes. Elder could imagine her with her mother, in town Saturdays shopping arm in arm, the two of them increasingly alike.

The eyes that looked at him now were tinged with violet, palest blue. She would have listened to Atkin like that, intense and sympathetic, pained. Whose hand would have reached out first, who would first have comforted whom?

Maureen came to the end of her expressions of condolence, regret.

'You were having an affair with him,' she said. 'Paul Atkin. A relationship.'

Connie sniffed and said yes.

'And this relationship, how long...?'

'A year. More. Thirteen months.'

'It was serious, then?'

'Oh, yes.' Her expression slightly puzzled, somewhat hurt. What else could it have been?

'Mr Atkin, was there... was there any suggestion that he might leave his wife?'

'Oh, no. No. The children, you see. He loved the children more than anything.'

Maureen glanced across, remembering the faces, the pillow, the bed. Killed with kindness: the proverb eddied up in Elder's mind.

'Have you any idea why he might want to harm them?' Elder asked.

'No,' she gasped, moments ahead of the wash of tears. 'Unless... unless...'

Joanne was in the living room, feet tucked beneath her, watching TV. Katherine was staying overnight at a friend's. On screen, a bevy of smartly-dressed and foul-mouthed young things were dissecting the sex lives of their friends. A laughter track gave hints which Joanne, for the most part, ignored.

'Any good?' Elder asked.

'Crap.'

'I'm just going out for a stroll.'

'Okay.'

'Shan't be long.'

Glancing towards the door, Joanne smiled and puckered her lips into the shape of a kiss.

Arms swinging lightly by his sides, Elder cut through a swathe of tree-lined residential streets on to the main road; for a moment he was distracted by the lights of the pub, orange and warm, but instead walked on, away from the city centre and then left to where the houses were smaller than his own and huddled together, the first part of a circular walk that would take him, an hour or so later, back home.

Behind the curtains of most front rooms, TV sets flickered and glowed; muffled voices rose and fell; the low rumble of a sampled bass line reverberated from the windows of a passing Ford. Haphazardly, dogs barked. A child cried. On the corner, a group of black youths wearing ripped-off Tommy Hillfiger eyed him with suspicion and disdain.

Elder pictured Gerry Saxon leaning up against a darkened tree, his hands trembling a little as he smoked a cigarette. Almost a year now since he had given up himself, Elder fumbled in his pocket for another mint.

He knew the pattern of incidents similar to that at the Atkins' house:

the man – almost always it was the man – who could find no other way to cope; debt or unrequited love or some religious mania, voices that whispered, unrelenting, inside his head. Unable or unwilling to leave his family behind, feeling it his duty to protect them from whatever loomed, he took their lives and then his own. What differed here was the intensity of the attack upon the wife, that single fierce and slashing blow, delivered after death. Anger at himself for what he had done? At her, for giving cause?

A cat, tortoise shell, ran two-thirds of the way across the road, froze, then scuttled back.

'She was seeing someone, wasn't she?' Connie Seymour had said, voice parched with her own grief. 'Lorraine. His wife, Lorraine. Paul was terrified she was going to leave him, take his kids.'

No matter how many times he and Maureen had asked, Connie had failed to give them a name. 'He wouldn't tell me. Just wouldn't tell. Oh, he knew all right, Paul knew. But he wouldn't say. As if he was... you know, as if he was ashamed.'

Maureen had got Willie Bell sifting through the house to house reports already; tomorrow Matt Dowland and Salim Shukla would start knocking on doors again. For Karen Holbrook the task of contacting Lorraine Atkin's family and friends. Elder would go back to the house and take Maureen with him.

Why? That's what you clever bastards are going to find out.

Joanne was in the bathroom when he got back, smoothing cream into her skin. When he touched her arm, she jumped.

'Your hands, they're like ice.'

'I'm sorry.'

The moment passed.

In bed, eyes closed, Elder listened to the fall of footsteps on the opposite side of the street, the window shifting uncertainly inside its frame. Joanne read for ten minutes before switching out the light.

They found a diary, letters, nothing of real use. In a box file shelved between two albums of photographs, Maureen turned up a mish-mash of guarantees and customer instructions, invoices and bills.

'Mobile phones,' she called into the next room. 'We've had those checked?'

'Yes,' Elder said, walking through. 'He had some kind of BT cellphone leased by his work, she was with – who was it? – One to One.'

'Right.' Maureen held up a piece of paper. 'Well, it looks as if she might have had a second phone, separate account.'

'Think you can charm some details out of them, recent calls especially?'

'No. But I can impress on them the serious nature of the situation.'

'You sure you want to do this alone?' Maureen said.

They were parked in a lay-by on the road north from the city, arable land to their left shading into a small copse of trees. Lapwings rose sharply in the middle distance, black and white like an Escher print.

'Yes. I think so.'

'You don't want…?'

'No,' Elder said. 'I'll be fine.'

Maureen nodded and got back into her car and he stood there, watching her drive away, rehearsing his first words inside his head.

It was a square brick-built house in a street full of square, brick-built houses, the front of this one covered in white pebble dash that had long since taken on several shades of grey. Once council, Elder assumed, now privately owned. A Vauxhall Astra parked outside. Roses in need of pruning. Patchy grass. Close against the kitchen window, a damson tree that looked as if it rarely yielded fruit.

He rattled the knocker and, for good measure, rang the bell.

No hesitation in the opening of the door, no delay.

'Hello, Gerry,' Elder said. 'Late shift?'

'You know,' Saxon said. 'You'd've checked.' And when Elder made no further remark, added, 'You'd best come in.'

It was tea or instant coffee and Elder didn't really want either, but he said tea would be fine, one sugar, and sat, mug cradled in both hands, in the middle of the cluttered living room while Saxon smoked and avoided looking him squarely in the eye.

'She phoned you, Jerry. Four days ago. The day before she was murdered. Phoned you when you were on duty. Twice.'

'She was upset, wasn't she? In a real state. Frightened.'

'Frightened?'

'He'd found out about us, seen us. The week before.' Saxon shook his head. 'It was stupid, so fucking half-arsed stupid. All the times we… all the times we saw one another, we never took no chances. She'd come here, afternoons, or else we'd meet up miles away, Sheffield or Grantham, and then this one bloody Saturday she said let's go into Nottingham, look round the shops. He was supposed to be off taking the kids to Clumber Park and there we are coming out of the Broad Marsh Centre on to Lister Gate, and they're smack in front of us, him with the little kid on his shoulders and the other one holding his hand.'

Saxon swallowed down some tea and lit another cigarette.

'Course, we tried to pass it off, but you could see he wasn't having any. Ordered her to go home with them there and then and of course, when they did, there was all merry hell to pay. Ended up with him asking her if she intended leaving him and her saying yes, first chance she got.' Saxon paused. '"You'll take the kids", he said, "over my dead body".'

'She didn't leave?'

'No.'

'Nor try to?'

Saxon shook his head. 'He seemed to calm down after the first couple of days. Lorraine, she thought he might be going to get over it. Thought, you know, if we lay low for a spell, things'd get back to normal, we could start up again.'

'But that's not what happened?' Elder said.

'What happened was, this idea of her taking the kids, he couldn't get it out of his head. Stupid, really. I mean, I could've told him, a right non-starter.' Saxon looked around. 'You imagine what it'd be like, two lads in here. Someone else's kids. Place is mess enough as it is. Anyway...' Leaning forward now, elbows on his knees, '...you know what it's like, the kind of life we lead. The hours and all the rest of it. How many couples you know – one or both of them in the Force, children – how many d'you know make it work?'

Elder's tea was lukewarm, tannin thick in his mouth. 'The last time she phoned you, you said she was frightened. Had he threatened her or what?'

'No. I don't think so. Not in as many words. It was more him coming out with all this guff. Next time we're in the car I'll drive us all into the back of a lorry. Stuff like that.'

'And you didn't think to do anything?'

'Such as what?'

'Going round, trying to get him to talk, listen to reason; suggesting she take the boys away for a few days – grandparents, somewhere like that?'

'No,' Saxon said. 'I kept well out of it. Thought it best.'

'And now?'

'What do you mean, and now?'

'You still think it was for the best?'

The mug cracked across in Saxon's hand and tea spilled with blood towards the floor.

'Who the fuck?' he said, on his feet now; both men on their feet, Saxon on his feet and backing Elder towards the door. 'Who the fuck d'you think you are, coming in here like you're some judge and fucking jury, some tin-pot fucking god? Think you're fucking perfect? That what you think, you pompous sack of shit? I mean, what the fuck are you here for anyway? You here to question me? Arrest me? What? There was some fucking crime here? I committed some fucking crime?'

He had Elder backed up against the wall, close alongside the door, the sweat off his skin so rank that Elder almost gagged.

'Crime, Gerry?' Elder said. 'How much d'you want? Three murders, four deaths. Two boys, four and six. Not that you'll be losing much sleep over them. I mean, they were just a nuisance, an irrelevance. Someone to mess up this shit-heap of a home.'

'Fuck you!' Saxon punched the wall, close by Elder's head.

'And Lorraine, well, you probably think that's a shame, but let's face it, you'll soon find someone else's wife to fuck.'

'You bastard!' Saxon hissed. 'You miserable, sanctimonious bastard.'

But his hands fell back down to his sides and slowly he backed away and gazed down at the floor, and when he did that, without hurrying, Elder let himself out of the house and walked towards his car.

He and Joanne were sitting at either end of the settee, Elder with a glass of Jameson in his hand, the bottle nearby on the floor; Joanne was drinking the white Rioja they had started with dinner. The remains of their take-away Chinese was on the table next door. Katherine had long since retreated to her room.

'What will happen?' Joanne asked. It was a while since either of them had spoken.

'To Saxon?'

'Um.'

'A bollocking from on high. Some kind of official reprimand. He might lose his stripes and get pushed into going round schools, sweet-talking kids into being honest citizens.' Elder shook his head. 'Maybe nothing at all. I don't know. Except that it was all a bloody mess.'

He sighed and tipped a little more whiskey into his glass and Joanne sipped at her wine. It was late but neither of them wanted to make the first move towards bed.

'Christ, Jo! Those people. Sometimes I wonder if everyone out there isn't doing it in secret. Fucking one another silly.'

He was looking at Joanne as he spoke and there was a moment, a second, in which he knew what she was going to say before she spoke.

'I've been seeing him again. Martyn. I'm sorry, Frank, I...'

'Seeing him?'

'Yes, I...'

'Sleeping with him?'

'Yes. Frank, I'm sorry, I...'

'How long?'

'Frank...'

'How long have you been seeing him?'

'Frank, please...'

Elder's whiskey spilled across the back of his hand, the tops of his thighs. 'How fucking long?'

'Oh, Frank... Frank...' Joanne in tears now, her breath uneven, her face wiped clear of colour. 'We never really stopped.'

Instead of hitting her, he hurled his glass against the wall.

'Tell me,' Elder said.

Joanne foraged for a tissue and dragged it across her face. 'He's... he's got a place... up here, in the Park. At first it was just, you know, the odd time, if we'd been working late, something special. I mean, Martyn, he wasn't usually here, he was down in London, but when... Oh, Frank, I wanted to tell you, I even thought you knew, I thought you must...'

She held out a hand and when Elder made no move to take it, let it fall.

'Frank...'

He moved quickly, up from the settee, and she flinched and turned her face away. She heard, not saw him leave the room, the house, the home.

It wasn't difficult to find out where Martyn Miles lived when he was in the city, a top-floor flat in a '70s apartment block off Tattershall Drive. Not difficult to slip the lock, even though stepping across the threshold set off the alarm. 'It's okay,' he explained to an anxious neighbour. 'I'll handle it. Police.' And showed his ID.

He had been half-hoping Miles would be there but he was not. Instead, he searched the place for signs of... what? Joanne's presence? Tokens of love? In the built-in wardrobe, he recognised some of her clothes: a dove-grey suit, a blouse, a pair of high-heeled shoes; in the bathroom, a bottle of her perfume, a diaphragm.

Going back into the bedroom, he tore the covers from the bed, ripped at the sheets until they were little more than winding cloths, heaved the mattress to the floor and, yanking free the wooden slats on which it had rested, broke them, each and every one, against the wall, across his knee.

Back in the centre of the city, he booked into a hotel, paid over the odds for a bottle of Jameson and finally fell asleep, fully clothed, with the contents two-thirds gone. At work next day, he barked at anyone who as much as glanced in his direction. Maureen left a bottle of aspirin on his desk and steered well clear. When he got home that evening, Joanne had packed and gone. *Frank – I think we both need some time and space.* He tore the note into smaller and smaller pieces till they filtered through his hands.

Katherine was in her room and she turned off the stereo when he came in.

Holding her, kissing her hair the way he didn't think he'd done for years, his body shook.

'I love you, Kate,' he said.

Lifting her head she looked at him with a sad little smile. 'I know, but that doesn't matter, does it?'

'What do you mean? Of course it does.'

'No. It's mum. You should have loved her more.'

Two weeks later, Joanne back home with Katherine and Elder in a rented room, he knocked on the door of the Detective Superintendent's office, walked in and set his warrant card down on the desk, his letter of resignation alongside.

'Take your time, Frank,' the Superintendent said. 'Think it over.'

'I have,' Elder said.

THE RIO DE JANEIRO PAPER

REGINALD HILL

This is one of only two stories in the present volume to have been published previously. I first read it almost twenty years ago. Having enjoyed one of the early Dalziel and Pascoe novels, I sought out a short-story collection entitled *Pascoe's Ghost*. This story was included in that volume and it struck me as immensely enjoyable. Yet it is one of Hill's less well-known works and when I asked the author if he would be happy for me to give it a new lease of life in this book, I was surprised to learn that it has never been reprinted since its first appearance. Connoisseurs of bibliographic trivia may like to know that Reg Hill decided to make a couple of changes to the final two pages of the story. Thus it is the first time that *precisely* this version of 'The Rio De Janeiro Paper' has ever appeared.

Mr Chairman, Ladies and Gentlemen,

It has been the custom at the International Criminological Conference to save the best for the last. At least this was the policy pursued by your committee before ill health forced my resignation from it. I think of the men who have occupied this spot in years gone by and I tremble at my effrontery. But perhaps today there is no need. Perhaps during my recent illness the policy has been changed and the last full session of Conference is now reserved for broken-down old professors on the edge of retirement!

Forgive my flippancy. I am deeply moved by the honour you have accorded me. And more than a little scared. Not that I don't like the view from up here. Through that huge window at the back of the hall I can see right across the harbour. The Sugar Loaf seems but a step away and I fancy that if I cared to strain my eyes just a bit, in this clear air, I could see clean across to Africa. It's really quite splendid.

It's only when my gaze drops to take in your own politely expectant faces that I begin to feel afraid.

But I have spoken elsewhere of the psychology of terror and that is not my subject today.

No, today I want to examine a simple proposition that seems to me to derive naturally from any serious criminological study of modern society, and one that has implications that must be relevant to all your specializations.

It is that every husband would like to see his wife dead.

Let me start by being non-scientific.

How many married men sitting here in this hall can look into their own hearts and say they have never felt personally the truth of this proposition?

Come on. Don't be shy. There are no hidden cameras spying on you. Two, three. I can see three. No, four. Thank you, sir. Definitely four. Well, I am disappointed. I had hoped to find greater powers of self-deception among so many eminent men!

So, it seems there might be some popular support for this proposition: *every husband would like to see his wife dead*. Certainly, as I'm sure that Captain Ribeiro of the Rio de Janeiro Police Research Bureau – whose stimulating paper caused so much debate on Tuesday – would confirm, if you show a policeman a female corpse the first thing that comes into his mind is, where's the husband? *Cherchez le mari!* I can't manage it in Portuguese!

I think Dr Egermann, in his excellent paper on *Women's Liberation and the Crime of Violence*, put it succinctly when he said that men are killed for many reasons, but women usually because they are women.

In other words, because of sex.

Lust, jealousy, disgust, frustration; potency fears, mother fixations, homosexual repression, transvestite envy – you will all recall Dr Egermann's list of the sources of sexual violence. And is it not self-evident that the marriage relationship, as it is understood in Western society, reinforces all these causes where they exist, creates many of them where they do not, and provides, in E K Charleshead's well-known phrase, the provocation of opportunity?

To Egermann's list, I myself would add one non-sexual motive to support my present assertions, and that is material gain. In her unpublished PhD thesis on *The Sociology of Wills,* Edna Botibol of Yale shows that while a man is rarely left money by his mistress, wives tend to be much more generous. (A form of compensation, I shouldn't wonder!) But it certainly brings marriage well into our professional view. For it seems to me that, in many ways, all that Conference has been discussing for the past week, some might say for the past decade, is: which of the two great areas of criminal motivation should be our prime concern – the sexual or the economic? Marriage, I would suggest, unites them uniquely and deserves much more attention from all the criminological specialists gathered here today than it has ever received in the past. It may not be putting it too strongly to say that, in marriage, there is no such thing as accidental death.

Every husband would like to see his wife dead.

I can see several dubious expressions, and many more that have that air of bright interest with which students are wont to conceal advanced torpor. Perhaps I am being too general. 'When in doubt, present a theoretical model' has always been a good maxim for the social scientist and that is what I shall do now.

First, we need a husband. Let's call him Smith. I am, after all, trying to demonstrate, not deceive! But let's bring him within the experiential range of everyone here by making him an academic; Professor Smith, a moderately eminent scholar at a moderately obscure university, the kind of man who, at the age of sixty, is pretty well known to his contemporaries but will hardly be remembered by their successors. But his voice will be listened to while he speaks.

Now, Professor Smith is a man who values marriage. He must do. He tries it twice. The first marriage follows a conventional course, and the professor reaches his half-century with little cause for complaint and some for congratulation; indeed, he looks an unlikely source of evidence to support my contention that every husband would like to see his wife dead. His children have grown up without too much drama; his first heart attack is still five years away; and his home is comfortably and efficiently managed by his comfortable and efficient wife, a still attractive woman, who is a good economist, likes gardening, laughs at his jokes and cooks a fair, if underseasoned, *canard en croûte* for special occasions.

It is on such a special occasion, the day let us say that his promotion from assistant to full professor is confirmed, that the Smiths first meet Miss X. Christine, let us call her. It sounds less sinister. Christine X.

Christine is eighteen years old, with long, blonde hair; a fresh, glowing complexion; and the kind of beauty God only gives to eighteen-year-old girls.

She has just joined one of the professor's classes and is enthralled by his material and manner. That day she stays behind to check a reference and, flattered by her interest, Smith takes her home to lend her a book.

She stays to dinner. She is delighted with the *canard en croûte,* which pleases Mrs Smith. She is also clearly delighted with the professor, which pleases him and amuses his wife, so that after Christine has gone they laugh about it over the washing-up.

The following day Christine X calls on the professor in his office. She is very serious. They talk for an hour. Then they make love on the floor between a filing cabinet and a bookcase, with the girl's head pillowed on a pile of examination scripts.

A week later the professor leaves his wife.

In an earlier period there would now have existed a situation in which the professor might very well have wished his wife dead. Such goings-on once could have caused an academic all sorts of problems in his social and professional relationships. But things have changed. I refer you to E K Charleshead, who I see has just entered the hall – yes, please do give him a round of applause; it is rare for one so young to achieve such distinction; let praise be unstinted – I was just referring, Dr Charleshead, to your monograph on *The Bourgeois Ethic in the Swinging Sixties.* Stimulating. Provocative.

To continue. No, it is not Professor Smith's abandonment of his wife that raises people's eyebrows, it is the ruthlessness with which he expedites the divorce in order to remarry! Who marries these days, except if the accountants advise it?

But once remarried, the professor's happiness seems complete. The only flaw in it is the apparent total alienation of his children. His two daughters shun him completely, while his son suffers some kind of breakdown and is caught in the British Museum Reading Room defacing some of the professor's books with obscene drawings and obscener words.

Smith is filled with guilt and takes all the blame on to himself until five or six years later he has a series of heart attacks that nearly kill him. When he discovers that, as he lay at death's door, not one of his children made enquiry after his state of health, though the doctors had informed them all, his guilt disappears and is replaced by an uncomprehending pain, which might have hardened into resentment were there not other, more pressing matters to occupy his mind and soul.

His health has been deeply undermined. From being a vigorous, handsome, athletic man in the prime of life, he has become a semi-invalid, fast slipping down the vale of years. He is not confined to bed or anything as extreme as that, but he has to take great care. He must carry a box of pills with him wherever he goes; he must always use the lift, never the stairs; and he knows that love's little death might for him very easily become the real thing.

The passing years change Christine, too.

She wears her hair short and it now strikes the eye with the burnish of ripe barley rather than the soft gold of early corn. Her skin, too, has lost something of its freshness but cunning make-up can highlight the dark eyes and the full lips as well as nature ever did. She, too, has entered the academic life, and when her enemies murmur that she owes her rapid advance to her husband's influence, her friends retort that she is twice as clever as he ever was, and ten times as clever as he has become.

In other words, in ten years he has grown old and she has grown up.

You begin to see the shape of our model? Triangulation maps lives as well as landscapes.

Professor Smith, his first wife, and Christine – there's one triangle. Now the time has come for another.

Let's keep things nice and close for the sake of tidiness. Just as in our basic triangle it made sense to locate the second female among the professor's students, now it makes sense to locate the second male among his colleagues. Let us call him C, a young lecturer whose research has won much acclaim and who looks set for a promising career. C has perhaps little grounds for liking or even feeling loyal towards Smith, who (so C alleges) has made a ham-fisted effort to appropriate to himself some of C's research results. We have all been research assistants in our younger days and know how narrow the line is between following instructions and finding out new directions for ourselves. Thus there is a cloud between C and the professor, which perhaps obscures the moral issue (if moral issues still exist after this morning's seminar on *The Chemistry of Good and Evil!*).

C and Christine are thrown into each other's company, are mutually attracted, at first refuse to admit the attraction, then struggle against it, and finally bring it out into the open to overcome it, which as any student of criminology knows is like stripping a woman naked to combat the temptations of a revealing gown!

The precise circumstances of their fall are not important. It happened, shall we say, two years ago? They are both discreet people, thrown naturally together by their job, and if C has no great concern about the pain he might cause the professor, Christine has enough for both of them. She takes every precaution against discovery and is resolved to stay with her husband until, as seems not unlikely, another heart attack carries him off. He loves her as dearly as ever, so if our starting proposition is to apply here, something must happen to show him the truth.

It is really very simple. C is a friend of the professor's son, the one who had the trouble at the British Museum. One night they are drinking together and the son, David let's call him, is still complaining after all this time about his father's treatment of his mother. C is happy to join in a general condemnation of Professor Smith at all levels, but when David turns his attention to Christine, he angrily springs to her defence. David is intrigued and either guesses at, or is told of, the relationship. He retails the news to his mother next time they meet and his mother, after a day and a night spent in close discussion of the information with no more than ten or twelve friends, persuades herself that it is her duty to do something. I refer you to the chapter in Arturo Bellario's *Crime In The Third Reich* on 'Duty as Pseudo-Motivation'.

So the first Mrs Smith telephones her ex-husband. He is enraged. He slams the phone down. It is a tissue of lies. His former wife is a monster. He will ring the police. He will ring his solicitor and issue a writ for slander. He will summon Christine and invite her to join in his anger. He will not hurt her by telling her anything. He trusts her absolutely. He trusts C. But not absolutely. C dislikes him. He feels uneasy with C. Christine and C spend a lot of time together. C is young. Christine is young. He is old. It is a year since he made love to his wife.

For the time being his thoughts stay there. That night he attempts to make love and fails. Christine assures him it does not matter. He turns away and lies, open-eyed, in the dark. Suddenly he knows it is true.

Of course, as an academic and a scientist he will seek objective evidence. But this is not hard to find.

Captain Ribeiro told us yesterday something of the psychology of interrogation. Two people cannot long deceive a third, especially if they are not yet aware that he suspects them.

So there we have our model complex. I'm sorry if I seem to have laboured over its construction. And I am sorrier still if you feel that all my labour has just brought forth a mouse. For what is he going to tell us now? you ask. That Professor Smith, a sick old man in the throes of jealousy, would like to see his wife dead? Possibly he would! More likely, he would prefer to see C dead. But wishes are not crimes!

No, but they may be translated into crimes. And in this model, it seems to me very likely that the translation would take place.

The situation is more complex than might at first appear. It is not simple jealousy that is at work. Let us examine all the courses that are open to Professor Smith and see that, if he does opt for murder, it is not through a shortage of alternatives.

First, he might carry on as before, concealing his knowledge and hoping that his health might improve or that of the affair deteriorate.

Secondly, he might confront his wife and try to shame her or argue her into giving up her lover.

Thirdly, he might institute divorce proceedings, either as a noble gesture aimed at freeing Christine from an intolerable situation, or as a salve to his own hurt pride.

Why does he choose none of these?

Not simply because he is unbalanced by jealousy. On the contrary, he thinks he is behaving perfectly rationally. No, the true reason for his decision to murder his wife might seem odd to a layman but the eminent criminologists here assembled will recall the wise words spoken by E K Charleshead in his seminar on *Recidivism as Onanistic Impulse:* 'One motive may be more *uncommon* than another, but no motive is more *unlikely* than another.'

Professor Smith decides to murder Christine because of the acute pleasure he knows the situation must be giving his first wife and his estranged children.

Better then, you may say, he should murder his first wife. Yes, he thinks of that, of course; but she is distant, access is difficult, he has no desire that his deed should produce consequences unpleasant to himself.

So it has to be Christine.

Thus our model now shows us an extremely complex situation, and perhaps I should now extend my opening proposition thus: *a man who has more than one wife would like to see them all dead.*

It has always seemed a shame to me that social scientists discard their models so readily once they have served their purpose. Anything that man has laboured to create deserves more than instant relegation to the scrap-heap and I hope you will bear with me if, having brought Professor Smith so far along his road, I follow him a little further.

In any case, just as *the wish to see dead* is not the same as the *decision to kill,* so the decision is still not the deed. Professor Smith now needs a method.

Well, if the professor moved in the same circles as we all do, he would not have far to look, for if there's one thing that regular attenders at these conferences get in plenty, it's methods of murder! It's a standing joke, isn't it, how well the homicide seminars are always attended. Of course, what we are considering on these occasions are the sociological and psychological problems, but what one remembers most vividly are things like Herr Doktor Schwarz's diagrams of pressure points, Señor Martinez's dexterity with knife and gun, or (more mundane but no less fascinating) Madame Rive's list of eighteen toxic substances in common domestic use. Whatever the professor's own discipline, such information as this is readily accessible to the academically trained mind. The first thing we all had to learn was how to find things out, was it not? Equally accessible would be all our treatises on police method and police psychology, and Professor Smith would know as well as I do that when a wife dies in suspicious circumstances, the first thing the police do is look closely at the husband.

So his first task would, of course, be to create circumstances that did not appear suspicious.

As scholars yourselves, you can easily imagine the meticulous care with which he would approach the task. He would, I'm sure, have read widely enough to know that it is in fact reactions, not circumstances, which usually cause suspicion. I see from your smiles that you recognize I am quoting from my own book, *Crime in Our Time,* the chapter on 'Information', though lest I be accused of egotism I should point out that many of my findings were soon afterwards confirmed by no less a talent than E K Charleshead. The first thing the provident murderer must do is choose, or arrange, a time when those likely to create an atmosphere of suspicion are as far removed as may be from the sphere of influence. In this case, that would be (in descending order of potential troublesomeness) Christine's lover, C; his son, David; and his first wife. His daughters present little problem, the younger being in California and the elder in a clinic for rehabilitation of alcoholics in, let us say, Yorkshire.

The academic mind always prefers the most elegant solution, so let us create one for our model.

Imagine Professor Smith to have close connections with, say, a Japanese university, whose vice-chancellor, an old friend, is currently visiting England. It is not difficult for him to arrange that C should be invited, on very favourable terms, to spend a term there – particularly as C is a young man of great promise and growing reputation. The necessary study leave presents no difficulty as it is to all intents and purposes, in Professor Smith's gift. But the real elegance of the solution lies in his contriving that the Japanese vice-chancellor, who knew him in his pre-Christine days, should also invite his son and first wife to pay him a visit. C's proposed trip, plus the opportunity en route for visiting the younger daughter, are large inducements respectively, and the ill-assorted trio set off on the same plane.

I do not think we need to exercise our minds much on the method the professor chooses for disposing of Christine. If, as E K Charleshead has suggested in his fascinating analyses of death statistics in the decades immediately before and after the Second World War, as much as one per cent of natural causes and up to two point five per cent of domestic accidents are suspect, murder of relatives is second only to Monopoly as a popular family game. Someone as well organized as Professor Smith could have the deed done, the necessary enquiries carried out and the body cremated before word of the tragedy filtered through to Japan, where C incidentally has made such a good impression, the university authorities have offered him a Chair.

Now, it was my intention, having constructed this elaborate model, to use it to illustrate the wider criminological implications of my opening contention. But, alas, I fear my recent ill health sapped my strength even more than I was aware. No, no, please, do not agitate yourselves, I am not ill now, just a trifle exhausted and I fear that this, my last lecture, will have to remain more open-ended even than I had intended. Perhaps a happy result of this will be to permit a very free-ranging discussion. The psychologists among you might like, for instance, to consider whether Smith would be able to resist the temptation to make a confession, however obliquely. Academics are notoriously eager to publish their results! But I shall not stay for the discussion. I feel I have earned a good, long rest.

And this leads me to conclude on a very personal note.

As you all know, I am due to retire from my post at the end of next term. But I have decided for various reasons to bring the date forward and, as from the end of this Conference, I shall cease to hold my Chair of Criminology. I have spoken to my vice-chancellor on the telephone and he has agreed to accept my resignation, reluctantly he says. I hope – no, I am sure – he will not be so reluctant to accept my nomination of a successor. Indeed, there can only be one man for the job, the associate professor of criminology at Tokyo University, my former research assistant and my dear friend, E K Charleshead.

Finally, let me say that it is not my intention to return to England. I have few ties there since my recent bereavement, and my resignation has just about cut the last one. I am contemplating settling down here in Brazil and the authorities have indicated that they would make me most welcome. The attractions are many: a benevolent climate, a beautiful landscape, a lively culture, a sympathetic tax system; perhaps even, as Captain Ribeiro told us in his talk yesterday, the absence of a clearly defined treaty of extradition with the UK! Well, forgive an old man's joke. But I like it here, and here, God willing, I shall rest.

Thank you for the kindness of your invitation, the courtesy of your hearing, and the comfort of your friendship.

I shall not soon forget you. And I hope that I shall be in all of your minds at some time.

And perhaps in some of your minds for ever.

I thank you.

Thank you.

Goodbye.

ELSEWHERE

BILL JAMES

Bill James is best known for his long-running and highly successful series featuring those memorable cops, Harpur and Iles. He is, though, a writer of considerable versatility – check out his books for The Do-Not Press as well as those he has written under the by-line of David Craig – and 'Elsewhere' finds him on top form. This is a witty and cleverly contrived story, which is likely to stick in the reader's mind for a considerable time.

Campion certainly did not realise he had strayed into a murder. All he experienced – or all Graham *thought* he experienced – was a sad voice answering the early morning phone call he'd made in search of comfort. That kind of call he often made lately.

Naturally, slaughter is out there always in the city – in all cities: London, Los Angeles, Leeds; Miami, Marseilles, Marrakesh. For most people it remains remote and generally unencountered, thank God, not part of our daily... well, intercourse. Yet most of us have heard how a killing can abruptly shatter what previously had been the peaceful, carefully ordered, even joyous lives of a family or group. Graham had always appreciated crime as the subject of novels and stories, but thought few such tales caught this constant, huge variability of things in our actual world: the jolting, savage moves from normality to violence and from near-farce to full tragedy.

Listening to the dawn voice on his telephone, Graham could not know that one of these terrible shifts had happened again. Afterwards, when newspapers reported the street stabbing, and Graham recognised some names, he did begin to think a bit, though even now he is not totally sure. And it would be unwise to ask for explanations, wouldn't it?

Graham had a lover named Alison who lived in St John's Wood, on the other side of London, in a considerable avenue, and who telephoned him very late most nights at his flat in Brixton, a distance away socially and otherwise, though, of course, part of the same city. Obviously, *he* could not ring *her* because she was married and her husband might get suspicious. But, on the pretext of washing her hair or reading in bed, she would often slip upstairs to their extension and make this call for romantic talk, while Raymond, her husband, watched television. A short, whispered chat could occur. She always used the land line, regarding mobiles as insecure after that famous tapped conversation between Prince Charles and Camilla Parker-Bowles. The point was, Graham had to be at the other end, waiting every night in case Alison came through, and this had begun to bug him. He felt damn cornered, utilised. Wasn't he larger than that?

It was the same when Alison decided to visit. He had given her a key to his place and she would drop in without warning and expect him to be at home, vivid with welcome. Generally he managed this, but lately had come to feel he was too available. Surely it should be women who sat anxiously, hopefully waiting, not men? His sense of meek passivity seemed worse because Alison and Raymond had all that money: three-dimensional, metropolitan-scale money.

For himself, Graham ran an adequate business selling novelties: love-spoons, cards and London-scene watercolours, mostly to tourists from overseas. However, he was making no pile and, since his divorce, lived solo in the Brixton flat. It might also be termed adequate, yet lacked all the grandeur of Ray's and Alison's property – and you could call that a property, without sounding absurd. The area boasted many such places. Yes, boasted. He had driven past a couple of times to gaze at their home, as much as he could through those thrivingly thick hedge ramparts.

On the other hand, Graham's own street and district were... say, problematical. It's true that parts of Brixton had shaken off their previous harsh image and become almost fashionable, especially among those who despised far-out suburbia but could not afford Kensington, or even St John's Wood. Upgrading had not quite reached the patch where Graham lived, though.

As a means of upgrading *himself* – since he could not, on his own, upgrade one whole segment of London – Graham planned to make two changes: he would acquire some new business allure, and he would arrange to become more scarce. Just before the time that Alison might ring, he took to dialling a number he knew would be unanswered – the office of his accountant, Jack Brabond, in the nearby district of Lewisham, sure to be empty so late. This gave Alison the busy tone. To take the receiver off the hook would not do because eventually that produced the 'unobtainable' wail to callers, and she would deduce what he had done, and be hurt and/or ratty-contemptuous – most likely ratty-contemptuous – and become sexually punitive for at least weeks. Not to answer would have produced interminable questioning from Alison on why he was out late. She could be darkly possessive.

He would leave the call ringing at Jack Brabond's for twenty minutes or so at about the right time, then replace the receiver. It did not always work, but often when Alison was eventually able to get through on these nights she asked why his phone had been engaged. He would reply that he'd had a fairly urgent business call from Seattle or Denver, where they were hours behind us and still in their offices.

He felt this arrangement gave him commercial brilliance: internationalised him, as well as ensuring that he was not endlessly and gratefully on tap. Also, in some mysterious, even mystical, way the imperturbable steady ringing tone at Brabond's office brought a sense of contact with the world, and a fiscal, important world at that. It told him he was not, after all, discarded and alone and flimsy in his drab corner of the city. Never mind that the call remained unanswered. It was specifically targeted and would have reached someone, had someone only been

there. This potential communion buttressed him. Occasionally, if
Graham awoke around dawn, miserable again in his deeply unshared
bed, he could re-solace himself by dialling Jack Brabond's number again,
sure it was now only a few hours before someone would reply. Clearly,
he did not let the ringing go on for that long; but, having been soothed by
the prospect of an answer, he would put the receiver back and find sleep
once more as morning arrived.

Now and then, Jack Brabond took women back to the office after an
evening at a club or the casino. He was married and supposed to be
seeing important clients of his firm in their houses on these nights, so
patently could not ask the women home. He kept some drink at the office
and had a five-seater leather sofa in his room for when he might be con-
ferring with several client directors. Jack needed regularity; a stable, reliable pattern: from home to work at the office, home again at the end of
the day, then out to the club or casino in the evening, perhaps to the office
once more – but for a delightful sojourn now, not work – and finally
home again. He had a dread of what he termed to himself the Outside,
meaning more or less anywhere or anything in the city – in cities generally – which did not fall within the tidy, charted realm he'd fashioned.
He recalled Sodom and Gomorrah, the Bible's 'cities of the plain', locations replete with danger and uncorralled evil. Jack feared cities,
although he had to live in one: knew they were trouble, knew you must
look after your defences.

Recently, on some occasions when Jack had returned to the office late
in the evening with a woman friend, his direct-line phone would ring very
close to the sofa at unfortunate, crux moments. God knew who would be
calling now. It enraged and unnerved him: perhaps an intrusion from
that threatening Outside. Without interrupting anything major, Jack
would reach down behind the sofa and yank the plug from its socket.
Whoever was ringing would get a 'no reply' sound, and never know they
were cut off. Several women found his decisiveness with the plug fero-
ciously sexy and grew even more loving, otherwise he might have pulled
it before they began.

Tonight, though, he was having trouble with a murderously articu-
late, very beautiful woman called Helen, whom he had asked back for
the first time. Jack gave her a couple of brandies and patiently listened as
she elaborated a thesis she began in the Grand Manner Club about the
way to achieve solid poise in badminton by playing well back from the
net and wearing heavier-type training shoes. He blamed himself for this
impasse, since he had mentioned to her that his only child, Ivor, played

badminton for Leeds university: with Jack, it was an unwavering rule to be honest and let women know early that he had a wife and admirable family, and was devoted to them. His family were as much an antidote to the infected Outside as were these cheery episodes, after hours, in the office.

In fact, now and then, if a girl had come back more than once with him and seemed liable to grow what he termed 'clingy', Jack would take a few moments of relaxed, post-coital time to ring Ivor – reconnecting the phone briefly if necessary – while she looked on and listened. The lad seemed to be living these days with his girlfriend, Sally, which was fine by Jack, and he might chat comfortably to one or both of them on such late-night calls. Ivor's student flat, full of love, sporting gear and academic industry, was one part of the Outside Jack felt happy about, akin in some ways to his own setting. Ivor, like Jack, had to contend with the perils of a city – a smaller, northern city, but still a city, with all its accumulated peril. Jack was glad Ivor had established a refuge for himself and Sally there, just as Jack had built a couple of refuges for himself in *this* city: his home and the office.

When Jack put his hand on Helen's skirt now, as the survey of bad-minton footwear seemed about to close, she did not tangibly flinch or freeze but glanced down at it and smiled momentarily, as if indicating that this advance was laughable enough and anything additional would be grotesque. As summing-up, she listed again some brands of heavier trainers she favoured and then said: 'I must be off soon, Jack, dear. I only came for a last drink and to see your set-up here. AS YOU KNOW.' The telephone rang. Jack, alert for it, leaned over the back of the sofa and, using his free hand, would have disconnected with standard, aphrodisiac flair.

'Don't do that,' Helen snarled.

Shamefaced, he removed his other hand from her thigh area, while continuing his effort to kill the phone.

'No, keep doing that, you dolt, but don't do that to the telephone,' she went on, a throaty tremor touching her words. She picked up his non-plug hand and put it back on her skirt, rather higher up.

'It can't be anyone so late,' he said.

'Oh, yes, so late, so late! A caller out there in the noble dark of the thrillingly complicit city, trying to get through.' Her voice still thrummed with excitement. She put one of her hands over his on her body and pressed down confirmingly. 'Mysterious. It's as if there were a spectator, a witness.'

'You like that?'

'It's special.'

He felt terrorised by the continuing din but moved his hand from under hers, then down her skirt, then quickly up and beneath it.

In a moment she remarked: 'There. Now you see what I mean about it tuning me up. The brilliant clamour, Jack – that brutal insistence, the forlorn echo through an empty building. One loves it so.'

Christ, how long would this benign, lubricating racket last? On all previous calls he had disconnected almost at once. Urgently, he began to undress her, then himself. Seize the jangling moment.

'Oh, if only he knew the threesome he makes,' she cried. 'I'm sure it's a he. Perhaps somehow, somewhere in the city, he senses what's happening here.'

The ringing went on long enough, though Jack was not sure he did. After all, the circumstances produced some strain. Nevertheless, he felt there had been progress, and, in fact, a few nights later Helen agreed to return with him to the office. 'But no messing about,' she said.

'Certainly not.'

Things went pretty well exactly the same again, though: coolness, titanic discourse and then those sudden hots from Alexander Graham Bell's bell. Above the sound of the ringing, she muttered into his ear on the sofa, 'You really reach me, Jacky, love.' Yet he feared that once more he had been too hurried, nervous all the time that a reversion to arid silence might abruptly end her zing.

When next he took Helen to the office, he found a smart way to avert this pressure. They were sitting sedately while she gave some detailed, very up-to-date, rather uncompulsive news on a great-aunt in Tasmania and her knitting prowess. He said suddenly that he must check he had locked the outer door. In fact, he hurried down the corridor to the room of his partner, Hugh Stitson. Hugh had a separate outside line and on it Jack dialled his own office number. Then he left Hugh's receiver off. When he returned to his room, the telephone was doing its fine, now wholly reliable bit, and Helen had shed her clothes and forgotten Tasmania. 'He's with us again, Jack – our blessed adjunct,' she sighed contentedly. 'Never, never stop, dear Wonderman,' she cried, gazing at the telephone.

'No, I won't,' Jack replied, but short of breath.

When Graham Campion, as usual, called Jack's office number that night he found it busy. Crazy. This did not interfere with his tactic for stalling Alison, since as long as he kept the call in to the accountant she would still get the engaged note from him, too, if she rang. But he loathed the aggressively sharp tone of Jack's *Busy* sound. It made him feel rejected rather than potentially in touch. Who the hell phoned an accountant at this time of night, except him? Or who the hell would be working down there and ringing out so late? He looked in the directory to check he had not made a mistake and found Jack's business had two numbers, obviously one for each partner. Immediately, he rang the other. Jesus, this was engaged, too. Did they now and then have big, emergency audit work, or similar, that kept them at it into the small hours? They actually bothered clients by phone around midnight? Replacing the receiver, he thought urgently of some second-choice subscriber where there would be no answer out of office hours and decided on his solicitor: those buggers hardly ever turned up, even *within* office hours. He was looking for the name in the directory when his own telephone rang. Answering was inescapable. Alison said: 'I got straight through to you. No big-deal calls tonight?'

'Later,' he replied. But he feared his image had taken a body blow. She did not talk for long and said she was going to bed. He felt diminished.

At the office, Jack and Helen eventually let things reach their rich conclusion, although his telephone continued to ring, and then they began to dress. While she was putting herself to rights in the women's staff cloakroom, Jack went to Hugh's office and replaced the receiver.

'Oh, it's stopped at last,' Helen said, reappearing in his room, ready to leave.

'Farewell then, Splendid Presence,' he said, addressing the handset in Helen's reverential style. And he meant it. He was coming to terms. 'You look so lovely, Helen.' He put out a hand to touch her face gently, affectionately.

'Now, don't start all that damn smoochy stuff,' she snarled.

At home, Graham felt a mixture of curiosity, hellish disorientation and anger over what had happened earlier. He thought that when the night had gone he might give one of his dawn calls, confident that by then at least there would be access to Jack's office. Graham craved this reassurance and notional companionship. But in a while he decided he could not wait until dawn and must try once more now, immediately, in the hope of settling himself for sleep. This time the number rang. Thank heavens! Had he been mis-dialling both numbers before?

In the office, Jack and Helen were about to leave. He had thought of

giving Ivor a late call, just so that she would get no notions about eternal
linkage with Jack on the basis of a few damn office evenings, but felt all-
in and eager for bed, meaning sleep. When the bell reblurted, she cried
warmly: 'Oh, he's with us once more, Jack. Does he never falter, never
lose concern for us?' She put her arm around his neck and drew him back
towards the sofa. 'We must not fail him.'

Fuck, he thought. Possibly.

Graham decided there was no point in letting the phone ring at Jack's for
long, since Alison would not be calling again tonight. The damage to his
aura had been done. This call was merely a final, rather desperate check:
he saw now that his earlier failures to get through must have been some
sort of freak breakdown on the lines. He replaced the receiver and went
to bed.

When the bell ceased in the office, Helen looked at her illuminated dial
watch – she never took that off – and said: 'I must get home, Jack. You,
too. It's an outrageous time.'

'Not quite yet,' he muttered, into irreversible countdown again.

'I must.' As brusquely as his former unplugging, she drew away from
him and swung her magnificent legs off the sofa.

'What was that?' he cried.

'What?'

'I thought I heard someone in the foyer. An intruder. Wait here, darling.'

Jack ran swiftly, naked, still creditably aroused, down the corridor
to Hugh's office and dialled his room again. He took true solace from
these little in-house trips – part of a nicely managed, tidy life, over well-
known ground, a portion of his wonderfully safe, niche habitat. When
he returned, Helen was lying back, haloed with appetite, and did not ask
about the supposed intruder. 'Our eternal accompanist from some
region of the grand Elsewhere,' she purred, pointing to the noisy phone.
'This time, lift the receiver off, Jack. Let him hear our joys. Let him be
truly with us.'

'But, sweetness, it will stop the ringing,' he replied.

'It's not the bell that gets to my spirit, it's the sense of SOMEONE' –
this was a big, pulsating, echoing word – 'some Night Person of our City,
some Anon, some Enigma from the Streets, some Garnering Ear; yes,
some Presence, as you so justly called him.'

Jack took the receiver off and laid it on the desk. Why not? The
sounds would be going nowhere except to an empty office. Again, the

sense of that small, private circuit pleased him. It had nothing to do with Night Persons of their city. Night Persons of their city, or of any city, would scare him tremulous. In a while Helen gave some grand groans and shrieks, and so did he. Staring with affection at the receiver, she said: 'Jack, wouldn't merely selfish ecstasy seem so skinflint? To share it is an act of blessedness.' She did not suggest actually speaking into the phone, thank heaven. He could imagine her asking the supposed listener in a Florence Nightingale voice if he'd taken therapy from his call.

Before they left Jack carried out a quick but thorough examination to see that Hugh's phone was not switched on to Record. If it were, Stitson's secretary, Martha, would be expecting only workaday messages about self-assessment and allowable expenses. She had a weak heart and should be spared shocks.

A night or two later, when Jack and Helen were seated on the sofa with drinks, he inadvertently mentioned he used to wear a tooth brace as a child, and afterwards waited anxiously for a small break in her account of the many types of these now available, so he could get down to Hugh's room and set up the contact. He had left her in mid chat the other night and felt it would be impossibly rude to do so again. His phone started to ring before she had completed her round-up.

'Ah!' she said. 'Take the receiver off, Jack.'

'But—'

'I must feel we are with him again, enveloping him, not just having him badger us through a damned meaningless bell. That's *so* one-way. Jack, don't deny me this. Don't shroud our love. I know you, too, yearn for this alliance with our plangent city.'

No, no, NO. But he lifted the receiver and placed it on the desk.

Shocked to have his call responded to, Graham almost dropped the phone. Covering the mouthpiece he listened carefully. At first there was virtual silence, except for some rather feverish rustling noises and then, possibly, subdued voices, perhaps a woman and a man. He could not tell if the man was Jack: Graham usually heard Brabond pronounce words like 'docket', not the kind of word on his lips now. Shortly afterwards, though, came unmistakeable sounds, and particularly from the woman.

Graham realised, of course, that these exclamations were not directed primarily at him, yet also felt in some gratifying way implicated, welcomed, yes, embraced. This, too, was another life extension for him. He decided it would be friendly to drive down to Jack's office and see whether he could approach a little closer, show extra fellowship. He did not replace his telephone, in case Alison rang and got no reply in his absence. To tell her where he had gone would be impossible, since that would give away his whole tactical system. She would hear a nice 'engaged' tone again.

Alison's husband Raymond telephoned her from Rotterdam to say there were delays in some deal and he would not after all be home that night. It seemed a lovely opportunity to call on Graham. She took the Volvo and not long afterwards let herself quietly into the flat, gently cooing his name. There was no reply but, standing in the little hallway, she thought she heard sounds coming from behind the part-open living room door. For a second she listened and then her rage soared. Graham had a woman there – was having a woman there. Bursting in, though, she was relieved to find the room empty. Then she saw the telephone had been left off the hook and went to pick it up. Meaningful noises still issued. For a while she listened: it must be one of those endless, dirty recorded calls for the lonely and maladjusted. So this must be the number he rang every night – nothing to do with love-spoon orders from the States! Graham Campion was a pervert. Tonight, he had obviously grown so excited by what he heard that he had been obliged to rush out and gratify himself with a girl, too hurried even to put the receiver back. She banged it down herself now.

Helen, in the office, was having a small spell of silence and quiet enjoyment and heard a click from the receiver, lying out of its cradle on the desk, as the call was abruptly cut. Leaning across deftly from under Jack, she picked up the instrument and listened. There was not the humming sound of an open line but the beep, beep, beep that showed they were no longer connected. 'Time we were away,' she snapped.

'What?' Jack gasped.

'Please. Don't be tiresome. This is an accountant's prestige premises, for Christ's sake, in close touch with the Inland Revenue. Have some decorum.'

Graham arrived in the street just in time to spot the two cars drive away. The office looked entirely dark. He knew he was too late and sadly went home, feeling solitary. Entering, he grew puzzled: he could have sworn he had not replaced the telephone when he left for Jack's office, yet it was back now. He rang Jack's number to seek a re-run of the previous effects, but there was no reply. Inevitably there was no reply! Hadn't he just seen the participants leave? He replaced the receiver.

A little later, as he was preparing to turn in, his telephone rang. When he picked it up he could hear vigorous sounds very like those that had intrigued him earlier, though louder and even more appreciative. Between the happy yelps a woman eventually said: 'Sauce for the gander is sauce for the goose, Graham.'

'Alison?'

'So you like earholing this sort of thing, do you?' she replied. 'You deserted me, bastard. I was bereft.'

'Where are you, darling?'

'In a public phone box, with a friend I've just met. It's so easy to get a booth when you urgently want one these days and nights, because everyone's got mobiles. And this *was* urgent.'

'Which friend?'

'A friend in need and a friend in deed.'

Jack Brabond went home and climbed into bed with his wife, Olive. She stirred, half asleep, and low down put out her hand inquiringly towards him. He turned away, deeply spent. Not long afterwards, he was awoken by the telephone ringing with fierce persistence downstairs. After a while, to his amazement, he found himself aroused by it. Delighted, he realised he had at last learned the full, spirit-lifting lesson from Helen and come to see the city and, indeed, the world around, not as hostile but as an inspiration. A phone bell at night would turn him on. Lovingly he edged towards Olive.

'You'd better answer the call first,' she murmured.

'No, it will spoil things. I'll go in due course.'

'In due course it will have stopped.'

'I don't think so.'

'What?'

'Believe me. I've an instinct about such matters.' Like Helen, he had come to feel that a magnificent source of desire and power out there was sending its restorative power to him: Elijah's mantle on Elisha.

The ringing stopped, then resumed, as if someone suspected they had mis-dialled. Olive said: 'Please, Jack. I can't relax while it's shrieking like that.'

'Doesn't it intrigue and thrill you? The Someone from the Brooding City. The Mystery from its Streets? The Presence?'

'You gone mad? Just get the sodding thing, will you?' she replied.

He would be considerate. One could not reasonably expect every-body – could not expect Olive – to be instantly in touch with these unspoken, vibrant messages from Outside; any more than he had been instantly in touch with them himself previously. A slow revelation was needed.

He climbed out of bed and went down to the phone in the hall. Always he had resisted having an upstairs extension in case one of his more personal calls was overheard by Olive. Expecting no voice – this would be the magnificent Presence who was a Non-Presence, after all – he picked up the receiver. For Olive's sake he was committed merely to stopping the bell. He did not even lift the phone to his ear. Just the same, he heard his name spoken. It was a woman's voice and for a moment he thought Helen's. What did she mean ringing him here at this hour, the wild cow? Now, he did raise the instrument and said: 'Yes, it's Jack. What?'

'Mr Brabond? Sally. I'm phoning from Leeds.'

'Sally? Sally?'

'Ivor's girlfriend.'

'Oh, yes, dear, of course. I was expecting a… But what is it?'

She seemed to be weeping. 'Oh, Mr Brabond, a terrible fight, outside in the street.'

'Outside?'

'In the street. They had broken into the flat to thieve. We came home and surprised them. Mr Brabond, there were three, with knives, and they held us prisoner for a while. They would have used me, but Ivor beat them off. So courageous. The fight spilled on to the pavement. He wanted to draw them away from me, I know it. People saw but by the time help came Ivor was—' She sobbed.

'Dead? Dead. Oh, why did you choose to live in a city?'

'What? Universities usually *are* in cities, Mr Brabond.'

'Just the same.'

'The police will tell you face to face. They don't telephone such news. But I thought you'd want to know even so late.'

'Yes. I'm used to late calls.' In those idiotically cheerful telephone conversations from the office, why had he never stressed to Sally and Ivor the foul hazards of Outside, the *de rigueur*, galloping evil of cities?

'And the robbery was so pointless, so trivial,' she said. 'All they got away with were a couple of badminton racquets and his trainers.'

Trainers? Were they the heavy style? Although the crazy thought broke into Jack Brabond's head, he stopped himself from speaking it. The banal and the horrific could mingle, as everybody knew, but he did not have to cave in and help them do it.

When Jack went back upstairs, Olive was snoring. Why wake her? Keep the grief to himself till morning. He dressed and drove around the streets, pathetically hoping to escape his own grief that way. At dawn, he found himself near the office, went in and lay blankly awake on the big sofa. The phone rang. He picked it up and said: 'Look, Presence, this is no good to you now. I'm utterly alone.'

'What about me?'

GROUND ZERO

PETER LEWIS

Peter Lewis is by profession an academic, and is also a publisher of distinction. With his wife, the writer Margaret Lewis, he runs Flambard Press, a highly regarded, small publishing company, which has sometimes dipped a toe in criminous waters. And finally, he is an occasional writer of quirky and entertaining short stories, which often verge on novella length. Here, like another contributor to this book, he turns his attention to the events of September 11th 2001, but the treatment is oblique. I found it interesting when reading through the stories submitted by CWA members for this volume that September 11th had evidently made an impact upon them. Quite apart from the two stories in this book that deal directly with the terrorist outrage, several other submissions made reference to it. Yet – most unusually – not a single American CWA member submitted a story this time around. It is as if the effect of the attacks has been to cause American writers to reflect long and hard on their approach to their craft. Undoubtedly, the impact of the crimes in New York and Pennsylvania will be felt for many years to come, in the field of fiction as elsewhere.

'Think big,' they told her, 'think big.'

Or words to that effect.

'Expand. Widen out. Spread your wings. Think Antony Gormley, think *Angel of the North*.'

Or variations on that theme.

When one of the older Fine Art lecturers urged her, in his somewhat archaic slang, to 'let it all hang out', she imagined herself with her intestines pouring from her belly button like a high-speed Cumberland sausage. That's what happened if you were hung, drawn and quartered, although the first time she'd come across that phrase as a child she couldn't for the life of her understand how drawing could contribute to an execution – unless, for some reason, it was important to have a visual record.

'Relax,' they said. 'Let yourself go. Open up. Let rip.'

Her university teachers might have been recommending a laxative, she thought, urging her to move her bowels, not encouraging her to take more risks with her painting. Made her think of the Italian artist who'd exhibited cans of his own shit – were they properly labelled? Not something you'd want to open by mistake – or that young British painter who daubed some of his colourful canvases with grassy dollops of elephant dung. Not curds and whey for him, but turds and hay. The irony was that no one in the art world turned a hair anymore at work involving excrement or bodily fluids or animals sawn in half, although it could *épater* the wider public, but if *she,* Morag, suddenly produced something of that sort or sado/masochistic or whatever, she'd send shock waves through her Department – staff and students alike.

Once, working late in the almost deserted Department, she'd overheard two of her tutors in the corridor outside her studio, unaware of her presence, actually call her 'tight-arsed'.

'Morag could be really good, get an excellent first, don't you think,' one of them said, 'if she took her corsets off? Just needs to be less—'

'Constipated? Scottish? Edinburgh? Presbyterian?'

'Don't be racist. Anyway, she's Catholic, isn't she?'

'Rosary in one hand, brush in the other. Explains a lot. How about tight-arsed, then? I think that's what you mean. Agreed. High time she lapsed a bit.'

'Or lap danced a bit.'

'How about that? Just imagine. Think you could persuade her? She certainly needs to let her hair down. There's enough of it. Rapunzel. Typical of her that she usually wears it in a bun. Contained. Controlled.

Probably goes to bed with her knickers on. Nuns' knickers. Chastity drawers.'

'One pair? Or two?'

They laughed as they moved away and she couldn't make out any more of what they said. After a couple of years at university, she was so familiar with this view of her as inhibited and repressed, even frigid, that it no longer bothered her as it had done when she was a teenager. She didn't pretend to be much of a party girl, although she was a good dancer – and not just at Scottish country dancing. But she didn't swing. She never got drunk. And she usually kept her knickers on; which didn't mean that she wasn't capable of giving herself orgasms when her libido got the better of her, a talent she'd acquired early in her convent school. Guilt-free orgasms, at that. She thought of herself as a very liberal Catholic, and with a home full of older brothers, there wasn't much about sex she hadn't picked up. At school, Biology was her favourite subject apart from Art.

From an early age she'd enjoyed drawing and it soon became obvious to her parents and others that she was unusually talented. 'Precocious' they called her, without implying anything derogatory. And she was. She particularly liked drawing flowers and birds, but she was good too at animals and people. She could produce excellent likenesses, and her parents lined up various members of her extended family – uncles and aunts and cousins – to sit for their portraits in pencil or charcoal, which several of them framed. She was every bit as good, they said, as those street artists in Montmartre and Florence – places like that – who rattled off sketches of people in no time flat. Except Morag was slow, meticulous and painstaking. She'd speed up with practice, they told her, and when she was older she'd be able to make a small fortune during the summer, sketching tourists and holidaymakers in some arty city on the Continent.

Discovering the beautiful, as well as scientifically accurate, botanical drawings and paintings of those draftsmen and artists who accompanied people like Captain Cook on voyages of exploration in the eighteenth and nineteenth centuries, she felt she would have been ideally equipped for such a role – had she been born a boy, of course. That was the rub. It wasn't a fate she'd wish on herself or any other female, even those she disliked. Being a girl was bad enough. But to have all that testostuff rushing through your system, causing you to rise and fall like a demented yoyo, up-down-up-down-up-down, was, she thought, devoutly to be avoided and more than flesh and blood could bear – although come to think of it, expanding flesh and widening blood vessels were what it was all about.

As for painting, she'd splashed, splurged, splodged, spilt, spattered and splattered her way through kindergarten and infant school with the best of them. To her teachers, she actually was the best of them: juxtaposing colours in an eye-popping way that would have made even the Fauves blink. But as her drawing skills developed, her use of paint became more restrained and fastidious and finicky. She put shackles on her childhood imagination. When she was older and had discovered William Blake, she diagnosed what had happened to herself as the move – the fall – from Innocence into Experience.

Although she gradually acquired the knack of turning out good watercolours, the medium didn't come easily to her since it required speed and fluidity, as opposed to the patient revising and dithery re-revising she brought to her drawings: putting lines in, then taking them out, then restoring them, then... Oils suited her much better since she could fiddle and faddle and diddle and daddle and twiddle and twaddle to her heart's content, until she achieved what she wanted. And she preferred to work on a small scale. When she first saw the exquisite miniature pictures by such Elizabethan and Jacobean limners as Nicholas Hilliard, she felt she'd found her artistic roots and regretted that she'd not been born in the age of Shakespeare – until she remembered that to succeed she'd have had to be a boy. And that was definitely not a price worth paying. So limited. And having to put up with a demented yoyo, like her brothers. Think of that.

In her closeted girls' school, where she was the outstanding Art student, her teachers complimented her work as delicate and feminine, but when she moved to a sixth-form college in the north of England, the same words were almost insults. Suddenly she was exposed to full-of-themselves boys and à-la-mode girls who gabbled about Conceptualism and Postmodernism and installations and video-art and multimedia, about which she knew little and sometimes nothing at all. She was much better at what she specialised in than they were, but then they regarded what she did as pedantic, conservative, backward-looking. And it was true that given the choice of visiting the Uffizi in Florence or MOMA in New York, she would have gone to the former; the same with the National Gallery or the Tate Modern in London.

She had, it seemed, been taken out of a small paddling pool and thrown into the deep end of an Olympic one. Sink or swim? She swam. She caught on, caught up. Had to, to survive. But at first she presented an easy target for show-off teasers. Did she know there'd been art since Giotto? Since Praxiteles? Since neolithic cave painting? If she hadn't been a quick learner, she might have dropped Art to avoid such ritual humiliation, but she soon acquired enough of the current jargon to pass muster and was able to toss around the right 'in' names – while not revealing what she actually thought of them.

Gradually her painting changed, becoming less delicate, less feminine, more adventurous, less cautious, but nothing remotely like the stuff the sixth-form avant-gardists perpetrated. Crimes against art, she thought some of it, but didn't say so. Not just out of politeness, but because she thought that the fault might somehow be hers, an inability to appreciate work so different from her own. And this self-doubt shook her confidence, making her question seriously for the first time her long-held conviction that what she wanted to do at university was Fine Art. Was she good enough? Was she up to it? Fortunately one of her teachers reassured her, and also pointed out that since she was deeply interested in Art History and would almost certainly get top grade in her A-level, she could combine her creative work with a career as a curator or gallerist or academic, or other possibilities in this field of study.

For her degree course she favoured Newcastle, which was pleased to have someone with four top grades at A-level. Why not somewhere in London, like Goldsmith's or the RCA? Partly the expense, but more because she found the city intimidating and overwhelming, and felt that she'd be lost in the crowd. Newcastle was cheaper, cosier, much nearer home. She knew it fairly well and felt comfortable there.

The first time she visited the university, still a sixth-former, she called into the Hatton Gallery and saw its most famous exhibit, the large *Merzbau* Kurt Schwitters had been creating on the wall of an old, dry-stone barn near Ambleside at the end of his life. She learned that Richard Hamilton had rescued this *Merz Barn* by having the entire wall transported to Newcastle and erected in the Hatton. She gazed at it for some time, uncomprehending. But once she was a Fine Art student, she saw it regularly and gradually came to like and admire it more and more. This growing appreciation of what she'd once considered beyond her typified how she changed during the first two years of her degree course, but nothing prepared anyone in the Department for what happened after 11 September 2001.

In fact, what happened after 11 September didn't come out of the blue the way the two hijacked passenger planes did on the day itself, when suicide terrorists flew them into the Twin Towers of the World Trade Center in Lower Manhattan. The work Morag produced, in an extraordinary explosion of creative energy was the continuation, but on a much larger sale, of something she'd devoted the entire long vacation to. Two somethings, really – related somethings – related by death – two deaths.

The first was not unexpected; that of her favourite grandparent, her mother's mother, who had been fighting cancer for years but finally lost the battle. But it was Morag's first death and first funeral, the first time she'd experienced adult grief. Not long after, she found herself engaged on a series of small, semi-abstract paintings of places and objects particularly dear to her grandmother. It began spontaneously rather than consciously, but she soon realised that she was painting the absence of presence – or was it the presence of absence? At first she incorporated shadowy images of her grandmother, but then she painted these out to leave the merest suggestion of her, the most ghostly of ghosts, the faintest of palimpsests. Would anyone apart from herself know they were there? No matter. She named the series *Absence Is a Form of Presence*, and called the individual paintings *Unfinished I*, *Unfinished II* and so on. For her to label a painting *Unfinished* was revolutionary, because she normally fussed around ad nauseam – or so her fellow students thought – before saying, 'That's it... I think.'

The second death, shortly after, was totally different, completely unexpected. The teenage brother of Morag's best friend Chloë was found dead at home, hanging from a banister and dressed in his sister's clothes, down to stockings and suspenders and a bra stuffed with tights. It was an autoerotic experiment that went as wrong as wrong can go. The family might as well have been hit by a smart bomb, their devastation was so complete. Chloë was inconsolable, unable to get her mind around what had happened. Morag got her mind around it by resorting to creativity, as she had with her 'granny pictures', as she called them, and to her surprise she produced an installation for the first time in her life. She didn't mean to at first, but that's the way it developed, the form it eventually took: a construction involving a variety of female clothing, from a G-string to a wedding dress with a long train she concocted herself. All the items were suspended in such a way that they implied the presence of a body although this was conspicuously absent. She called her installation *Requiem*, but it might just as well have been *Absence Is a Form of Presence II*. And like the granny pictures, it was unfinished, or at least open-ended since it could be added to ad infinitum.

What she couldn't do was show *Requiem*, or even mention it, to Chloë – or anyone else, come to that. Not for a while. It was her secret, almost a dirty secret. Even as she assembled it, she was uneasy about what she was doing, making art out of pain and suffering and anguish. Nothing new in that, of course. As old as art itself. But in this case, the emotions were still very raw.

On 11 September 2001 Morag was at home, getting ready to return to university, when Chloë phoned her and told her to put the TV on. She didn't say why: 'Just do it. You won't believe it. It's impossible.'

Impossible it wasn't, but incredible it most certainly was. Could she believe her eyes? Should she believe her eyes? Morag watched and watched and watched. The video footage was repeated and repeated and repeated. And then the first tower collapsed with the ease of a house of cards, followed by the second. Not impossible, but beyond belief. After all, she'd stomped around the top of the World Trade Center with other tourists the previous summer, during an extended visit to New York. How could buildings like those fall down? They just couldn't. Except they did. It had happened. It was happening again and again and again as she viewed. Unless the whole thing was some kind of TV spoof equivalent to Orson Welles's famous radio version of *The War of the Worlds*, which had people sixty years ago believing there really was an invasion by aliens. But that really was impossible. No, it had happened right enough. By far the most destructive and murderous terrorist attack ever carried out. The New York skyline transformed in a trice. And it was the only thing people talked about for days. Weeks even.

This was crime in the city, with a vengeance. It was *the* crime in *the* city. Supercrime in the supercity. Megacrime in the megametropolis. The ultimate crime in the ultimate city. The crime of the year, according to the media. Of the decade, the century, or even the millennium, according to the tabloids – claims that seemed premature since they assumed that nothing worse was going to occur for a very long time indeed.

They were still talking about it when she returned to Newcastle, but she could barely believe her ears at some of the talk, especially among the post-postmodernists who prided themselves on their sophisticated, nihilistic irony.

'All we're getting is ethics and morality and politics,' said Dave, 'but what about the aesthetics of the Twin Towers?'

'You mean the guys piloting the planes didn't like the buildings and were making a statement about modern architecture?' Ian said. 'Direct-action criticism rather than verbal?'

'No, I mean that watching the planes fly into the towers was an aesthetic experience. There was something beautiful about it. Apocalyptic beauty. If someone had created a virtual-reality video of gleaming, shimmering planes flashing through that perfect blue sky and scything into the towers like that, you'd call it a dazzlingly original piece of twenty-first century art.'

'How can you talk like that about a catastrophe, an atrocity, about thousands of deaths?' This was Morag, who knew they were winding her up but was also aware that their cynicism wasn't just an act. 'All those people in the planes. Far more in the buildings. Think of the people you could see falling or jumping out of windows high up.'

'We're all going to die, Morag,' Dave said. 'No big deal. Keats may have thought his nightingale wasn't born for death, but we are.'

'But not like that. Not like those.'

'Homo sapiens is hardly an endangered species, Morag, and there are plenty more planes where they came from, not to mention skyscrapers.'

'I don't believe I'm hearing this.'

'But you are, darling Morag. Humanism was blown out of the water many years ago. And as for Catholic humanism, don't ask. Philosophy's moved on a bit since the three A's, you know: Aristotle, Augustine and Aquinas. How about Nietzsche, Heidegger, Derrida? We're all post-humanists now. If not anti-humanists. And another thing. As well as the aesthetics of terror, there's also its erotics.'

'I don't think I want to hear this. I'm off.' Morag got up to go.

'Very briefly then. September the eleventh was a kind of rape fantasy made real. Violent penetration. Twice. From different directions. One plane, then the other. Penetrations followed by huge explosions. Just like... you know. And then the most colossal detumescences in recorded history.'

Morag was through the door, but not quickly enough to avoid this résumé of the erotics of terror. Later, when she was hard at work on her *Ground Zero* series, she thought that the rage she felt at some of her fellow students for being so icily inhuman was, paradoxically, one of the spurs that drove her to begin it. And once she began, there was no stopping her.

The words 'Ground Zero' were those used in New York to describe the scene of total devastation where the Twin Towers had once stood. The absence of what had been present. Nothingness. Or nothing but rubble and occasional body parts. Morag didn't contemplate depicting the site itself. That would have been sacreligious, a form of blasphemy. An exploitation of the disaster. An insult, not a tribute, to the dead. But a memorial was possible, and her solution came to her while she was messing around with a pile of photographs she'd taken of Hadrian's Wall, or what was left of it. A presence, but also an absence, and her ghostly photographs taken at dawn and dusk hinted at a past that had long been absorbed into the landscape, life transmuted into still life – and death.

What if she were to take images well known to most people, endlessly reproduced images of man-made structures, and 'disappear' them, just as the hijacked planes had 'disappeared' the Twin Towers? With the crucial difference that, as an artist, she could accomplish removal without demolition. As if by magic. Now you see it, now you don't. She began with another Tower, the Eiffel, taking a familiar postcard shot of it and subjecting it to two different treatments. In one, she blew the image up to an enormous size and painted out the Tower itself to leave an extraordinarily naked cityscape. By re-photographing this, she produced an alternative version devoid of brushstrokes. But she also used computer graphics to 'disappear' the Eiffel, thus ending up with three variants of Paris minus its Tower, all on a scale she'd never attempted before.

Word soon went around the Department that Morag had gone barking bananas – 'always was a bit of a virginal fruitcake, though nothing that couldn't be cured by a good old-fashioned you-know-what' – and was suffering from the delusion that the Pope had commissioned her to re-do the Sistine Chapel. They nicknamed her Michelangela. Suggested that even if they all vacated the Department and left it to her, it wouldn't be big enough. But there was no stopping her.

After Paris came Berlin: Unter den Linden without the Brandenburg Gate. Of course, Berlin had undergone a process of 'disappearing' when the Wall came down, but that was as nothing compared with the Brandenburg Gate. Then there was the Mall in London, but no Buckingham Palace or statue of Queen Victoria at the end of it. And how about San Francisco without the Golden Gate Bridge? Or Pisa minus the Leaning Tower? The Sphinx but no Pyramids? Washington less the Capitol? The Taj Mahal without the Taj Mahal? She thought of ridding the Vatican of St Peter's, but whether she was inhibited by her Catholicism or – her fellow students' view – Michelangela needed to keep in with the Pope so that she wouldn't lose the commission to redecorate the Sistine, she refrained.

'Think big,' they'd advised her, but now that she was doing what they said – and how – they were perplexed. It was as though Gwen John had begun to paint like her brother Augustus. Unthinkable. Morag's abrupt conversion to works the size of American Abstract Expressionist paintings at their most expansive caused nearly as much incredulity in her Department as the events of 11 September themselves. Even her friends didn't know what to make of her, except that she must be travelling down her personal road to Damascus. Saul becoming Paul. Morag becoming… Who knows?

One of the post-postmodernists, Dave, suggested she was an artistic terrorist, indulging in a vicarious form of criminal annihilation, to which she replied: 'In that case, every writer from Shakespeare and Dostoevsky who's included a murder in their work would be a vicarious killer, and as for Agatha Christie – she'd be a genocidal maniac, wouldn't she?' Another, Ian, accused her of being exploitative, of cashing-in on tragedy, to which she answered: 'If that's the case, the entire tradition of Crucifixion painting and sculpture amounts to cashing-in on suffering, doesn't it? Including versions by Rembrandt and other Old Masters who included themselves as guilty participants in Christ's death.'

Defiant as she was, their remarks made her question herself about the origins of her *Ground Zero* series. Since she never started from a preconceived plan but followed her instincts and imagination where they led, it was only in retrospect that she was ever able to reach any conclusions about the subconscious sources of what she'd been creating. With her 'granny paintings' and her installation *Requiem*, the death of someone she knew had been a stimulus, but now it was a more general sense of loss and transience, the impermanence of the apparently permanent, the seeming victory of destructiveness. Was she – as one of her tutors suggested – metaphorically 'disappearing' God, depicting His absence? Had she perhaps absorbed more of fashionable nihilism than she realised? Had 11 September undermined what faith she still had?

Yet she still believed in her art. How, otherwise, could she have worked on such a scale, thought so big, thought Antony Gormley, thought *Angel of the North*? Since becoming a student, she'd seen his *Angel* often enough, on train journeys south and from the road, but she'd never bothered to visit it properly so as to lay hands on it. After all, like the figure of Christ high above Rio, it was designed to be seen from a distance, not in close-up. But now she did. Lying flat on her back underneath the colossus, she herself, she thought, was ground zero. With wings like those of a large passenger plane – or were they the outstretched arms of a figure nailed to a cross or about to embrace a multitude, like Rio's Christ? – the figure was vast, seemingly indestructible, as the Colossus of Rhodes must have seemed long ago, as the Twin Towers seemed when she'd stood on the roof and assumed they'd be there for – well, not for ever, not in Manhattan, but for a long time; much longer than their mere thirty years. But Gormley's *Angel* would one day cease to be. It would probably take centuries, but not long before 11 September, the largest figures of the Buddha in the world, carved out of rock fifteen hundred years ago, had been demolished by the Taliban in Afghanistan. Another feat of destruction. The two giant Buddhas of Bamian, twin towers of a sort, had survived Muslim conquests, even Genghis Khan, but these 'idols' had finally been reduced to rubble. *Ars longa*, but not everlasting. Just longer than *vita brevis*.

Leaving the *Angel*, she considered what the site would look like without it, now that it had become a familiar presence, a part of the land-scape. A few years ago, no one would have paid any attention to the little hill on the edge of Gateshead where it had since been erected, but if it were to disappear there would be an absence, a sense of loss. Even those who didn't particularly welcome it would miss it. From what she'd heard in Manhattan, the Twin Towers had never been popular with New Yorkers the way that the Chrysler or the Empire State Buildings were, but they'd become an essential part of New York. The entire city had been violated by their bizarre demolition. Viciously raped. Perhaps the post-postmodernists had a point after all when they talked about the erotics of terror.

As she crossed the Tyne back to Newcastle, she imagined some kamikaze fanatic flying a plane low enough over the river to crash into as many of the seven, closely bunched city-centre bridges as possible. No longer unthinkable. And since the Tyne Bridge itself was sacred to Geordies, this would be more than a crime. It would be akin to deicide. She, of course, could 'disappear' all the bridges in her studio, just as she could 'disappear' the *Angel*, but that was totally different. Nothing to do with destruction. She was memorialising and lamenting absence.

Or was she? That's what she'd been telling herself. But was she?

Suddenly she experienced a stab of jarring doubt. The prospect of a bridgeless Tyne triggered in her a flash of panic. Had she been deluding herself about the inspiration of her *Ground Zero*? *Requiem*, too, come to that. Were Dave and Ian perhaps right after all about the forces within her driving her recent work? Had these emerged from the murky depths of her subconscious? She remembered feeling uncomfortable, even a little guilty, about *Requiem*, but she'd been so carried away and intoxicated by her own creativity in recent months that she'd hardly thought it through.

She'd been appalled to hear about the viewing platforms erected near the site of the World Trade Center to enable sightseers to view Ground Zero. That struck her as the height of macabre voyeurism. Positively ghoulish. Yet might her *Ground Zero*, whatever her motives, itself be construed as voyeuristic? Interpreted as condoning, even celebrating, violence and destruction? Art as a form of complicity? That was the ques-tion Dave and Ian had raised, although she'd tended to treat it as a provocative tease rather than a serious point. Now she wasn't sure. Not sure at all.

But if her doubts had substance, what to do? Could she still live with it? Better to destroy the entire series, she thought, to ground-zero her

Ground Zero. It would, of course, be an act of lunacy, but at the same time there was a perverse excitement at the prospect of wiping it out, obliterating it. Zap, zap, zap. The destruction of art devoted to destruction.

Would she be able to carry this out, if she came to the conclusion that there was something fundamentally sick about her entire project? There was only one way to find out. She'd intended returning to her flat in Jesmond after visiting Gormley's *Angel*, but now she stayed on the urban motorway until the next exit, which would take her to the Department. She had no difficulty in parking, but then remained sitting in her car, immobile, wanting to move but not moving, paralysed by the impossibility of making up her mind and reaching a decision.

THE STOOGE

PHIL LOVESEY

Like his distinguished crime-writing father, Peter, Phil Lovesey combines a flair for the mystery novel with an abiding enthusiasm for the short story. When I was seeking contributions to this volume, I was keen to encourage CWA members to think laterally about the theme of 'Crime in the City'. Too heavy an emphasis on metropolitan *noir* and stories set in contemporary London would, I thought, result in an imbalance and a failure to display the range of crime-writing talents within the CWA. But I must admit that I did not imagine Welwyn Garden City as a likely setting. Happily, Phil came up with a story idea that suits his chosen backdrop admirably.

For many – most notably architectural purists – the mere existence of Welwyn Garden City represents one of the biggest English crimes of the century.

Set in some of Hertfordshire's blandest countryside, this urbane urban development is perhaps one of the only places truly worthy of derogatory terms muted behind closed Royal fists – 'monstrous carbuncle' being the most apt. Indeed, the very word 'city', when applied to the sprawling block-systemed new town, seems beyond all cultural and architectural optimism. Where, the unfortunate casual visitor might enquire, is the classic city denominator – Welwyn Garden's cathedral? Birds flying overhead find no cosy resting place amongst stone gothic gargoyles. Indeed, the briefest look around the pathologically tendered, geometrically laid-out roadways reveals nothing of visual interest over forty feet high, save for the vast, steel roasting towers of the Weetabix plant overlooking the eastern fringes of the town. Welwyn Garden City, whose 'cathedral' plays host to the general synod of breakfast cereals – wheat worship; stripped, baked and shaped twenty-four hours a day.

The 'city' centre masquerades as an enclosed, two-storey shopping mall fronted by a long (and predictably straight) lawn, home to weakly bubbling fountains, parking zones, dog-shit receptacles and coned plastic bus-stops. But say what you like about the place (and believe me, I could go on at length), Welwyn Garden City is by and large a clean place. Spotlessly clean. Maniacally clean. Unrealistically clean, a town ritually swept clean of the detritus of its inhabitants, as if they will only be tolerated provided they leave absolutely no impression whatsoever. A graffiti-reader's nightmare.

However, the one thing in Welwyn Garden City's favour is its crime rate. Perhaps it's the overpowering regimental effect of the place that subdues the criminal urges of its inhabitants. A quick look through the records of the Hertfordshire County Courts reveals just six cases brought against Welwyn Garden residents in the last four years. Three of these involved physical affray in connection with border-fencing disputes (Welwyn Gardenees are passionate gardeners); one concerned a rogue firework let loose in the shopping mall; the final two being lewd offences committed by the same felon in conjunction with lingerie and washing lines. Capone's Chicago it isn't.

Inevitably, the 'Garden City' is often looked upon as a model of effective policing. Uniformed officers still patrol the streets (two pairs, strolling the wide boulevards and shopping malls, eyes peeled for litter droppers), proudly claiming that it's their presence that deters felonious activities, when in fact this isn't altogether the case. The phenomenally low crime rate can be traced to another, altogether more practical social experiment – The Bricklayers Arms.

Architectural historians in the irritating 'know' will no doubt bore you with the temperance history of Welwyn Garden City. A city born out of revulsion of the demon drink, whose immaculate streets and toy-town houses were built by Quakers in order that they be a haven from alcohol of all sorts. However, times changed. Corporate breweries gradually moved in on the stubborn right-wing council with many plans (and frankly bribes) in order that their products find a small, frowned-upon market in the town. Even so, by any modern city's standards, WGC is possibly the worst place in England for a pub-crawl. Just two hostelries grace the town – one a steak-house affair, all corporate beams, salad-bar and uniforms; the other, The 'Layers.

And it's in the truly horrible confines of the latter that the wisdom of the city council finally reveals itself. They realised that regardless of how quickly one could clean the streets, they couldn't ever fully eradicate the anti-social underclass of their beloved town. Granted, there were only three dozen at most – considered modest under-achievers by fellow crims elsewhere – but exist they did. And in the same manner in which a skate-board park is reluctantly agreed upon as recreation for dispossessed youth, The 'Layers, sandwiched as it was between the back end of John Lewis and a disused office space, was allowed to continue trading more as a policy of containment than as appeasement. During opening hours, the shoe-borne bobbies could rest safe in the knowledge that all the town's scallies were safely getting hammered there. Any trouble outside could easily be dealt with by a few heavy-handed enquiries at the bar after the event. Typical of small-time losers, there wasn't a single regular who wouldn't sell out a mate for a few pints loosely disguised as a liquid Community Action Trust reward.

Stranger still, the degenerates themselves loved the place. Pick any day bar Sunday, and by half-eleven in the morning there'd be over a dozen regulars finishing their first pint or starting their second. Stick a nervous head round the boarded door at one, and the place would be playing damp, sticky, nicotine and bleach-smelling host to its full complement of boozers. Indeed, the regulars at The 'Layers were probably the most loyal bunch of semi- and full-blown alcoholics in Southern England. Mostly living on the fringes of the town, poured into scarce, crumbling council accommodation (screened by a thankful border of hardy conifers), Welwyn Garden City's scarred, tattooed and largely unimaginative criminal underside spent the majority of their lives exactly where the city fathers wanted them – out of their heads in The 'Layers.

So, there you have it then, the location for our city crime tale, The 'Layers – a dog-turd in the encrusted temperance jewel of Welwyn Garden City. A threadbare, lozenge-shaped boozer, home to the town's entire sub-culture – and on one memorable April afternoon, home once more to Billy Adams the moment he put his shock of fair hair round the door.

'Hello bastards, I'm home!'

A subdued cheer weakly rippled round the lounge. Undeterred, Welwyn Garden City's most famous (and most unsuccessful) rocket-assisted robber strode to the bar.

'All right, Irene?' he asked of the middle-aged redhead filing her nails behind the bar. He checked out her bust. 'Jesus wept, Irene, I swear they get bigger every month.'

Irene, always one to accept even the crudest of compliments, rewarded him with a smile. 'Fine. You all right, Billy, love?'

'Champion.'

'When they let you out, then?'

'S'morning.'

'But they give you six months for that firework thingy, didn't they?' The firework *thingy*. Remember the WGC list of shame: the fencing punch-ups; knicker thief (twice); and the rocket let off in the shopping mall? Billy Adams lit the touchpaper.

'Got off on good behaviour, didn't I,' Billy winked, watching as Irene poured his pint.

She set it on a damp beer towel. 'Just can't see you as a good boy, Billy,' she suggestively replied. 'Never have done.'

'Just goes to show then, don't it?' he said, taking the first five inches straight out of his pint, and looking around the room. 'Jesus, same old faces. Some things never bleedin' change, eh?'

'You've only done three months' bird, Billy. Anyone listening to you'd think you'd just done a ten-stretch for bank robbing.'

At which point Billy tapped the side of his not-unhandsome nose. 'Speaking of which, got plans, ain't I?'

She sighed. 'Just leave it out, love, eh? A mug like yours is too pretty to end up behind bars.'

He smiled. 'Met some right tasty geezers in there. The real deal, Irene. Proper cons – legends, some of them – not like this bloody shower of no-hopers.' He took down the rest of his pint, returning to stare at her bust while she poured another. 'Give it a couple of months and I'll be out of this toilet, sunning myself somewhere exotic, believe you me.'

'Two sixteen,' she said, holding out a heavily jewelled hand. 'First one's on the house, the rest you pay for.'

Billy handed over the money. 'No worries, pet. Tell you what, eight weeks from now, I'll be bloody rolling in folding.'

At any given moment, understanding the working and motivating drives of the human mind is a near-impossible task. Introduce a colossal amount of alcohol into said mind and it becomes hopeless. Even the finest shrinks shrug and give up. So it was with Billy Adams' brief on the evening after his ill-fated rocket attack upon the premises of Mr Shoes in the precinct. Although his legal-aid client was still clearly pissed out of his box, any explanation as to why he undertook this pyrotechnic suicide mission was utterly beyond his psychology-student understanding. He went instead to Billy's last port of call – The 'Layers – and, at immense personal risk, enquired after Billy's state of mind shortly before the incident. There, the shocked young lawyer was told in no uncertain terms about Billy's mental state:

'Kid's a nutter.'

'Always off his head.'

'Bang the useless twat up. Throw away the soddin' key.'

Undeterred, Billy's brief returned to Hertford nick and got hold of Adams' file, sitting down to read a list of similarly bizarre, unsuccessful hold-up ventures stretching back to the boy's early teens. Two hastily-scrawled social worker and juvenile probation officers' reports reached the same conclusion as the pub regulars – Adams was a loner, prone both to drink and grand fantasies concerning his criminal status.

The following morning, while Adams sobered up in his cell, his brief tried his diplomatic best to break the news that this latest fracas would most likely bring about a custodial sentence.

'Finally!' Adams shouted, making a fist. 'Someone's taking me bloody seriously!'

For many angel-faced 22-year-old lads, the prospect of their first stretch inside would fill them with dread. But not Billy Adams. Oblivious to some of the more unsavoury aspects of his incarceration, and long experienced in the rigours and regimes of institutionalised life, he thought he had finally made the big time, been justly promoted into the premier league of persistent offenders. The sentence was proof. Shackled to the plastic seat in a mini-cell in the stale confines of a Group 4 security bus, he regaled the disinterested driver and assistant through the thin grey walls.

'Course, I'm related to the firm, you know.'

'Really,' came the muffled reply.

'Me dad was a cousin of one of the great train robbers. Straight up, me mum told me.' Which she had, many a time on her various infrequent visits to whatever juvenile home or bang-up Billy was currently guest at. 'He just met her one night, chatted her up, then nine months later – Bob's your mother's brother – out I pop. So, you know, I've got them gene things, ain't I? Can't help myself.'

He served out his sentence at HMP Chelmsford, spending twenty-three hours out of every twenty-four in a small Victorian cell with one Jimmy Taverner – forty-four, bearded, six-seven, with terrible teeth and seventeen years porridge already under his belt. Which, to wide-eyed Billy, was nothing short of a revelation. Day after day, the mentally unbalanced Taverner would regale his young charge with fictional tales of his own criminal prowess, before encouraging the lad to kip on the top bunk with him as it was 'the only way to keep out the cold, like'.

One morning, after a particularly athletic body-warming session, Billy got to telling Taverner of his own brief pyrotechnic foray into the world of the sophisticated heist.

'See, where you went wrong,' Taverner assured him, aware the youngster was hanging on his every word, 'was the identification thing.'

'And the drink,' Billy added.

'Well, obviously.'

'If I hadn't been out of my box, I'd never have lit the bloody thing. I only threaten 'em with it. But seeing as they was just sort of standing there, to open the till, what choice did I have?'

Taverner spent nearly a minute fighting a hacking cough, before beginning work on his first roll-up. 'Like I said, kid – identity. That's where you blew it.'

Billy sat quite still, hypnotised by his lanky mentor, oblivious to the obvious – that as a crim, Taverner's prison record pointed to a less than successful career in the trade himself. 'What you saying, then?'

'Well, see, way I would have pulled a caper like that was to disguise myself as another geezer entirely. Walked in in someone else's clobber, for example, their hat and coat, you know, someone recognisable as not being me.'

Briefly, Adams wondered how many of Hollywood's top make-up and prosthetic artists it would take to make Taverner's horribly gaunt grey face look like anyone else on the planet. Yet, in the same instant, the bearded sage's words hit a nerve of inspiration. The old lag was right. There was a guy in The 'Layers who'd have made the perfect fall guy for the failed rocket robbery. Dave 'the Dip' Baxter. A good deal older than Billy, but still with a shock of blonde hair, around the same body size –

and more importantly, known throughout the Welwyn Garden City area for always wearing the same tattered red ski-jacket with white stripes down both arms. Billy quickly re-played the dismal hold-up scene with the new wardrobe, saw himself strolling to the precinct in Baxter's jacket and a balaclava, the out-of-date *Starblaster!* rocket from Singh's in one hand, green plastic disposable lighter in the other. Adding swirling, impressive music, he approached the bewildered Mr Shoes counter-staff, pointed the massive firework threateningly and made his demands in the best imitation of Baxter's fag-shot voice that he could muster.

And this time, much to his amazement, the blagg worked! Take-two saw petrified staff assessing the threat quite differently. No stifled giggles this time, sideways glances or tapping of the head. This time (because in take-two, he was also straight-as-a-die sober) they knew he wasn't messing – or rather *Baxter* wasn't messing. Cash was duly nervously handed over, and Billy fled the precinct, a winner at last. (In a final denouement, Billy had the police turning up at The 'Layers to nick a bewildered, protesting Baxter for the crime, while the great robber himself sipped casually on his pint at the bar.)

Disguise – what could be simpler, more assured of success than that?

Over the next few weeks of his sentence, Billy Adams began at the brute stone of a vague plan, mentally chiselling, chipping and polishing it into the prime cut diamond that was to be his next caper. Fuelled by Taverner's many criminal insights, and powered by the overwhelming genetic confidence he felt as the son of a loosely connected mobster, day by day the heist took shape.

Nights, too, were spent privately obsessing over the fine details. As a result Taverner began losing interest in his young protégé, no longer inviting him up into the top bunk. To the old lag, Adams was simply a young dreamer – frankly one of the dimmest he'd ever met – and thus, as Taverner preferred something more of a challenge in his menfolk, he set his mind on Adams' release and the exciting arrival of his next new cell-mate (who, unfortunately for the bearded con, would turn out to be a pathological homophobic martial-arts expert from Yorkshire. Taverner would spend much of the next six months in the confines of the prison hospital, wondering how it all went so lamentably wrong).

So, on Billy's appointed day of release, he strolled from HMP Chelmsford to the town's bus station to catch the first green and yellow double-decker back to Welwyn Garden City full of hope, excitement and enthusiasm. He felt wiser, more experienced, initiated into the real world – and most importantly, he had a plan.

Looking back on the rocket misadventure (everyone makes mistakes, he assured himself) he now realised the full folly of it all. Mixing explosives and drink wasn't too smart even by his standards. What every successful crime needed was a germ of simplicity. The Mr Shoes debacle was far too complicated. The next blagg wouldn't merely embrace simplicity, Billy decided, it would take it for a candlelight dinner, woo it with whispered small talk, then make love to it passionately under a star-strewn sky.

Smash-and-grab at John Lewis. In a disguise – specifically Dave ('the Dip') Baxter's signature red and white anorak. Brilliant. Brilliantly *simple*. Simplicity enjoying a post-coital cigarette after finally surrendering to weeks of seduction in Billy's mind.

Location was the key, specifically the back entrance to the grandiose department store and the many cases of expensive jewellery just inside said doors. Both within a short sprint of The 'Layers. All he'd need do was somehow persuade (or nick) Baxter's jacket from him while the old pickpocket sank a few in The 'Layers, belt round to the front entrance of John Lewis, cruise through the store with his head down (a masterstroke, this – Billy realising the full value of the overhead CCTV cameras getting a blurred evidential shot of 'Baxter' making his way towards the rear of the store), put on a balaclava as he approached the jewellery counter, out with the concealed mini lump-hammer – POW, SMASH! – in goes Billy's hands as he pulls out a glittering fistful of priceless swag. Then leg it as fast as possible through the back doors. Seconds later, trouser pockets bulging with looted gems, he removes Baxter's jacket, slips back into The 'Layers – (and frankly, here came the tricky bit) – somehow engineers Baxter's jacket back on to the oblivious owner's chair, then joins the throng at the bar in wondering what all the sirens and excitement are about. Time taken to complete the task? Round about two minutes, from leaving the pub until returning. Foolproof.

And it didn't stop there. This was a plan that had had weeks to mature and fester inside Billy's genetically-distant criminal mind. Even the after-touches were nothing short of genius. When the police would eventually arrive at The 'Layers to arrest a protesting Baxter, a quick search of his anorak would reveal an incriminating gem left purposefully in one pocket, and the yellow balaclava (a present from Billy's mother for his eighteenth) in the other. He estimated he'd then have thirty-six hours before the police would eliminate Baxter as the culprit – 'the Dip' being something of an opportunist felon himself, and all alibi witnesses in the pub unlikely to be initially believed by plod, either. Thirty-six hours. An escape window, during which time the young master criminal would fence the gems to a bloke he knew in Hatfield, before fleeing the country for sunnier climes armed only with some swimming trunks, passport, a wad of cash and a dog-eared copy of *Costa Del Crime – Where the Hardmen Live*. In less than a month, Billy felt sure he'd be the chief guest at Ronnie Knight's pool-side barbecues.

All that now remained was to put his plan into action.

'All right, Dave? How's it all going, mate?'

Dave 'the Dip' Baxter looked up from his copy of *Railway and Signals Monthly* with some suspicion.

'Not still reading that old crap, are you?' Billy asked, seating himself at the small, round table known collectively as 'the Dip's spot'. 'Signals and trains, eh? Dull as bloody ditchwater to me.'

Baxter did what he always did when others invaded his space – simply glowered at the intruder, then carried on with his mag, re-immersing himself in a well-written piece about the inherent signalling problems bought about by the track-laying activity in the Southampton area in the late '50s.

''Course,' Billy went on, undefeated, 'there's been many a man like you and I that's made a pretty few bob on the railways, eh?' He tapped at the side of his nose just in case Baxter hadn't got the reference. 'Bit of red gel over a green light late at night, a dozen geezers by the trackside, one cosh – whack! – whoops, there goes the money from the overnight mail train.'

'Just bugger off, son, while you still got the legs to do it on.'

Anxious not to let so small a thing as imminent physical violence blight his criminal progress, Billy remained seated. 'Now is that the way to treat a lad who's just done a six-stretch at Her Maj's pleasure?'

For once, breaking his own cardinal rule, Baxter allowed his eyes to travel back up from the magazine to the young idiot before him. Lad by the name of Billy Adams, he knew that much. The pratt with the rocket in the shopping centre and the loose line of eternal chat about how his mother got banged up by a distant relative of Biggs and co, now grinning at him like a lobotomised chimp. A kid who'd never sat opposite him in his life, but who suddenly professed an interest in bonding through a railway magazine. 'What the hell are you after?'

Billy pulled mock-offended. 'Just a chat.'

'We've had it. Now sod off.'

Undaunted, Billy devoted the next few days to patching some of the larger holes in his plan. Firstly there was the matter of the police. Aware of the two travelling pairs of plod cruising the immediate vicinity of both the pub and John Lewis, he began his own covert surveillance operation, looking for any routine or pattern to their beats. He felt not a little unlike those good British fellows in Colditz, timing the goon-runs, working out the best moment to pull off their audacious escapes: except the Welwyn Garden City police didn't take Nazi prison-camp guard duty as a model for their own patrols. Sadly, there appeared to be no fixed routine for their ambling. One day they walked clockwise about the town, the next anti-clockwise. Another day all four would stop for a cup of tea and a doughnut in the precinct, whereas the following day neither pair would meet. It began to look like Billy would have to give up to sheer mother luck that on his big day neither patrol would be within a hundred yards of John Lewis (the time he estimated it would take him to reach the post-heist safety of The 'Layers), or he would surely be spotted and nicked.

The more he followed the police, the more their seemingly slap-dash approach to beat patrol both depressed and annoyed him. Their very lack of a routine could puncture his whole plan – nay, career. And what an ignominious end that would make – Billy Adams, nicked at the very beginning of his lifetime's commitment to superior criminality, simply because PC bloody-nobody had decided to stop for a BLT at the sandwich bar on the afternoon in question, It was a risk, he realised with increasing gloom, that he simply couldn't afford to take.

Likewise, things weren't exactly progressing smoothly on the 'befriending Baxter' front. If he'd had thinner skin (and a sharper mind) Billy could well have given up by now, identifying Baxter's obvious annoyance as the real thing. Certainly, the old pickpocket seemed loath to surrender to Billy's charms. But the one quality the aspiring robber had in abundance was persistence. Bundles of it. Annoying great wodges of it, as Baxter, not normally a violent man but who'd been pushed damn close by the young pretender, was finding out in spades.

It was around this time that an inspirational thunderbolt crashed across Billy's clouded sky. Exactly a week after his release, he came to the sudden conclusion that perhaps both of these thorny problems could be solved at the same time. Two birds with the one stone. Granted, it would mean sacrificing a little of the loot – but hell, this was his first proper job after all.

Billy's new plan owed a lot to his genetic inheritance – or rather, the fact that the train robbers acted as a gang, an outfit, a firm. It was an audacious plan, and had taken a group of men to hold up the train, not merely one kid in someone else's anorak. So it was, then, that Billy decided the only way forward was to – three deep breaths – invite 'the

Dip' in on the scam. And surely, once he was fully aware of the raw simplicity of this imminently successful crime – how could the man resist his
own small part in it?

The following afternoon, Billy explained all to Baxter. The 'Layers
was predictably full of regulars and fag smoke, so once or twice he had to
raise his voice above the stage whisper he thought suitable for such occasions. At the end of it, Baxter (who'd never taken his eyes from a
humorous piece about the lost-and-found office at Dudley Central)
closed his magazine and looked up coldly.

'That is without a doubt,' he said slowly, 'quite the stupidest scheme
I've ever heard in my life.'

Billy leant forward. 'Ah, but *brilliantly* stupid, eh?'

'Oh, undeniably.'

'Well?'

'Well what?'

Billy leant in even closer. 'Are you in, or what?'

'Let me get this straight, you were going to implicate me in all this
mess?'

'Only temporarily, like. The coppers would soon have guessed it
couldn't have been you. No hardship, is it?'

Baxter shook his head wearily. A brief internal 'what the hell are the
kids of today coming to?' monologue flashed across his mind. The boy
was simply beyond all help. And quite possibly the most useless partner
in crime since Frankenstein's assistant robbed the wrong brain for his
creation. And yet... and yet...

It's interesting to focus in on Dave 'the Dip' Baxter for a moment,
because, despite all the small-fry drifters in The 'Layers, the Cockney
railway-obsessed pickpocket was in reality an extremely successful criminal. Emphasis on *was*. Unlike the others, Baxter didn't measure his success on the amount of prison biro tattoos he had on his forearms – rather
it was the fact that despite committing *over four thousand* separate
offences during a twenty-five year spree, he'd never been caught, never
spent a single day inside. It was, quite simply, a legendary feat, well
known, respected and grudgingly admired on both sides of the law
throughout central London – but largely unheard of in Welwyn Garden
City. Which suited Baxter fine.

He'd come to the place seven years previously, honouring a vow he'd
always made to himself to retire from 'the business' on his fortieth
birthday. The signs were all there, classic pointers that all dips dreaded –
the hands getting slower, heavier, the crowds on the Underground wising

up to pickpocketing generally. He considered himself lucky to have got away with it for so long (sometimes in heavy disguise right under the noses of the London Transport Police so desperate to nail him), and resolved to retire as king-of-the-dips while he was still on top. The news shocked the criminal underworld. Baxter had become something of an institution. They even had a leaving do for him in a South London club. Three DIs and an Assistant Police Commissioner turned up to anonymously shake the hand of the man who had outwitted them for so long.

How had he got away with it for over twenty years? It was a mixture of things: dedication, a clean bachelor lifestyle, persistent practice – and most fundamentally, never going back on his own word. Thus, when Baxter decided his fingers had earned a rest, he stuck by it, heading out for Welwyn Garden City – a place he suspected (quite accurately) would be devoid of serious temptation for the retired pickpocket.

So confident was he of his new law-abiding status that on his second week in the Garden City, he'd walked right up to one of the beat-patrol officers and politely introduced himself, before giving them a brief rundown of the London years. Hurried phone-calls were made from Hertford nick to the Met. Next, Baxter found himself summoned to the offices of one DCI Corkerham, Hertford CID, where it was explained in no uncertain terms that from now on, Welwyn Garden's patrolling officers would be keeping a careful eye on his every move.

'No problem,' Baxter reassured the nervous DCI. 'You'll always know me. I've left that life behind, burnt all the wigs, beards, glasses and silly disguises. I even got rid of my favourite jacket the other day – it had a completely false arm holding a rolled-up copy of the *Evening Standard*. Would have been worthy of a place in the dips' hall of fame. All gone. From now on,' he reached down by his chair, pulled out a red and white anorak from a John Lewis bag, 'I'll always be wearing this,' he smiled. 'So I'm going to stick out like a bleedin' sore thumb, ain't I?'

And so began his long and daily acquaintance with the trademark garment. True to his word, he wore it whenever he ventured out, still smiling politely at the suspicious bobbies on the beat on his way to The 'Layers. Inside the pub, the regulars largely remained in ignorance of his true status. Granted he'd shown them a few bodged 'dips' early on, but since then had done what he enjoyed the most, sat quietly at his table, supping a pint and reading railway mags. And up till fairly recently, it had been a largely satisfying, uneventful retirement. He'd slipped unnoticed into Welwyn' s criminal fraternity, and had enjoyed his time there. He lived frugally, interest from shrewdly managed investments feeding and clothing him, but of late Dave Baxter had found another feeling rising steadily and overwhelmingly within. Boredom. There were no two ways to describe it; the quiet man with the glowering eyes, the 'right-on geezer' who'd lived more, done more and achieved more than the others would in forty lifetimes, was colossally bored. And he knew the impending price of it. Sooner or later, he'd be tempted back into his previous ways. If he didn't do something smartish, he'd be getting the first train back to London, trying to pick up and dip into a career he'd left well behind. How much better it would be, he often mused, to catch the train the other way, up North, head for a new beginning somewhere quaint and quiet – Bridgnorth, perhaps; put down a deposit on a small terrace within whistling distance of the Severn Valley Steam Railway. But he'd need some funds, a few grand to tide him over, and he was reluctant to untie his investments for what was really little more than a pipe-dream.

And then, of course, he met Billy Adams.

Over the following week, young Billy began to see the true wisdom of the modification to his plan. Involving Dave 'the Dip' had been an inspirational masterstroke. The man, Billy was fast realising, was something of a dark horse. Billy even reckoned that if the old fella had been born with a little more confidence, a pinch of extra savvy (in short, not a lot unlike himself) he might really have made something of himself.

It hadn't surprised him, either, the speed at which The Dip had agreed to his part in the plan. After all, here was the old boy's chance to finally have a go at a real caper, not another of his watch-removing circus tricks. And he was growing into the role just fine, coming up with all sorts of ideas to improve the heist. Like the daily John Lewis run, for instance. Quite clever, this. The Dip had persuaded Billy that in order for the plan to work, it wasn't simply a matter of disguise (another area the old guy seemed to know tons of crucial stuff about!), but also, ironically, recognition. He reckoned that if he went through the store every day at around the same time, staff on various counters would become used to seeing him. Thus, come the big day, when Billy donned the anorak, staff would naturally assume it was The Dip on his daily round, cementing the identity confusion even further. Wow! See, Billy just knew the guy had the makings of something in him.

Sometimes, as the big day grew closer, the two of them would meet over at The Dip's flat, where Billy would be schooled how to imitate the same limp Baxter had been putting on as he walked through the store. The same hand gestures, too. A right-hand wave to the young girl on cosmetics, left to the old girl selling china cottages, two shakes of the right to the stuffy old geezer on menswear. He'd drawn up plans too, had The

Dip. Overhead renderings of the layout of the jewellery section, marking
out the entry route, chosen gem counter, the best side for smash and
grab, and exit route. It almost got to the stage whereby Billy wondered
who was most committed to the project – him or The Dip. He began to
wonder if the guy wasn't getting a little too fanatical, especially when he
began setting clandestine 'homework' written and verbal tests to ensure
Billy had the whole damn thing down pat. Whatever – Billy didn't really
mind. The way he saw it, it was the old boy's final fling, but his first shot.
Sure the geezer wanted to get it right, but next time Billy resolved to pick
a slightly less obsessive partner. Perhaps, he wondered mournfully, late
one night as he re-rehearsed his limp for the sixty-third time, perhaps the
railway magazines should have been some sort of clue.

As time went on, however, one issue remained unresolved in Billy's hopelessly overcrowded mind. What the hell were they going to do about the
flaming police patrols? Billy broached the subject one afternoon in The
'Layers.

'I mean, it's important, isn't it?' he moaned. 'It only takes a couple of
plod to be arsing about nearby when I come belting out with the gear,
and it's curtains.'

Baxter nodded, made as if to be giving the matter his most serious
thought. 'I'm already on to it, Billy.'

'And?' A group nearby burst into loud laughter.

'What we need is a diversion.'

Now this sounded good. 'Go on.'

'Way I see it,' Baxter explained. 'If we can tie up those four coppers
on some kind of phoney operation at the other end of town, then there's
no chance they're going to be bumping into you at this end.'

Genius! 'Took the words out of my very mouth,' Billy fudged.
'Diversion. Classic tactic. Winner every time.' He took a meaningful sip
at his pint. 'So... er... how are we going to, you know...?'

Baxter resumed reading the article in his mag. 'Already working on
it, Billy,' he quietly replied. 'Already working on it.'

Now at about this time, Welwyn Garden City fell prey to the begin-
nings of perhaps the most devastating potential crime in its largely
trouble-free history. A real crime, proper stuff rendering rocket attacks,
garden-fence disputes and knicker nicking pathetic in its wake.

A secretary at the Weetabix plant arrived early one morning to find a
large brown envelope in her in-tray. Opening it, she was shocked to discover an empty packet of razor blades and the following note, fashioned
from single cut-out letters:

TEN GRAND IN LOCKER NUMBER SEVEN AT THE
STATION BY 2:30PM ON MAY 26TH – OR THE NATION
STARTS WAKING UP TO SOMETHING SLIGHTLY
SHARPER IN THEIR BREAKFAST
NO POLICE – OR THE BLADES GO IN.
I'LL BE WATCHING!

Being a loyal employee, the breathless secretary immediately showed it to her boss, who (also being a loyal company man, and hence fully aware of procedures in such cases) alerted Hertford CID within minutes.

Within four hours, the note was undergoing full forensic testing at the National Crime Lab in Milton Keynes. Six white-coated officers gave it their full and undivided attention before passing the note back to Hertford CID with their findings.

At two that afternoon, DCI Corkerham sat in the smallest of the three Weetabix conference rooms addressing a nervous executive.

'Well, gentlemen,' he said. 'Firstly, let me congratulate you on turning the matter straight over to us.'

Smiles all round.

'So, do you want the good news, or the bad?'

No response, so Corkerham pressed on.

'We'll start with the bad. Firstly, I can tell you that it's probably not a hoax.'

Someone groaned from the other side of the large table.

'It was clean of prints and grammatically correct, two pointers I always look for.' Corkerham stressed the 'I' part, keen to impress upon the executive not only a completely false line of experience in company blackmail (it was his first time), but also to imply that the conclusion was his alone. As he saw it, they didn't really need to know that he'd spent the majority of the day sitting on his backside waiting for the boffins to work their magic.

'So we're going to have to pay up then, are we?' the chiefest-looking executive asked. 'Give in?'

Corkerham smiled, milking the silence. 'The next thing I noticed, however, was the first of this blackmailer's mistakes. He'd...'

'Or she'd,' a short woman at the other end of the table who Corkerham hadn't spotted before, suddenly piped up.

'Or she,' Corkerham conceded, 'had most probably used letters cut from the same few pages of the same magazine.' He handed round colour copies of the note. 'See how many brown letters there are, same size and typeface, all against a blue background?'

The executive collectively nodded. 'And that's some sort of pointer, is it?' one asked.

'It is when you re-arrange them,' the beaming DI replied, handing round a second series of colour copies, each with *'END OF THE LINE FOR THE STEAM AGE,'* constructed from the aforementioned brown letters. 'A short enquiry revealed your blackmailer constructed his note from last month's copy of *Railway and Signals Monthly,'* Corkerham announced, in a rather more dramatic fashion than the chaps at Milton Keynes had previously told him over the phone. 'And when I looked into the availability of said publication in the Welwyn Garden City area, I discovered that this opportunist isn't a disgruntled member of your staff...'

'Inspector,' the old guy interrupted. 'I can assure you none of my staff are disgruntled.'

Corkerham let it pass. 'He is instead one Dave Baxter – the only local to actively reserve a copy of the magazine from New-News in the precinct.'

A brief silence settled over the room, no one seemingly able to move the conversation on. Finally, the boss spoke again. 'And you're sure it's him, are you?'

'He's an old-time crook, believe you me,' Corkerham replied. 'We've been keeping our eye on him for a while.'

'Seems like quite a blunder to make,' the boss continued, scanning both copies on the table in front of him. 'I mean, surely he should have chosen a few different, less incriminating magazines to make his note from.'

Corkerham smiled, thinking – people like these, when will they ever learn? 'Thing is, in most cases, your average crook's a pretty dumb animal. Baxter's like all the rest. He's kept his head low for a few years, nose clean, but now he's getting restless, greedy, making mistakes. He's like an old prize-fighter on a comeback trail – ring-rusty. Only this time, he's going to get walloped.'

'But what if,' objected the woman, 'he's simply having a joke with us?'

'An empty razor-blade pack?' Corkerham replied. 'Is that something you can afford to joke about?'

She blushed slightly.

'And I take it you've arrested this man, Inspector?' the boss asked.
'Not yet, no.'

Which was met by a few raised eyebrows. 'Can I ask why not?'

'What for? All he's done is send a threatening letter. Even if we could make the charge stick, chances are all he'd get is a JP slapping him on the wrist. No, the plan is this: to do exactly as the letter asks – then nick… er, arrest Baxter when he shows up and collects the money. Bingo – he'll be doing five years minimum.'

There was a collective murmur at this one, before all eyes deferred to the boss once more. 'Inspector,' he said calmly. 'Are you saying you want this company to comply with this lunatic's request?'

Corkerham nodded.

'You want us to leave ten thousand pounds in a bag in a railway locker?'

'Where's the harm? I'll have the place watched by the entire City police force. Nothing will get into the station without our knowing. And the moment he gets his hands on the bag, we'll swoop and slap the cuffs on him.'

It was the woman again. 'Surely we should mark the money in some way,' she suggested. 'You know, just in case?'

Corkerham tried his level best to disguise his irritation. 'Life, I'm afraid ' he slowly said, 'isn't as simple as your average episode of *The Bill*, Miss.'

'It's Mrs,' she fired back, stung by a stifled snigger to her left. 'And I don't have a television, either.'

Explained a lot, Corkerham thought, turning back to the boss. 'So, like I said, bit of bad news, buckets of good. Rustle up the money, and we'll have your blackmailer. And think of the press mileage you'll get out of that.'

The boss nodded, already way ahead of Corkerham on that one.

'So,' Baxter said, on the night before the big job. 'Let's go over it one more time.'

Billy sighed, tired, let his eyes give out a 'do I have to?' expression.

'For me, son,' Baxter urged. 'Just to put my mind at rest.'

Billy nodded, sat a little straighter on Baxter's sofa. He supposed that's how it was with some people – the little guys like The Dip – nerves creeping in the night before a job. Which is precisely why he was one of the other guys – the big guys – casual, assured of success. But he'd do it, anyway, just to calm the guy down.

'We meet in The 'Layers at one. Have a couple. Around one-forty-five, you're going to slip out in my coat to pull off your little diversion thing. Five to two, I nip out in your jacket, stroll round to the front of…'

'Limp round,' Baxter stressed. 'As we practised.'

Billy nodded, stifled a yawn. Jesus, the guy was taking it seriously. 'Limp round to the front of John Lewis, walk through the store, do all the waving and greeting stuff…'

'Head down this time, though. Don't let them get too good a look at you.'

'Head down,' Billy conceded. 'Then stick the balaclava on as I approach the gems, out with the lump-hammer, do the business, leg it out back to the boozer. You're back, waiting outside the back door. We swap coats, and I take the gems. You go in the back, I walk round and wander back in through the front with a bacon sandwich in my hand asking everyone what all the alarms are about.'

'Don't forget to buy the bacon sarny on the way to the pub, either.'

Billy tapped at the side of his head. 'It's all in here, don't worry.'

'And then what?'

'I contact you through a postcard in a couple of weeks, you fly out and we split the loot fifty-fifty.'

Baxter smiled. 'Go it in one, son,'

They were both silent for a moment, dreaming their separate dreams.

Adams slumped back on to the sofa. 'The old diversion thing going to work then, is it?'

'Like clockwork, son, don't you worry. Those dozy coppers won't be within five-hundred yards of you.'

'How d'you manage that then?'

'Less you know the better.'

Billy nodded, conceding the point. As it was, his head was already crammed to capacity with detail. The guy looked confident, so he'd have to trust him.

And basically, wasn't the diversion part of the plan the least important part? Billy reckoned it was only right to let The Dip covet it as his. For himself, he had the serious stuff to worry about. Now, what was it again – left-hand wave to the girl on cosmetics, or right...?

'Know what?' he said lazily. 'You're all right, you are.'

Baxter said nothing.

'I mean, when I met you, like, I thought you was a bit of a nobody, you know, like the others. And there's not everybody who could pull off the stooge role. Make it their own, like you have. Perhaps, in a few months, we could try it again, somewhere else. If you're up for it, like.'

'We'll see, Billy. We'll see.'

One o'clock the following day, and the main players had already taken their opening positions. A group of six men are trying to look anonymous in the lobby of Welwyn Garden City station, comprising DCI Corkerham, two jumpy executives from Weetabix and three out of the four uniformed officers normally out patrolling the streets. Incredibly, they all chew gum. Ten minutes previously, they had deposited the blue holdall full of money in locker number seven as instructed, and now stand in a loose group fifteen yards away, waiting. Corkerham himself took command of the locker key, pocketing said item with an air of ruthless efficiency.

'Thing is,' the smaller of the two Weetabix men explained in a hushed whisper. 'I don't understand how this Baxter chap ever expects to even get the money. What's he going to do, blow the locker open?'

'Another classic mistake,' Corkerham reassured him. 'Typical crim, doesn't think these things through. Most probably reckons the note will have scared you enough not to tell us about it. Then all he needs is a couple of minutes with a tool, and he's jimmied the lock, grabbed the cash and *fled.*'

'But he's not going to do that, is he?' the second cereal-man asked, fearful of a career-ending calamity if the money moved so much as an inch from the locker. 'Maybe Lilian was right,' he whispered. 'Maybe we should have marked the cash.'

Corkerham merely gave him a look.

Billy Adams walked into The 'Layers at three minutes after one, mini lump-hammer and balaclava in one coat pocket; a bagged, warm bacon sandwich in the other. It had been a mistake, he now realised, to ask the girl to add extra brown sauce. The smell was slightly more than obvious.

As agreed, Billy gave only the briefest of nods across to The Dip whilst ordering a beer. His heart began to race as he saw the 'okay' signal (Baxter scratching the side of his head) being returned.

'Two sixteen, Billy love.' It was Irene, holding out a hand for her money.

'Oh, sure,' Billy flustered. 'Miles away.'

'You all right, love?'

''Course. Why?'

'Only you haven't said nothing about my tits or anything.'

Billy cleared his throat. 'Well, you know... they're great. As they always are.'

She looked at him quizzically. Then sniffed. 'Can you smell bacon in here?'

A trickle of sweat ran down his back. 'Bacon? No. I don't think so.'

'Only if you're thinking of coming in here and eating your own food, you can forget it.'

'Not me, Irene. Never.' He went and sat at a table across from Baxter, glad of the beer to ease his wretchedly dry mouth.

Half-past one, and Corkerham made a discreet radio call to the last member of the Welwyn Garden City police. 'Turnip, you there?'

PC Andrew Turner's voice cracked back: 'In position, Sir. At the back of The 'Layers. About thirty yards from the doors. Freezing me nuts off, truth be told.'

'You got a good view of Baxter'?'

'I can see him through the back windows. Calm as a bloody cucumber. Got in there about forty minutes ago, ordered a pint. He's been sat down ever since.'

Corkerham nodded. It was all going amazingly well to plan. Turnip had the guy eye-balled, the money was in the locker, now they were waiting for Baxter's every move. 'Don't take your eyes off him, son. You call me the moment he leaves, understand?'

'Copy on that, sir.'

'Over and out.' Corkerham slid the radio back into his pocket, turned to the other four men and gave them a brief thumbs-up.

Eight minutes to two, and Billy spotted The Dip strolled casually over to the gents. Leaving it for twenty seconds, he took a last swig of his drink and followed. Inside, they were thankfully alone. They silently exchanged coats, Billy slipping into the only stall.

'Six minutes,' Baxter whispered, pulling up the collar on Billy's long greatcoat and handing him the sandwich, lump-hammer and yellow balaclava. 'Good luck, son.'

Billy nodded, closing the door and zipping up Baxter's red and white anorak. He just about heard The Dip's retreating footsteps over his own beating heart. He sat on the closed toilet lid and tried to steady his nerves, eyes totally fixed on the ticking secondhand of his watch.

One minute…

Two minutes…

Three minutes… and someone banged on the door of the cubicle…

Four minutes… they gave up waiting and wandered away muttering obscenities…

The longest fifth minute in the history of time…

Finally – thankfully – the second hand climbed to the end of the sixth minute.

Billy stood, shook his head to clear it, crossed himself, checked his pockets, flushed the toilet, then stepped out to begin his genetic date with criminal destiny.

'That's him, Guv, he's leaving the premises now!'

Corkerham felt the adrenaline rush through him as he gripped the radio. 'Sure? You sure it's Baxter?'

'Affirmative. Red and white jacket, same limp as the boys at security in John Lewis tipped us off about.'

Corkerham punched the air, mouthed 'He's coming!' to the others. The radio crackled again. 'Hang about, Sir.'

'What is it?'

'I don't know... he's...'

'What?'

'Heading into John Lewis, Sir .'

'John Lewis?' A sudden, dark dread fell over the excited detective.

'What the hell's he...?' What if – and it completely pained him to think about it – what if he'd been wrong? What if the dozy Weetabix woman had been right? What if the whole blackmail note was simply a seam, some sort of hoax?

'He's going in, Sir. What shall I do?'

Corkerham's mind raced. Something was very wrong here. Baxter, going into John Lewis? He'd already been tipped off by shop security that Baxter had been cruising through the store most every day. What if?... But still it was too devastating to think about, too unbelievable. Had Baxter had the jump on him all the time? Never. Things like that simply didn't happen. Not to him, the great DCI Corkerham. All crims were dim and DCI Corkerham could never be conned, ever. 'Stay on him, Turnip,' he barked, avoiding the others' curious glances. 'Just don't lose him, understand!'

Next came a distant sound that would haunt Corkerham and blight his CID career path for the next few years. Just a quiet tinkling at first, difficult to make out above the incoming train announcement nearby. Turning ashen, Corkerham realised what it was. An alarm.

The radio crackled into life once more. 'Sir! Something's gone off in the store! Bloody alarms all over the place!'

'Jesus Christ!' Corkerham exclaimed, turning to the others. 'He's only gone and stuffed us, hasn't he? Pulled a bloody job on the other side of town while we've been stood here like bloody puddings!' He turned on the three officers. 'John Lewis – now!'

The two Weetabix men watched in stunned bemusement as all four police rushed from the station lobby. The smaller one winced as Corkerham collided with a bottle-glassed trainspotter just outside, landing in an undignified heap. His taller colleague couldn't help but

Phil Lovesey

laugh at the scene, then, feeling a sense of public duty, wandered over to the bewildered spotter and gentlemanly helped the poor loser on to his feet.

'You all right, sir?' he politely asked.

The spotter brushed himself down. 'What's the bleeding hurry then?'

'Police business.'

'Well, they should be more careful.'

The Weetabix man was saved replying by a minute's madness of the incoming train and arrival of several dozen passengers. After the lobby finally cleared and the train journeyed on, he looked across at his colleague, the familiar face now deathly pale, an arm loosely pointing to the open door of locker number seven. Empty.

Neither man said a word.

It was another seven minutes before they turned off the alarms in John Lewis.

And on the 2.02 from Welwyn Garden City to Birmingham New Street, a bespectacled trainspotter in a shabby dark overcoat, vaguely smelling of brown sauce, sat holding a blue holdall on his lap and smiling at a private joke the other passengers could only guess at.

WHITE KNIGHTS, BLACK MAGIC

VAL McDERMID

This was the very first contribution I received after I'd invited CWA members to let me have 'Crime in the City' stories for consideration. Although each year the editor of the CWA anthology receives many more manuscripts than can possibly be included in a single volume, there was never any doubt in my mind that this particular story would be one of the highlights of this collection – and not just because of its unusual setting and plot. From the gripping first sentence to the menacing conclusion, Val McDermid's story exemplifies modern crime writing at its most compelling.

When night falls in St Petersburg, the dead become more palpable. In this city built on blood and bone, they're always present. But when darkness gathers, they're harder to escape. The frozen, drowned serfs who paid the price for Peter the Great's determination to fulfil Nostradamus's prediction that Venice would rise from the dead waters of the north; the assassinated tsars whose murders changed surprisingly little; the starved victims of the Wehrmacht's 900-day siege; the buried corpses of lords of the imagination such as Dostoevsky, Borodin and Rimsky-Korsakov – they're all there in the shifting shadows, their foetid breath tainting the chilly air that comes off the Neva and shivers through the streets.

My dead too. I never feel closer to Elinor than when I walk along the embankment of Vasilyevsky Ostrov on a winter's night. The familiar grandeur of the Hermitage and St Isaac's cathedral on the opposite bank touch me not at all. What resonates inside me is the sound of her voice, the touch of her hand, the spark of her eyes.

It shouldn't be this way. It shouldn't be the darkness that conjures her up for me, because we didn't make those memories in the dead core of winter. The love that exploded between us was a child of the light, a dream state that played itself out against the backdrop of the White Nights, those heady summer weeks when the sun never sets over St Petersburg.

Like all lovers, we thought the sun would never set on us either. But it did. And although Elinor isn't one of the St Petersburg dead, she comes back to haunt me when the city's ghosts drift through the streets in wraiths of river mist. I know too that this is no neutral visitation. Her presence demands something of me, and it's taken me a long time to figure out what that is. But I know now. Elinor understood that Russia can be a cruel and terrible place, and also that I am profoundly Russian. So tonight, I will make reparation.

Three summers ago, Elinor unpacked her bags in the Moscow Hotel down at the far end of Nevsky Prospekt. She'd never been to Russia before, and when we met that first evening, she radiated a buzz of excitement that enchanted me. We Russians are bound to our native land by a terrible, doomed, sentimental attachment, and we are predisposed to like anyone who shows the slightest sign of sharing that love.

But there was more than that linking us from the very beginning. Anyone who has ever been in an abusive relationship has had their mental map altered forever. It's hard to explain precisely how that manifests itself, but once you've been there, you recognise it in another. An almost imperceptible flicker in the eyes; some tiny shift in the body language; an odd moment of deference in the dialogue. Whatever the signals, they're subconsciously registered by those of us who are members of the same club. In that very first encounter, I read that kinship between myself and Elinor.

By the time I met Elinor, I was well clear of the marriage that had thrown me off balance, turned me from a confident, assured professional woman into a bundle of insecurities. I was back on even keel, in control of my own destiny and certain I would never walk into that nightmare again. I wasn't so sure about Elinor.

She seemed poised and assertive. She was a well-qualified doctor who had gained a reputation for her work on addiction with intravenous drug users in her native Manchester. She was the obvious choice for a month-long exchange visit to share her experiences with local medical professionals and voluntary sector workers struggling to come to terms with the heroin epidemic sweeping St Petersburg. She exuded a quiet competence and an easy manner. But still, I recognised the secret shame, the hidden scars.

I had been chosen to act as her interpreter because I'd spent two years of my post-graduate medical training in San Francisco. I was nervous about the assignment because I had no formal training in interpreting, but my boss made it clear there was no room for argument. The budget wouldn't run to a qualified interpreter, and besides, I knew all the technical terminology. I explained this to Elinor over a glass of wine in the half-empty bar after the official dinner with the meeting-and-greeting party.

Some specialists might have regarded my confession as a slight on their importance. But Elinor just grinned and said, 'Natasha, you're a doctor, you can probably make me sound much more sensible than I can manage myself. Now, if you're not rushing off, maybe you can show me round a little, help me get my bearings?'

We walked out of the hotel, round the corner to the Metro station. Her eyes were wide, absorbed by everything. The amputee war veterans round the kiosks; the endless escalator; the young woman slumped against the door of the train carriage, vodka bottle dangling from her fingers, wrecked mascara in snail trails down her cheeks; Elinor drank it all in, tossing occasional questions at me.

We emerged back into daylight at the opposite end of Nevsky Prospekt, and I steered her round the big tourist sights. The cathedral, the Admiralty, the Hermitage, then back along the embankment to the Fontanka Canal. Because she was still operating on UK time, she didn't really register the White Nights phenomenon at first. It was only when I pointed out that it was already eleven o'clock, and she probably needed to think about getting some sleep, that she realised her normal cues for waking and sleeping were going to be absent for the next four weeks.

'How do you cope with the constant light?' she said, waving an arm at a sky only a couple of shades lighter than her eyes.

I shrugged. 'I pull the pillow over my head. But your hotel will have heavy curtains, I think.' I flagged down a passing Lada and asked the driver to take us back to the hotel.

'It's all so alien,' she said softly.

'It'll get worse before it gets better,' I told her. I dropped her at the hotel and kept the car on. As the driver weaved through the potholed streets back to my apartment on Vasilyevsky Ostrov, I couldn't escape the image of her wide-eyed wondering face.

But then, I wasn't exactly trying.

Over the next week, I spent most of my waking hours with Elinor. Mostly it was work, constantly stretching my brain to keep pace with the exchange of information that flowed back and forth between Elinor and my colleagues. But in the evenings, we fell into the habit of eating together then strolling round the city so she could soak up the atmosphere. I didn't mind. There were plenty of other things I could have been doing, but my friends would still be there after she left town. What I wasn't allowing myself to acknowledge was that I was falling in love with her.

On the sixth night, she finally started opening up. 'You know I mentioned my partner?' she said, filling our wine glasses to avoid my eyes.

'He's a lawyer, right?' I said.

Her mouth twisted up at one corner. 'He's a she.' She flicked a quick glance at me. 'Does that surprise you?'

I couldn't keep the smile from my face. For days, I'd been telling myself off for wishful thinking, but I'd been right. 'It takes one to know one,' I said.

'You're gay?' Elinor sounded startled.

'Labels are for medicines,' I said. 'But lately, I seem to have given up on men.'

'You have a girlfriend?' Now, her eyes were on mine. I didn't know what to read into their level stare, which unsettled me a little.

'Nothing serious,' I said. 'A friend I sleep with from time to time, when she's in town. Just fun, for both of us. Not like you.'

She looked away again. 'No. Not like me.'

Something about the angle of her head, the downcast eyes and the hand that gripped the wine glass told me my first instinct had been right. Whatever she might say next, I knew that this apparently confident woman was in thrall to someone who stripped her of her self-esteem. 'Tell me about her,' I said.

'Her name's Claire. She's a lawyer, specialising in intellectual property. She's very good. We've been together ten years. She's very smart, very strong, very beautiful. She keeps my feet on the ground.'

I wanted to tell her that love should be about flying, not about the force of gravity. But I didn't. 'Do you miss her?'

Again, she met my eyes. 'I thought I would. But I've been so busy.' She smiled. 'And you're such good company, you've kept me from being lonely.'

'It's been my pleasure. Where would you like to go this evening?'

Her gaze was level, unblinking. 'I'd like to see where you live.'

I tried to stay cool. 'It's not very impressive.'

'You don't have to impress me. I'd just like to see a real Russian home. I'm fed up with hotels and restaurants.'

So we took the Metro to Vasileostrovskaya and walked down Sredny Prospekt to the 10th Line, where I live in a two-roomed apartment on the second floor. Buying it took every penny I managed to save in the US, and it's pretty drab by Western standards, but to a Russian, it feels like total luxury to have so much space to oneself. I showed Elinor into the living room with some nervousness. I'd never brought a Westerner home before.

She looked round the white walls with their Chagall posters and the second-hand furniture covered with patchwork throws, then turned to me and smiled. 'I like it,' she said.

I turned away, feeling embarrassed. 'Interior design hasn't really hit Russia,' I said. 'Would you like a drink? I've got tea or coffee or vodka.'

'Vodka, please.'

There is a moment that comes with drinking vodka Russian-style when inhibitions slip away. That's the time to stop drinking, before you get too drunk to do anything with the window of opportunity. I knew Elinor had hit the moment when she leaned into me and said, 'I really love this country.'

I pushed her dark hair away from her forehead and said, 'Russia can be a very cruel place. We Russians are dangerous.'

'You don't feel very dangerous to me,' she whispered, her breath hot against my neck.

'I'm Russian. I'm trouble. The two go together like hand in glove.'

'Mmm. I like the sound of that. Your hand, my glove.'

'That would be very dangerous.'

She chuckled softly. 'I feel the need for a little danger, Natasha.'

And so we made trouble.

Of course, she went back to England. She didn't want to, but she had no choice. Her visa was about to expire, she had work commitments at home. And there was Claire. She had said very little about her lover, but I understood how deeply ingrained was her subservience. The clues were there, both sexually and emotionally. Claire wasn't physically violent, but emotional abuse can cause damage that is far more profound. Elinor had learned the lesson of submission so thoroughly it was entrenched in her soul. No matter how deep the love that had sprung up between us, in her heart she couldn't escape the conviction that she belonged to Claire.

It didn't stop us loving each other. We emailed daily, sometimes several times a day. We managed to speak on the phone every two or three weeks, sometimes for an hour at a time. A couple of months after she'd gone back, she called in distress. Claire had accepted a new job in London, and was insisting Elinor abandon her work in Manchester and move to the capital with her. I gently suggested this might be the opportunity for Elinor to free herself, not necessarily for me but for her own sake. But I knew even as I spoke it was pointless. Until Claire decided it was over, Elinor had no other option but to stay. I understood that; I had only managed to free myself when my husband had grown tired of me. I wanted to save her, but I didn't know how.

Three months later, they'd moved. Elinor had found a job at one of the London teaching hospitals. She didn't have the same degree of autonomy she'd enjoyed in Manchester, and she found it much less challenging. But at least she was able to use some of her expertise, and she liked the team she was working with.

I was actually reading one of her emails when my boss called me into his office. 'You know I'm supposed to go to London next week? The conference on HIV and intravenous drug use?'

I nodded. Lucky bastard, I'd thought, when the invitation came through. 'I remember.'

'My wife has been diagnosed with breast cancer,' he said abruptly. 'They're operating on Monday. So you'll have to go instead.'

It was an uncomfortable way to achieve my heart's desire, but there was nothing I could do about my boss's misfortune. A few days later, I was walking through customs and immigration and into Elinor's arms.

We went straight to my hotel and dived back into the dangerous waters. Hand in glove. Moths to a flame.

Four days of the conference. Three evenings supposedly socialising with colleagues, but in reality, time we could steal to be together. Except that on the last night, the plans went spectacularly awry. Instead of a discreet knock at my bedroom door, the phone rang. Elinor's voice was unnaturally bright. 'Hi, Natasha,' she said. 'I'm down in reception. I hope you don't mind, but I've brought Claire with me. She wanted to meet you.'

Panic choked me like a gloved hand. 'I'll be right down,' I managed to say. I dressed hurriedly, fingers fumbling zip and buttons, mouth muttering Russian curses. What was Claire up to? Was this simply about control, or was there more to it? Had she sussed what was going on between Elinor and me? With dry mouth and damp palms, I rode the lift to the ground floor, trying to hold it together. Not for myself, but for Elinor's sake.

They looked good together. Elinor's sable hair, denim-blue eyes and olive skin on one side of the table, a contrast to Claire's blonde hair and surprising brown eyes. Where Elinor's features were small and neat, Claire's were strong and well defined. She looked like someone you'd rather have on your side than against you. While Elinor looked nervous, her fingers picking at a cocktail coaster, Claire leaned back in her seat, a woman in command of her surroundings.

As I approached, feeling hopelessly provincial next to their urban chic, Claire was first to her feet. 'You must be Natasha,' she said, her smile lighting her eyes. 'I'm so pleased to meet you.' I extended a hand, but her hand was on my shoulder as she leaned in to kiss me on both cheeks. 'I've been telling Elinor off for keeping you to herself. I do hope you don't mind me butting in, but I so wanted to meet you.'

Control, then, I thought, daring to let myself feel relieved as I sat down at the table. At once, Claire stamped her authority on the conversation. How was I enjoying London? Was it as I expected? How were things in Russia? How was life changing for ordinary people?

By the time we hit the second drink, she was flirting with me. She wanted to prove she could own me the way she owner her lover. Elinor was consigned to the sidelines, and her acquiescence to this confirmed all I believed about their relationship. My heart ached for her, an uneasy mixture of love and pity making me feel faintly queasy. I don't know how I managed to eat dinner with them. All I wanted was to steal Elinor away, to prove to her she had the power to take her life back and make of it what she wanted.

But of course, she left with Claire. And in the morning, I was on a plane back to St Petersburg, half convinced that the only healthy thing for me to do was to end our relationship.

I didn't. I couldn't. In spite of everything I know about the tentacles of emotional abuse, I found it impossible to reject the notion that I might somehow be Elinor's saviour. So I kept on writing, kept on telling her how much I loved her when she called, kept on seeing her face in my mind's eye whenever I slept with other people.

More weeks trickled by, then, out of the blue, an email in a very different tone arrived. 'Natasha, darling. Can you get to Brussels next weekend? I need to see you. I can arrange air tickets if you can arrange a visa. Please, if it's humanly possible, come to Brussels. I love you. E.'

I tried to get her to tell me what was going on, but she refused. All I could do was fix up a visa and collect the tickets from the travel agent. When Elinor opened the hotel room door, she looked a dozen years older than when I'd seen her in London. My first thought was that Claire had discovered our affair. But the truth was infinitely worse.

We'd barely hugged when Elinor was moving away from me. She curled up in the room's only armchair and covered her face with her hands. 'I'm so scared,' she said.

I crouched down beside her and gently pulled her hands away from her face. 'What's wrong, Elinor?'

She flicked her tongue along dry lips. 'You know I'm mostly working with HIV patients now?'

It wasn't what I'd expected to hear, but somehow, I already knew what was coming. 'Yes, I know.'

A deep, shuddering breath. 'A few weeks ago, I got a needle stick.' Her eyes filled with tears. 'Natasha, I'm HIV positive.'

Intellectually, I knew this wasn't a death sentence. So did Elinor. But in that instant, it felt like the end of the world. I couldn't think of anything else that would assert her right to a future, so I cradled her in my arms and said, 'Let's make love.'

At first, she resisted. But we both knew too much about the transmission routes of the virus for the idea of putting me at risk to take deep root. Sure, it meant changes for how we made love, but that was a tiny price to pay for the affirmation that her life would go on.

We spent the weekend behind closed doors, loving each other, talking endlessly about what she'd have to do to maximise her chances of long-term health. At some point on Sunday, she confessed that Claire had refused to have sex since the diagnosis. That made me angrier than anything I'd previously known or suspected about the abuse of power between the two of them.

That parting was the worst. I wanted to take her home with me. I wanted our passion to be her cocoon against the virus. But realistically, even if she'd been able to leave Claire, we both knew her best chance for access to the latest treatments would be to remain in the West.

Oddly, in spite of the cataclysmic nature of her news, nothing really changed between us. The old channels of communication remained intact, the intensity between us diminished not at all. The only difference was that now we also discussed drug treatments, dietary regimes and alternative therapies.

Then one Monday, silence. No email. I wasn't too worried. There had been days when Elinor hadn't been able to write, but mostly those had been on the weekend when she'd not been able to escape Claire's oppressive attention. Tuesday dragged past, then Wednesday. No reply to my emails, no phone call. Nothing. Finally, on the Thursday, I tried to call her at work.

Voicemail. I left an innocuous message and hung up. Friday brought more silence. The weekend was a nightmare. I checked my email neurotically, every hour, on the hour. I was afraid to go out in case she called, and by Sunday night, my apartment felt like a prison cell. Monday, I spoke to her voicemail again. Desperation had me in its grip. I even considered taking the chance of calling her at home. Instead, I hit on the idea of calling the department secretary.

'I've been trying to contact Dr Stevenson,' I said when I finally got through.

'Dr Stevenson is away at present,' the stiff English voice said.

'When will she be back?'

'I really can't say.'

I'd been fighting fear for days, but now my defences were crumbling fast. 'Look, I'm a personal friend of Elinor's,' I said. 'From St Petersburg. I'm due to be in London this week and we were supposed to meet. But I've had no reply to my emails, and I really need to contact her about our arrangements. Can you help me?'

The voice softened. 'I'm afraid Dr Stevenson's very ill. She won't be well enough to have a meeting this week.'

'Is she in hospital?' Somehow, I managed to keep hold of my English in the teeth of the terror that was ripping through me.

'Yes. She's a patient here.'

'Can you put me through to the ward she's on?'

'I'm… I'm sorry, she's in intensive care. She won't be able to speak to you.'

I don't remember ending the call. Just the desperate pain her words brought in their wake. I couldn't make sense of what I was hearing. It ran counter to all I knew about HIV and AIDS. It was a matter of months since Elinor had been infected. For her to be so ill so soon was virtually unheard of. People lived with HIV for years. Some people lived with AIDS for years. It was impossible.

But the impossible had happened.

I spent the next couple of days in a frenzy of activity, staving off my alarm with action. I couldn't afford the flight, but I managed to get the money together by borrowing from my three closest friends. I couldn't explain to my boss why I needed the time off and we were under pressure at work, so there was no prospect of making it to London before the weekend. The rest of my spare time I spent trying to sort out a visa.

By Thursday evening, I was almost organised. The travel agent had sworn she would call first thing in the morning about last-minute flights. I'd managed to persuade a colleague to cover for me at the beginning of the following week so I had a couple of extra days in hand. And the visa was promised for the next afternoon.

I'd just walked through the door of my apartment when the phone rang. I ran across the room and grabbed it. '*Da?*'

Breathing rasped in my ear. 'Natasha.' Elinor's voice was little more than a whisper but there was no mistaking it.

'Elinor.' I couldn't speak through the lump in my throat.

'I'm dying, Nat. Pneumocystis. Drug-resistant strain.' She could only speak on the exhalation of her shallow breaths. 'Wanted to call you. Brain's fucked, couldn't remember the number. Claire wouldn't... bring me my organiser. Had to get nurse to get it from my office.'

'Never mind. We're talking now. Elinor, I'm coming over. At the weekend.'

'No. Don't come, Nat. Please. I love you too much. Don't want you to remember... this. Remember the good stuff.'

'I want to see you.' Tears running down my face, I struggled to keep them out of my voice.

'Please, no. Nat, I wanted you to know... loving you? Best thing that ever hit me. Wanted to say goodbye. Wanted to say, be happy.'

'*Ya tebyeh lublu,*' I gulped. 'Don't die on me, Elinor.'

'Wish I had... choice. Trouble with being a doctor... you know what's happening to you. A couple of days, Nat. Then it's... DNR time. I love you.'

'I know.'

The breathing stopped and another voice came on the line. 'Hello?

I'm sorry, Dr Stevenson is too tired to talk any more.'

'How bad is it?' I don't know how I managed to speak without choking.

'I shouldn't really speak to anyone who isn't immediate family,' she hedged.

'Please. You saw how important this call was to her. I'm a doctor too, I know the score.'

'I'm afraid her condition is very serious. She's not responding to treatment. It's likely we'll have to put her on a ventilator very soon.'

'It's true she's signed a DNR?'

'I'm very sorry,' the nurse said after a short pause.

'Take good care of her.' I replaced the phone as gently as if it had been Elinor's hand. I'd spent enough time in hospitals to read between the lines. Elinor hadn't been mistaken. She was dying.

I never went to London. It would have been an act of selfishness. Claire never called me, which told me that she knew the truth. But the nurse from intensive care did phone, on the Sunday morning at 9.27 am. Elinor had asked her to let me know when she died. A couple of weeks later, I wrote to Claire, saying I'd heard about Elinor's death from a colleague and expressing my sympathy. I'm not sure why I did, but sometimes our subconscious paves the way for our future actions without bothering to inform us.

Grief twisted in me like a rusty knife for a long time. But everything transmutes eventually, and slowly it turned to anger. Generally when people die, there's nobody to blame. But Elinor's death wasn't like that. The responsibility for what happened to her lay with Claire, impossible to dodge.

If Claire had not ruled her with fear, Elinor would have left her for me. If Claire had not stripped her of her self-confidence, Elinor would have stayed in Manchester and someone else would have suffered that needle stick. However you cut it, Elinor would still be alive if Claire had not made her feel like a possession.

For a long time, my anger felt pointless, a dry fire burning inside me that consumed nothing. Then, out of the blue, I had an email from Claire. 'Hello, Natasha. I'm sorry I never got in touch with you after Elinor's death, but as you will imagine, it was not an easy time for me. However, I am attending a conference in St Petersburg next month, and I wondered if you would like to meet up for dinner. I have such fond memories of the evening we spent together in London. It might bring us both some solace to spend some time together. Let me know if this would suit you. Best wishes, Claire Somerville.'

The arrangements are made. Tonight, she will come to my apartment for dinner. I know she will seduce me. She won't be able to resist the challenge of possessing the woman Elinor loved.

But Claire is a Russian virgin. She doesn't understand the first thing about us. She will have no sense of the cruelty or the danger that always lurks beneath the surface, particularly in this city of the dead.

She will not suspect the narcotic in the alcohol. And when she wakes, she won't notice the scab on the vein in the back of her knee. The syringe is loaded already, thick with virus, carefully maintained in perfect culture conditions.

It's almost certain she'll have longer than Elinor. But sooner or later, the black magic of those White Nights will take its revenge. And perhaps then, my dead will sleep.

THE FALLEN CURTAIN

RUTH RENDELL

Ruth Rendell has written many acclaimed short stories, but 'The Fallen Curtain' was one of the earliest. It first appeared in *Ellery Queen's Mystery Magazine* and it subsequently earned an Edgar from the Mystery Writers of America. It is a story of enduring power, which to my mind offers a very distinctive spin on the theme of 'Crime in the City'.

The incident happened in the spring after his sixth birthday. His mother always referred to it as 'that dreadful evening', and always is no exaggeration. She talked about it a lot, especially when he did well at anything, which was often as he was good at school and at passing exams.

Showing her friends his swimming certificate or the prize he won for being top at geography: 'When I think we might have lost Richard that dreadful evening! You have to believe there's Someone watching over us, don't you?' Clasping him in her arms: 'He might have been killed – or worse.' (A remarkable statement, this one.) 'It doesn't bear thinking about.'

Apparently, it bore talking about. 'If I'd told him once, I'd told him fifty times never to talk to strangers or get into cars. But boys will be boys, and he forgot all that when the time came. He was given sweets, of course, and *lured* into this car.' Whispers at this point, meaning the glances in his direction. 'Threats and suggestions – persuaded into goodness knows what – I'll never know how we got him back alive.'

What Richard couldn't understand was how his mother knew so much about it. She hadn't been there. Only he and the Man had been there, and he couldn't remember a thing about it. A curtain had fallen over that bit of his memory that held the details of that dreadful evening. He remembered only what had come immediately before it and immediately after.

They were living then in the South London suburb of Upfield, in a little terraced house in Petunia Street, he and his mother and his father. His mother had been over forty when he was born and he had no brothers or sisters. ('That's why we love you so much, Richard.') He wasn't allowed to play in the street with the other kids. ('You want to keep yourself to yourself, dear.') Round the corner in Lupin Street lived his gran, his father's mother. Gran never came to their house, though he thought his father would have liked it if she had.

'I wish you'd have my mother to tea on Sunday,' he once heard his father say.

'If that woman sets foot in this house, Stan, I go out of it.'

So gran never came to tea.

'I hope I know what's right, Stan, and I know better than to keep the boy away from his grandmother. You can have him round there once a week with you, so long as I don't have to come in contact with her.'

That made three houses Richard was allowed into: his own, his gran's, and the house next door in Petunia Street where the Wilsons lived with their Brenda and their John. Sometimes he played in their garden with John, though it wasn't much fun as Brenda, who was much older, nearly sixteen, was always bullying them and stopping them getting dirty. He and John were in the same class at school, but his mother wouldn't let him go to school alone with John, although it was only three streets away. She was very careful and nervous about him, was his mother, waiting outside the gates before school ended to walk him home with his hand tightly clasped in hers.

But once a week he didn't go straight home. He looked forward to Wednesdays because Wednesday evening was the one he spent at gran's, and because the time between his mother's leaving him and his arrival at gran's house was the only time he was ever free and by himself.

This was the way it was. His mother would meet him from school and they'd walk down Plumtree Grove to where Petunia Street started. Lupin Street turned off the Grove a bit further down, so his mother would see him across the road, waving and smiling encouragingly, till she'd seen him turn the corner into Lupin Street. Gran's house was about a hundred yards down. That hundred yards was his free time, his alone time.

'Mind you run all the way,' his mother called after him.

But at the corner he always stopped running and began to dawdle, stopping to play with the cat that roamed about the bit of waste ground, or climbing on the pile of bricks the builders never came to build into anything. Sometimes, if she wasn't too bad with her arthritis, gran would be waiting for him at her gate, and he didn't mind having to forgo the cat and the climbing because it was so nice in gran's house. Gran had a big TV set – unusually big for those days – and he'd watch it, eating chocolate, until his father knocked off at the factory and turned up for tea. Tea was lovely; fish and chips that gran didn't fetch from the shop but cooked herself, cream meringues and chocolate eclairs, tinned peaches with evaporated milk, the lot washed down with fizzy lemonade. ('It's a disgrace the way your mother spoils that boy, Stan.') They were supposed to be home by seven, but every week when it got round to seven, gran would remember there was a cowboy film coming up on TV and there'd be cocoa and biscuits and potato crisps to go with it. They'd be lucky to be home in Petunia Street before nine.

'Don't blame me,' said his mother, 'if his school work suffers next day.'

That dreadful evening his mother left him as usual at the corner and saw him across the road. He could remember that, and remember too how he'd looked to see if gran was at her gate. When he'd made sure she wasn't, he'd wandered on to the building site to cajole the cat out of the nest she'd made for herself among the rubble. It was late March, a fine afternoon and still broad daylight at four. He was stroking the cat, thinking how thin and bony she was and how some of gran's fish and chips would do her good, when – what? What next? At this point the curtain came down. Three hours later it lifted, and he was in Plumtree Grove, walking along quite calmly ('Running in terror with that Man after him'), when whom should he meet but Mrs Wilson's Brenda out for the evening with her boyfriend. Brenda had pointed at him, stared and shouted. She ran up to him and clutched him and squeezed him till he could hardly breathe. Was that what had frightened him into 'losing his memory'? They said no. They said he'd been frightened before – ('Terrified out of his life') – and that Brenda's grabbing him and the dreadful shriek his mother gave when she saw him had nothing to do with it.

Petunia Street was full of police cars and there was a crowd outside their house. Brenda hustled him in, shouting, 'I've found him, I've found him!' and there was his father, all white in the face, talking to policemen; his mother half-dead on the sofa being given brandy; and – wonder of wonders – his gran there too. That had been one of the strangest things of that whole strange evening, that his gran had set foot in their house and his mother hadn't gone out of it.

They all started asking him questions at once. Had he answered them? All that remained in his memory was his mother's scream. That endured, that shattering sound, and the great open mouth from which it issued as she leapt upon him. Somehow, although he couldn't have explained why, he connected that scream and her seizing him as if to swallow him up, with the descent of the curtain.

He was never allowed to be alone after that, not even to play with John in the Wilsons' garden, and he was never allowed to forget those events he couldn't remember. There was no question of going to gran's, even under supervision, for gran's arthritis had got so bad they'd put her in the old people's ward at Upfield Hospital. The Man was never found. A couple of years later a little girl from Plumtree Grove got taken away and murdered. They never found that Man either, but his mother was sure they were one and the same.

'And it might have been our Richard. It doesn't bear thinking *of*, that Man roaming the streets like a wild beast.'

'What did he do to me, mum?' asked Richard, trying.

'If you don't remember, so much the better. You want to forget all about it, put it right out of your life.'

If only she'd let him. 'What did he *do*, dad?'

'I don't know, Rich. None of us knows, not me nor the police nor your mum, for all she says. Women like to set themselves up as knowing all about things, but it's my belief you never told her no more than you told us.'

She took him to school and fetched him home until he was twelve. The other kids teased him mercilessly. He wasn't allowed to go to their houses or have any of them to his. ('You never know who they know or what sort of connections they've got.') His mother only stopped going everywhere with him when he got taller than she was, and anyone could see he was too big for any Man to attack.

Growing up brought no elucidation of that dreadful evening but it did bring, with adolescence, the knowledge of what might have happened. And as he came to understand that it wasn't only threats and blows and stories of horror that the Man might have inflicted on him, he felt an alien in his own body or as if that body were covered with a slime that nothing could wash away. For there was no way of knowing now, nothing to do about it but wish his mother would leave the subject alone, avoid getting friendly with people and work hard at school.

He did very well there, for he was naturally intelligent and had no outside diversions. No one was surprised when he got to a good university, not Oxford or Cambridge but nearly as good – ('Imagine, all that brainpower might have been wasted if that Man had had his way') – where he began to read for a science degree. He was the first member of his family ever to go to college, and the only cloud in the sky was that his gran, as his father pointed out, wasn't there to see his glory.

She had died in the hospital when he was fourteen and she'd left her house to his parents. They'd sold it and theirs and bought a much nicer, bigger one with a proper garden and a garage in a suburb some five miles further out from Upfield. The little bit of money she'd saved she left to Richard, to come to him when he was eighteen. It was just enough to buy a car, and when he came down from university for the Easter holidays, he bought a two-year-old Ford and took and passed his driving test.

'That boy,' said his mother, 'passes every exam that comes his way. It's like as if he *couldn't* fail if he tried. But he's got a guardian angel watching over him, has had ever since he was six.' Her husband had admonished her for her too-excellent memory and now she referred only obliquely to that dreadful evening. 'When you-know-what happened and he was spared.'

She watched him drive expertly round the block, her only regret that he hadn't got a nice girl beside him, a sensible, hard-working fiancée – not one of your tarty pieces – saving up for the deposit on a house and good furniture. Richard had never had a girl. There was one at college he liked and who, he thought, might like him. But he didn't ask her out. He was never quite sure whether he was fit for any girl to know, let alone love.

The day after he'd passed his test he thought he'd drive over to Upfield and look up John Wilson. There was more in this, he confessed to himself, than a wish to revive old friendship. John was the only friend he'd really ever had, but he'd always felt inferior to him, for John had been (and had had the chance to be) easy and sociable and had had a girl to go out with when he was only fourteen. He rather liked the idea of arriving outside the Wilsons' house, fresh from his first two terms at university and in his own car.

It was a Wednesday in early April, a fine, mild afternoon and still, of course, broad daylight at four. He chose a Wednesday because that was early closing day in Upfield and John wouldn't be in the hardware shop where he'd worked ever since he left school three years before.

But as he approached Petunia Street up Plumtree Grove from the southerly direction, it struck him that he'd quite like to take a look at his gran's old house and see whether they'd ever built anything on that bit of waste ground. For years and years, half his lifetime, those bricks had lain there, though the thin old cat had disappeared or died long before Richard's parents moved. And the bricks were still there, overgrown now by grass and nettles. He drove into Lupin Street, moving slowly along the pavement edge until he was within sight of his gran's house. There was enough of his mother in him to stop him parking directly outside the house – ('Keep yourself to yourself and don't pry into what doesn't concern you') – so he stopped the car some few yards this side of it.

It had been painted a bright pink, the window woodwork picked out in sky blue. Richard thought he liked it better the way it used to be, cream plaster and brown wood, but he didn't move away. A strange feeling had come over him, stranger than any he could remember having experienced, which kept him where he was, staring at the wilderness of rubble and brick and weeds. Just nostalgia, he thought, just going back to those Wednesdays that had been the high spots of his weeks.

It was funny the way he kept looking among the rubble for the old cat to appear. If she were alive, she'd be as old as he by now and not many cats live that long. But he kept on looking just the same, and presently, as he was trying to pull himself out of this dreamy, dazed feeling and go off to John's, a living creature did appear behind the shrub-high weeds. A boy, about eight. Richard didn't intend to get out of the car. He found himself out of it, locking the door and then strolling over on to the building site.

You couldn't really see much from a car, not details, that must have been why he'd got out, to examine more closely this scene of his child-hood pleasures. It seemed very small, not the wild expanse of brick hills and grassy gullies he remembered, but a scrubby little bit of land twenty feet wide and perhaps twice as long. Of course it had seemed bigger because he had been so much smaller, smaller even than this little boy who now sat on a brick mountain, eyeing him.

He didn't mean to speak to the boy, for he wasn't a child any more but a Man. And if there is an explicit rule that a child mustn't speak to strangers, there is an explicit, unstated one, that a Man doesn't speak to children. If he had *meant* to speak, his words would have been very dif-ferent, something about having played there himself once perhaps, or having lived nearby. The words he did use came to his lips as if they had been placed there by some external (or deeply internal) ruling authority.

'You're trespassing on private land. Did you know that?'

The boy began to ease himself down. 'All the kids play here, mister.'

'Maybe, but that's no excuse. Where do you live?'

In Petunia Street, but I'm going to my gran's... No.

'Upfield High Road.'

'I think you'd better get in my car,' the Man said, 'and I'll take you home.'

Doubtfully, the boy said, 'There won't be no one there. My mum works late Wednesdays and I haven't got no dad. I'm to go straight home from school and have my tea and wait for when my mum comes at seven.'

Straight to my gran's and have my tea and...

'But you haven't, have you? You hung about trespassing on other people's property.'

'You a cop, mister?'

'Yes,' said the Man, 'yes, I am.'

The boy got into the car quite willingly. 'Are we going to the cop shop?'

'We may go to the police station later. I want to have a talk to you first. We'll go...' Where should they go? South London has many open spaces, commons they're called. Wandsworth Common, Tooting Common, Streatham Common... What made him choose Drywood Common, so far away, a place he'd heard of but hadn't visited, so far as he knew, in his life? The Man had known, and he was the Man now, wasn't he? 'We'll go to Drywood and have a talk. There's some chocolate on the dashboard shelf. Have a bit if you like.' He started the car and they drove off past gran's old house. 'Have it all,' he said.

The boy had it all. He introduced himself as Barry. He was eight and he had no brothers or sisters or father, just his mum who worked to keep them both. His mum had told him never to get into strangers' cars, but a cop was different, wasn't it?

'Quite different,' said the Man. 'Different altogether.'

It wasn't easy finding Drywood Common because the signposting was bad around there. But the strange thing was that, once there, the whole layout of the common was familiar to him.

'We'll park,' he said, 'down by the lake.

He found the lake with ease, driving along the main road that bisected the common, then turning left on to a smaller lane. There were ducks on the pond. It was surrounded by trees, but in the distance you could see houses and a little row of shops. He parked the car by the water and switched off the engine.

Barry was very calm and trusting. He listened intelligently to the policeman's lecture on behaving himself and not trespassing, and he didn't fidget or seem bored when the Man stopped talking about that and began to talk about himself. The Man had had a lonely sort of life, a bit like being in prison, and he'd never been allowed out alone. Even when he was in his own room doing his homework, he'd been watched – ('Leave your door open, dear. We don't want any secrets in this house') – and he hadn't had a single real friend. Would Barry be his friend, just for a few hours, just for that evening? Barry would.

'But you're grown up now,' he said.

The Man nodded. Barry said later when he recalled the details of what his mother called that nasty experience – for he was always able to remember every detail – that it was at this point the Man had begun to cry.

A small, rather dirty, hand touched the Man's hand and held it. No one had ever held his hand like that before. Not possessively or commandingly – ('Hold on to me tight, Richard, while we cross the road') – but gently, sympathetically – lovingly? Their hands remained clasped, the small one covering the large, then the large enclosing and gripping the small. A tension, as of time stopped, held the two people in the car still. The boy broke it, and time moved again.

'I'm getting a bit hungry,' he said.

'Are you? It's past your tea time. I'll tell you what, we could have some fish and chips. One of those shops over there is a fish and chip shop.'

Barry started to get out of the car.

'No, not you,' the Man said. 'It's better if I go alone. You wait here. OK?'

'OK,' Barry said.

He was only gone ten minutes – for he knew exactly and from a distance which one of the shops it was – and when he got back Barry was waiting for him. The fish and chips were good, almost as good as those gran used to cook. By the time they had finished eating and had wiped their greasy fingers on his handkerchief, dusk had come. Lights were going up in those far-off shops and houses but here, down by the lake, the trees made it quite dark.

'What's the time?' said Barry.

'A quarter past six.'

'I ought to be getting back now.'

'How about a game of hide-and-seek first? Your mum won't be home yet. I can get you back to Upfield in ten minutes.'

'I don't know… Suppose she gets in early?'

'Please,' the Man said. '*Please,* just for a little while. I used to play hide-and-seek down here when I was a kid.'

'But you said you never played anywhere. You said.'

'Did I? Maybe I didn't. I'm a bit confused.'

Barry looked at him gravely. 'I'll hide first,' he said. He watched Barry disappear among the trees. Grown-ups who play hide-and-seek don't keep to the rules, they don't bother with that counting to a hundred bit. But the Man did. He counted slowly and seriously, and then he got out of the car and began walking round the pond. It took him a long time to find Barry, who was more proficient at this game than he, a proficiency that showed when it was his turn to do the seeking. The darkness was deepening, and there was no one else on the common. He and the boy were quite alone.

Barry had gone to hide. In the car the Man sat counting – ninety-eight, ninety-nine, one hundred. When he stopped he was aware of the silence of the place, alleviated only by the faint, distant hum of traffic on the South Circular Road, just as the darkness was alleviated by the red blush of the sky, radiating the glow of London. Last time round, it hadn't been this dark. The boy wasn't behind any of the trees or in the bushes by the waterside or covered by the brambles in the ditch that ran parallel to the road.

Where the hell had the stupid kid got to? His anger was irrational, for he had suggested the game himself. Was he angry because the boy had proved better at it than he? Or was it something deeper and fiercer than that, rage at rejection by this puny and ignorant little savage?

'Where are you, Barry? Come on out. I've had about enough of this.'

There was no answer. The wind rustled, and a tiny twig scuttered down out of a treetop to his feet. God, that little devil! What'll I do if I can't find him? What the hell's he playing at?

When I find him I'll – I'll kill him.

He shivered. The blood was throbbing in his head. He broke a stick off a bush and began thrashing about with it, enraged, shouting into the dark silence, 'Barry Barry, come out! Come out at once, d'you hear me?' He doesn't want me, he doesn't care about me, no one will ever want me.

Then he heard a giggle from a treetop above him, and suddenly there was a crackling of twigs, a slithering sound. Not quite above him – over there. In the giggle, he thought, there was a note of jeering. But where, where? Down by the water's edge. He'd been up in the tree that almost overhung the pond. There was a thud as small feet bounced on to the ground, and again that maddening, gleeful giggle. For a moment the Man stood still. His hands clenched as on a frail neck, and he held them pressed together, crushing out life. Run, Barry, run... Run, Richard, to Plumtree Grove and Brenda, to home and mother who knows what dreadful evenings are.

The Man thrust his way through the bushes, making for the pond. The boy would be away by now, but not far away. And his legs were long enough and strong enough to outrun him, his hands strong enough to ensure there would be no future of doubt and fear and curtained memory.

But he was nowhere, nowhere. And yet... What was that sound, as of stealthy, fearful feet creeping away? He wheeled round, and there was the boy coming towards him, walking a little timidly between the straight, grey tree trunks *towards* him. A thick constriction gripped his throat. There must have been something in his face, some threatening gravity made more intense by the half-dark that stopped the boy in his tracks. Run, Barry, run, run fast away.

They stared at each other for a moment, for a lifetime, for twelve long years. Then the boy gave a merry laugh, fearless and innocent. He ran forward and flung himself into the Man's arms, and the Man, in a great release of pain and anguish, lifted the boy up, lifted him laughing into his own laughing face. They laughed with a kind of rapture at finding each other at last, and in the dark, under the whispering trees, each held the other close in an embrace of warmth and friendship.

'Come on,' Richard said. 'I'll take you home. I don't know what I was doing, bringing you here in the first place.'

'To play hide-and-seek,' said Barry. 'We had a nice time.'

They got back into the car. It was after seven when they got to Upfield High Road, but not much after.

'I don't reckon my mum's got in yet.'

'I'll drop you here. I won't go up to your place.' Richard opened the car door to let him out. 'Barry?'

'What is it, Mister?'

'Don't ever take a lift from a Man again, will you? Promise me?'

Barry nodded. 'OK.'

'I once took a lift from a stranger, and for years I couldn't remember what had happened. It sort of came back to me tonight, meeting you. I remember it all now. He was all right, just a bit lonely like me. We had fish and chips on Drywood Common and played hide-and-seek like you and me, and he brought me back nearly to my house – like I've brought you. But it wouldn't always be like that.'

'How do you know?'

Richard looked at his strong, young man's hands. 'I just know,' he said. 'Good-bye, Barry, and – thanks.'

He drove away, turning once to see that the boy was safely in his house. Barry told his mother all about it, but she insisted it must have been a nasty experience and called the police. Since Barry couldn't remember the number of the car and had no idea of the stranger's name, there was little they could do. They never found the Man.

A FRIEND IN NEED

KATHRYN SKOYLES

The long-term health of the CWA, like that of any other organisation, depends not merely on the success of its leading lights, but also on the zest and talent of its younger members. Kathryn Skoyles, formerly a partner in a large solicitors' practice, has in recent years sought to combine a career in business with first steps along the road to success with fiction. But, like many of us with a day job that is far removed from the world of literature, she faces the challenge of finding enough time to write. As a result, her first novel has been on the stocks for quite a while – but I am delighted that, in the meantime, she seized the opportunity presented by this book to write a short story featuring the protagonist of that novel, Sarah Marshall.

As the women walked down the alley towards Fleet Street, two men emerged from a hidden doorway. They went for Sarah first, perhaps because she was the smaller of the two. They punched her in the stomach and she crumpled to the ground. Laura was next. She stumbled and threw up her arms to protect her head as she hit the pavement. There was a flash in the darkness and a slithering sound as one of the men cut the strap of her handbag and it whipped around his wrist like a snake. The other one stepped across Laura's body, grasped her jaw in a hand as big as a dinner plate and shoved her face down hard. As he crouched to scoop up the tan leather briefcase still in Laura's hand, Sarah launched herself at him. He headed for the street and she missed him but she held on to the briefcase. She heard the screech of a car ignition and then the squeal of tyres as the car sped off towards St Pauls.

'Are you a relative?'

'No, a – a friend,' said Sarah. She hesitated. 'We came in together. Is she okay?'

'She's bruised and shocked but she'll live. We've stitched up her leg. You can both go home as soon as the nurse has finished up. She's just next door.' The doctor finished writing his notes with a flourish. 'There's a policeman waiting,' he added as he left. 'I'll send him in.'

Sarah collected her belongings and went to find Laura.

'How are you feeling?' she asked.

'A bit better than you, by the looks of things,' Laura replied. She might have said more, but they were interrupted.

'Ms Laura Johnson?' A hand, a head and then a policeman in uniform poked around the edge of Laura's curtain. 'I wonder, may I have a word?' He stepped inside the cubicle without waiting for an invitation. 'PC Colin McCulloch,' he said proudly. He looked at Sarah with the repressed eagerness of a young officer let out on his own for the first time and consulted his notebook. 'And you must be Ms Marshall?'

Sarah nodded half-heartedly as he expressed his regrets for the attack.

He turned to Laura and made an obvious effort to contain his excitement. 'What exactly happened?' he asked.

'We were coming out of Stationer's Hall. A lecture on human rights. We're both solicitors.' Laura smiled apologetically. 'I bumped into Sarah in the lobby. We haven't seen each other in years. We decided to go on for a drink, but we didn't get very far, I'm afraid.'

Laura looked at Sarah as she spoke. 'There were two of them,' she continued. 'I didn't really see their faces. It was dark and it all happened very fast. They must have wanted our handbags, but Sarah scared them off. That's it really.' Laura smiled sweetly at the policeman. Sarah kept quiet.

'What about you, Ms Marshall?'

'I... er...'

'You didn't see anything either, did you, Sarah?' said Laura.

'No, I suppose not.'

The policeman asked more questions but elicited no further information. Looking disappointed, he left his card with them, 'just in case you think of something else'.

'What's going on, Laura?' said Sarah as soon as he'd disappeared down the corridor.

'What do you mean, what's going on?' whispered Laura as she collected her belongings and lowered herself gingerly off the trolley. 'Nothing's going on.'

'They had knives, for Christ's sake. And they were waiting for us.' Sarah thought about that. 'For you? You must have got a good long look – he was standing right over you. Why didn't you say anything?'

'I just didn't want to make a fuss, that's all. You know they'll never catch anyone, so what's the point? Anyway, keep your voice down, will you?' She parted the curtains of the cubicle and nodded past Sarah's shoulder. The policeman was still loitering in the corridor by the waiting room. He was deep in conversation with another man, who was dressed in a dark suit and was muttering into the mobile phone he held like a walkie-talkie between his shoulder and his left ear. Plain clothes, Sarah guessed.

Sarah watched as a male nurse marched over to the two men, wagging a finger at the mobile phone. Laura was already heading for the exit. She was limping. Sarah grabbed her bag and followed.

They stood silently together on the pavement to wait for a cab. 'It's been a long time,' said Sarah.

'And still you haven't forgiven me?'

Sarah didn't reply and the cab was a long time in coming. Laura began to falter so Sarah offered an arm in support, but Laura shrugged it away.

'Where are you living now?' Laura said eventually, as if by way of apology. 'I forgot to ask.'

'Isle of Dogs,' replied Sarah. 'But we're taking you home first.'

Laura started to protest, then saw the look on Sarah's face. 'Fournier Street,' she said to the driver as she clambered in and pulled Sarah after her.

It was three in the morning when the taxi pulled up in front of Christ Church, Spitalfields. 'Save me getting into the one-way,' said the cabbie hopefully. Laura leant forward to get out and grimaced in pain. Sarah stepped out after her and quickly handed some cash to the driver.

'Don't be daft, Sarah. You won't find another cab round here at this time of night.'

'Then you'll just have to put me up for the night,' said Sarah firmly as she pocketed her change.

The house was in darkness apart from a lamp left on in the hall. Sarah realised that Laura was in no mood for girlish confidences over cocoa. They went straight to bed, Sarah in a spare room off the hallway. She hesitated when she realised that Laura was planning on taking the sofa in the room opposite, but Laura dismissed her protests.

'It's comfortable enough, believe me. And I don't want to wake Josh up,' she said.

Sarah looked puzzled.

'My partner. He's got a lot on his mind,' Laura explained. 'And Steve – my brother – he's in the other bedroom.'

Sarah was still at a loss.

'He's been staying with us for a while,' Laura continued. 'He'll want to do the caring, sharing bit. I don't think I can take that tonight.'

Sarah woke very early. At first, she thought it was just the unfamiliarity of her surroundings that had disturbed her but then she heard a low murmur from the sitting room. Laura, on the phone, Sarah thought. She drifted back to sleep. When she woke up again, it was mid-morning and Laura was gone.

Signalling failure meant that the trains were out of action again and it took Sarah over an hour to get home. She showered quickly, got dressed and hurried out of the flat. Her office was a few minutes' walk away, somewhat down-at-heel, but conveniently located above a row of shops in Manchester Road, between the chippie and the all-night grocer. She had already got the key in the lock when someone tapped her on the shoulder. She whirled round, scared.

'I'm so sorry,' he said. 'I didn't think.' It was the man with the mobile phone. He rifled through a leather satchel and produced a business card, discreet, the type that smart West End lawyers used to have before they hired graphic designers. All small letters and gilt-embossed typeface.

'Jackman. I'd like to ask you a few questions, Ms Marshall. About last night.'

'A private detective? I thought...' Sarah said warily.

'Can we go inside?'

Curiosity overcame her caution and Sarah invited him in. 'How did you find me?' she asked.

'Easy,' he boasted. 'You're a solicitor. The Law Society website?' He sat down, placed the satchel on the floor between his knees and retrieved a fistful of papers from it.

'And what do you want?'

'Laura Johnson. A routine enquiry,' he said as he shuffled his papers into order. 'Laura acts for my client. I'm looking into the, er, disclosure of some information. When I heard about last night...'

'It wasn't just her that got hurt,' replied Sarah archly.

'I guess that's why I'm here. How long have you known Laura?'

Sarah couldn't decide whether to boot him out or answer his questions. Curiosity again got the better.

'Long enough. We were at the LSE together, then did our articles at the same firm.'

'But you left there in...' he checked his papers '...1994?'

'Yes,' said Sarah. She wondered if that was on the website too.

'And now you're doing legal aid and she's still in the City?'

Sarah shrugged and waved her hands around the shabby office.

'Have you seen much of her recently?'

'Recently? No, our paths didn't cross.' Sarah laughed grimly. 'I bumped into her at the lecture.' She hoped he didn't notice her face flushing. She wasn't lying exactly, but she didn't feel like a lot of explanations. 'By accident,' she added.

'Do you know where we can find her now?'

'No. Do you?' Sarah thought about Laura's attitude at the hospital and about the early morning phone call. 'Where is she?'

'I promise you, we're as anxious to find her as you are. Maybe more. She has a lot of things to tell us.' He paused. 'We know all about it, you know. Your friend, Laura Johnson. Her – shall we say – indiscretion and your departure from the firm. Word is, she dropped you right in it.'

'There were lots of reasons to leave. And it's none of your business.'

'It might be. She's done it again. This time, she's cost us a lot of money. And not a small amount of embarrassment. She just can't keep her mouth shut.'

'Laura?'

'We checked. She had access. And this brother... '

'Steve?'

'Yeah, that's him. Calls himself a journalist but trades in shit, basically. He peddles nasty little stories about his elders and betters.' He waved his papers at her. 'And then you turn up again. Makes me wonder if we shouldn't be looking at you as well.'

'Is that a threat?'

'Threat? Oh, no, love, we don't do threats. We just want to know what else she's told them. Damage limitation and all that. Her partners will do the rest. She'll never work in the City again.' He bent to put his papers back in the satchel. 'Help us find her and maybe I'll forget about you.'

'Help you? Why should I do that, if Laura's such a good mate? Anyway, you've got it all wrong. Laura had no choice back then.' Sarah hesitated. 'Neither of us did.'

'Think what you like, love. But give her a message from me. Tell her I'll find her. That's all.'

'Actually, he's right. I am the leak.' Laura crossed her elegant legs and leaned back cautiously into the same tatty sofa that Jackman had occupied only a few hours before. Sarah couldn't help smiling wryly to herself at her unexpected popularity that day. After Jackman, Steve had called, and then Josh had turned up looking for Laura. Normally, Laura would have died rather than travel east of Tower Bridge, but now she was here too.

'Why're you telling me?'

'You're my friend, Sarah.'

'And?' Sarah replied without acknowledging Laura's unspoken question.

'And I need your help,' Laura confessed.

'My help?'

Laura leaned forward and spoke quietly, so that Sarah strained to hear.

'I need you to get Jackman off my back. Till this all gets sorted. It wasn't supposed to go this far. Josh promised me...'

'Promised you what?'

'That he'd leave me out of it. That we had to do something. They're in it up to their necks, you know. Child labour, dumping their shit products in Third World countries. We only wanted to publicise what was going on.'

Sarah stared in silence.

'I forgot,' said Laura eventually. 'That one won't work, will it?'

'It's what you said the last time,' said Sarah. 'I believed you. Made what came afterwards seem worth it somehow.'

Laura reddened. 'I'm so sorry,' she said. 'I didn't know where to turn. I've been so scared.' She burst into tears.

Sarah was unmoved. Laura had tried the tears last time, too. She stood up to show Laura out. 'It's Josh,' said Laura hurriedly. 'He'll kill me.'

They fished Laura's body out of the river two days later. Sarah said nothing then about her final meeting with Laura, nor did she give evidence at the inquest. Jackman waited for three months before he came to see her.

'She must have set the whole thing up from the beginning,' he said. 'The mugging, at least.'

'It might've worked,' said Sarah. 'You were sniffing around and she needed a way to hand the stuff over without bringing the roof down on her. They were just supposed to thump her a little, then grab the briefcase. No one really got hurt and the rest was all for show. Only I turned up and grabbed the briefcase back and everything went wrong from there.'

'I don't believe it was suicide,' he said. 'All that crap about the job.'

Sarah paused before responding. 'She told me Josh was going to kill her,' she said after a while.

'And did you believe her?'

'It was Laura's fault I had to leave, you know. Dad was so proud of me. "My daughter, the City lawyer." Afterwards, he wouldn't speak to me for a year. Mum died, and he didn't even tell me about the funeral. But through it all, I thought we were doing the right thing. Only then Josh came here to see me. He was angry. Thought I was poking my nose in.' Sarah laughed, a hollow tone in her voice. 'I think he assumed I knew all about it after last time. That they'd had a nice little earner going. Prying out secrets in his office and hers, and selling them to the highest bidder.'

Sarah breathed in deeply. 'So, do I think he killed her? Honestly? He was pissed off, but I don't know. Do I care? No.' She shook her head as if in disbelief at her own words. 'No, Mr Private Detective, I don't give a shit. She was a lying cow who wrecked my life without a second thought and then just walked away.'

'Why didn't you say anything?'

Sarah didn't answer at first. 'It's a different world out here, you know. It took me a long time to work that out. Five miles from the City and a planet away. I had no evidence it wasn't suicide and I wasn't prepared to look for any. So, what would I have said?'

'But she was your friend?'

'Friend?' said Sarah. 'Forget it.'

D O A

CATH STAINCLIFFE

This short, sharp and dark little story may come as a surprise to those who know of Cath Staincliffe through her series of books featuring the single mother turned private eye Sal Kilkenny. But despite her association with that series, Staincliffe is a writer keen to experiment and explore the boundaries of her craft and this piece is the result. There is one link with the Sal Kilkenny books, however: they too are set in Manchester.

DOA.
Johnny saw. Johnny saw blue.
Deep blue, blue as bone. Cold.

Like some place deep in the ocean with little light, full of neon fish. Bill used to have fish in a tank like that at his place, he reckoned they were good for the head. If you were wired, losing it, paranoid or whatever, Bill recommended a decent spliff, a carton of double-chocolate ice cream and an hour or so watching the fish dart and float in the tank.

Bill was away now. Someone had grassed him up and the Es in the back room got him four in Strangeways. Bill had asked Headcase to sort the house out but Headcase had got cabbaged in town and gone off to Blackpool with some girl who had a scam going. Time Headcase gets back the leccy's run out and all Bill's fish have frozen to death. Or boiled. Or suffocated. Something they needed from the little motor in the tank.

Johnny saw blue circles, spinning above, like light from a propeller. Loud light that whooped at him. Mint FX. Well cool. Maybe he was swimming except he couldn't feel water, no silky waves rocking him, no ripples or splashes, no chlorine or salt spray. Not warm. Not cold. Zero. Just the light above and below…?
    …a snake of fear needled through him, left him lurching but when he tried to trace it, to name it, he came up empty…
    …Below? The nearest he could get was air, like he was a hovercraft. Wished he could remember what he'd taken because this was a real mind-fucking trip.

Johnny spinning on a plate. Blue noise whipping him fast, like the lads on the Waltzers did with the talent: giving them a faster spin, something to get them squealing. All excited in among the hot smell of candyfloss and the gut-thump of boom-boxes.
    Johnny saw Lola spilling off the rides, breathless already, into his arms. Eyes teasing, violet eyes. Lola, legs apart and eyes wide open, moaning in her throat, hands on his back, on his arse.

Changed when she had Kim. He was made-up at first. Lovely girl like Lola, sweet baby. But it all unravelled. She was on at him all the time. Do this, do that, get this, get that. Endless bloody weeks of never enough of anything, never enough fags, or chips, or money. Not enough love. Dreams shrinking to the size of a crappy 14-inch repo set with a moody video.

Lola in tears or having a fit. Kim likewise. Did his best. Shifts at the airport, loading bags, seventeen years old, not even minimum wage. Job made no sense when Headcase or Bill could set him up with a nice little earner, score a month's pay in a night. Then Victor-bloody-Meldrew, supervisor in his poxy uniform accuses him of inefficiency. Jesuschrist, the bags got on or off or they didn't and he wasn't going to kill himself working up a sweat about it. Stuff the job.

Lola kicked him out at Christmas. Maybe he walked. Hard to tell.

You don't know how to be a father.

You never give me the chance.

Kim bawling.

Fuck off Johnny…

…Just like your fuckin' father.

His Mam calling him now. But he wasn't. Wasn't anything like his Dad who'd spent more time inside than out and spent his whole life being sorry, saying sorry, feeling sorry – for himself mainly. A wash-out of a man. No charm, no nous, no bloody point.

I'm not, Johnny had yelled, nothing like him. Freaked at the way his voice cracked and his eyes stung. Turning away. She could at least have stuck up for him. Her only son. Seen that he had done his best, done what he could to be a man and provide for them in this shit-heap. What more could he have done? Even the robbin' was for them, wasn't it?

You never gave us a chance, he told his Mam.

I had yer, didn't I? Fed you, clothed you?

Not enough.

It wasn't easy for me either.

You owe me…

What Johnny? Just what exactly?

Johnny saw but couldn't speak. There were moths in his throat. Large and blurry and soft. Saw how it should have been. Felt it, in the space between his ribs, in the back of his skull and the pit of his belly, that he deserved more, if only…

…spike of fear again. The blue swimming red and Johnny closing his eyes. Not liking the gush of the red, the colour clotting his vision.

Johnny listened instead to the whirl of sound, a spiral like a wolf's cry. Baying for him. Johnny danced with the sound, arms flung out, head back, reeling. The two-tones slowing and Johnny heard Lola moaning as they fucked, Lola screaming before they took her in for the Caesarian. Kim's wail cracking a thinner sound. Two notes over and over. Johnny, wheeling, heard the horns play; saxophones and trumpets chasing round each other.

Played in a Silver Band once, when he was a little kid; French horn and a blue uniform. Marching round the estate, neighbours out and smiling. Didn't last. Half the time it sounded like he'd stepped on the cat's tail or farted. Couldn't read the words, never mind the music. Never got on with reading. And the bigger lads began to take the piss. They worked out this plan to nick the instruments. Johnny had to tell them what the setup was. He told them about the padlocks and the metal cabinets and the bars across the doors. Not exactly a soft touch. They spent an hour at it with hammers and iron bars, Johnny as look-out. Then the neighbours came nosing and they were out of there. Total waste of time. And after, thinking where would they have got rid of twenty-three horns and bugles? Crap idea. Better stick to stuff that's easy to shift. VCRs, fags, sound systems, cameras, drugs, mobile phones.

In the whirl of sound Johnny heard an old train hooting. Then an owl. There'd been an owl in the park for a while where he and Lola went before Kim. Fuckin' spooky sound, that. Made you think of wild places, moors and haunted houses, not the city with the smell of rogan josh in the air and the drone of the traffic and carrier bags and takeaway trays blowing across the concrete.

Lola said it meant death, the cry of the owl.

For a mouse maybe...

Aw, fuck.

Johnny fell. Back into the space beneath him. Pictures tumbling through him like bloody Lottery balls.

A Beemer.

Headcase getting them in, disabling the alarm.

Not a job, just a laugh. Go for a spin.

Barrelling down the Parkway. The city falling away behind them.

Some Ragga on the CD player. M56. Pretty quiet. Dark. Headcase gunning it. Johnny rolling a fat one. No plan. A buzz from the speed and the smoke and the cheek of it.

Headcase sees the Old Bill first, races away. Fast as fuck. A whump and they're flying. Outer space, stars like rain.

Falling.

Voices.

Stretcher.

Ambulance.

In the blue Johnny cartwheels up, a satellite revolving through the howling. Fear bucking, protest rising.

No. Fuck no. Not enough. Please.

Then the wolf falls quiet, the blue fades, bleaches to white. Crystal light. Fear gone. Hope gone. All gone.

CLOSER TO THE FLAME

JERRY SYKES

Jerry Sykes is another of the contributors to this volume who represents the new generation of crime writers. Yet he already has a number of successful short stories, as well as the acclaimed anthology *Mean Time*, to his credit. Here he ventures much further afield than usual – to Austin, Texas. It is difficult, even in a relatively long short story, to present multiple viewpoints effectively, but here Sykes pulls off the trick. The result is a police story of considerable depth.

In the distance the surface of the Colorado River shimmered like snakeskin in the late afternoon sun. Small tufts of mist broke on the pebble shores and lifted into the air like tender smoke. On the near bank, the interstate rose out of the mosaic of motels and office blocks at the foot of the Convention Center, stalked across the river and disappeared into the emerald ripples of land that bordered the city to the south.

Dennis Lane stared out across the hill country where it seemed he had spent his entire childhood, alone and afraid, waiting for his father to return home with the latest form of discipline he had discovered to help him in his responsibility as a sole parent. His mother had died when Dennis was three and his father had struggled to look after him on his own. A willing student, he had listened to everyone from the school principal and the local doctor to his unmarried sister down in Galveston and his friends on the bowling team for advice. Not that it made any difference, in the end he had always fallen back on his hands, and Dennis had soon come to resent the people who had made his father feel such a failure: left to his own devices and free from second-hand expectations, he probably would have fared much better and Dennis himself would have been much happier. He closed his eyes for a moment and shook the memories from his head and then turned away from the hills.

Reflected in the side of the Convention Center he could see the dome of the State Capitol, an Austin landmark for over a hundred years. Built from pink granite quarried at nearby Marble Falls, the building had once been the seventh largest in the world and still drew an impressive number of visitors each year, but still nowhere near as many visitors as the building on which he himself now stood.

The sun broke free from the shade of the thunderheads that had started to bunch overhead, and he blinked at the sudden shock to his pupils and dropped his head to look out across the clipped spread of lawn at the foot of the tower. School had been out a couple of months but a number of students still decorated the area. In the far corner of the lawn a man dressed in purple tracksuit pants practised Tai Chi, calm and deliberate in his actions. To his left, a couple of jocks in UT colours hurled a football back and forth to the annoyance of a plump girl in red jeans trying to read a fat paperback. Beneath the shade of a cedar tree a couple of female students chatted quietly, and then all of a sudden one of them tossed back her head and fell flat on her back. She spread her arms in a sudden burst of emotion and stretched her thin limbs into the shape of a star, and at that Dennis felt a chill run up his spine.

On the first day of August 1966, a former marine named Charles

Whitman climbed into the observation deck of the University of Texas Tower and, armed with an assortment of weapons, started to snipe at unwary students and teachers on the campus. In what was then the largest simultaneous mass murder in American history, Whitman managed to shoot forty-five people, killing fourteen of them, before a pair of Austin police officers stormed the deck and killed the sniper himself.

Dennis recalled his father telling him about how he had listened to the incident live on KTBC, a cub reporter crouched behind the mobile news vehicle out on Guadalupe telling people to keep away from the UT Tower. Later in the broadcast, the reporter had read out a list of the victims to the anchorman in the studio. The anchor had listened in silence for a couple of moments and then broken in and said: 'Read that list again, please. I think you have my grandson on that list.'

Dennis could tell from his tone that his father had been impressed with the man's dedication to his job, his professionalism, but to Dennis the cold-bloodedness of the anchor's words struck a far greater chill in his young heart than the fatal actions of the killer himself. And it was a feeling that had stayed with him across the years. He took a deep breath and stepped back, reached out and ran his hand across the memorial plaque attached to the inside of the stone balcony. It had taken the people of Austin a long time to come to terms with the tragedy of that day over thirty years ago, and now another mass killer had struck at the heart of their city.

Bonnie Lane: Former Wife

He used to feel my period pains. Every month he'd get these cramps in his stomach at the same time that I started my period. And he always knew when it was going to happen. The same every month, as if he could sense what my body was going through. And I'm not one of those women that're that regular, y'know, so it's not like he could work it out or anything like that. I wouldn't have to tell him, and I never used to turn into some kind of monster with PMS so that it'd be obvious, it was as if he just knew. I mean, I never heard of that before, y'know. You hear about groups of women that live together – nuns, you hear about nuns – you hear about groups of women that live together falling into the same cycle – but guys and sympathetic pains? Uh huh. But Dennis was different. Oh, nothing serious, but a couple of times I remember that he couldn't eat anything for a day or so. And sometimes, sometimes he used to smoke pot to help ease the pain. He said it was as good as any painkillers you could buy in the drugstore. He used to bring home some of the stuff he'd confiscated from kids out on the street. Skim a little off the top, nothing too real, nothing too noticeable. Personal use, y'know. He tried to turn me on to it, but I... The only time I tried it I got sick and I never tried it again.

Griffin Clark, Austin PD: Partner, Homicide Division
    I remember driving back to the station with Dennis one night, sometime around the start of the hunt for the Smiler. It had just turned one and it came on the radio that another body'd been found. I don't know, it must've been the second or third, I don't recall. No, that's right, it was the third. Anyhow, it was the time that the press came up with the name – Smiler. The press thought that it might help focus the public and help us out, or at least make people more wary: the guy was still out there, no doubt about that. A couple of lovebirds'd stumbled across the body in a picnic area out in McKinley Falls State Park, hidden behind some cherry trees. Hancock, Blake Hancock. He was a teacher at the junior high on the other side of the park. His neck had been cut from ear to ear, 'like some horrific kind of weird smile,' the kids'd said. And Dennis? Man, I've never seen him so juiced up. When he heard that the guy'd been a teacher he just started in on this shit about how he understood – that's the very word he used, understood – about how he understood what was goin' on in this guy's mind, the Smiler. What was in his head, why he was doin' what he was doin' and how he was now goin' to catch the guy.

Marc Louris, Austin PD: Classmate, Police Academy
    Dennis was never the brightest of guys bookwise – he seemed to float around average the whole time we were in the academy – but he was always the first to pick up on the practical side of things: dismantling weapons, surveillance techniques, all that kind of stuff. Most times, he just had to watch the instructor once and that was it – he had it.

Ethan Robinson, Austin PD: Former Partner, Robbery Division
    I wouldn't call him a kleptomaniac – that's not fair and it wouldn't be true. But whenever we worked a burglary together, particularly if it was at someone's home, most times he'd end up taking something from the scene. He told me once that it was a way of getting inside the perp's head, tuning into the same vibes that'd stirred him up in the first place. Made him commit the crime. Oh, nothing major – a photograph or a lighter, something small that he could slip into his pocket. Personal stuff. But it's not as if he was the first. No sir, I've worked with guys that'd steal the cash from a dead man's wallet, pocket his credit cards and sell 'em on the street. All kinds of shit like that. But with Dennis it was always

*personal stuff. And it seemed to work, he always got his man. Dennis
was a good cop.*

The unmarked police car pulled to a halt in front of the condo on San
Jacinto and Dennis Lane climbed out and stretched his arms in the air.
He nodded at the uniform in front of the place and then looked up and
down the street. The sun had started to set behind the hotels lined up on
the shores of nearby Town Lake and the area was bathed in a sulphurous
sheen. On the corner a man in a lilac polo shirt and headphones fiddled
with a broken sprinkler on his lawn, and across the street a couple of kids
in bulky shorts jumped in the heat and rattled the roof of the family car
with a basketball.

Ethan Robinson opened his door and flipped his smoke on to the hot
tarmac, climbed out of the car and followed Lane into the cool of the
condo's lobby.

The door to an apartment on the third floor stood open a fraction, a
slice of sun on the carpet outside the apartment like a sundial snapshot
of the time of the break-in. Robinson pushed the door open a little
further and a sheet of hot air curled around his torso and he felt a catch
in his throat. 'Jesus Christ,' he said. 'We should be able to lock this guy
up just for havin' no aircon, man, victim or not. S'like a fuckin' desert in
here.'

In the far corner of the room a man in a rumpled T-shirt and blue
shorts sat on a chair in front of the window and stared out into the street.
At the sound of Robinson's voice he turned and looked at the pair of cops
with flat eyes.

'This your apartment?' said Robinson.

The man stood and stepped closer to Robinson. 'That's right,' he
said, a touch of defiance in his voice. 'This is my home.'

'And you are?'

'Michael Usher.'

'You live here alone, Mr Usher, there's no… you're not married?'

The man shook his head. 'Just me.'

Robinson looked into the shade that buffeted the walls, the rubble of
broken china and furniture that littered the floor. 'You know what happened, Mr Usher?'

Usher hiked his shoulders, pursed his lips. 'No,' he said. 'I just came
home and found the place like this.'

'Kids,' said Lane. 'Most likely kids after a quick score.'

Robinson looked across at his partner and let out a short breath,
rubbed the heel of his hand across the perspiration on his forehead. He

took a notebook and a pencil out of his pocket. 'You know what's been taken?'

'The TV for a start,' said the man, and pointed to a dusty space in the corner.

'I'll check out the rest of the apartment,' said Dennis, and disappeared into the dark stretch of hall that led to the rooms at the rear of the apartment.

Dennis padded into the bedroom, picked up scattered clothes and at once dropped them in the same place. He lifted a slat on the blinds and peered out into the street at the rear of the condo. Heat and dusk had cleared most of the area and all he could see was an Hispanic kid in yellow trunks rolling a watermelon on the sidewalk.

He picked up a photo frame from the sill: a blond boy of about three or four squinted into the sun, a stretch of sun-kissed beach behind him. He had the same flat forehead as the man in the front room: father and son, Dennis reckoned, and slipped the frame into the inside pocket of his jacket.

Couple of hours later, Dennis took a detour on his trip home and headed out past the condo. He pulled into the kerb across the street and peered up at the dark and silent front of the apartment: the man in the T-shirt and shorts had headed out to his local bar to bitch about the fall of the area to his buddies, the invasion of treacherous kids.

Dennis jumped out of the car, lifted a holdall from the back seat and headed into the condo. He took the stairs at a run, and on the third floor took a pocket knife from his coat and popped the lock on the door in less than a minute, slipped into the apartment and left the door ajar.

He stood in the centre of the front room and looked around. The tenant had attempted to clean up the place a little, but it still looked like the local kids had bounced a basketball around the place. Dennis scoped each aspect of the room in turn and then crossed to a bookcase and dropped a silver Buddha statue into the holdall. He ran his hand across a line of CDs on another shelf, pulled out ones that he knew and dropped them in the holdall with the Buddha.

He crossed to the bureau and rifled the compartments, scattered papers and documents across the floor. He came across a passport and a driver's licence and bundled them into the holdall; a pack of unopened photos still in the store's envelope and a pocket calculator landed on top of the passport and the driver's licence.

In the bedroom he added a couple of Ralph Lauren shirts and a pair of faded Levis to the haul; a pair of battered loafers and a fresh pair of white Reeboks trailed the clothes.

He hitched the holdall across his shoulder and left the apartment, left the front door open and tilted to ten o'clock, the time of his escape.

Harvey Carter, Lawyer: Racquetball Partner

No matter how busy we were, we always used to try and meet up about once a week to play racquetball. I work for a law firm downtown and I use the sport to ease a lot of the stress that builds up in the job. I think Dennis felt the same about being a cop, that he needed some kind of release. I remember one time the game had been pretty competitive, more competitive than usual, and as I went for a low backhand I slipped and fell and sprained my wrist. Dennis took me down to the Emergency Room and then drove me home. But then just before we were due to meet the following week, I had this call from his wife, Bonnie. She said that Dennis still had some pain in his wrist and that he couldn't make it. I didn't know what to say, I didn't understand what she was talking about. I mean, it was me that'd sprained my wrist, right?

Griffin Clark, Austin PD: Partner, Homicide Division

I remember the time Dennis first told me his theories about the Smiler, about the reason he cut people's throats from ear to ear. He told me that it was because... Dennis had this idea that the guy had been abused as a kid and that all he could remember was this smile on his abusers' faces as they... y'know, you understand what I'm tellin' you? The smile that told him that it was over? That they'd done with him? You do? Good. I don't know where that came from; it was never raised in the nine months I worked the case and it was not an idea that made it into the paperwork.

Kent Burke: Crime Reporter, Austin Star

There was a dark side to Dennis that he kept hidden from most people. It was something that you could maybe catch a glimpse of if you caught him off guard. Fifteen months ago, a friend of mine – his daughter was raped one night after a trip to the movies, right on campus. Nineteen. Straight-A student heading to be a doctor. Pretty, sweet and pretty, just like her mother. She was badly beaten and a couple of bones in her left hand had been broken. I don't know, maybe she put up a fight, but she'd also been hit around the head and suffered a fractured skull. Terrible. Couple of nights later I ran into Dennis out at that cops' bar down near the river, the Lantern. I used to hang out there quite a lot, meet up with a couple of guys who'd tipped me stories in the past. On this particular night someone pointed me in his direction, told me that he

*was the primary on the case and that maybe I should introduce myself,
buy him a beer. Well, I never met this guy before, and he was friendly
enough, but there was something about him that made me take a step
back. I asked him about the rape case, asked him what had happened and
how the investigation was going. I never told him that I was a friend of
the family, I didn't want him to feel that he couldn't tell me the truth. I
don't know, maybe it was because he was half-cut – he had this kind of
dull stare and his breath stank of Jack Black – but the way he talked
about the girl, about her breasts and stuff, made me think that maybe his
sympathies lay elsewhere.*

Dennis took a pull of cold Bud, put the bottle back on the bar and then
looked across at the woman in the Ryan Adams T-shirt that had been
clocking him for the last hour. She was kind of pretty in a raw way, with
thick black hair that fell like a stream at dusk across her shoulders, but
her face held a sadness that hinted at a lifetime of mistakes and missed
opportunities. Dennis had spotted it the moment he saw her and he had
felt no inclination to add to her woes, but after three or four drinks his
defences had slipped and he shot her a lopsided smile and nodded at the
vacant stool beside him.

The woman smiled and looked into the faces of her friends for a
second, then snaked around the far end of the bar and hitched herself up
on the stool beside Dennis.

'Hey,' said Dennis. 'Get you a drink?'

'Yeah, thanks,' she said, and shuffled around on the stool a little.

'Cold Bud okay?'

'Sure, what else you gonna drink when it's as hot as this?' she said,
and blew a jet of air up across her face, flapped her hand in front of her
face. She smiled and her teeth reflected neon sparks from the mirror
behind the bar.

Dennis turned and raised his hand to the bartender, ordered a couple
of bottles of Bud and then spun back around on his stool.

The woman held out her hand to him and said, 'Marnie. Marnie
Stead.'

'Ethan,' said Dennis, and took her hand and kissed it.

Dennis followed Marnie up the path that led from the street to a staircase
at the rear of the house, his footsteps dull echoes in the moon silence. She
had told him that she lived in a studio apartment on the fourth floor, invited him up for coffee after he had treated her to take out steak burritos from
the Little City Café on the ride home. They had eaten in the car and after,

she had kissed him and tasted chilli and bourbon on his lips; rubbed the band of soft white skin on the third finger of his left hand to let him know that she wasn't after commitment beyond the next few hours.

Sodium lamps cast a pale ochre sheen across the main street, but the foot of the path faded into darkness behind the house and he could just make out her outline ten feet ahead of him, the softness of her ankles and the easy hitch of her buttocks. To his left, knotted rose bushes lined the back wall of a car-parts warehouse, the path itself patched in dusted oil and littered in flattened soda and beer cans. Brilliant stars sparked from a hot, clear sky and the moon looked like a chipped blue marble.

Marnie reached the end of the path, spun on her toes and tossed Dennis a smile just as a security light came on above her head that turned her face the colour of burnt copper. It seemed to hover in the air for a moment, and then she disappeared around the corner and a couple of seconds later he heard her feet hit an iron staircase.

Dennis broke into a run, felt his blood rise in his heart and in his limbs and start to thump in his ears. He chased after Marnie and at the foot of the staircase he reached up and snatched hold of her hair and yanked her back down on to the path.

Marnie let out a startled cry and her limbs bucked in a spastic attempt to hold on to the iron rail, but her efforts were in vain. Her hands clutched at thin air as the back of her head hit the path with a hard and sickening thump. Before she could climb to her feet, Dennis straddled her at the hips, pinned her to the concrete and punched her in the face. Her head hit the path once more and then seemed to shake for a brief second before it slumped to the side; a trickle of blood curled out of her nose and pooled in the hollow of her shoulder, and her eyes rolled up in her head.

Dennis took hold of her ankles and pulled her into the darkness at the rear of the house, shot a look out to the street in both directions. He dropped to his haunches and took hold of the front of her jeans and snatched at the buttons, tore the T-shirt from her chest. He ripped the pair of battered Nikes from her feet and tossed them further into the darkness, slid jeans and panties from hips that felt both hot and cold in his hands and dropped them on the path. His breath came in harsh rasps and he paused for a second and then fell back on his heels and peered out once more at the street for a shift in the atmosphere, potential witnesses to the attack. He looked into the four corners of darkness around him and then, satisfied that he acted in isolation, dropped his hands on to the path and stared into the woman's face. Tortured, bloodied, pained and silent. He lifted a thick bunch of her hair and spread it across her eyes with tenderness, closed her mouth with the palm of his hand.

Griffin Clark, Austin PD: Partner, Homicide Division

Dennis had this idea that the places where the Smiler had picked up his victims held some kind of significance for him, something that reminded him of his childhood. But most of the places were not the kind of places that you'd normally associate with kids – playgrounds, schools, swimming pools, those kinds of places. No, Dennis believed that the killer'd been lonely and abused as a kid and that the places he picked his victims from were the kinds of places that a lonely and abused kid'd hang out – libraries, bookstores, the airport – places where there were loads of other people around, loads of adults, loads of parents. I mean, like he said, why else would the Smiler pick up his victims in places where sometimes there would literally be hundreds of witnesses? I had the impression that the reason Dennis believed this was because he himself had been a lonely child and that these were the kinds of places that he'd hung out in.

Bonnie Lane: Former Wife

Another thing he used to do – and this'd just drive me crazy – was copy me when we were talking. At home in the den watching TV; having a meal in a restaurant or a drink in a bar; even at my mother's, for God's sake. Gestures, hand movements, the way I sipped a cup of coffee or smoked a cigarette – everything. If I crossed my ankles, he'd cross his ankles; if I scratched my head, he'd scratch his head. It was like looking in a mirror, one of those creepy mirrors that you find at old-fashioned funfairs. I don't think he knew that he was doing it but it used to drive me crazy.

Griffin Clark, Austin PD: Partner, Homicide Division

After we found the third victim – Blake Hancock, the teacher – and we knew that we had a serial killer on our hands, Dennis became obsessed with the Smiler and spent all his waking hours on the case. As well as the official reports, he started to keep this scrapbook of all the newspaper clippings that he could find – not just from the local papers but from the New York Times and the Washington Post as well. And every so often he'd tell me about one of the little theories that he'd come up with about the Smiler. Like the fact that all his victims were – and I think this is what he said, but don't quote me – 'figures of assumed authority', although I've no idea what he meant by that. I even heard that he'd turned a room at home into some kind of command centre with crime-scene photos and all that kind of shit pinned to the wall. He never mentioned it to me, so it could just have been a rumour, but it wouldn't have surprised me. I do know that he had this map of the city pinned

above his desk in the squadroom with little coloured pins in it where he
reckoned the Smiler would strike next.

Dennis rolled the napkin into a ball and tossed it into the trash can on the
sidewalk. He rubbed his hands on his pants and then lifted a pack of
Camels from the dash and put a match to one, snapped the flame out of
the match and dropped it out on the tarmac. He took a pull on the Camel
and behind the smoke he could taste the barbecue smoke that drifted
from one of the concession stands on the banks of Town Lake.

Ten minutes earlier he had heard the applause for the final act of the
annual Aquafest rise and fall, and people had now started to drift from
the site. The moon lit the mass of communal bonhomie that bubbled into
the street and split it into smaller and smaller packs until faces started to
form out of the darkness. Dennis let his eyes drift across the faces that
appeared for a minute or so and then stopped on a couple as they halted
to let a '50s Oldsmobile pull out from the kerb in a crescendo of noise
and fumes and Buddy Holly.

The pair seemed familiar, but it took Dennis a moment to identify
them as the couple that he had come across outside the Continental Club
a month or so earlier. He had responded to a disturbance call only to
arrive at the bar to find a paramedic bunched over the woman, and the
kid already cuffed and in the back of a cruiser. The woman had a fresh
bruise on the side of her face that matched the shape of the knuckles on
the kid's right hand, but even after Dennis had spoken to her she had still
refused to press charges and he had had no choice but to turn the kid
loose. The woman had been a trainee parole officer and he remembered
wondering at the time if it had been part of her training to date a jerk.

The couple walked down the street to an old blue Honda. The kid
unlocked the car and then took hold of the woman's arms and tried to
push her inside, but she held her arms stiff at her sides and refused to
move, her mouth a firm line of defiance. The kid's mouth opened in a
shout lost in the pack and his face turned crimson.

Dennis fired up the car, tapped the pedal and eased across the street,
pulled up behind the Honda. He climbed out of the car and walked
around to the front of the Honda, rested his hand on the roof as if he
intended to hold it back if the kid tried to drive away.

'Hey, haven't I seen this movie before?' said Dennis.

The kid turned to look at him, bunched his face into a question.

'Hey, Detective Lane,' said the woman after a moment, a clear and
hopeful smile on her face. He noticed that fear coloured her pupils black.
'Been enjoying the music?'

Dennis felt his head turn from her in embarrassment and he understood at once that he had not misinterpreted the scene. 'You remember what we talked about the last time we spoke?' he said to the kid.

The kid shot a look across the street at the audience that had started to pool on the kerb, turned back to Lane. He opened his mouth to speak, but then he seemed to pull back into himself and he snapped his lips shut.

'This is not –' started the woman, but Dennis cut her off with a raised palm.

'Look,' he said, and pointed at her upper arm where bruises had started to rise in the skin. 'You may not think that you deserve better than this little piece of shit…'

'Hey,' interrupted the kid, but the woman punched him on the arm and he fell quiet.

Dennis smiled and took a step closer to the woman. 'Connie?' he said, and she nodded. 'Look, Connie, you've got a kind face; you look like the kind of person that'd give someone a second chance. But I reckon that this here piece of shit's had just about all the second chances that he could take. That so, kid?'

The kid looked into the cop's face, hit steel, and his mouth crumpled into a sneer.

'Smells like you've had a few drinks, too,' said Dennis.

'Couple of beers or so,' replied the kid.

'And the rest,' said Dennis. 'Still, what the hell do I care if you still want to jump behind the wheel – it's too much like bullshit to write up a DUI on a night like this. But there's no way I'm going to let you drive this lady home. C'mon,' he added, and pointed into the Honda, 'climb in the car and get the fuck out of here before I change my mind.'

The kid reached out to the woman but she stepped aside and his hand snatched at air. 'Travis, no,' she said and turned her back on him. Her shoulders seemed to have lifted a couple of inches and her voice had a clarity and strength that hadn't been there a moment earlier.

The kid snarled at her and then climbed into his car, stoked up the motor and laid rubber on the tarmac as he shot out from the kerb and headed in the direction of the interstate.

Dennis trailed him with his eyes until he disappeared and then turned back to the woman and said, 'That was very brave of you, Connie. But the way you treated him'll prey on his mind, so you'd be wise to bear that in mind the next few days.' He took a pack of Camels from his pocket and offered her one. She declined his offer and he put the pack back in his pocket. 'You need me to call you a cab?' he said.

She looked at his face, turned aside. 'That's okay,' she said. 'I think I saw one of my girlfriends back there. I can catch a ride from her.'

Dennis looked at the tail-enders coming out of the park, the dark spaces behind them. 'You sure she's still here?' he said. 'Looks like most folks've already upped and left. You want me to give you a ride home? It's the least I could do in the circumstances.'

The traffic on Barton Springs Road was thick in the heat of the summer. The tarmac shimmered in front of them like an oasis, and the air that hit his face felt like it had been shot from the tailpipe of one of the semis that roared in the blind distance. Kids in more open top autos from the '50s cruised the street and, at the junction of Bouldin, Dennis saw a man cross the intersection with a red-faced toddler asleep in the front seat beside him. The man looked like he hadn't slept in a month, ashen and drawn.

For a couple of miles, Dennis chatted about the kind of music he liked to listen to, the fresh bands that had come up in Austin of late, the old-timers he had seen rise and fall and rise once more. Connie listened in silence for a time, but then he noticed that she had started to squirm a little in her seat. 'Hey, don't let the kid rattle you.'

'I just ran into him at the Aquafest,' she said. 'I had no idea he was still in Austin. Last time I spoke to him – after… after that time at the Continental Club I told him I didn't want to see him any more – he told me that he'd been offered a job down in Corpus Christi and he planned to move down there.'

He turned and offered her a smile, noticed a tear on her cheek. 'You want to stop and talk about it? There's a quiet bar… '

'I'm in no fit state to be out in public,' she said.

'Okay, how about Barton Springs?' said Dennis, his tone loose and casual. 'Couple of tins of cool beer from the liquor store before I drop you back home.'

Connie looked at him in surprise – she never expected to be hit on by a cop, even one that had just pulled her out of a difficult situation. She still felt a little jumpy from the encounter with Travis, but as she looked at the cop once more she felt a kind of loyalty come upon her. He's only trying to be kind, she told herself. 'Sure, that'd be nice.'

Dennis purchased some beers at a store near the entrance to Zilker Park and then took the car to a spot that overlooked Barton Springs, the natural swimming pool in the park. It had been a hot day and three or four people still bobbed in the water on the far side of the lake, brilliant specks under a fresh moon. He parked the car a hundred feet from the only other car in the lot, then popped one of the beers and handed it to Connie. He turned to take another beer from the paper sack on the back seat and took the chance to look around the dirt lot and the rest of the immediate area.

Connie picked up on his actions and said, 'What're you looking for? You expecting someone?'

'No, but you can never be too careful with the Smiler still out there.'

Shock filled her features. 'Hey, you're not using me as some kind of bait, are you? Is that why you brought me out here?'

'Hey, c'mon,' said Dennis. 'You know that's not true. You know why we came out here.'

Connie shuffled in her seat, uncomfortable in the car all of a sudden. She looked out across the lot to where a bunch of people climbed up the hill from the side of the water, towels draped across their shoulders. She took a sip of beer and put the can on the dash. 'Well, thanks for the beer but I really should be getting back.'

'Okay,' said Dennis, and touched her on the forearm. 'Let's not talk about the Smiler no more.'

Connie pointed at a young couple beside a blue sedan. 'Hey, look, there's Reba Ball,' she said, a quiver in her voice once more. 'She lives just across the street from me. That must be her new boyfriend. I heard they were staying with her folks for a couple days.'

'Let's just finish our beer and then I'll take you home,' said Dennis.

Connie opened the door and dropped a foot on to the dirt lot. 'I'll just go ask if I can get a ride home,' she said, and quickly stepped out of the car and started to walk in the direction of the blue sedan.

'Hey, hold on a minute,' cried Dennis, and snapped open the door and hurried around to the other side of the car. He felt his heart thump deep in his chest and his breath came in hard bursts. 'C'mon, I'm sorry, okay.'

But Connie had started to run, and in a moment pulled up in front of the young couple. Dennis could tell at once from their curious faces that they had never seen her before. She started to speak and after a couple of seconds the man peered across her shoulder at him, a look of deep concern on his face. The woman continued to stare into Connie's face, and then she reached out and took Connie's hand and helped her into the back seat of the car and then climbed in beside her. The man shut the door behind them and then slid into the driver's seat. He stoked up the motor and pulled out of the lot in a cloud of dust. Connie did not look back, did not offer him a smile of thanks.

Dennis stood and stared after the car until the red tail-light sheen faded from the pecan trees that surrounded the lot, then shook his head and turned to look out across the lake. The people on the far shore had packed up and left and he found himself alone under the moon. Raccoons and rabbits bundled around in the brittle shrubs beneath the pecan trees, and in the distance he could hear the mournful cries of a bluebird. He strolled around the hill a short distance and tossed some pebbles into the lake and smoked a couple of Camels, kicked at the hard earth in frustration and headed back up to the car.

He had just put his hand on the door handle when he felt his head jerk back and a coldness prick the skin beneath his left ear. On instinct he tried to turn, but before he could shift his feet or lift his hands to his head, the coldness had spread across to his other ear and he felt his throat start to burn. Intense pain spread across his chest and out into his arms, shot across his torso and in seconds he dropped to his knees and then fell flat on his face in the earth. Darkness filled his head and drained across his face, blacked out his vision. His other senses started to fail one at a time, and his last sensation was of the smell of pecans returning to the earth.

Bonnie Lane: Former Wife
Do I think that Dennis was the Smiler? No, of course not. Oh, I know that the murders stopped once that Dennis himself had been murdered, but there's not one shred of physical evidence to prove that Dennis had anything to do with any of the murders.

Ethan Robinson, Austin PD: Former Partner, Robbery Division
No.

Griffin Clark, Austin PD: Partner, Homicide Division
You're asking me if I think that another cop found out that Dennis was the Smiler and took him out? What kind of ridiculous question is that? Dennis just had a hair up his ass on this one and ended up too close to the flame, that's all. End of story.

WAITING FOR MR RIGHT

ANDREW TAYLOR

Ever since his first novel won the CWA John Creasey Memorial Award for the best debut of the year, Andrew Taylor has appeared to be destined for eminence in the genre. His work is quirky and often original, yet these qualities are not always fully appreciated by the critics. Happily, last year saw *The Office of the Dead*, the final entry in Taylor's stunning Roth Trilogy, awarded the CWA Ellis Peters Historical Dagger. Taylor writes short stories infrequently, but when he does, the results are always compelling, as this thoroughly enjoyable tale – which plays on the 'Crime in the City' theme with great ingenuity – illustrates to perfection. And the last line is one of my all-time favourites.

I live in a city of the dead surrounded by a city of the living. The great cemetery of Kensal Vale is a privately-owned metropolis of grass and stone, of trees and rusting iron. At night, the security men scour away the drug addicts and the drunks; they expel the lost, the lonely and the lovers; and at last they leave us with the dark dead in our urban Eden.

Eden? Oh yes – because the dead are truly innocent. They no longer know the meaning of sin. They can never lose their illusions.

Other forms of life remain overnight – cats, for example, a fox or two, grey squirrels, even a badger and a host of lesser mammals, as well as some of our feathered friends. At regular intervals, those splendid security men patrol the paths and shine their torches in dark places, keeping the cemetery safe for its rightful inhabitants. Finally, one should not forget to include, perhaps in a special sub-human category of their own, somewhere between life and death, Dave and the woman Tracy.

In a place like this, there is little to do in the long summer evenings once one's basic animal appetites have been satisfied. Fortunately I am not without inner resources. I am never bored. In my own small way I am a seeker after truth. Perhaps it was my diet, with its high protein content, which helped give me such an appetite for learning. In my youth, I taught myself to read. Not for me the sunlit semi-detached pleasures of *Janet and John*. My primers were the fruity orotundities of funereal inscriptions, blurred and sooty from decades of pollution. Once I had mastered my letters, though, I did not find it hard to find more varied reading material.

We live, I am glad to say, in a throwaway society.

It is quite extraordinary what people discard in this place, either by accident or design. The young prefer to roam through the older parts of the cemetery, the elderly are drawn to the newer. Wherever they go, whatever their age, visitors leave their possessions behind. Litter bins have provided me with a range of periodicals from *The Spectator* to *Marxism Today*. The solar-powered, palm-top personal organiser on which I am typing this modest memoir was carelessly left behind among the debris of an adulterous picnic on top of Amelia Osbaston (died 1863).

I have also been fortunate enough to stumble upon a number of works of literature, including *Jane Eyre* and *Men Are From Mars, Women Are From Venus*. Charlotte Brontë is, without doubt, my favourite author. How could she peer so penetratingly into the hidden chambers of the heart? Jane Eyre and I might be twin souls.

On one occasion, after an unexpected shower, I came across a damp but handsomely illustrated copy of *Grave Conditions*, a scholarly survey of Victorian funerary practices. This enabled me to identify the Bateson's Belfry of Kensal Vale.

Perhaps the term is as unfamiliar to you as it was to me. Bateson's Belfry was a Victorian invention designed to profit from the widespread human fear of being interred alive. In essentials it consisted of a simple bell pull, conveniently situated in the coffin at the right hand of the corpse, which would enable one, should one find oneself alive and six foot under, to summon help by ringing a bell mounted above the grave.

Usually, and for obvious reasons, Bateson's Belfries were designed as temporary structures. But there were circumstances in which a longer-lasting variant was appropriate. Thanks to *Grave Conditions*, I learned to look with fresh eyes at what I had previously assumed was a purely decorative feature of the mausoleum of the Makepeace family.

The mausoleum, which is illustrated in full colour on page 98 of *Grave Conditions,* was situated in a relatively remote corner of the cemetery, an area where the dead lie beneath a coarsely-woven shroud of long grass, thistles and clumps of bramble. A flight of steps led down to a stout, padlocked door leading below the monument into the chamber itself, which measured perhaps eight feet square. Two banks of four shelves faced each other across the narrow gangway. Only three of the shelves were occupied – with the remains of the Reverend Simon Makepeace, the first incumbent of St George's, Kensal Vale; his wife, Charlotte, and their son Albert Victor, both of whom had predeceased him. The rest of the family had apparently preferred to make other arrangements. On ground level there was a rather vulgar monument consisting of four weeping angels clustered round the base of a miniature campanile, at the top of which hung the bell.

Having studied *Grave Conditions*, I was not surprised to find that a fine brass chain passed from the top of the bell through a pipe that penetrated the roof of the chamber. It emerged at the end of the gangway, opposite the door, within easy reach of the upper ends of the coffins. I imagine Mr Makepeace stipulated that the lids should not be screwed down.

During the day, especially around lunchtime and in the early evening, the cemetery can become almost crowded. But the gates are locked half an hour before sunset, and once the security men have done their sweep (and they are commendably efficient at this) the only people left are – or rather were – Dave and Tracy in their cottage by the gates in the majestic shadow of the cemetery chimney. Dave and Tracy did not get on – and as Dave was very deaf, owing to a passion for the music of Aerosmith, Black Sabbath and Led Zeppelin, one sometimes heard his wife's trenchantly expressed opinions about his sexual inadequacy and his low income. Tracy was tall and big breasted, with dyed blonde hair, sturdy legs and a taste for very short skirts. She and Dave rarely had visitors and never indulged in nocturnal rambles through the cemetery. Often Tracy would go off by herself for days at a time. I sometimes surprised myself by entertaining a certain sisterly regard for her.

So, given their habits and the secluded nature of a cemetery at night, you will understand my surprise when I saw Tracy arm in arm with a tall, well-built man, guiding him through the gravestones by the light of a small torch. At the time I was sitting on a table monument, and eating a light snack of Parma ham and wholemeal bread. I was interested enough to discard my sandwich and follow the couple. Tracy led the man to the Makepeace vault. Her companion was carrying a briefcase. They went down the steps together, and I heard a rattle as she unlocked the padlock.

'Christ,' I heard the man say in a hoarse whisper. 'You can't leave me here. They're coffins, aren't they?'

'There's nothing here could harm a fly,' Tracy told him. 'Not now. Anyway, beggars can't be choosers, so you might as well get used to it.'

'You're a hard woman.'

For an instant she shone the torch on him as they stood at the foot of the steps. He was broad as well as tall, with a stern, dark face. I noticed in particular his big eyebrows jutting out above his eyes like a pair of shelves. I am not a sentimental creature, but I must confess a jolt went through me when I saw those eyebrows.

'Stay here, Jack,' Tracy said. 'I'll get you a sleeping bag and some fags and stuff.'

'What about Dave?'

'He wouldn't hear if you dropped a bomb on him. Anyway, he's drunk a bottle of vodka since tea time.'

She left Jack with the torch. I slipped under the lowest shelf on the right-hand side and watched him. When he thought he was alone, he squatted down and opened the briefcase. I was interested to see that it contained an automatic pistol and piles and piles of banknotes. He rummaged underneath the money, took out a mobile telephone and shut the case.

He stared at the telephone but did not use it. He lit a cigarette and paced up and down the gangway of the vault. Despite his agitation, he was a fine figure of a man.

My hearing is good, and I heard Tracy's returning footsteps before he did. She dropped a backpack on to the floor of the vault. It contained a sleeping bag, several cans of Tennents Super Lager, a plastic bucket, some crisps and a packet of Marlboro cigarettes. Jack watched as she unrolled the sleeping bag on one of the lowest shelves and arranged the other items on the shelf above.

'Listen,' he said when she had finished. 'Get some passport photos done and go and see Frank.' He snapped open the case, took out a wad of notes and slapped it down on the shelf. 'That'll cover it.' He took out another wad and added it to the first. 'Buy a motor. Nothing flashy, maybe two or three years old. There's a place in Walthamstow – Frank'll give you the name.'

Tracy stared down at the open briefcase. 'And where do we go then, Jack? Shangri-fucking-la?'

'What about Shangri-fucking-Amsterdam for starters? We take the ferry from Harwich, then move on from there.'

'I got nothing to wear. I need some clothes.'

He scowled. Nevertheless he gave her another bundle of notes. 'Don't go crazy.'

'I love it when you're masterful.' Tracy dropped the money into the backpack. 'Careful with the torch. You can see a glow round the edge of the door. And I'm going to have to lock you in.'

'What the fuck are you talking about?'

'The security guys check the door at least twice a night. We had a bit of trouble with kids down here earlier in the summer. Orgies and what-not. Pathetic little bastards.'

'You can't just leave me here,' Jack said.

'You got a better idea?'

'I can't even text you. There's no signal. So what do I do if I need you?'

'I can't bloody wait,' she said. 'Big boy.'

'For Christ's sake, Trace. If it's an emergency.'

She laughed. 'Ring my bell.' She leant over and touched the handle that hung between the shelves. 'You pull that, and the bell rings up top.'

'Sure?'

'We had this weirdo from the local history society the other month who tried it. Built to last, he said. But for God's sake, Jack, don't use it because if anyone hears it but me, you're totally fucked.'

Tracy put her hand on his shoulder and kissed his cheek. 'See you tomorrow night, all right? Got to get my beauty sleep.'

She slipped out of the vault and locked the door. Jack swore, a long monotonous stream hardly above a whisper. His torch beam criss-crossed the vault and raked to and fro along the dusty shelves. Finally he reached floor level and for an instant the beam dazzled me. He let out a

screech. I dived into the crack between two blocks of masonry that was
my usual way in and out of the vault. A moment later, as I emerged into
the cool night air, I heard the frantic clanging of the bell.

Tracy came pounding through the graves. She ran down the steps and
unlocked the door.

'Jesus, Jack, what the hell are you up to?'

He clung to her, nuzzling her hair. He muttered something I couldn't
hear.

'Oh, for God's sake!' she snapped, drawing away from him. 'I bet it's
a damn sight more scared than you are. Give me the torch.' A moment
later, she went on, 'There you are – it's buggered off.'

'Can't you do something? Can't you put poison down?'

'It won't be back,' she said as though soothing a child. 'Anyway, they
seem to like poison. I'm sure there's more of them than there used to be.'

'I can't stay here.'

'Then where the hell else are you going to go? It's not for long.'

'How am I supposed to sleep? They'll crawl all over me.'

'Jesus,' said Tracy. 'And I thought women were the weaker sex. It
won't be back.'

'How do you know?'

'You probably scared the shit out of it. Listen, I tell you what I'll do: you
can have some of Dave's pills. A few of those and you'll be out like a light.'

Off she went again, and returned with a handful of capsules, which
Jack washed down with a can of lager. He insisted she stay with him,
holding his hand, while he went to sleep. Yet despite this display of weak-
ness, or perhaps even because of it, there was something very appealing
about him. I came back down to the vault and listened to them billing
and cooing. Such a lovely deep voice he had, like grumbling thunder. It
made something deep within me vibrate like a tuning fork. Gradually his
words grew thicker, and slower. At last the voice fell silent.

There was a click and a flare of flame as Tracy lit a cigarette. Time
passed. Jack began to snore. Edging out of my crack into the lesser shelter
of the space beneath the lowest shelf I had an extensive, though low-level,
view of the vault. I saw Tracy's legs and feet, wearing jeans and trainers.
The cigarette fell to the floor. She ground it out beneath her heel.

I saw the briefcase, and Tracy's left hand with its blood-red nails and
big flashy rings. I watched in the torchlight as her fingers made a claw and
hooked themselves through the handle of the case. The trainers moved
across the vault. The door opened and softly closed. The padlock grated
in its hasp.

After a while, I scaled the rough stone wall to the shelf where Jack lay.

I jumped lightly on to his chest and settled down where I could feel the beating of his heart. I stared at his face. Through my breast surged a torrent of emotions I had never known before.

Was this, I wondered, what humans felt? Was this love?

So it began, this strange relationship, and so it continued. I do not intend to chart its every twist and turn. There are secrets locked within my bosom that I shall never share with another soul.

Late in the afternoon of the day after Jack's arrival, I happened to glance through a copy of the *Evening Standard* that I had found in a litter bin on the other side of the cemetery. His face loomed up at me from one of the inside pages. The police, it seemed, were anxious to interview John Rochester in connection with a murder at the weekend in Peckham. The dead man was said to have been a prominent member of a south London gang.

On the second day, the police arrived. They interviewed Dave in the lodge cottage. They did not search the cemetery. Halfway through the morning, Jack finished his lager, his crisps and his cigarettes, in that order. Early in the evening, the bucket overflowed. He tried to ration his use of the torch, but inevitably the battery died. Then he was alone with me in the darkness.

Is it not strange that a grown man should be so scared of the dark? If only I could see, he would mutter, Christ, if only I could see. I have no idea why he thought the faculty of sight would have improved his plight, but then I have found little evidence to suggest that humans are rational animals.

Just before dawn on the third day, it occurred to Jack – bless him, he was not a fast thinker – that Tracy might not be coming back, and that he would be able to escape from this prison and move into one of Her Majesty's if he rang the bell in Bateson's Belfry long enough and loud enough.

Alas for him, I had anticipated just such an eventuality.

The bell wire was sound for most of its length, I believe, but at the end of its length it met a metal flange that was, in turn, attached to the spindle from which the bell depended. Where the wire had been inserted, bent and twisted into a hole in the flange, rust and metal fatigue had already caused many of its constituent strands to snap apart. All one needed to deal with the remaining strands was a certain physical agility, perseverance and a set of sharp teeth. So it was that when Jack gave the bell wire a sharp tug, all that happened was that he pulled the wire down on top of him. He clenched his fists and pounded them against the oak and iron of the door. That was one of the occasions when he wept.

Later, after he had sunk into an exhausted slumber, I licked the salty tears from his cheeks, my tongue rasping deliciously on the abrasive masculinity of his stubble. It was one of those small but intimate services that seem to be peculiarly satisfying to the females of so many species.

The days passed, and so did the nights, and they passed agreeably enough for me. When he was awake, Jack was increasingly distraught, and was still terrified of me. Are we always scared of those who love us? When he was asleep, though, and defenceless, he became mine. I spent as much time as possible with him – indeed, if possible on top of him or curled into some crevice of his person.

Can one ever be close enough to the man one loves? Oh, that oft-imagined bliss of perfect union! One soul, one flesh!

Sometimes he screamed, and banged on the door, and yelled, and wept; but no one except myself heard him. On one occasion, Dave was only twenty yards away from the vault when Jack began to wail, but of course Dave was too deaf to hear.

There remained a possibility that a passer-by might hear his cries, even in this remote and overgrown quarter of the cemetery. Here, however, the British climate played its part. Rain fell with unlovely determination for most of three days. As a result, Kensal Vale attracted far fewer visitors than usual.

Among those who braved the weather was a brace of middle-aged ladies from Market Harborough searching, without success, for the last resting place of an ancestor. They left me the remains of a very acceptable chicken mayonnaise salad and – even more to the point – they discarded their newspaper. For hard news and sound principles one cannot do much better than the *Daily Telegraph*.

My eye fell on a short but intriguing item to the effect that Jack Rochester and an unnamed lady friend were believed to be in Rio de Janeiro. Knowing Tracy as I did – a special sort of knowledge unites two females with a man in common – I had little doubt that this was a false trail designed to throw the authorities off the scent.

I come now to the final act in my story, to a resolution that is both melancholy and edifying. All passion spent, blind in his own darkness, my poor Jack sank slowly into a coma. I grieved and rejoiced in equal measure. I sat on his chest and felt the beat of his heart growing slower and feebler. My night vision is good, and I gazed for long hours at his manly features. A lover is like a beloved city. I explored Jack's public squares and great thoroughfares. I strolled through tree-lined suburbs and splendid municipal parks. I wandered through twisting side streets and lost myself in the labyrinth of his bazaar.

In his final hours, as he drifted inexorably towards another city, to the dark heart of this metropolis of the dead, Jack rested his hands on my warm fur. Then, to my inexpressible joy, he stroked me.

Soon afterwards, the life left him altogether – or very nearly so. And then?

Reader, I ate him.

AUTHORS'
BIOGRAPHIES

Andrea Badenoch lives in Newcastle. She has been a lecturer and co-editor of an annual anthology, *Writing Women*. Her published crime novels are *Mortal*, *Driven* and *Blink*.

Ann Cleeves lives in West Yorkshire with her family. She is best known for her Inspector Ramsay novels set in Northumberland, but she has recently turned to non-series novels of psychological suspense and both *The Crow Trap* and *The Sleeping and the Dead* have earned considerable critical acclaim. As a member and bookings secretary of the collective 'Murder Squad', she works with other Northern writers to promote crime fiction.

Mat Coward was born in 1960 and became a full-time freelance writer and broadcaster in 1986. Having written all manner of material for all manner of markets, he currently specialises in book reviews, magazine columns and short stories – crime, SF, humour, horror and children's. His first crime story was shortlisted for a CWA Dagger and he has also published two novels: *Up and Down* and *In and Out*.

David Stuart Davies is both a magazine editor and the author of several books, both fiction and non-fiction, concerning Sherlock Holmes. They include *Bending The Willow*, an account of Jeremy Brett's portrayal of Holmes. His novels include *The Scroll Of The Dead*.

Carol Anne Davis has been described as 'an uncompromising new literary talent'. Four reviewers chose her mortuary-based novel *Shrouded* as their début of the year in 1997 and its successors include *Safe As Houses*. Most recently, she has published a study of female serial killers, *Women Who Kill*. Carol's short stories have appeared in anthologies and magazines and have been placed in national competitions. Her dark crime collection is available for publication and she says that no reasonable offer will be refused.

Eileen Dewhurst was born in Liverpool, read English at Oxford, and has earned her living in a variety of ways, including journalism. When she is not writing, she enjoys solving cryptic crossword puzzles, and drawing and painting cats. Her latest novel is *No Love Lost* and her other works include *A Private Prosecution, The House That Jack Built*, and *Death In Candie Gardens*. She wrote five novels featuring the policeman Neil Carter; currently, her principal series detective is the actress Phyllida Moon.

Martin Edwards has written seven novels about the lawyer and amateur detective Harry Devlin; the first, *All The Lonely People*, was shortlisted for the CWA John Creasey Memorial Dagger. He has published a collection of his short fiction, *Where Do You Find Your Ideas? and other crime stories*, and has edited eleven crime anthologies, including *Murder Squad*. He is also the author of seven non-fiction books on legal topics. In 1999 he was commissioned to complete the late Bill Knox's police novel *The Lazarus Widow*. His latest book is a non-series novel of psychological suspense, *Take My Breath Away*.

Jürgen Ehlers works as a geologist at Hamburg State Geological Survey. Since his graduation from Hamburg University, he has published more than fifty articles in scientific journals as well as five books about Ice Age geology. In addition, he has contributed to a number of anthologies published in German.

Marjorie Eccles was born in Yorkshire and spent her childhood there and on the Northumbrian coast. Later, she lived for many years in the Midlands, where her crime novels are set. Her series featuring Detective Chief Inspector Gil Mayo has achieved an enthusiastic following; titles include *The Superintendent's Daughter*.

Kate Ellis was born and brought up in Liverpool and studied drama in Manchester. She has worked in teaching, marketing and accountancy, and first enjoyed literary success as a winner of the North West Playwright competition. Keenly interested in medieval history and 'amateur' archaeology, she lives in North Cheshire with her family. Her novels featuring Detective Sergeant Wesley Peterson include *The Merchant's House*.

John Harvey is a poet and dramatist, as well as a novelist. He is best known for the series of crime novels featuring the world-weary cop

Charlie Resnick. After many years spent in Nottingham, he now lives in London.

Reginald Hill is the author of over forty books, including the internationally acclaimed Dalziel and Pascoe series, which has been successfully adapted for BBC television. His other series character is the Luton private eye Joe Sixsmith. His many awards include the CWA Diamond Dagger and the CWA Gold Dagger for *Bones and Silence*.

Bill James lives in his native South Wales. He is married with four children and is the author of a critical work on Anthony Powell, as well as many thrillers and crime novels. His well-regarded Harpur and Iles series includes titles such as *Top Banana* and *Eton Crop*, whilst, as David Craig, his books include the Cardiff-based crime novel *Bay City*.

Peter Lewis has lived in the North East for more than 30 years. He is an academic and teaches courses in crime at one of the institutions for which Durham is famous. Among his books are critiques of Eric Ambler and John le Carré; the latter received an Edgar Allan Poe award from the Mystery Writers of America. He and his wife Margaret run Flambard Press, which has published *Northern Blood 2*, an anthology of regional crime stories, collections of the work of Chaz Brenchley and H R F Keating, and novels by crime writers such as Maureen Carter and Meg Elizabeth Atkins.

Phil Lovesey is the son of another notable crime writer, Peter Lovesey. Born in 1963, Phil took a degree in film and television studies and had a career as London's laziest copywriter at a succession of the capital's most desperate advertising agencies. He turned to 'proper' writing in 1994 with a series of short stories, and was runner-up in the prestigious MWA 50th anniversary short-story competition in 1995. His first novel, *Death Duties,* was published in 1998 to excellent reviews, and has so far had two successors.

Val McDermid grew up in a Scottish mining community, then read English at Oxford. She was a journalist for sixteen years and is now a full-time writer based in South Manchester. Her series featuring private investigator Kate Brannigan has been much praised, as was the non-series *Killing The Shadows*. The latest of her psychological thrillers featuring criminal profiler Tony Hill is *The Last Temptation*. This series is now being televised, with Robson Green in the lead role.

Ruth Rendell, under her own name and as Barbara Vine, has won both critical and popular acclaim for her achievements in showing the rich potential of the crime novel. Her first book about the Kingsmarkham policeman, Reg Wexford, *From Doon with Death*, appeared in 1964. Her non-series novels under her own name include *A Demon in my View*, which won the CWA Gold Dagger in 1976, and *A Judgement in Stone. Lake of Darkness* won the Arts Council National Book Award for Genre Fiction in 1981. The much-praised Vine novels include *A Fatal Inversion* (another CWA Gold Dagger winner) and *The Brimstone Wedding*.

Kathryn Skoyles is a qualified solicitor who enjoyed a successful career in the London legal profession before moving into the business world. A long-time enthusiast for crime fiction, at present she is combining active involvement with a group of London writers with work on a first novel featuring Sarah Marshall.

Cath Staincliffe is the author of six novels featuring Sal Kilkenny. She is based in Manchester, the setting for her books, and is also a playwright, community arts worker, mother of three children and founder member of 'Murder Squad'. Her latest Sal Kilkenny book is *Towers Of Silence*.

Jerry Sykes's stories have appeared in diverse magazines and anthologies, including *Cemetery Dance*, *Crime Time*, and *Love Kills*. He edited the collection *Mean Time – New Crime For A New Millennium* and with his wife runs a small press, Revolver.

Andrew Taylor grew up in East Anglia and went to the universities of Cambridge and London. He now lives in Gloucestershire with his wife and two children and writes full time. His first novel about William Dougal, *Caroline Minuscule*, won the CWA John Creasey Memorial Award and the third, *Our Father's Lies*, was short-listed for the Gold Dagger. He has also written an espionage trilogy, books for younger readers, the Roth Trilogy, non-series novels and a series of mysteries set in the post-war era and located in the border town of Lydmouth. He is a member of the writers' collective 'The Unusual Suspects'.

BLITZ
by Ken Bruen

The fast moving follow-up to the 'White Trilogy'

ISBN 1899344 00 X   paperback (£6.99)

ISBN 1899344 01 8 hardcover (£15.00)

> 'Irish writer Ken Bruen is the finest purveyor of intelligent Brit-noir' *The Big Issue (London)*

The South east London police squad are suffering collective burn out:

- Detective Sergeant Brant is hitting the blues and physically assaulting the police shrink.
- Chief Inspector Roberts' wife has died in a horrific accident and he's drowning in gut-rot red wine.
- 'Black and beautiful' WPC Falls is lethally involved with a junior member of the National Front and simultaneously taking down Brixton drug dealers to feed her own habit.

The team never had it so bad and when a serial killer takes his show on the road, things get progressively worse. Nicknamed 'The Blitz', a vicious murderer is aiming for tabloid glory by killing cops.

From absinthe to cheap lager, with the darkest blues as a chorus, The White Trilogy has just got bigger. 'Getting hammered' was never meant to be the deadly swing it is in this darkest chapter from London's most addictive police squad.

Also published by THE DO-NOT PRESS

I've Heard The Banshee Sing by Paul Charles

ISBN 1899344 02 6 paperback (£7.50)

ISBN 1899344 03 4 hardcover (£15.00)

WHEN the butchered and dismembered body of an elderly man is discovered in Camden Town's famous Black Cat Building, Detective Inspector Christy Kennedy finds this is no ordinary murder. Initial investigation produces not a single clue but an article by Kennedy's sometime lover, ann rea (whose name always appears in lower case), reveals a couple of potential leads in Kennedy's Northern Ireland birthplace.

Kennedy and ann rea head over to Portrush: she to work on a follow-up to her story, Kennedy to try and make sense of the bizarre, ritualistic killing. Assisted by Ulster Detective McCusker, Kennedy's investigation takes him through the Irish countryside and back in time to World War II. *I've Heard The Banshee Sing* is Paul Charles at his very best.

'Masterful sleuthing'
What's on in London

Also published by THE DO-NOT PRESS

Kiss Me Sadly
by Maxim Jakubowski

A daring new novel from the 'King of the erotic thriller'
Time Out

ISBN 1899344 87 X   paperback (£6.99)

ISBN 1899344 88 8   hardcover (£15.00)

Two parallel lives: He is a man who loves women too much, but still seeks to fill the puzzling emptiness that eats away at his insides.

She grows up in an Eastern European backwater, in a culture where sex is a commodity and surviving is the name of the game.

They travel down separate roads, both hunting for thrills and emotions. Coincidence brings them together. The encounter between their respective brands of loneliness is passionate, heartbreaking, tender and also desolate. Sparks fly and lives are changed forever, until a final, shocking, epiphany.

Also published by THE DO-NOT PRESS

Double Take
by Mike Ripley

Double Take: The novel and the screenplay (the funniest caper movie never made) in a single, added-value volume.

ISBN 1899344 81 0 paperback (£6.99)

ISBN 1899344 82 9 hardcover (£15.00)

Double Take tells how to rob Heathrow and get away with it (enlist the help of the police). An 'Italian Job' for the 21st century, with bad language – some of it translated – chillis as offensive weapons, but no Minis. It also deconstructs one of Agatha Christie's most audacious plots.

The first hilarious stand-alone novel from the creator of the best-selling Angel series.

'I never read Ripley on trains, planes or buses.
He makes me laugh and it annoys
the other passengers'
Minette Walters

Pick Any Title
by Russell James

RUSSELL JAMES was Chairman of the CRIME WRITERS' ASSOCIATION 2001-2002

PICK ANY TITLE is a magnificent new crime caper involving sex, humour, sudden death and double-cross.

ISBN 1899344 83 7 paperback (£6.99)

ISBN 1899344 84 5 hardcover (£15.00)

'Lord Clive' bought his lordship at a 'Lord of the Manor' sale where titles fetch anything from two to two hundred thousand pounds. Why not buy another cheap and sell it high? Why stop at only one customer? Clive leaves the beautiful Jane Strachey to handle his American buyers, each of whom imagines himself a lord.

But Clive was careless who he sold to, and among his victims are a shrewd businessman, a hell-fire preacher and a vicious New York gangster. When lawyers pounce and guns slide from their holsters, Strachey finds she needs more than good looks and a silver tongue to save her life.

A brilliant page-turner from 'the best of Britain's darker crime writers'
The Times

Thirteen – photographs by Marc Atkins

'Revealing, occasionally disturbing and often erotic.'
Daily Express

ISBN 1899344 86 1 paperback (£13.00)

'13' is a unique juxtaposition of imagery: photographic nudes by Marc Atkins 'illustrated' with text specially commissioned from thirteen internationally-acclaimed writers.

Aside from his celebrated solo work, Atkins is also known for collaborations with the likes of poet and critic Rod Mengham, lexicographer and essayist Jonathon Green, and novelist Iain Sinclair.

The authors 'illustrating' Atkins' photographs in '13' range from twice Booker Prize nominated novelist Julian Rathbone to New York columnist Maggie Estep via Bill Drummond (best known for his part in pop/art unit, KLF) and Groupie author, Jenny Fabian. Some, like Nicholas Royle and Stella Duffy, are rising stars of British literature; others, such as writer and biographer James Sallis and writer/journalist Mick Farren are seasoned veterans. All thirteen were given a nude portrait and asked to write about what they saw. The results are revealing, occasionally disturbing and very often breathtaking – descriptions which also fit Atkins' images perfectly.

Also published by THE DO-NOT PRESS

Middleman by Bill James

The brilliant new thriller from the creator of the bestselling Harpur & Iles series

ISBN 1899344 95 0 paperback (£6.99)

ISBN 1899344 96 9 hardcover (£15.00)

Times are tough for 'middleman' Julian Corbett.

He operates as a half-respectable, half-crooked businessman in what was once the rough dockside of the Welsh capital. But a multi-billion-pound redevelopment is transforming the seafront into the stylish Cardiff Bay marina-style housing and shopping area, and Corbett is determined to grab a piece of that action.

At first, Corbett thinks the opportunity to help shady developer Sid Hyson dispose of his lakeside casino/hotel/nursing home complex is his road to riches, but he soon realises that all is not well. Hyson is suddenly worried the sea might come flooding in, and before that happens he wants to 'liquidate' his assets.

Corbett knows that if he doesn't find an acceptable buyer – and quick – he's as good as dead. The body of one failed 'middleman' has already washed up on a nearby beach. Then Corbett realises he's negotiating with people twice as ruthless as Sid Hyson.

> "Bill James is British mystery fiction's finest prose stylist"
> Peter Guttridge, *The Observer*

Also published by THE DO-NOT PRESS

Mr Romance
by Miles Gibson

An epic tale of love, lust, jealousy, pain and purple prose

ISBN 1899344 89 6   paperback (£6.99)

ISBN 1899344 90 X hardcover (£15.00)

'Miles Gibson is a natural born poet' –
Ray Bradbury

Skipper shares his parents' boarding house with their lodgers: lovely Janet the bijou beauty and Senor Franklin, the volcanic literary genius. Life is sweet, until one night the lugubrious Mr Marvel seeks shelter with them.

Who is the mysterious fugitive and what dark secret haunts him? Skipper sets out to solve the riddle. But then the astonishing Dorothy Clark arrives and his life is thrown into turmoil. Skipper falls hopelessly in love and plans a grand seduction. He'll stop at nothing. But Dorothy is saving herself for Jesus…

Also published by THE DO-NOT PRESS

The Jook
by Gary Phillips

AS GOOD AS WALTER MOSLEY OR YOUR MONEY BACK!

ISBN 1899344 91 8   paperback (£6.99)

ISBN 1899344 92 6 hardcover (£15.00)

> "Gary Phillips writes tough and gritty parables about life and death on the mean streets. His is a voice that should be heard and celebrated."
>
> *Michael Connelly, author*

Zelmont Raines has slid a long way since those winning touchdowns brought him lucrative endorsement deals. Crack, barrels of booze, a paternity suit, a hip injury, groupies and some shady investments in gangsta rap; can things get any worse?

Enter Wilma Wells, the leggy and brainy lawyer for the Los Angeles Barons' professional team. She just happens to be of a mind to pull off a job on her mob-connected bosses. When Zelmont is enlisted in her schemes, he soon learns that the violence he experienced on the field was just a warm-up to the dangers he faces with a woman more than his match, sexually and amorally.

The Do-Not Press
Fiercely   Independent   Publishing

Keep in touch with what's happening at the cutting edge of independent British publishing.

Simply send your name and address to:
The Do-Not Press (Dept. CITC)
16 The Woodlands, London SE13 6TY (UK)

or email us: jk@thedonotpress.com

There is no obligation to purchase
(although we'd certainly like you to!)
and no salesman will call.

Visit our regularly-updated web site:

http://www.thedonotpress.com

Mail Order

All our titles are available from good bookshops, or (in case of difficulty) direct from The Do-Not Press at the address above. There is no charge for post and packing for orders to the UK and EU.

(NB: A post-person may call.)